★

**Praise for the Lena Jones series by
Betty Webb**

"A must read for any fan of the modern female
PI novel."
—*Publishers Weekly* on *Desert Noir*

"If Betty Webb had gone undercover and written
Desert Wives as a piece of investigative journalism,
she'd probably be up for a Pulitzer... The factual
details...are eye-popping."
—*New York Times*

**Praise for the Owen Keane series by
Terence Faherty**

"The intermingling of past and present, and the
presentation of the truth are handled masterfully
by Faherty...powerful."
—*Mystery News* on *Orion Rising*

"Faherty is a crafty writer with a...style that
is delicious."
—*Washington Post Book World* on *The Ordained*

★

BETTY WEBB
TERENCE FAHERTY
NANCY BAKER JACOBS
JONATHAN HARRINGTON

DESPERATE
JOURNEYS

WORLDWIDE®

TORONTO • NEW YORK • LONDON
AMSTERDAM • PARIS • SYDNEY • HAMBURG
STOCKHOLM • ATHENS • TOKYO • MILAN
MADRID • WARSAW • BUDAPEST • AUCKLAND

DESPERATE JOURNEYS

A Worldwide Mystery/May 2004

ISBN 0-373-26491-7

DESERT DECEIT Copyright © 2004 by Betty Webb.
THE FIRST PROOF Copyright © 2004 by Terence Faherty.
STAR SEARCH Copyright © 2004 by Nancy Baker Jacobs.
DEATH ON THE SOUTHWEST CHIEF
Copyright © 2004 by Jonathan Harrington.

CONTENTS

DESERT DECEIT

by Betty Webb

Author's Note

The Little Grand Canyon, as described in this novella, does not exist. Readers familiar with Arizona's topography, though, will find that the fictional Little Grand resembles the combined beauty of both the Salt River Canyon and the Verde River Valley.

—B.W.

ONE

THE BLOOD on Stephen MacPherson's face mirrored the canyon's crimson walls, but didn't look nearly as attractive. Not that it mattered. Arizona's beauty had been wasted on the media magnate, anyway.

I leaned over to inspect his wounds more closely, while next to me, Clinton Clayburn, MacPherson Communications' senior vice president, shifted his considerable weight from one sore foot to the other. "Thank God you happened to be riding by, Lena. It's like I told you. I found the body when I came back here to take a leak, and even though I don't know much about horses, it's obvious that devil he's been riding trampled him to death. Too bad no one has a gun, or we could shoot it."

My plan to find a high point from which to watch the sunset now canceled, I inspected MacPherson's formerly handsome face. Jagged indentations traveled all the way from the top of his head to what remained of his chin—wounds that bore no resemblance to a horse's hooves.

Clayburn limped closer, his wide feet encased in too tight, too expensive cowboy boots. "You see? That damned animal must have gone crazy on him. The person responsible for putting Stephen on that horse is looking at the mother of all lawsuits."

I doubted it. Slim Papadopolus, owner of Happy Trails Dude Ranch, had mounted MacPherson on Moonglow for the ten-day cattle drive only after insisting on a signed waiver in which MacPherson swore he had not only grown up with horses but won several ribbons on the horse-show circuit, as well. After watching MacPherson ride, we all realized he'd lied. Still, if Moonglow had killed the idiot, I was Mick Jagger, skinny hips and all.

Tuning out Clayburn's mutterings about lawsuits, I looked around for the vanished horse. At first I saw only the nearby scrub oak glade that sheltered the wagon carrying the Porta-Johns. Behind the oaks rose the sheer canyon wall, its orange and scarlet hues rapidly deepening to violet by the setting sun. Then, approximately one hundred yards farther down the narrow canyon and half hidden by a scraggly mesquite, I spotted the pale shimmer of a cream-of-wheat palomino: Moonglow.

Left to his own devices, the big gelding would probably wander back to camp to find solace among the other horses, but I didn't want to take the chance. If frightened enough, he might attempt to lope the sixty miles back to the dude ranch we had left five days earlier.

"Stay here," I told Clayburn. "Don't get any closer, and certainly don't touch the body."

"A little bossy, aren't we?" he muttered. But he turned away from the mess on the ground.

I walked cautiously toward Moonglow and he rewarded me with a tremulous snort. At first he leaned away from my outstretched hand, his eyes white-rimmed with fear. But then he decided to stand his ground and even lowered his head to let me take firm grasp of his bridle.

"You didn't do anything evil, did you, boy?" I whispered.

Moonglow fluted his nostrils again and closed his eyes. He seemed to enjoy the look of MacPherson's corpse no more than I, and was content to have a human take control of the situation. Relieved, I hooked my left arm through his reins, bent down and tapped his near front hoof with my right hand.

"Foot," I commanded.

Like any seasoned riding horse, Moonglow lifted his foot obediently. His iron shoe was clean of blood; so was the frog, the soft inner part of the hoof. His white fetlocks remained unstained, too. I repeated the inspection process with his other three legs and found a similar story. The horse was innocent of any crime other than skittishness.

MacPherson's killer had been human.

But how much should I reveal to Clayburn or his other MacPherson Communications' compatriots? We still had more than sixty miles to go on the cattle drive before we reached the summer grazing grounds near Flagstaff, and I didn't relish the thought of traveling through the long, desolate canyon with a killer alert to my suspicions. The more I thought about our situation, the more I suspected it might be wiser to pretend to buy Clayburn's theory. Presumed ignorance, in this case, would be bliss. Or, at least, relative safety.

After giving Moonglow a reassuring pat on the neck, I led him back to Lady, my own horse, and ground-tied him beside her. Then I rejoined Clayburn.

"Go back to camp and tell Slim to bring me some rope," I said, my mind already envisioning the next few hours. "Oh, and a camera."

He looked at me with eyes suddenly as spooked as Moonglow's. "What for?"

"I need to take pictures of the, um, accident scene before it's disturbed by..." I trailed off, not sure how much he needed to know about desert predators. "Before it's disturbed. I'll use the rope for sealing off the area. Once the sheriff is notified, he'll helicopter in to get the body. And the insurance company will probably want to look around."

Ah. Insurance claims he could understand. He nodded in

agreement. "Okay, sweetie. That's not bad thinking for a woman, but you can relax now and let us men take over."

I tried not to let my irritation show. As an ex-cop, and now a licensed private detective, I knew what needed to be done until the sheriff arrived. And I didn't appreciate Clayburn's blatant sexism.

"Mr. Clayburn, why don't you just hustle on back to camp like a good boy? It can't be more than three city blocks away, so I'm sure you can manage it, even in those silly boots. By the way, don't call me 'sweetie' again."

He opened his mouth as if to argue, then thought better of it. As a member of MacPherson Communications' board of directors he might have been a big deal back in Boston, but out here he was just the new kid on the block. Arizona was my territory. I'd lived here all my life. Well, make that all my *known* life. God knows where I had lived before I had been found at the age of four lying beside a Phoenix road with a bullet in my head.

After Clayburn disappeared around a bend in the canyon toward camp, I knelt beside MacPherson's body. Rigor had not yet stiffened his extremities, but death's matte film already covered his eyes. I touched his neck again. Cooling, but not by much. He had probably lain here less than an hour, hidden from the many Porta-John visitors by a yellow-bloomed creosote bush.

I frowned at his battered face. Along with the standard ain't-nobody-home look of the recently dead, he wore an odd half smile, which made me suspect he hadn't been afraid of his killer. Rather, it appeared that his last emotion had been disdain. Knowing the man for only a few days, I wasn't surprised. Like so many of the powerful men I'd met in the course of my work, MacPherson viewed money as the sole measure of human worth. I doubted if ninety-nine percent of humankind ever made a blip on his radar. The trail hands on this pseudo cattle drive remained beneath his notice, but intriguingly, so did his own board of directors, the three men and one woman he'd bullied into accompanying him to Arizona. As for his wife and stepdaughter, from what I could see, he merely tolerated them. And me? Let's just say that underneath his wolfish leers lurked an even creepier contempt.

I touched the scar on my forehead. When MacPherson— standing too close for comfort—had asked me how I'd received it, I related the story of my childhood shooting. He raised his eyebrows, but not in sympathy.

"Get the scar removed," he said, his eyes already traveling south along my body. "It spoils the package."

His own package was spoiled now, the chiseled nose crushed, the capped teeth broken. Even the tip of one perfect ear had been ripped half off.

"How the mighty are fallen," I murmured, remembering the biblical verse taught to me by Reverend Giblin, my fifth foster father. Or had the Rev been my sixth? No matter. Those old prophets could certainly sum up the human condition. Stephen MacPherson, with his cable television networks, radio stations and newspaper chains, reigned in life as one of the mighty, but in death he was little more than biological refuse.

In Arizona's April heat, such refuse presented a problem. Namely, what to do with the body? Strapping it to a horse and hauling it for another five hot days along the trail to Flagstaff was out of the question. The decomposing flesh would spook the horses, not to mention our herd of four hundred cattle. I didn't think the dudes would appreciate the smell, either.

If only we could pick up a cell phone and call for help.

I ground my teeth in frustration. Tempted by an off-the-books cash bonus, Slim had acceded to MacPherson's request to ban all cell phones and laptops from the drive.

"If I let them bring their little toys, they'll conduct business as usual,'' MacPherson had said, with his charming but empty smile. ''And if you bring yours, they'll find a way to borrow them, too.''

He explained that several acrimonious mergers and acquisitions had nearly brought his board of directors to blows, and now they needed what he termed a ''healing experience.''

''Slim, my man, what better way can there be to soothe the soul of the corporate beast than to return him to the nondigital days of yesteryear?''

MacPherson's final argument had been accompanied by an additional roll of bills.

So now here we were, out in the back end of beyond, several days' ride away from the nearest authorities, with a rapidly decomposing body on our hands.

And a murderer among us.

Behind me, Lady snuffled and Moonglow gave a quizzical whinny. A few minutes later voices began drifting through the narrow canyon. I took a deep breath, turned my back to MacPherson's body and stationed myself five yards in front of him: the guardian of the dead.

The entire party trickled into view, first a grim-looking Slim, a large coil of rope slung over a shoulder; Jessop, the trail boss; then the cowhands. The four members of the MacPherson Communications' board of directors, all limping from their unaccustomed Western boots and long days in the saddle, trailed behind.

Where was MacPherson's wife? Or for that matter, his stepdaughter?

I raised my hands as they neared. ''Please don't come any closer,'' I called. ''We need to keep the accident scene as pure as possible.''

''That woman's got control issues,'' I heard Clayburn mutter to Slim as they came to a halt. The comment had been just loud enough for me to hear. On purpose, probably.

"Oh, stuff it, Clayburn," Dusty, my sometimes boyfriend, snapped before the more diplomatic Slim could shush him. Dusty had lured me onto the cattle drive by promising me a week of R and R away from Desert Investigations. Some vacation it had turned out to be. Thanks to the dictatorial MacPherson, the first five days had been hell. Now it was about to get worse.

Regardless of Clayburn's bruised ego, I needed to establish some semblance of order. So even though I hated the pompous way I sounded, I took a deep breath and plunged in.

"Mr. Clayburn, I'm a licensed private detective and, unfortunately, I'm also the closest thing we've got for a law-enforcement officer within sixty miles. Whether you like it or not, I'm placing myself in charge of this accident investigation until we get to Flagstaff and alert the Coconino County sheriff."

Luck was with me there. Sheriff Orson Nakai had spent ten years with the Scottsdale Police Department, five of them working side by side with me. We still shared a high degree of mutual respect, and I knew he would take my allegations of murder seriously.

Clayburn thrust his head forward at a pugnacious angle and started toward Dusty. He might have been carrying too many pounds, but it looked like the extra weight of an aging athlete, not a couch potato. "Listen, cowboy…"

A high, theatrical wail froze Clayburn in his tracks. The grieving widow had finally arrived.

Renée Rodgers MacPherson, her red hair artfully windswept, dashed toward her husband's body. "My beloved! My beloved!" Only Dusty's restraining hand kept her from entering the crime scene.

In all my years in law enforcement, I'd never heard anyone refer to a spouse as "beloved," but then again, I'd never socialized with an Oscar-winning actress before. Even if I hadn't seen any of Renée's movies, there would still be no mistaking her profession. The woman's every action, every gesture, reeked of drama, whether ordering whole-wheat-Texas-toast-no-butter for breakfast, flirting with the flattered trail hands, or—as she'd done the day before—screaming that her beloved should rot in hell for dragging her out West with his company toadies.

Yet with all Renée's emoting, I'd never seen her show the slightest sign of affection toward her husband. Or for her daughter, Tiffany.

I looked around for the girl and finally found her at the back of the crowd, her pretty but too thin face ashen with shock. As usual, she was being completely ignored by everyone.

But not Miss Hollywood.

"Renée, Renée." Clayburn rushed over to the hysterical actress and wrapped her in his beefy arms. "He's gone. There's nothing you can do."

Renée struggled backward, breaking his hold. "If he's dead, I don't want to live anymore!" When she turned toward me, I noticed that her eye makeup remained perfect. "Oh, Lena! Can it be true? Can my beloved truly be gone?"

Feeling guilty about slandering poor Moonglow, I answered with a lie. "I'm sorry, Renée. It looks like his horse trampled him."

"Trampled?" The shock still didn't travel all the way to her eyes, but then again, her acting skills might have deteriorated in the twenty years since she won her Oscar. "What do you mean *trampled?*"

"I'm thinking the horse spooked and he fell under its hooves. Or maybe he did something that, uh, annoyed it."

"Hey, let's just wait a minute here before we start placing blame!" Slim detached himself from the others and regardless of my earlier warning, jogged over to MacPherson's body. He took one quick look at the wounds, then turned to me, his face indignant. "Lena, what you just said is a pile of..."

I interrupted before he ruined my plan. "Horses are known for having bad tempers, and it doesn't take much to set them off, does it, Slim?"

Slim narrowed his eyes. "What are you talking about?"

I turned my back to the dudes and leaned toward him, shaking my head as if in sorrow. "Such a tragedy!" I said loudly, then more quietly to Slim alone, "Just play along for a few minutes, okay? We'll talk later."

"Well, I hope you know what you're doing," he murmured back. But Slim, an old friend, had seen me work before, too. He raised his voice. "If Moonglow did this, then I'll put him down. But you have to prove it first."

With no more ado, he handed me the camera he used to create a photo album for the ranch's guests, then unwound the rope from his shoulder. While I snapped pictures of MacPherson's body from every angle, including the rocky area that surrounded him, Slim closed off the crime scene.

As he neared me again, I whispered, "You and Dusty can stay here, but I don't want the paying guests to know what we're doing. We need to look for the murder weapon, which I'm guessing is a big rock."

Slim nodded and issued his instructions to the trail hands, who then began rounding up the dudes much as they did the cattle. After only a few protests and some fresh wails from Renée, the group headed back up the canyon to camp.

The crime scene now secured, I explained the true situation to Slim and Dusty. After a hurried consultation, we began searching the canyon floor in ever-widening circles. The sun, which had already dipped behind the canyon walls, created deep shadows and made our search more difficult, but in spite of the failing light, Dusty eventually found the murder weapon. The killer, obviously in a hurry, had tossed the rock mere yards from his victim, probably thinking no one would look further for cause-of-death than poor Moonglow.

"Want me to rope off this area, too?" Slim asked, motioning toward the prickly pear cactus that had failed to hide the weapon.

I nodded. "Yes, but give me a chance to take a few photos over there first. By the way, do you have any plastic on you?"

Slim thought for a moment, then dipped into his shirt pocket. "Will a Ziploc do? I always carry one for my cheese and pita."

Soon the murder weapon, a jagged piece of bloodstained quartz, had been bagged and tagged and stashed in one of Lady's saddlebags with the rest of my private gear. I would turn over the rock and the crime scene photographs to Sheriff Nakai when we reached town. I didn't expect the rough-surfaced rock to yield any fingerprints, but there was always a chance that the rock had scratched its user and thus carried the killer's DNA. Murder tended to be a messy business for both victim and perpetrator.

The details seen to, the bigger problem remained.

"Okay, guys, what are we going to do with Mac-Pherson?" I asked.

Neither answered for a minute, nor did they need to. We all knew what had to be done.

"We have to bury him," Slim finally said.

Dusty nodded. "Deep enough so that the coyotes don't get at the body."

"But shallow enough so that Nakai's crime-scene specialists can dig him back up without too much trouble," I added.

Slim gave me a bleak smile. "I'll go back to camp and fetch us a tarp and shovels. We're going to have ourselves an old-fashioned trailside funeral."

I sighed. "Looks like Stephen MacPherson got his real Wild West experience, after all."

IT TAKES A LONG TIME to dig a hole deep enough to bury a man. By the time MacPherson had been wrapped in a tarp and safely tucked into the ground, night had long since chased any remnants of light from the sky. After Slim mumbled a few words over the fallen magnate, his still-wailing wife scattered the purple lupine and gold Mexican poppies she'd collected earlier in the day across the grave. But his stepdaughter revealed no sign of grief. Or even respect.

With no more ado, Dusty erected a quickly constructed wooden cross to serve as a headstone, and we filed back to camp for a late dinner. As the desert darkness wrapped us in its velvet folds, we huddled around the campfire, chewing on our cooled franks and beans. No songs. No jokes. No cowboy poetry. Just strained silence broken only by Renée's banshee cries.

When Cookie began clearing away the remains of the barely eaten food, Slim hooked his arm through mine and tugged me toward the privacy of the trees.

"Lena, we've got to talk." The receding firelight cast Slim's Grecian face into statuary shadows. An ex-jockey, he may have stood little more than five feet, but his deep voice carried a rare authority.

Once we were out of earshot, he made an admission. "You might as well know, I do have a cell phone."

"What? MacPherson made you guarantee—"

"Oh, I took his little bonus, all right, but I wasn't about to endanger anyone by cutting us off from civilization like that. The problem is, I kind of outsmarted myself. I've been trying for the past two hours, but these damn cliffs are keeping me from getting a signal out."

The brief spark of hope I'd felt died. The canyon we were in, the Little Grand, cut a deep gouge through the desert for almost a hundred miles. Throughout the land rush of the last century, its sheer inaccessibility had kept it unpopulated except for mule deer and elk. The rock walls on both sides of us, so scenic earlier, now appeared hostile.

"Send a rider ahead for help," I proposed. "We can't continue on as if nothing's happened."

He shook his head. "This terrain's too dangerous for a lone rider, especially if he's riding fast. If the horse goes down, the rider could break a leg. Or get bit by a snake. Hell, anything could happen, and he'd just lie there until we caught up with him. Now, if one of the dudes needed an emergency appendectomy or something, I might risk it, but MacPherson's already dead. A few days in the ground isn't going to make any difference to him."

"Slim, MacPherson was murdered."

"You're the cop."

I held up my hands. "Ex-cop."

"Yeah, yeah, but still a detective. You just keep a handle on that side of things, and I'll call the authorities as soon as I can get a signal out. By the way, why don't you want anyone else to know MacPherson was murdered? Do you mind sharing? Or is it just a cop thing?"

A horned owl swooped low across the glade, drawn by the distant firelight. Then it veered off into the trees to continue his hunt. Some small animal would die tonight.

"Those folks are scared enough already," I said, gesturing toward the campfire. "Just imagine what they'd be like if they knew the truth. But back to that lone rider business. Okay, maybe riding sixty miles alone is risky, but isn't there a ranger station about twenty miles from here? One of your ranch hands, maybe even Dusty, could make for that. He certainly knows how to take care of himself."

Slim shook his head again. "Twenty miles as the crow flies, but a horse isn't a crow. The trail to that ranger station goes almost straight up those cliffs, and counting the switch-backs, it's more like forty miles. Forty very dangerous miles.''

"What about ranches? Surely there's one around some-where.''

He gave a low laugh that held little humor. "Oh, yeah, there's a ranch just a few ridges over, all right. The problem is, slides closed the one road leading out of the Little Grand last week, and now we can't reach it. Not without outfitting a horse with rock-climbing gear.''

Remembering the high lava, sandstone and granite ridges that stretched for miles on both sides of us, I realized Slim was right. "So you're saying we're stuck, that we can only go forward.''

He put a reassuring hand on my arm. "Or back. But since we're already at the halfway point, I say forward. Regard-less of everything, I still have to get these steers up to the ranch. Look, if everything goes smoothly from here on, we'll reach the Mormon Lake cutoff in three days. I'll send a rider out then, with the phone. Trust me, Lena. It'll work out fine.''

I wished I could believe him.

Once we settled ourselves back at the campfire, Slim tried to ease the strain by telling a few stories about the old Ar-izona Territory. No one listened. Once, when a piece of wood split with a gunshot crack, Tiffany shrieked and fi-nally began to sob. Her mother ignored her, but took the opportunity to turn on her own waterworks again.

"Renée, don't you think you should go to your tent and get some rest, now?'' Clayburn said. "You're going to need your strength in the morning.''

That was all Renée needed. Her face assumed a tragic but brave expression. "You're right, Clinton. I must be strong.'' With that, she stood and, with head lifted nobly, walked toward the tents.

Dusty and I made our excuses and did the same.

"Have any idea who murdered the bastard?" Dusty whispered as we nestled against each other in our tent. After five days on the trail, our double sleeping bag combined the scents of Old Spice, L'Aire du Temps and Eau de Horse.

"Everyone wanted to murder the bastard. Even you."

I'd meant it as a joke, but his chuckle sounded forced. "Oh, come on, now! We didn't get along that bad."

"Really? Then what were you two arguing about by the chuck wagon last night?" I had just returned from the Porta-Johns when I heard the two snarling at each other near MacPherson's tent.

"We weren't arguing, Lena, we were just having a spirited discussion."

Knowing Dusty as I did, I realized there was no point in pressing the issue. Instead, I nibbled at his ear.

He surprised me by nibbling back. "Do you want to talk or do something else?"

I'm not stupid, so I stopped talking.

LATER, AS DUSTY SNORED beside me, I thought back to the previous night's argument. What had I actually heard? Due to the high wind rattling though the pines that night, only a phrase or two carried.

"Keep away…" MacPherson.

"…a fool if…" Dusty.

"…warning you…" MacPherson.

One complete sentence had reached me, and it now kept me awake.

"Keep on and you're liable to wake up dead some morning." Dusty.

Others had probably heard those raised voices, too. Once Sheriff Nakai began his homicide investigation, the dudes would surely be eager to finger anyone but themselves. If Dusty opened up to me first, I might be able to help him, but there was the rub. The man never told me anything, which created an ongoing problem in our relationship. Then again, we both kept too many secrets.

Why did I always love the wrong people?

The answer was easy. In light of where I'd come from, a few secrets, a little distrust, the ever-present specter of infidelity—such problems seemed minor. With all Dusty's many flaws, I knew that his good qualities far outweighed the bad. Hell, compared to some of the people in my life, the man was a near saint.

Faces from my past haunted me: the foster father who raped me, the foster mother who beat me, the meth freak who shot me, the murderer who left me to die in the desert...

Considering all the ghosts that continued to haunt my dreams, it was a miracle I could still love at all.

As I stared into the darkness, I could hear Renée's sobs drifting through the night. Try as I might to summon up sympathy for the woman, her grief still sounded too theatrical to be real. I tuned her out and fixed instead on the cattle lowing to one another as they settled in for the night. From farther down the canyon, I heard the call of a nightbird, the yip of a coyote.

I wondered if we'd dug MacPherson's grave deep enough.

TWO

THE SUN ROSE on one of those unique Arizona mornings, highlighting a sky so clear that the few red-tailed hawks riding the thermals stood out in dark contrast. Below them, humans did what they could to spoil the day's serenity.

"I'm really sorry, hon," Dusty said, hugging me as we stood outside our tent taking in the pine-scented air. "I thought this cattle drive would be a good way for you to relax. You've had such a rough time lately, what with that last case of yours and all."

I leaned against him, trying to still my concerns. "It's not your fault." At least I hoped not. My sleep had been fitful, and during the long night, I'd remembered something: Dusty admired redheads. Since he was a good-looking man with his tall, spare frame and brilliant blue eyes, it had been obvious to me right from the start that Renée admired him right back.

Had MacPherson noticed?

"Keep away…"

I broke his embrace.

"What's up?" He drew me to him again. "You just got the strangest look on your face."

There was no point in stirring up any more man-woman trouble for the present, so I gave him a quick peck on the cheek. Then, to disguise my real thoughts, I said, "There's something about this cattle drive that's not quite right, but I can't put my finger on it. Tell me the truth, Dusty. Hasn't this whole thing been a mess from the very start?"

"Any mess in particular you're thinking about?"

Dusty had known me for five years, ever since I'd been a uniformed police officer and given him a speeding ticket. Our relationship had never been easy, but after more break-ups than I cared to count, we always wound up back together. Maybe that meant something. Or maybe we were just too crazy or lazy to find anyone else. Still, the man knew me well and usually demonstrated an uncanny ability to zero in on my vague anxieties and ease them.

"Which mess in particular? Oh, I don't know," I said, still trying to cover up my worries about his confrontation with MacPherson. "Name me something around here that's not a mess."

He smiled. "Horses. The smell of hay in the morning. The creak of saddles in the afternoon."

"My life's not that simple. I'm a detective, remember? I see dead people."

"Yeah, you and that kid in the movie."

I waved his flippancy aside. "Dusty, there's a dead man out there and somebody murdered him. Why did it happen here? Why not in Boston?"

Unless a cowhand was the killer, I wanted to add.

He shrugged. "Don't ask me, Lena. You're the detective. But as delightful as this conversation has been, I've got horses and cattle to see to, unless they took off during the night. Hell, I wouldn't blame them if they did."

As he walked across the clearing, his spurs jingling, I ducked back into the tent and tucked clean jeans, shirt, bra and panties under my arm. I stuck my bare feet into my Tony Lama boots, trudged across the dew-spangled clearing, then several hundred yards down the trail to the mesquite grove where Jessop, Slim's gritty trail boss, had jerry-rigged a couple of solar showers for the women. Unfortunately, I could see MacPherson's grave just beyond them. To mask my thoughts, I tried to think about the smell of hay in the morning.

It didn't work.

The problem with solar showers, I mused as icy drops raised goose bumps all over my body, is that to work, they had to suck up a couple hours' worth of sun. This made it tough on we folks who rose at dawn.

I had almost finished showering when I heard footsteps. "This one's occupied!" I called, my teeth chattering.

"I'll use the one next to yours, okay?" Tiffany, Renée's daughter. Her voice trembled, and I didn't think it was from the cold.

Curious, I looked over the shoulder-high canvas shower surround. When she started to strip the bathrobe away from her near-anorexic body, I hurriedly averted my eyes.

"After what happened, I don't want to shower by myself," she added, not quite whimpering, but pretty close to it.

I didn't bother to ask why she didn't wait for her mother.

As Tiffany stepped into the canvas stall next to me, I tried to ease her fears. "We'll be back in civilization before you know it. But until then, I can assure you that you're perfectly safe."

Especially now that MacPherson was dead.

The first night out, I'd seen him sitting much too close to her at the campfire during dinner, whispering something that made her blush. When she tried to edge away from him, he moved closer. A couple of times she tried to attract her mother's eye, but Renée was too busy flirting with the cowboys to pay her any attention. So Tiffany threw a tantrum about the food.

Behavior problems, sure. But it didn't take a psychologist to figure out why.

"Why do you think that horse killed my stepfather?" she asked. "Was he torturing it?"

Shocked, I stared at her over the canvas surround. "Torturing it? What makes you think…"

I drew in my breath. Was I just imagining things, or did

those red welts across her bone-thin back resemble belt tracks?

"Tiffany, who beat you?"

"Oh, is that what it looks like?" Her face, peeping over her soapy shoulders, held no expression.

"A leather strap about one inch wide, am I guessing right?" I tried to keep my voice steady.

She didn't say anything for a while, just scrubbed and scrubbed, attacking her body as if she hated it.

"Maybe," she said finally.

Without another word, Tiffany toweled herself off, shimmied back into her robe and trotted back toward camp. I remembered that she had tucked her solitary tent so far into the trees that she almost appeared to be hiding. But from whom? Her overbearing stepfather or her neglectful mother?

A few minutes later I heard the jangle of Cookie's bell. The smell of spiced sausage, blended with onions, drifted down the canyon, and to my surprise, I heard my stomach rumble. Not even murder could put Lena Jones off her feed, especially when someone else was doing the cooking.

Back at the fire circle, Tiffany pointedly ignored me. She had flashed her wounds just enough to pique my suspicions, then returned to her former sulky self. As she so often did, she took out her unhappiness on the food. How could she be certain, she whined to Cookie, that her egg-and-pepper omelet hadn't been cooked in the same pan as the sausage? She wouldn't let up until he returned to the chuck wagon and brought back a Teflon pan. Scratched into its black handle was the word "vegetarian."

"No meat ever gets in here," he growled.

As Tiffany sniffed the pan suspiciously, I thought back to some of the other cases I'd worked on. Belt marks usually meant parental abuse, but not always. I had once come across a teenager who'd regularly flagellated herself with the cat-o'-nine-tails she found in her parent's nightstand drawer. Could Tiffany be so disturbed that she received a sick kick out of parading self-inflicted wounds? But she could be a genuine abuse victim. And victims had been known to turn on their tormentors. Still, it was hard to imagine a vegetarian murdering someone. They were opposed to the taking of any life.

Then I remembered that Hitler had been a vegetarian.

After a hasty breakfast, we broke camp, loading the tents and supplies onto the packhorses and wagons. That done, each rider took up his position. Slim and Jessop rode point at the front of the herd, Dusty and the other trail hands at the flanks, the dudes rode drag at the rear. Today was my turn to baby-sit them.

The trail hands worked in earnest now, no longer content to let the amateurs attempt to round up the strays. They'd all seen MacPherson's face and, unlike the Boston contingent, understood what his wounds truly signified. What worried me was that the cowboys' tension could affect the cattle. Yes, a killer rode with us, but cattle could kill, too, especially when herded along canyons as narrow as the Little Grand. Most of the trail hands, at some point in their lives, had experienced the terrifying power of a stampede. Jessop, our trail boss, had once lost a brother when a herd spooked at a lightning strike.

Regardless of my concerns, Jessop hurried everyone along, the animals with snaps of his long bullwhip, the humans with curt commands. Although anxiety remained high among the riders, no one quarreled with him, not even the hyperaggressive Clinton Clayburn. He knew better.

As MacPherson's grave fell farther behind, his widow remembered to cry. Her wails reached the decibel levels of the previous night.

"Jesus, Mother, you'll scare the cows," Tiffany said, her tone biting in that way that only rebellious teenagers can manage. "The way you're acting, you'd think there was a camera around."

But Tiffany's tone couldn't disguise the very real tears in

her own eyes. Had she, after all, truly cared for her step-father? If so, it certainly wouldn't be the first time an abused child loved its tormentor.

Renée, obviously stung by Tiffany's perceptive comment, snapped back, "Don't you talk to me like that, miss!"

Tiffany wiped her eyes—a little too theatrically?—and fell silent again. Maybe she really was her mother's daughter. Or perhaps I was being unkind. It was clear to me that Renée was too self-absorbed to notice her daughter's obvious psychological problems. In fact, I doubted that Renée Rodgers MacPherson ever noticed more than her own reflection in the large, battery-lit mirror that, despite Slim's protests, she had packed along on the ride.

Desiring to put a little distance from the dysfunctional pair, I spurred Lady forward and rode up alongside Vern Pincus, another member of MacPherson Communications' board of directors. Pincus's gaunt, dewlapped face and watery gray eyes appeared even more morose than usual, but then again, the poor man always looked as if he were on his way to a hanging. With MacPherson's death, he had a real reason to be sad.

"How are you doing, Vern?" I asked in as gentle a voice as I could summon yet still be heard over the rattle and creak of the nearby chuck wagon. "I understand that Mr. MacPherson was an especially dear friend of yours. Losing him must be hard on you."

He gave me a woeful look. "You have no idea, Lena. No idea. Stephen and I, we've known each other, *knew* each other, since we were kids. We went to school together, got married together. Started MacPherson Communications together. Hell, we even went through our first divorces together and remarried around the same time. Life's funny, isn't it?"

A laugh riot. "Are your, uh, current wives friends, too?"

He shook his head. "Different worlds, different generations. Renée is, well, she's Renée. Big stars don't have much time for girl talk.''

Somehow I kept myself from wincing at his dismissive attitude toward female conversation, which these days ranged anywhere from quilting patterns to global tariffs and nuclear fission. But I pushed onward. The way men discussed their wives revealed much about the men themselves.

''It doesn't surprise me that Renée doesn't have much in common with your wife,'' I said. ''I doubt if she has much in common with many people. So what's your wife like, Vern? She's pretty, I bet.'' And a safe bet it was, too. Once they attained financial success, plain men like Pincus almost always sought out the young and beautiful, as if they needed physical proof of their changed status in the world.

Pincus didn't disappoint me. His hangdog face lit up.

''Stacey's a beautiful girl, and just as smart as she is beautiful! She used to run the exercise program in the gym at the MacPherson Building, but last fall she opened her own place in the Back Bay. It's doing so well that she's expanding into two more locations. She's so brilliant that I told her that if I'd waited a few more years to meet her, I'd probably be the one marrying for money, not—'' He stopped abruptly, turning red. ''I didn't mean…''

''Of course you didn't,'' I murmured.

He rushed ahead, eager to clear up the picture he'd inadvertently painted of his young gold digger. ''I know what everyone thinks about these May-December marriages, but a lot of girls prefer an older, settled man. Fewer problems, if you get my meaning. They think we're less inclined to roam, and they're probably right. Anyway, that's what Stacey told me when I started working out in that company exercise program Stephen signed us all up for.''

I almost laughed. ''Stephen MacPherson signed you up for an exercise program?''

''The entire board.'' Pincus flapped his hand at a horsefly, a common annoyance when riding drag. ''He told us he didn't want heart attacks carrying off his board of directors, so regardless of how much we whined, he made us all go down to the same gym he used and work out every afternoon for an hour. Isn't that something?''

It was something all right. And Clayburn accused *me* of having control issues.

"Well, I'm glad he did," Pincus added. "It turned out Stacey was just getting over a bad relationship. When we started opening up to each other, some of the things she told me about her ex-boyfriend gave me the creeps. Not only was he unfaithful to her, but he was, uh, a little rough. No actual hitting, mind, but well…''

He trailed off, but his blush made me suspect sexual sadism.

"Stacey was ready for a new relationship, and there I was, Johnny-on-the-spot! I'm a lucky man. They don't get any more beautiful than that girl. Here, see for yourself.''

He reached into his shirt pocket and slipped out a photograph. Then he handed it across to me, almost falling into the space between our horses as he did so. Repressing a smile, I glanced at the picture. Love certainly was blind. Perhaps Pincus saw beauty, but I saw something else. The softly lit studio photograph revealed a suspiciously busty, thin-nosed blond with greed-narrowed eyes and collagen-plumped lips. Not even her forced smile could disguise the lines of dissatisfaction around her mouth.

"Lovely," I said, handing back the picture.

He beamed. "I took one look at her and fell in love at first sight. Later she told me it had happened to her, too.''

In other words, he fell for her implants, she for his billfold. "How sweet.''

He winked at me, all trace of his earlier gloom vanished. "Know what's even sweeter?''

I groaned inwardly, fearing that he was about to tell me she was a chili pepper in bed.

"We're pregnant!''

Once I recovered from my surprise, I noticed his more liberated use of "we." Stacey might be more progressive than I'd thought. "Why, congratulations, Vern. When's the baby due?"

"September. We've already decorated the nursery."

"Boy or girl?" Everyone these days, it seemed, knew in advance.

Pincus shrugged. "We don't know. Stacey's superstitious about that sort of thing. She says it's best to let nature take its course."

Remembering Stacey's surgically designed face and breasts, I doubted she held any deep-seated attachment for nature's wisdom, and filed the information away for further reference. In a murder investigation, you never knew what could turn out to be important.

As the sun rose higher in the sky, the cattle continued northward. Toward noon, we temporarily emerged from the narrow canyon onto an elongated meadow of scrub oak. The confining cliff walls left behind, everyone relaxed. Even the cattle became more attentive to the cowboys' "Hut! Hut!" as we wound along the broad, tree-lined trail.

Tired of Pincus's paeans to his ladylove's plastic beauty, I allowed Lady to lag behind. In the way of horses, she had become partial to the big sorrel gelding ridden by Hester Showalter, the lone female on MacPherson's board of directors. In the few conversations I'd had with her, I had found Hester to be both intelligent and observant. When the dirt fell on MacPherson's tarp-wrapped body, Hester had brushed her beauty-salon-blond hair back and muttered, "'My name is Ozymandias, king of kings: Look on my works, ye Mighty, and despair!'"

The blank looks on the other board members' faces revealed their ignorance of Shelley. Interesting, considering that Boston was supposed to be the pinnacle of American sophistication. Hell, they even taught the Romantics at my own alma mater, Arizona State University. Then I reminded myself that businessmen tended to prefer spread sheets to poets.

Except for Hester.

"This must be a difficult time for you, Hester," I said as soon as Lady had positioned herself next to her buddy. "From what I hear, Vern and you have been with Mac-Pherson since he started the company."

Actually, I'd heard a lot more than that. Renée, in a particularly catty mood before we left the ranch, had intimated there had once been more to Hester's relationship with MacPherson than business.

Hester didn't reply at first, nor turn to face me. She kept her eyes on the broad expanse of cattle rumps ahead of us, only becoming animated when a wayward cow and her calf headed off into the bushes.

"Shouldn't we go after them?" she finally asked.

Before I could answer, one of the trail hands reined his muscular Appaloosa toward the runaways. Within seconds, horse and rider caught up with the miscreants and turned them back toward the herd.

"Now that's what I call teamwork," Hester said. "The horse instinctively knew what his rider wanted."

"A lot of training went into that 'instinct,'" I pointed out. "But in a way, you're right. Some horses seem to be born wanting to please their riders."

"Like good secretaries?"

I smiled at the simile. "Hester, now that MacPherson is, um, gone, what will you do? Stay with the company or find something else?"

She finally turned her face to me and delivered my second surprise of the morning. An attractive woman despite her fifty-plus years, Hester appeared to have aged a decade overnight. Shadows now haunted her perfect oval face and lines of despair furrowed her formerly smooth cheeks. Even her ash-blond hair drooped.

She forced a smile. "Why would I leave the company

just because Stephen is dead? MacPherson Communications needs me more now than ever.''

I shrugged. ''My mistake.''

But I had obviously hit a nerve. A hard edge crept into her voice. ''Let me guess. You think that just because I'm a woman my loyalties have to be to a person. If so, you're wrong. As a board member, my loyalties remain with the company and its stockholders. These are perilous times we live in, and financial decisions have to be made with more caution than usual.''

Perhaps. But that didn't keep me from thinking that Hester's poorly disguised grief appeared more personal than corporate.

''So you'll stay with MacPherson Communications then?'' I asked.

She turned away from me again, making a big show out of looking for strays. ''Didn't I just say that? Now, if you'll excuse me, I need to keep my eye on those cows. With Stephen gone, we're short one trail rider.''

Remembering MacPherson's overenthusiastic but ineffectual attempts at herding, I didn't worry about it. Besides, something in Hester's entire conversation hit a false note. Although she made a big show out of her loyalty to MacPherson Communications, I noticed she seldom sought out the company of the other board members.

Why?

THREE

OUR LUCK with the weather ran out just before noon. While the low desert of mid-Arizona usually enjoyed sunny skies, we had already moved the cattle far enough north to enter a more tempestuous climate. At least the drizzle that soaked the riders did so gently and remained unaccompanied by lightning. No stampedes today.

Happy Trails' guests didn't appreciate the rain's tenderness, though. They pulled their rain slickers tightly around them and complained until the frustrated trail boss made Cookie pull over the chuck wagon for an early lunch.

"What a bunch of babies," Jessop said with a sneer as he tethered his horse next to mine at the rear of the supply wagon. I noticed, though, that he made sure none of the babies heard him. Like all the other cowboys at Happy Trails, he had been drilled in the Golden Rule of dude ranches everywhere: keep the guests happy at all costs, no matter how much they whined, carped and fussed.

"Don't underestimate them," I said, following him over to a flat, treeless area to help set up the chuck tent. "They're probably tough enough on their own turf."

While Vern Pincus struck me as a lust-blinded doofus, and the puffed-up Clinton Clayburn appeared little more than the standard corporate blowhard, I knew that no one ever rose to the boardroom heights without some mean business skills. Truth be told, I'd rather meet a drunken cowboy in a dark alley than a lit-up company vice president. At least the cowboy would come at me from the front.

When I shared my observation with Jessop, he laughed. "You got something there, Lena. I been in plenty of barroom brawls, but I never once hit a man from behind. Not even that time…" His face closed down and his voice trailed off.

Not even that time…? Jessop's mention of his involvement in barroom brawls surprised me, because I had always envisioned Slim's trail boss as the epitome of self-control. Yes, I was well aware that he held strong emotions, but I had never once seen them displayed in anything stronger than a frown. Now, as he worked beside me, I studied him more carefully.

Like many professional cowboys, Jessop was not tall, but he was solidly built, with a muscular torso that could have belonged to a much taller man. His deeply crevassed face reflected years underneath burning desert skies, and his stocky, bowed legs bespoke of long acquaintance with horses. I noticed that those massive hands of his, when opened, spread almost to the size of dinner plates and that his crooked fingers had obviously been broken more than once. A silvery network of scars led all the way from his dirt-encrusted fingernails to his thick wrists. Had those scars been inflicted by something other than horses and hard work?

The rain-soaked earth made driving the tent stakes into the ground easier than usual, and within mere minutes, our amateur cowboys had crowded under the tent without even waiting for Jessop and me to clear our gear away.

Clinton Clayburn immediately began hounding Cookie about the food. Death and lousy weather had made no inroads on his huge appetite.

"You'll get it when you get it," Cookie snarled back. "Now back off and let me cook."

"Cook?" Clayburn sniffed. "That's not cooking, that's cremating."

As I watched the big man annoy Cookie, I remembered that Clayburn had never expressed anything but anger over being forced along on the trail drive. He had constantly complained about his horse, his saddle, the heat and even the scenery.

"So where's that great Arizona outdoors Stephen promised us?" he growled. "Miles and miles of cattle asses, that's all I've seen."

The others apparently agreed with him, but were less vocal in their unhappiness. As MacPherson had prophesied, they proved themselves loathe to leave their jobs behind in Boston. Especially Vern Pincus, who after a surprisingly quick recovery from his shock over MacPherson's death, returned to his favorite topic of conversation: corporate buyouts.

"You think the FCC's ready to rule on FUN Cable yet?" Pincus asked Clayburn, shoveling beans into his mouth.

At first the dude's discussions of the Federal Communications Commission had intrigued me, especially since it appeared that MacPherson had tendered a near one-billion-dollar bid on a nationwide cable network that aired children's television shows. Nothing but Captain Kangaroo, Teletubbies and Ninja Turtles, all day long. But as soon as the group left the specifics—their company's ongoing troubles with the FCC's regulatory board and reeled into a mind-numbing recitation of Nielson ratings and audience shares— I grew bored.

Leaving Jessop to finish up, I wandered over to the supply wagon where Slim, as usual, was the last to tether his horse.

"Tell me about Jessop," I demanded.

"Ah, come on, Lena. Jessop's been with me even longer than Dusty. I'd trust him with my life." I noticed that Slim wouldn't look at me.

"That's all very touching, but I'd appreciate more concrete information. Jessop gave me the impression that he's been in more than his share of fights. Has he ever hurt anyone seriously?"

Slim took me by the arm and led me behind the supply wagon and out of the others' sight. "Look, I don't want you poking into my employees' pasts, okay? You know what ranch life is like. Somebody looking for work shows up, if he can handle horses, cows and tourists, I try him out for a couple of weeks. If he's done okay, I assign him to a bunk. As for background checks, hell, I'm not the FBI. But I can assure you that none of my guys are responsible for MacPherson's death. Especially not Jessop. That's a good man there."

Slim's defensive tone revealed more than he'd meant to. I made a wild guess. "Jessop's done time, hasn't he?"

"Oh, hell, Lena!" But his stricken face said I was right.

I put my hand on his arm. "Slim, like it or not, this is a murder investigation. If Jessop has a sheet, Sheriff Nakai will find out. Tell me what you know, or I'll have to question him myself."

He threw me an infuriated look. "Oh, really? Well, Miss Big Shot Detective, after you finish with Jessop, are you going to start questioning Dusty? Or are you just going to let that slide, seeing how you're so sweet on him and all."

Just the thought of Dusty harming MacPherson or anyone else was ridiculous, so I didn't respond to the jab. I merely repeated, "Tell me about Jessop."

As the rain continued to fall gently around us, a very unhappy Slim confirmed that my suspicions were correct. Before hiring on at Happy Trails, Jessop had led a less than stellar life, although one not too unusual among the cowboy set. A former drinking problem, now under control, had once earned him a three-year stint for assault at the Arizona State Prison.

"Three years just for assault?" I wondered aloud. "I know murderers who received less time."

Slim got that defensive look again. "Well, the guy almost died."

Which might have made the original charge Attempted Manslaughter. "Jessop pled down, then."

Slim nodded. "Jessop's ex-wife, uh, they'd been divorced for a couple of years by then, she hired him a good attorney. They're still friends, so that should tell you something about the man. Besides, Lena, the other guy started it."

The other guy always did. "Give me the details."

Slim's long face looked glummer than usual. "He'd taken his ex-wife and one of his stepdaughters out for the girl's twenty-first birthday. They wound up at this dance bar in Cave Creek where some coked-up yokel grabbed the girl's ass. The whole thing continued on from there, and by the time it was over, the guy was on life support. He made it, though. Now for Christ's sake, let's go eat."

As I settled onto a camp stool, tin plate in my lap, I wondered why Cookie's barbecue beef had lost so much of its flavor. Gee, it couldn't be the company, could it? Sitting directly across from me was the entire MacPherson Communications' board of directors: Clinton Clayburn, looking more like a fullback than ever; Hester Showalter, sitting as far away from Clayburn as possible—a little history there, perhaps?—and Vern Pincus, patting his shirt pocket to make sure his bouncing baby bride was still along for the ride. They were all wolfing down the "cremated" barbecue as if it were Chateaubriand. Sitting slightly apart from them, his nose stuck into a paperback novel, was Bob Gately, the fourth member of the MacPherson board. During the ride we'd exchanged few words, but he seemed friendly enough. Maybe his male model looks had put me off. Men that gorgeous had no right to be millionaires, as, according to Slim, all the MacPherson Communications people were.

But there was plenty of time for me to talk to Mr. Beautiful. Four more days, in fact. Then Sheriff Nakai could do the talking.

To my right, the trail hands, including Dusty and Jessop, had scrunched themselves into a tight pack, turning their backs to the dudes. Sitting next to me were Renée and Tiffany.

Hail, hail, the gang's all here.

Every now and then Jessop stared at me over his shoulder, a bitter smile tugging at a corner of his mouth. Surely he couldn't have heard my conversation with Slim. Or had he? Good trail bosses sometimes demonstrated almost preternatural senses when cattle and humans were concerned.

To get my mind off Jessop's angry stares, I turned to Renée, who, thank God for small favors, had not indulged in hysterics all day. Although she no longer wore makeup, she still looked beautiful, reminding me that *People* magazine had once termed her "The Sexiest Woman in Hollywood." But that had been more than a decade earlier. Since then, a long line of younger actresses had bumped her off the front page of the entertainment magazines.

Come to think of it, I hadn't seen Renée in any movies recently, either. Perhaps that was because Hollywood was a young person's town, and she, although still striking, was no longer young.

Even before Renée's husband had been killed, the cattle drive had begun to change her appearance. When we first set out, her long hair fell straight down in silky red locks, and she attended to it as if she would be gracing a Hollywood premiere that very evening. This morning, though, she had merely pulled her hair into a primitive pony tail and anchored it with a rubber band, revealing the signature cosmetic surgery scars in front of her ears. With her husband dead, did Renée no longer care how she looked? Or was this simply a new way of dramatizing herself?

I tried to remember what I had read about her and MacPherson.

As with so many entertainment-industry marriages, her marriage to MacPherson had begun with throngs of paparazzi and helicopters hovering over the outdoor wedding ceremony at MacPherson's Martha's Vineyard estate. Now, after a decade, their marriage had begun to implode in an equally public manner. Not long before the cattle drive began, the *Tribune*—one of the few newspapers not recently purchased by MacPherson Communications—had printed a blurry shot of MacPherson snuggling up to a young blonde on an Aspen ski slope. The girl had born a startling resemblance to Tiffany, although the caption identified her as "teenage actress Heather Steele, starring in the title role of the new Walt Disney film *Tinkerbell*."

Maybe MacPherson liked them young. I looked at Tiffany, who hadn't yet touched the food on her plate, and thought about those strap marks on her back. Had a jealous Renée put them there?

Or had MacPherson?

I remembered a highly publicized case when a Boston massage therapist had brought charges against MacPherson for assault. She claimed he had called her to his penthouse to work on his tight back muscles, but that the session had turned unexpectedly brutal. The masseuse wound up with a broken arm and had the X-rays to prove it.

After titillating the nation's talk shows for a week or two, the woman suddenly dropped the charges. Rumors hinted at a large payoff, but no one could find her to ascertain if the rumors were true. She seemed to have dropped off the face of the earth.

As I sat there, watching Renée eat her barbecue, I couldn't help but wonder if MacPherson had also played his little S and M games with Renée. If so, it wouldn't be the first time a Hollywood star turned out to like the rough stuff.

Taking for granted, of course, that Renée had been a willing participant.

I might as well see what I could find out.

"I'm so sorry about Mr. MacPherson," I said to Renée, hoping my condolences wouldn't trigger those banshee wails again.

At first I didn't think she was going to answer me. She just took another nibble of barbecue. Then she looked up at me with eyes untouched by tears. "Thanks."

Encouraged by her calm demeanor, I continued with my questioning. "What will you do now? Stay out on the Vineyard or move back to California?"

She shook her head so hard that a long red tendril escaped from the rubber band and fell across her cheek. She didn't bother brushing it back. "The Vineyard is our summer home," she said. "The main house is in Boston, and frankly, I can't stand the damned city. I still have a home in Beverly Hills, thank God. As far as I'm concerned, you can have the entire Eastern seaboard. Too many old buildings for me."

Alert to the fact that Tiffany was watching us intently, I lowered my voice, hoping that Renée would, too.

"Does Tiffany share your feelings about Boston?"

Renée's face hardened and for a moment, I feared she would revert to hysterics again. But I was wrong.

"It doesn't matter what Tiffany likes or dislikes," she said, loud enough for the girl to hear. "I've been thinking about sending her to boarding school, anyway. There's a place in Switzerland that's supposed to work wonders with troubled girls."

While I was pleasantly surprised that the self-centered Renée had actually noticed her daughter's unhappiness, it angered me to hear her discuss the girl's problems in public. I was even more disturbed to discover that Renée thought the solution was to send the girl away. Most children would interpret such an action as out-and-out rejection. Then again, boarding school might be a move up after living with Renée and Stephen MacPherson.

With Tiffany obviously listening to our conversation, I changed the topic. "They say work helps take your mind off grief. Are there any good scripts out there you're interested in?"

Renée flashed me a Hollywood smile. "Why, yes, now that you mention it. I'm thinking about going back into legitimate theater. A couple of years ago I performed the Scottish play in New York, and now I've been asked to do it in London."

I blinked. "The Scottish play?"

Tiffany leaned around her mother and said, "Mom means *MacBeth*. Actors think it's bad luck to use the name, so they just call it 'the Scottish play.' It's just another one of those stupid actors' superstitions."

The thought of Renée doing Shakespeare surprised me, because I'd mainly seen her in romantic comedies. But then I remembered that she'd received her Oscar for performing the role of Sapphire, an ex-nun-turned-prostitute who murders her pimp. Improbable, maybe, but that was Hollywood for you.

I allowed myself to look astonished. "You performed Lady MacBeth?"

"Of course. She's one of the greatest female roles in all theater. I did win an Oscar once, you know."

Lady MacBeth was also the role of a woman who conspires to kill a king, which made me wonder if Renée was a Method actress. Considering the circumstances, it would be rude to ask, so I threw her another rude question instead. "Um, I don't know much about Hollywood or the stage, but don't film roles pay more than theater?"

To Renée's obvious discomfort, Tiffany answered for her mother again. In full hearing of everyone in the chuck tent, she said loudly, "Oh, Mother's too old to get good film roles anymore. The casting directors say she doesn't appeal to the 'right demographics,' which means people my age. We're the ones who buy most of the movie tickets. But it doesn't matter how little some goofy stage part pays, anyway. Stephen said he was going to divorce her, but since he died before he could, she'll be rolling in money. Not that Mother was all that broke before, but once you're used to driving around Hollywood in Bentleys, it's not real cool to switch to Toyotas."

As I opened my mouth to pursue this intriguing subject, Renée gasped, stood and turned to her daughter with her hand upraised. But before Renée delivered the intended slap, she saw Jessop's shocked face, saw him rise and start toward her. So she lowered her hand, spun on her heel and stalked wordlessly toward her tent.

But not before I noted that she wore a belt approximately one inch wide.

With a malicious smile, Tiffany watched her mother stride away. "Mothers can be so hysterical, can't they?"

Hysterical? Well, I wouldn't know.

Later that day, as the rain stopped and the sky cleared, we were able to push on more quickly toward Flagstaff across the greening hills. Tiffany's question had made me reflect on my own mysterious past. I'd never known my mother or father. A throw-away child, I couldn't remember either of them. Hell, I couldn't even remember my own name. After completing the physical therapy necessitated by the gunshot wound that had almost killed me, I'd been named by a rather uncreative social worker before she'd signed the papers shipping me off to my first foster home.

Hysterical? Perhaps that had been my mother's problem. Maybe in a fit of hysterics over some problem, real or imagined, she had shot me and left me to die by the side of that

Phoenix road. But if so, why hadn't my father done anything to prevent it?

As I looked up at the hard blue Arizona sky, I wondered where my parents were.

And if they had hurt anyone else.

FOUR

THE FURTHER NORTH we pushed, the higher and steeper the mountains alongside our narrow valley became. We had left the desert behind and entered tall stands of ponderosa pine. At the same time, the trail grew rougher, revealing porous expanses of lava poking out of the slick granite beneath our feet. It was unstable footing, to be sure, but easy enough to navigate as long as no one did anything stupid.

But of course someone did.

Just after we had successfully navigated the herd along a particularly treacherous stretch of trail that wound along the top of a rock fall, Clinton Clayburn, in an ill-timed rebellion from riding drag, attempted to move his horse toward the front. The horse, startled by his clumsy urgings and loud "Yee-haw!" shied. As the wall-eyed creature scrabbled about, it knocked into the nearest packhorse, a pinto, sending it skidding sideways along the granite. For a second the pinto teetered at the top of the rock fall. Then, overbalanced by its heavy pack, it fell over the edge and onto the scattered rocks ten feet below.

But it was a survivable fall. I dismounted quickly, letting Lady's reins drop to a ground-tie, and hurried over to the trail edge. With relief I saw that the pinto had regained his footing and, except for a few scrapes along his flank, appeared none the worse for wear.

Muttering imprecations under my breath about Clayburn's stupidity, I slid down the boulders on my rump until

I reached the shaken animal. Then I saw the more serious injury.

As the pinto had fallen, his cannon bone—the longest section of a horse's leg—had become entangled with the snapped rope that had connected it to the other pack animals. Now the leg hung uselessly, crooked at an odd angle.

"Oh, sweetheart." I sighed, as I attempted to calm the trembling animal. "I'm so sorry."

They say horses don't cry, but the pinto's eyes were as damp as mine when Jessop scrambled down the slide to join us. I said nothing as his huge hands gently inspected the damage, nothing when he gave vent to a long stream of curses that would have repulsed a pirate. I also said nothing when he threatened to kill Clayburn; I wanted to kill the idiot myself.

"What are we going to do?" I asked the trail boss when his curses finally wound down. "The horse is in pain. And you know…"

"Yeah, I know." To make the animal more comfortable, he removed its pack and set it to one side. After giving the dangling leg one final look, he said, "You wait here and keep him calm. I'll get Slim."

He climbed back up the rock fall to the trail, then paused for a moment to give Clayburn, who had dismounted to see what was going on, a hefty kick in the behind. As Jessop continued along the trail toward the front of the herd, Clayburn fell face forward onto the rocks. Unfortunately, he didn't slide over the edge into my waiting arms so that I could encore the butt kick.

"I'll sue your ass for that!" Clayburn shouted at the trail boss, who didn't even bother to look back. "I'll take every penny you have!" With that pointless threat—cowboys have no money, just calluses—Clayburn picked himself up and clambered back onto his horse. He still did not realize the damage he had caused.

Neither had any of the other city folk. They peered over the edge of the rock fall, providing an unwanted audience to the drama below.

Leaning my head into the pinto's glossy neck, I reached up and scratched his ears. He leaned back against me, making low, rumbling noises in his throat, a horse's version of sobs. I wished I knew his name, but all I knew about him was that he was sweet-tempered, liked to hang around Moonglow and always gave a joyous little buck when his pack was removed at the end of the day.

"We'll take care of you, boy, yes we will," I whispered to him. "We won't let you suffer."

But what could we do for him? When I had signed up for the ride, Slim had ordered me to leave my .38 behind. Yet there was no way we could simply leave the horse for the coyotes.

Sorrowing, I began to sing to the doomed animal.

> "Hush-a-bye, don't you cry.
> Go to sleep, my little baby.
> When you wake, you will see
> All the pretty little horses."

Soon Slim, accompanied by Jessop and Dusty, appeared at the top of the rock fall.

"Ah, hell, it's Jerry," Slim said as soon as they joined me. With a woeful look, he walked up to the pinto, who even in its pain, stretched its neck forward to nuzzle its master.

Slim stroked the velvety nose once, then bent down to inspect the leg. After a moment he straightened and stroked the pinto's nose again. "Oh, Jerry-boy, what am I going to do with you?"

But I knew what Slim was going to do with Jerry-boy. I had seen a holstered Bulldog .44 Special strapped to his thigh. Well, I should have known. Slim may have forbidden me to bring my gun on the ride, but he had obviously packed his own. It only made sense. No one knew what might happen on a trail ride.

Jerry's situation was hopeless. There was no chance that a cash-strapped rancher such as Slim would resort to the luxury of airlifting in a vet, even if we could get a call out of the canyon to one. Because of a horse's unique circulatory system, a broken leg was almost always fatal. Death remained the usual treatment. And no weapon—short of a syringe full of potassium cyanide—dealt such severe mercy more efficiently than a gun.

Slim cocked his revolver. "Everybody move back so Jerry doesn't fall on you."

We stepped back.

Slim leaned toward his horse again, the .44 pointed straight down. "We've had a good, long ride together, haven't we, Jerry? Well, I'll see you some day on the other side of the trail."

Calmed by his master, Jerry shut his eyes and fluted his nostrils in contentment.

With a swift motion, Slim raised the gun and pointed it at the horse.

I shut my eyes.

But I couldn't shut out the sound.

GRIEVING THE LOSS of his favorite packhorse, Slim kept us moving quickly throughout the afternoon, snapping at anyone who dared complain about the pace. For obvious reasons, we kept Clayburn away from him. Still not understanding the part he'd played in the tragedy, the big man continued to bluster until Renée told him to shut up.

"You are the most abysmally stupid man I've ever known, and I've known many," she snapped, her ponytail long collapsed into scraggily tendrils around her dust-caked face. "No wonder Stephen was getting rid of you."

"You're fantasizing as usual, Renée," Clayburn said, shifting his considerable bulk in his saddle. "Stephen wasn't getting rid of anyone except you."

"The hell you say. You were on your way out, and you know it. You think Stephen didn't tell me the truth about you and why you were always hitting him up for loans? Hell, the only reason you're not in jail for domestic abuse is because you used the money to buy off your ex-wives! You're disgusting, that's what you are. For that matter, you're *all* disgusting! Stephen thought so, too. He said that the entire board was dead weight, that none of you had any vision, and that he was calling in all those loans. Then he was going to…"

Sensing that Renée was about to embark upon a tirade that would rival Clayburn's deadly yee-haw, Vern Pincus attempted to sooth her. "Please, Renée. Things are difficult enough without fighting among ourselves."

As angry people tend to do, Renée turned on the peacemaker. "Ourselves? Don't include me with you pack of losers! And as for you, Vern, if it weren't for Stephen you'd be back where you started, doing other losers' taxes!"

Pincus winced. "Stephen always appreciated my accounting skills. That's why he appointed me chief financial officer."

Renée vented an ugly laugh. "Oh, you mean it wasn't because you're Kissass Number One at that miserable company? Ha! When he wanted to do an end run around the board, you were the person he always started with. For Christ's sake, Vern! How can you be so clueless?"

A shocked silence, then Bob Gately, looking more like a male model than ever, maneuvered his big blue roan between the two.

"Let's not scare the cattle," Gately said. "I realize that

we're all under a lot of tension, but there's no need to give in to it. Especially since we've got four hundred cattle in front of us, and they're looking jumpy.''

Renée cast a quick look at the herd. Even she could tell that the animals around her appeared more tense than before. With an obvious effort, she quieted.

But the merciful silence did not last long. Tiffany, who had been ominously quiet since Jerry's death, began to cry in great gulping sobs.

"Now look what you've done! You think you know so much, but—'' Clayburn said to Renée.

Hester interrupted. "Clinton, leave it alone. The girl's upset enough already.''

It was true. Tears streamed down Tiffany's face, and I feared they might be the harbinger of true hysterics, not her mother's theatrical kind. Motioning to the nearby cowboys to continue on, I grabbed her horse's reins and steered her over to the side of the trail.

"He…he…he was murdered!'' the girl wailed. "Right there! I…I saw the whole thing!''

I stiffened. Tiffany had seen her stepfather being killed? Why hadn't she spoken up before?

The girl's sobs grew louder and louder, until to my dismay, she slid off her horse and onto the ground. She lay there crying, facedown in the dirt.

"Oh, hell,'' I muttered. Not knowing what else to do, I dismounted, bent down and hauled her to her feet. As I did so, the affection-starved girl wrapped her arms around me and wailed onto my shoulder.

I let her cry for a few minutes, but when she finally regained some semblance of control, I seized the moment. "Who killed him, Tiffany?''

"Wha…what?'' The face she turned up to me was pathetic in its distress.

"I said, who killed your stepfather? You need to tell me.''

"Who killed my stepfather?" Bafflement replaced her bereft expression. "I thought Moonglow did."

"Then what did you mean when you said you saw him murdered?"

She sniffled. "I meant Jerry. The horse."

I tried not to show my annoyance. The girl was just fifteen, and the horse's death had probably been the first she had ever witnessed. Watching the event—it had taken two shots from Slim's .44 to dispatch the wretched animal—had even upset the adult members of the cattle drive. Especially the rough, tough cowboys.

Attempting to talk a little sense into her, I said, "Tiffany, what happened was very sad and I'm sorry you had to see it, but Jerry was a horse. Your stepfather was a human being."

She wiped her eyes with the hem of her shirt. "Human being? You didn't know him."

"Nobody deserves to be mur...killed."

The look she gave me then was canny, if a bit bleary. "You almost said murdered, didn't you?"

"Because that's what you said. I mean, what I thought you said. That you saw your stepfather being murdered." I hoped she bought it.

"But everybody said that Moonglow..." She trailed off again, then thought for a moment. "Do you think that maybe Moonglow didn't kill Stephen? That someone else did?"

With anyone other than Tiffany, I might have raised the possibility of murder, but her emotionally fragile state argued against it. "Moonglow's a pretty spooky horse, kid, and your stepfather shouldn't have been on him. It just wasn't smart."

No lie there. For all MacPherson's much-vaunted corporate genius, when it came to living creatures—by which I include both horses *and* humans—he had been as dumb as a rock.

Tiffany began to cry again, this time more softly. When she leaned against my shoulder, I patted her back, murmuring, "There, there," much as I had to poor Jerry.

My attention was so focused on the weeping girl that I didn't truly register the sound of nearing hoofbeats, the creak of a dismounting rider, the tat-tat-tat of hurried footsteps.

I ignored everything until someone jerked Tiffany out of my arms and slapped me hard across my face.

"Get your hands off her, you dyke!"

Renée, who had ridden back with one of the trail hands to collect her daughter, grasped the stunned girl's arm with one hand, then drew back the other to slap me again.

I blocked the blow easily, and for a second, thought about returning the favor. In the end, though, I decided that Tiffany had seen enough violence for one day. Taking a deep breath, I stepped out of slapping range and spoke as calmly as possible, given the situation. "Renée, your daughter was distraught, and I was merely comforting her."

Renée sneered, her beautiful face twisted into a gargoyle mask. "A likely story." But, perhaps noticing the look in my eyes, she did not raise her hand to me again.

Behind her, Tiffany snuffled. "Lena's telling the truth, Mother. I was upset."

Renée ignored her. "Miss Jones, when we get to Flagstaff, I'm filing charges against you!"

"For what? Showing compassion?"

"Indecent sexual overtures to a minor."

I almost laughed. "Oh, really, now, Renée. No judge will take that claim seriously."

But she wasn't finished. "Not only that, but I'm suing you for alienation of Stephen's affections, too. You weren't just trying to seduce my daughter, you also tried to seduce my husband!''

The trail hand who had brought Renée back to collect her daughter gasped. He would have plenty to talk about in the bunk tent tonight.

Was there no end to Renée's foolishness? "You can't be serious!''

"I saw him looking at you, Miss Big Tits! Don't tell me you didn't fall for him, too! Every woman does!''

Tiffany, tears vanished, entered the fray. "Oh, Mother, would you just stop? You always accused your husbands of fooling around. Even my father.''

Renée turned on her. "Shut your mouth about your father, you brat. You don't know anything.''

But Tiffany wouldn't be silenced. "I know enough! You think I don't remember, but I do. He died the same night you two had that big fight over some other stupid actress! And everybody says you killed him!''

Renée's face paled. "Tiffany, get on your horse. Now! I want you away from this woman.''

Tiffany obeyed, but not before throwing me a smile every bit as malicious as the one I had seen earlier in the chuck tent. Then the two rode off, leaving me standing there in the middle of the trail, mouth agape.

"Jesus, I hate city people,'' the trail hand muttered, breaking the sudden silence. "Even their females are jerks.''

Lady must have agreed with him, because as I remounted, she vented a snort. While we trotted to rejoin the others, I could not help reflecting upon my miserable "vacation.'' In less than a week we had not just lost a man and a horse, but had also accumulated three threatened lawsuits: one against Jessop for assault and two against me for being a nondenominational hussy. Yet we still had several days' journey left before we reached the high, green meadows of Flagstaff.

Surely the cattle drive had used up its store of bad luck.

FIVE

I WAS WRONG, of course. Bad luck continued to dog us as we climbed north through the verdant valley toward the still snowcapped San Francisco Peaks, which now loomed in the distance.

First, a yellow jacket stung Jessop as he answered a call of nature behind a creosote bush. Less than an hour later, Dusty's horse bruised the interior of his hoof clambering over a rock field, so he had to transfer his tack to Moonglow, whose high-strung temperament Dusty had little patience for. Then another rock slide blocked the trail ahead of us, necessitating a five-mile detour. A horse can walk five miles an hour, but a cattle herd isn't as quick on its feet. Given the cattle's grazing, meandering and basically brainless behavior, it took us a full three hours to pick up the trail again. By then, all the dudes—as brainless as the cattle—had begun to quarrel.

Hester complained to Clayburn that the stock tip he'd given her several months earlier had lost half its value already. Clayburn complained to Pincus that the newlywed should spend less time dreaming about his bouncing baby bride and more time thinking about MacPherson Communications' looming financial crisis. Not to be left out of the carping sweepstakes, Pincus told Renée it was about time she started pulling her own weight; namely, to start rounding up strays before the animals were left behind in the brush.

To my surprise, Renée did as Pincus suggested and moved up to join the flankers.

Not wanting to miss my chance, I rode up beside him.

"How much do you know about Renée?" I asked Pincus. "Her daughter said something odd earlier, that Renée's former husband, uh, died. In fact, she hinted that Renée actually killed him."

Pincus snorted. "Which husband was that? She's had quite a few, you know. She changes them with her wardrobe."

"I'm talking about Tiffany's father."

He nodded. "Oh, yeah. That one. I heard it was an accident, but I don't really know too much about all that ancient history stuff, just what I read in the tabloids." Then he smiled, some of his usual good nature returning. "And of course I don't read the tabloids, just *Barron's* and the *Wall Street Journal.* But if you really want to know the truth about that old scandal, you ought to talk to Bob Gately, not Tiffany. I'm no fan of Renée's, but I doubt if she ever killed anyone, not even a husband!"

Pincus laughed at his little witticism, then choked on the ever-present trail dust. "Lord, I hope I survive this," he rasped. "Anyway, I'm sure Bob would be glad to tell you all about it."

He gestured toward the other side of the herd at Mr. Beautiful.

"Bob's married to Jini Salsoza, one of the producers on the movie that was being filmed when the guy died. Jini's always hated Renée, so I'm betting Bob got the benefit of some pretty sizzling pillow talk around then. Hell, he probably knows more about Jeff's death than the police do!"

Intrigued, I began working my way around the herd to Gately, where Mr. Beautiful had formed an outrider trio with two of the cowboys. Unlike the rest of the dudes, Gately sat his horse with the ease of a lifelong rider.

I'd meant to talk to Gately earlier, but he seldom mixed with the crowd around the campfire. Instead, he was usually reading one of the paperback Agatha Christie and Patricia Cornwell novels he'd stored in his saddlebags. He had even brought a small, battery-powered reader's light so that he could continue his reading long after the rest of us were asleep. Once, when Renée had chided him for being anti-social, he had explained that his wife wanted him to see if any of the novels would serve as a Ben Affleck vehicle.

But Tiffany, true to form, had cattily disagreed. "He just doesn't want to be anywhere near you, Mom."

As I maneuvered Lady toward him, I hoped Tiffany's assessment had been correct. If Gately disliked Renée, he would be more inclined to dish the dirt.

"Howdy, cowpokes," I said, finally reining alongside the outrider trio.

Gately tipped his hat. "Howdy yourself, ma'am." A wink.

The cowboys smiled, but kept their eyes on the cattle.

Mr. Beautiful looked happy in the saddle, perhaps because unlike the others, his horse hadn't bit, stomped or kicked him. And that would have been a shame, for he could easily have earned a healthy living as leading man himself. His eyes were the color of the Arizona sky, his hair the same soft gold as desert sand. Although his facial features were almost too delicate for a man's, his large frame and broad shoulders lent him an impressive masculinity.

"You look like you ride a lot," I told him, to break the ice.

"Grew up on horses on my parents' farm in Virginia," he said, with his heartbreaker's smile. "I haven't done much riding since my school days, but it's like riding a bike. Once you learn, you never forget."

We talked about horses and their intriguing ways for a while, and shared a few words of sorrow over Jerry. Then

I edged into the real conversation. "I hear your wife's a movie producer."

He beamed. "Oh, yes. Jini's a brilliant, creative woman." There was genuine pride in his soft drawl as he proceeded to reel off her film credits. To my surprise, I had seen most of her movies, which contained fewer car chases than the standard Hollywood dreck.

I did not have to fake the admiration in my voice. "That's quite a résumé."

Gately nodded. "When I retire, Jini will keep me in the style to which I've become accustomed."

"You thinking about retiring?" For the first time I noticed the sun crinkles around his eyes, but decided that age had only added to his good looks.

"I wasn't before this. After Stephen's death, though... Well, let's just say I'm rapidly losing interest in the communications industry. I'd rather spend the rest of my days helping Jini find good film material. It's much more entertaining."

The perfect opening. "Speaking of film, Renée starred in one of those movies your wife produced, didn't she?"

Another nod. "Yes, Renée won an Oscar for her performance in *Hearts of Dust*. At first, the movie wasn't all that successful. You know, a little too artsy. But the week after the Academy Awards ceremony, box office receipts doubled."

"Wasn't there some kind of tragedy during filming?"

Mr. Beautiful's matinee idol smile faded. "One night Jeff, Renée's husband, fell down the stairs at their house and broke his neck. He died instantly. Fortunately, Renée had already filmed her major scenes. You know how, um, *dramatic* she can get, so you can imagine how she carried on when he died. She wound up spending a couple of months in a clinic."

I frowned. "I'm sure it was terrible for her, but what

happened to Tiffany during all this time? Did she stay with her grandparents?''

Gately shook his head. ''Both Renée's and Jeff's parents were dead, so my wife and I took the kid in. Talk about a troubled child!'' He shook his head. ''When Renée finally checked out of the clinic and came to pick her up, we told her the girl needed serious therapy, but she just ignored us. Renée doesn't worry herself about anything that doesn't directly involve Renée.''

I'd noticed. ''Say, wasn't there some rumor going around about Jeff and another woman?''

A flicker of distaste crossed Mr. Beautiful's face. ''That kind of gossip always dogs movie sets, but I doubt if it was anything serious, especially since Renée was the major breadwinner of the family. Jeff may have been just a stuntman, but he wasn't stupid. He liked money, and Tess, the lady in question, had none. Now, this may sound harsh, but Tess also wasn't talented enough or smart enough or pretty enough to get very far in Hollywood. She eventually left the business. The last I heard, she was working as the social director of some ski lodge in Aspen.''

We chatted for a few more minutes, then Gately tipped his hat to me again and rode off in pursuit of a maverick steer. He left me wondering how a professional stuntman could be clumsy enough to break his neck falling down his own stairs.

SLIM KEPT US MOVING forward all afternoon with no breaks, and by the time he finally called camp, dusk had fallen, shading the cliffs surrounding us a deep purple. Exhausted, most riders ate their dinner wordlessly, then staggered toward their separate tents.

As I neared mine, I heard steps behind me. I turned to see Slim, his face drawn with anxiety.

He took me by the arm and guided me toward the stand

of scrub oak at the edge of the clearing. His voice was an urgent whisper. "Lena, my gun's missing. So's the cell phone. You got anything you want to tell me?"

My mouth dropped. "Your *gun*'s missing? *And* the phone?"

"I had them both stashed in my bedroll. But I'm not worried about the damn phone—the battery was almost dead, anyway. The gun's a worse problem. When I unrolled my sleeping bag, it was gone. And, well, I kind of hoped that you…"

Maybe I should have been insulted that Slim suspected me of theft, but I wasn't. We were old friends, and he well knew my level of paranoia.

"I'm sorry, Slim. I didn't take it."

We just stood there for a few seconds, staring at each other. Then Slim began to swear softly.

Knowing what the missing gun probably meant, I joined him.

SIX

THAT NIGHT, Dusty didn't come to our tent until almost midnight. I lay awake waiting for him, listening to Renée's soft laughter answered by a man's indecipherable voice. It probably wouldn't have bothered me as much if I had not known Dusty's weakness for redheads.

The next morning, I rose and dressed in silence.

"Hey, hon, what's the matter?" Dusty's hand slipped up and down my spine, finally coming to a stop between my shoulder blades. He began to massage me there, in soft, circular motions. Ordinarily I would turn to him, but not now.

I stepped away. "Nothing's the matter."

He cocked his head. "Anyone ever tell you you're a lousy liar?"

"Only experts."

He blinked. "Hey, what's that supposed to mean?" His hand, which had remained in the air when I moved away from him, fell back.

"It means that it takes a liar to catch a liar." I opened the tent flap and stepped out, leaving him there, a puzzled look on his face.

Looks can lie, too.

"WE SHOULD REACH THE Mormon Lake cutoff by late afternoon tomorrow," Slim told me, as I joined him near the front of the herd after putting four hundred cows' worth of distance between me and Dusty. "There's a ranch only about ten miles up the cutoff, so when we near it, I'm sending one of the wranglers up ahead to call the sheriff from the ranch's landline."

I should have felt relieved, but I didn't. The missing gun bothered me and I told him so.

"Look, I've told the wranglers to keep an eye out for that gun, but I don't expect much," Slim told me. "Stay close to the herd and don't go wandering off anywhere by yourself. I think our guests are beginning to think you're too nosy. Cool it until we hook up with Nakai, okay?"

"Sure."

I doubt if he believed me. I didn't even believe myself.

Sneaking a quick look behind us, I saw that the dudes, as if seeking safety in numbers, had done exactly what Slim cautioned them not to do. The entire MacPherson Communications board of directors had bunched up and were now riding in a tight pack at the rear of the herd. Only Renée and Tiffany remained in their newly assigned mid-flank position, every now and then making a run at stray steers. As far as herding went, the board's clumped formation was inefficient, but I, for one, found it comforting. The gun thief couldn't get off a shot without the others seeing. Not only that, each member of the board had an unobstructed view of the grieving widow, too.

Slim's and my temporary safety assured, I began organizing my thoughts as the herd spread out through a gently rising valley brightened by yellow blooming creosote and pink filaree. Lady, ever alert to my tension, swiveled her ears back and forth, shying to the left when a covey of quail burst, chittering and squawking, from behind a stand of prickly pear cactus.

"Easy, easy," I whispered to her, leaning forward to scratch between her ears. "We don't want another broken leg on this ride, do we?"

Calmed by my voice, she settled down and soon moved along fluidly with the herd, her eyes watching for any untoward movement. I didn't calm. If anything, my anxiety grew as the morning progressed.

Stealing Slim's gun and cell phone had been a bold move. Considering the number of people on the ride, the constant walking back and forth between the tents, someone could easily have spotted the perp entering Slim's tent. In fact, I was puzzled as to why this hadn't happened. Other things worried me, too. Slim and I had pretended to accept MacPherson's death as an accident. Did the theft mean that the murderer suspected we knew the truth? And why would he steal a gun unless he meant to use it?

So many unanswered questions, so many complicated personalities. Yet beneath it all, murder tended to be the most simple of all crimes.

I had long ago learned that to understand a murderer, you must understand the victim. This placed me at a disadvantage, because although I'd read a lot about MacPherson in the newspapers, I hardly knew him personally. And what did I know, really? That his wife and stepdaughter hated him, probably for good reason. I'd also begun to suspect that his business associates—for all their crocodile tears at his trailside memorial—feared him.

But fear was a mainstay in the corporate world, wasn't it? From what I'd seen in some of my own cases, I knew that the average Brooks Brothers-suited businessman could be as vicious as any gangsta thug; he just initiated a hostile takeover instead of a drive-by. And speaking of hostile takeovers, hadn't I heard something recently about MacPherson Communications doing exactly that? From what I had overheard in the chuck tent, MacPherson's purchase of the children's cable TV network seemed relatively straightforward. But something else nagged at me. As the cattle flowed around us, I searched my memory.

Then I remembered.

About a year ago, television news shows broadcast exhaustive coverage of the Federal Communications Commission hearings. From what I could understand, the FCC had decided to ease its regulations on how many television stations and newspapers one corporation could own in a certain geographic locale. But limitations still remained, so private media companies still lobbied for greater freedom. MacPherson, certain the private sector would win, had already jumped the gun.

Several months back, at the bottom of the local ten-o'clock news, an inanely smiling newscaster updated the ongoing media struggle. MacPherson Communications had purchased the Arizona-based Taggart Enterprises, one of the U.S.'s sole remaining family-owned newspaper chains. A couple of weeks later, the same newscaster, still smiling, informed me that MacPherson Communications was now attempting to take over several Southwestern cable television companies, many of them covering the same areas as Taggart's twenty-one newspapers. Because this would give MacPherson a blatant monopoly on all media coverage in the Southwest, the FCC, as well as the Securities and Exchange Commission, launched an investigation.

My familiarity with the corporate world was little more than elementary, but even I knew that when the FCC and SEC started nosing around, savvy folks began quietly unloading their stock holdings. On a later news report, the same newscaster—his vanished smile tipping me off that he was now probably a MacPherson employee—informed me that the investigation had caused MacPherson stock prices to dive, and that even the company's 401K plan was in jeopardy.

Then something clicked into place, something that had once intrigued me but that I had let slide. The very fact that the insensitive MacPherson had engineered this cattle drive as a "bonding" experience for his board of directors signaled serious dissent in the corporate ranks. MacPherson, after all, was a man who apparently felt it was his right to invade every facet of his board's life, to the extent of even bullying them all into joining the same health club he belonged to.

Business problems, personal problems. Was there any area of MacPherson's life that had not operated at crisis point?

I looked at the cattle, now moving like a brown carpet across a green meadow, and saw Renée's bright red hair in the distance. *Beloved,* she had called MacPherson, but I had never seen any man less beloved. Or was I studying the problem from the wrong perspective? From personal experience I'd learned that love caused almost as many murders as hatred.

Who could have loved the unlovable MacPherson enough to kill him?

"Penny for your thoughts," Hester said as she rode up beside me.

Lady, jealous of her turf, took a quick nip at Hester's big sorrel gelding. It shied to the side, but Hester, now seasoned by a week in the saddle, rode it out like a veteran.

"Snot!" I smacked Lady on the rump, and she flattened her ears in irritation. She looked around at me, her upper lip atwitch, alerting me that she was considering revenge. "Don't even think about it," I warned her.

Lady plastered a "Who, me?" expression on her long face and returned her ears to normal.

Hester smiled. "You really know horses."

I smiled back. "They're not too different from people, just more straightforward."

The horses settled down and Hester rephrased her question. "What were you thinking about when I rode up? You had the strangest expression on your face."

After Slim's warning, I knew I had to be careful. "I was wondering why MacPherson was so adamant about bringing you all on this cattle drive. Other than Bob Gately, none of you seems to have much affection for life in the saddle. Neither did MacPherson, actually."

"But that was Stephen all over," she said, watching as one cow separated itself from the herd and trotted toward a grove of piñon pine. Just as she started to rein her gelding toward it, one of the trail hands cut the cow off and drove it back to the herd.

Hester returned her attention to me. "Stephen was brilliant in many ways, but he was impulsive to a fault. He'd get some crazy idea, and the next thing you knew, we were all marching along after him like kids behind the Pied Piper."

"Impulsive? That's surprising. I would have thought that men with his power planned everything."

As she shrugged, I noticed how deeply the Arizona sun etched the lines in her face. I could still tell, though, that she had once been beautiful.

"Oh, Stephen planned ahead, all right," she said. "Just in the wrong way. He believed that because he wanted something, he would automatically get it."

"I'd imagine that could be a dangerous trait in business."

"In other things, too." Sadness colored her voice.

Here was my chance. "Tell me if I'm sticking my nose in something that's none of my business, but I heard a rumor that you and Mac…Stephen used to be, well, involved."

She gave me a piercing look. "Yes, that is a little nosy, but you're quite the nosy woman, aren't you? Always asking questions, pretending to just be making conversation. But everyone back in Boston knows the truth about Stephen and me, so why not you? I love—*loved* the man. There was even a time I thought… Well, never mind what I thought. Women always dream dreams, don't they?"

Yeah, but for some of us, those dreams are nightmares. "What happened?"

"Wife number one happened, that's what," she said bitterly. "A Back Bay socialite who gave him the financial backing he needed to become a major player in the communications industry. Then wife number two came along, a *Playboy* centerfold. Stephen didn't need money quite so much then, just big boobs and an empty brain pan. When he tired of her, along came wife number three, Renée, with all that Hollywood glamour and glitter. Now I guess prospective wife number four will have to shed her tears in private and stay married to her husband number one."

"Prospective wife? Then it's true that he was going to leave Renée for someone else?"

Her voice took on an even harder edge. "Of course he was. Once he recovered from the thrill of being married to an Oscar winner, he began to realize how shallow she was. And shallow can get pretty boring after a while."

"Did Renée suspect?"

She nodded. "Renée's crazy, but she's not stupid. She may not have known how serious the relationship with the other woman had become. But it was as serious as you can get, if you catch my meaning."

I didn't, and I guess my bafflement showed on my face.

Hester sighed. "The girl told Stephen she was going to have his baby, and guess what? He was thrilled!"

My mind whirled. "Hester, didn't you say that, uh, prospective wife number four is married to someone else?"

"So? Since when did that ever stop Stephen?" She gave me a wry smile. "But Renée is convinced that the girl is nothing more than another of Stephen's usual blondes, faithfully waiting to sooth his saddle sores when he returned to Boston."

Usual blondes. I looked at Hester carefully. After MacPherson's death, she had stopped applying makeup every morning, allowing her almost-white eyebrows and eyelashes to remain undarkened. A natural blonde, now gone gray.

She noticed my stare. "Yes, Lena. *The usual blondes.* Stephen may have married a redhead and a brunette, but his bimbo of choice was always a blonde." She touched her own hair. "Considering my own coloring, maybe I shouldn't be so harsh about the poor girls."

I couldn't help feeling sorry for her. Loving an unfaithful man was always painful, but at least Dusty and I had managed to come to an understanding. Since I refused to commit to him—foster home survivors tend to be terrible at commitment—I told him he remained free to pursue interests elsewhere. As did I. My problem was that I'd never really cared for anyone other than Dusty.

Hester broke into my thoughts. "For a few years there at the beginning, when we were starting up MacPherson Communications, I though Stephen would eventually marry me. We even talked about it. But then he met the socialite. She was thinner than me, richer than me, and much, much quicker to get everything down on paper. I knew it wouldn't last, though."

Ah, the wisdom of hindsight. "How is that?"

She flashed her teeth, but it resembled a grimace more than a smile. "Before the ink dried on the marriage certificate, he was back in my bed. And he never really left."

With that, she kicked her sorrel ahead and left me behind with my mouth hanging open.

FOR THE REST of the afternoon, as the cattle flowed over valley after valley, I kept repeating the mantra, *understand the victim, understand the killer.* But every time I did, another part of me argued that Stephen MacPherson was too complicated a man to ever understand. Still, I had to try.

What did I really know about him? That he was a superb

businessman who managed to make billions, yet endangered it all by stretching FCC and SEC rules against media monopoly. A manipulator of both men and women who became an out-and-out bully when manipulation failed. An unfaithful husband and unfaithful lover.

Then there was his odd behavior with Tiffany, and the belt marks on her back. In addition to all his other faults, could MacPherson have been a child molester?

But Tiffany wasn't exactly a child, was she?

SEVEN

WHEN JESSOP CALLED a lunch break, I tethered Lady to the supply wagon by herself. In addition to her recent feud with Hester's gelding, she was now quarreling with every horse in sight. Before I could stop her, she had managed to sneak a bite out of Gately's blue roan and the unfortunate Moonglow.

"Bitch," I muttered at her as I secured her halter rope. "What's got into you?"

But I could guess. Horses are sensitive creatures, and the rising tension had affected them even more than it had the cattle. All the animals were afraid; they just didn't know what—or who—to pin their fear on.

Come to think of it, neither did I.

Noontime break was a hurried affair, but no one complained. Jessop gave us time enough to exercise the kinks out of our legs, which the dudes appreciated. Singly and in pairs, they walked in tight, nervous little circles around the camp, never once venturing beyond the supply wagon. What were they afraid of? An attack by wild Indians?

After wolfing down a few hot dogs and beans, we climbed back on our horses and continued north, pushing hard for the Mormon Lake cutoff. When I took my turn riding point at the front of the herd to help guide the lead steers along the rocky trail, the view—rolling meadows instead of cattle rumps—improved immeasurably. For a while, Lady and I simply ambled along, enjoying the change of scenery, but after an hour or two, I began to obsess about MacPherson again. By the time the sun began to drop behind the western cliff face, I was more exhausted from thinking than from riding. The dark-backed cattle blended into the deepening shadows so perfectly that during some stretches along the trail, I couldn't tell where the cattle left off and the canyon walls began.

A peaceful scene, disturbed only by the knowledge that the wrong person now had a gun.

But we only had a few more miles to go before we reached the cutoff. From there, one of the wranglers would make his run up the flat, safe surface of the road to a phone. Then the whole mess would be the sheriff's problem, not mine.

With a sense of relief, I eased back in the saddle.

Only to sit straight up again when I heard the gunshot.

At least I think it was one gunshot, but from the way the sound reverberated around the surrounding canyon walls, it could have been an entire artillery barrage. Lady shied to the side, but riding that out was easy. The true danger lay elsewhere.

Settling her, I snapped a look back, saw the white-rimmed eyes of the lead steers, and knew the worst was about to happen.

"Dudes ride out!" Jessop bawled, motioning for the drag riders to head for the safety of the trees.

Even as Jessop yelled, the terrified herd began to charge toward me.

Stampede.

"*Heeyaaaaw!*" I screamed at Lady and dug my heels into her flanks.

But she didn't need my urging. Even more terrified than the steers, Lady bolted away from the herd with her neck outstretched, ears flattened. Behind us I could hear the flankers shouting instructions to each other as they spurred their horses toward the front, hoping to turn the herd into a circle, then finally bring it to a halt.

A stampede was the one event every cowboy feared and did his utmost to prevent. In their panicked state, herds of thousands had been known to run off cliffs, drown themselves in rivers, or smash themselves against trees or canyon walls. God help any creature unfortunate enough to be caught in their path. I could only hope that Lady would outrun them, that as we fled down the trail in front of the herd she wouldn't fall and deliver us both to the savagery of sixteen hundred hooves. She was a fast horse, but I knew the uneven ground would work against us, offering up death with every twist and dip.

But we had no choice. We sped up the trail at a full gallop, a fool's pace. Even bent low in jockey position over Lady's neck, I could sense the trees whipping by on our right flank, the steep canyon wall blurring to our left. Collision with either spelled certain doom. All we could do was continue our mad pace forward, hoping that no more rock slides or other obstacles lay in our path.

In endurance and speed alone, a good horse could outlast any solitary cow, but a herd at full stampede was a separate species, nothing more than a killing machine that mowed down everything that lay in front of it. As we thundered along, I tried not to think about the stories I'd heard of cowboys and horses slashed to death under sharp hooves, their bodies reduced to red smears.

"Faster! Faster!" I yelled to Lady.

If there had been a couple of cowboys by my side, we could have pulled our rain slickers from our saddlebags and waved them in the lead steers' faces, thus slowing them. But a lone rider had no chance. The herd would just run me down.

I chanced a look to the right, where a scraggly stand of oak and pine began the forest's march up the mountain. If

Lady and I could just get far enough ahead of the stampede, I might be able to cut across at a diagonal, then slow her enough to guide her safely between the trees, using them as a life-saving buffer zone. Left to their own devices, the cattle would continue down the trail until the cowboys, now galloping hard up flank to turn the leaders, regained control.

A hasty look back proved that Lady and I had, indeed, gained twenty yards distance from the herd's vanguard. But as I increased the angle of her run toward the shelter of the trees, she stumbled and almost went down. I grabbed a fistful of mane and prayed.

Not only were there no atheists in foxholes, but damned few in stampedes, either.

Just as it seemed Lady would somersault, she righted herself and regained her gallop. But the stumble had lost us our precious lead, and the steers had gained ground so quickly that I could smell their rank odor and see the red linings of their flared nostrils. Still, I thought we might make it.

Then something strange happened.

At first I thought the trees had begun to tilt, and wondered in my frantic state if we were having an earthquake. Or had the pounding of the cattle loosened the pines' roots, causing them to topple? Then I realized, with a sickening sense of hopelessness, that the trees remained stationary; I didn't. My saddle had slipped, and I was falling, falling, ever so slowly it seemed, to the ground.

In front of all those hooves.

I tried to throw my arms back around Lady's neck, but it was too late. My center of gravity had shifted with the saddle and I'd slipped too far to the side to regain my balance. One hand still clutching a fistful of mane, I hung against her side for a second, feeling the saddle slip even farther. As the saddle finally completed the turn under her belly, she let out a bellow, then gave a high-air buck, tossing me away.

"Jesus!" This time, I prayed aloud as I crashed toward the ground.

Maybe Jesus heard me. For whatever reason, I hit the ground with the flat of my left shoulder blade, rolled, then leaped to my feet, screaming for my horse. But Lady had her own problems. Still bellowing, and with the saddle bouncing along between her legs, she veered toward the trees. Her gallop degenerated into a clumsy higgledy-hop. The herd was about thirty yards behind her, and closing fast.

And only twenty yards behind me.

I ran.

I almost made it.

I'd cleared the trail and almost entered the trees when the lead steer, a white-faced Hereford, hit me.

Even then my luck held. The steer's right shoulder gave me only a glancing blow, which knocked me through the air and spun me several feet to the left. This brought me even closer to the tree line. But my actual fall this time was rougher than my first.

I landed on my knees with my arms outstretched, then slid forward, eating bitter earth all the way. Momentum scooted me farther along, shale tearing at my hands and slashing through my jeans as I fought to clear my nose and mouth. Just as I lurched to my knees, another steer, a big dun monster, hit me square-on, sending me tumbling ass over end. As I crashed back to earth, he ran straight over me, and as his final favor, planted his rear hoof square onto my left thigh.

The pain, at first a dull thud, quickly blossomed into an electric dance, doing the cha-cha up my thigh, my stomach, across my chest, my head, even to the tips of my ears.

Had the son of a bitch broken my leg?

Knowing that I would surely die if I took the time to roll around in agony, I staggered to my feet once more and, spitting dirt and manure, hobbled and hopped toward the trees. The sentry pine was almost within touching distance when another cow barreled into me.

The third time, though, was a charm.

As the first steer had done, the black cow—her spotted calf trailing behind her—hit me at an angle and threw me the rest of the way into the trees. I landed on a nest of pine needles, but I didn't even attempt to get to my feet. Instead, I crawled to the lee side of a broad-trunked oak and crouched into a fetal position, my face between my knees, my hands clutched protectively at the back of my head.

Bile filled my mouth, whether from pain or my involuntary meal of cattle droppings, I couldn't tell. At that point, I didn't even care.

The only thing that mattered was that I was still alive.

It seemed an eternity that I huddled there, eyes clenched, listening to the dying rumble of cattle hooves, the bleating of the calves. Then callused hands touched me.

"Lena! Oh, Lena, honey, are you all right?"

I uncurled and looked up at Dusty, his face pale beneath a layer of splattered manure.

I had to swallow bile again before I could answer. "Oh, I'm doing as well as could be expected, what with getting trampled on and eating shit and all."

"I saw you go down. I was so afraid…" His voice faded into a croak.

"*You* were afraid? Oh, ha." Suddenly the world became dark, except for the bright pinpoints of light that sparkled at the edges. But instead of passing out, I turned my head and threw up.

After another eternity, my heaves came up empty and, with Dusty's help, I staggered to my feet. I tested my leg and discovered that while it might be bruised to the bone, it wasn't broken. Slim wouldn't have to shoot me.

"I'll probably fall down in a minute," I rasped, my throat raw from stomach acid.

"I'll catch you."

I leaned my head against his chest. "You always do."

We stood like that for a few moments, me wanting to sob, his own shoulders shaking suspiciously. But I finally had to call a halt to our Hallmark moment.

"Dusty, I need to find my horse. And my saddle."

He sniffled and cleared his throat. "Last I saw of her, she was heading past that bald pine. You okay to ride?"

Forcing a smile, I said, "Never felt better in my life."

Dusty mounted Moonglow and swung me up behind him. We headed deeper into the trees and within minutes we found Lady near a lightning-split oak. The saddle and, even more importantly, the saddlebags remained slung below her belly, held on only by the rear flank cinch. The latigo, the front cinch that actually secured the saddle to the horse, had torn in two and now dangled uselessly on the ground.

I hopped off Moonglow, taking care to land on my good leg. "You're a good girl, you are," I told Lady as I limped toward her.

She rolled her eyes at me but stood her ground with spraddled legs, as if terrified to even touch the bulky object between them.

Still murmuring sweet nothings, I looped her reins over my arm, then bent and unbuckled the flank cinch. When the saddle dropped away from her, she stepped aside with a delicate motion. "Yes, a good, good girl."

I studied the latigo girth carefully and found what I suspected. Someone had sliced it halfway through. The stress of Lady's life-saving gallop had torn away the rest.

Someone wanted to kill me.

EIGHT

AFTER PULLING my slicker out of my miraculously undamaged saddlebags, I donned it over my shredded clothes. Then I swung up on Lady's bare back with the saddle blanket and saddle bags balanced in front of me. We picked up the trail again and pushed north at a slow jog, the horses too tired to go faster. Within an hour we met up with the rescue party, fronted by Slim himself.

Slim fawned over me for a while, then told us that the cowboys had finally managed to stop the herd in a wide meadow by getting in front and turning them in increasingly tighter circles. The cattle were grazing now, exhausted as much by their fear as their breakneck run.

"That's it, we're through for the day," he said. "By the way, you guys come across any casualties back there?" He motioned behind us.

Dusty nodded. "Yep, two calves and a steer got trampled. They're about four miles back, in that gully. One was already dead, the others too injured to help."

"Ah, hell! Now that my gun's gone, what am I going to do for the poor bastards? Cut their throats?"

"Slim." I lowered my voice. "We already took care of them."

He widened his eyes at me. "Lena, that's rough, that's butchering stuff."

I shook my head. "Remember when you told me to leave my gun back at my apartment?"

He gave me a hard-eyed stare. "Yeah?"

"Well, I paid as much attention to your orders as you did to MacPherson's. My .38 was in my saddlebag all the time. When Jerry broke his leg, I was getting ready to shoot him before you turned up and did it yourself."

Slim didn't say anything to that. He just set his jaw, spun his horse around and rode back toward the herd.

WE MADE CAMP at the very place the cattle had stopped their suicidal run. As soon as the tents were up, Slim announced that he was no longer going to wait until we reached the Mormon Lake cutoff to send a rider ahead. He detailed Manuel Benecito, one of his most trusted wranglers, who was mounted on a speedy yet surefooted Appaloosa, to make the dash to the ranch.

"And if we come across you later lying by the side of the trail with a broken leg, well, Lena'll just shoot you," Slim told Manuel, throwing a mean look in my direction.

"There will be no more broken legs, not with this horse," Manuel said, swinging up on his Appaloosa. "I will let Lena save her bullets for the foolish man who fired that shot."

Alarmed by the stampede and what it meant, Slim wanted his ranch hands to be on guard, so he took them aside and told them the truth about MacPherson's death. Not that they hadn't already guessed. They had heard the shot that started the stampede, but the news that my saddle's girth had been cut through rankled them even more. Idiocy, if that's what the gunplay had been, they could excuse; straight-out murder, never.

I watched Manuel disappear down the trail, then let Dusty help me hobble to the solar shower, where he stood guard as I cleaned my wounds and congratulated myself on keeping my tetanus shots up to date. While I scrubbed, I also did some heavy thinking about the murderer's identity.

Everyone, it seemed, had a motive for killing Stephen

MacPherson. Not only his wife and stepdaughter, but as far as I was concerned, every single member of MacPherson Communications' board of directors. But who had the opportunity? I cast my mind back to the evening the media magnate had been killed, the constant bustle to and fro around camp. Theorizing is one thing, but which one of them really had enough time to hurry unseen to the Porta-John area, bash MacPherson's head in, drag him behind the creosote bush, then return—unseen again—to camp? A cattle drive is not exactly an exercise in the solitary life; watchful eyes were everywhere.

As the tepid water rained down on me, I fast-forwarded to the gunshot that started the stampede. Who had been alone then? Or had someone seen the shooter and for reasons of his—or her—own, was keeping quiet about it?

"You doin' okay in there, hon?" Dusty asked. "You're awful quiet."

"Just thinking," I told him. Then, baffled over the entire case, I decided to try something I had never tried before. If Holmes could have his Watson, and Poirot his Hastings, why couldn't I bounce my ideas off a nondetective friend, too?

"Dusty, let me ask you something. Who do you think murdered MacPherson?"

He answered without even stopping to think. "Renée. She's got more loose screws than a hardware store."

I nodded. "That's exactly what I thought you would say."

For a few more merciful minutes I simply stood there under the running water, listened to the distant bawling of the calves, the chatter of the dudes as they walked back and forth, Cookie's hammering as he erected the grub tent. Now that the cattle had calmed down, birds had returned to the Little Grand's surrounding pines. Their songs rang out over the lush valley with a simplicity that put the lie to the tangled lives of the humans below.

"Here's your towel, hon," Dusty said, lifting it over the shower's canvas surround. Then he looked down at my naked body and winced. Not his usual reaction. "That leg looks pretty bad. When we get back to Scottsdale, I think you'd better see the doctor. Might be a hairline fracture in there."

I followed his eyes. My right thigh sported a fiery but perfect imprint of a steer's hoof, and the edges were already beginning to turn black. I didn't mind, though. Bruises faded.

After toweling myself off, I donned the clean clothes Dusty held out. As the birds continued their treetop symphony, we walked back to camp.

Now that I had taken care of myself, I did what I should have done earlier—take care of my horse. One of the cowboys had tied Lady up next to Moonglow, and both their coats were a study in dust and dirt. Knowing that Dusty would shortly groom his horse, I started conscience-free on mine.

Lady leaned happily against me as I took a hoof pick and cleaned trail crud away from her iron shoes. Her feet clear, I brushed the dust off her coat, burnishing it to a deep, mahogany glow. To finish her off, I combed the briars out of her mane and tail until they rippled like a glossy, black waterfall. By the time I finished, Lady looked like a new horse.

And I knew who murdered MacPherson.

"Oh, Lady," I whispered to her. "Once you rule out the impossible, only the improbable is left."

She turned her head and gave me a sympathetic nudge.

"MR. JESSOP, I'm placing you under citizen's arrest for the murder of Stephen MacPherson," I said a few minutes later while two big cowboys grabbed their shocked trail boss by the arms. The rest of the wranglers hovered nervously in the background.

Jessop's face reddened and his mouth dropped. "Lena Jones, are you *crazy?*"

"Not at all," I said, my right hand resting on the holster now strapped openly to my thigh. "From the day we left Happy Trails, MacPherson kept digging at you, never letting up for a minute. It finally got to be too much, didn't it?"

I had read my man right. Jessop would give us trouble. Lots of it.

"Listen, you stupid woman…"

I unsnapped the holster and eased out my .38, making sure he and everyone else saw it. I didn't want any escape—or rescue—attempts. "Tell it to Sheriff Nakai, Jessop. If that horse of Manuel's is as fast as it looks, Nakai might even get here before dark, or at the very latest, first light tomorrow." I transferred my gaze to the cowboys. "Take him away, guys, and tie him to the latrine wagon."

Jessop's eyes goggled. "The latrine wagon? Why, you miserable…" He began to struggle in earnest, but the combined strength of the two young cowboys was too much for him. They dragged the trail boss, protesting and cursing, away.

The dudes had seen and heard it all.

"Sorry about the language, Tiffany," I told the obviously shaken girl, holstering my gun.

She tried hard to be blasé, but her trembling voice betrayed her. "Oh, like I've never heard those words before." She shot a look at Renée.

"Cowboy trash." Renée sniffed, missing her daughter's implied criticism. "I told Stephen this whole thing was a stupid idea, but no, he had to have his way."

"Stephen never listened to anyone," Hester said, her eyes filling with tears while she watched the cowboys tie Jessop to the latrine wagon. "He never even listened to the board when—"

"Stephen was a maverick, that's for sure," Vern Pincus interrupted, rubbing the shirt pocket where he kept his pregnant wife's picture. Then he looked around at the other dudes. "Well, why don't we go get us some something to eat? All this excitement has given me an appetite."

Not me. My unplanned meal of offal and disgust had put me off my feed.

Not to mention this murder case.

But I joined them, anyway. On our way to the chuck tent, only Clinton Clayburn asked the obvious question. "Nice gun, Ms. Jones. I've always been a fan of snub-nosed .38s, myself. They're so easy to hide. But tell me, why exactly did you take it upon yourself to initiate that citizen's arrest? Considering the fact that Happy Trails is Slim's company, I would have thought the arrest would be his job."

"Maybe it has something to do with my control issues," I said, then quickened my pace to leave him behind.

I had no taste for dinner, not that it mattered. All I wanted to do was baby my throbbing leg and get some sleep. If I could. Now that I had figured out who murdered Mac-Pherson and then tried to kill me via stampede, I should have been able to relax.

But relaxation would have to wait until Sheriff Nakai arrived and began the official arrest process.

Which meant I faced yet another sleepless night.

NINE

JESSOP CURSED LOUDLY throughout the night, and by dawn it looked like the sleepless dudes itched to take the law into their own hands and string him up to the nearest tree. He continued all the way through breakfast, stopping only to eat his own, which was hand-fed to him by a sympathetic cowboy.

The sun had barely peeked over the Mogollon Rim when the whup-whup-whup of helicopters pierced the morning air. Almost giddy with relief, I watched as the Coconino County sheriff's copters followed the canyon due south toward MacPherson's grave while taking care to keep their distance from the still-nervous herd.

"Looks like our boy came through for us," Slim said, forcing a smile. "Manuel's probably up there having the ride of his life."

I nodded. "That means Nakai will be along soon."

A fresh burst of cursing from Jessop brought a chorus of groans from the dudes.

"Would somebody please just knock that man in the head or something?" Renée whined. "I didn't get a wink of sleep last night, and I probably look like hell."

But I noticed she had applied makeup this morning, and her famous face was once again Hollywood fresh. Perhaps she was expecting photographers.

"Oh, shut up, Mother," Tiffany snapped at her. "This isn't about you."

I stared at the two. Ever since I could remember, I had wanted to find my birth parents, hoping against hope that once I found them, I could build some semblance of a family. But watching Renée and Tiffany tear at each other, I wondered if I should just leave it all alone and consign my missing parents to the past.

Maybe orphans were the lucky ones.

"Ladies, ladies," Slim said, stepping between the two. "Let's all just pack up and get ready to clear out, okay?"

"Well, if you think I'm going to continue riding with these stupid cows all the way to Flagstaff, you've got another think coming," Renée said. "Tiffany and I plan to drive back to civilization with the sheriff. The sooner we're out of this hellhole, the better."

Hellhole? I gazed around at the verdant forest, the crimson cliffs softened by lavender shadows. Some people, it seemed, saw only ugliness in the midst of the most exquisite beauty.

But that was their problem, not mine. With my hand resting on my unsnapped holster, I sat back, shut my ears to Jessop's curses, and waited for the sheriff.

TWO HOURS AFTER we'd last seen the helicopters, Sheriff Orson Nakai arrived with a fleet of deputies in four-wheel-drive vehicles. Given MacPherson's high public profile, I wondered how long it would take the press to catch up. Thinking about the media flap that was certain to ensue over this case, I shuddered.

"*Ya-tah-hey,* Lena," Nakai said, climbing out of his Jeep Cherokee. "I see you still can't stay out of trouble, even on vacation."

Flagstaff must have agreed with Nakai, because he didn't look a day older than he had ten years earlier, when he'd been my partner on the Scottsdale Police Force. Tall and lanky, his Navajo cheekbones leant angularity to an otherwise round face, and his seemingly relaxed demeanor hid a fierce competitiveness that had served him so well in his law-enforcement career.

From his spot near the latrine wagon, Jessop began to scream invectives again, this time infusing his scatological Anglo-Saxonisms with a few prime Navajo curses.

"Your suspect, I take it?" Nakai asked with a bemused smile. "That's a pretty good accent for a Bil-i-gan-nah."

"Can we talk in private, Orson?"

Nakai nodded, and after detailing a couple of men to see to Jessop, we huddled in his Jeep Cherokee. It took me a while to explain everything, but to my relief, he didn't call me crazy.

"That's quite a theory, Lena," he said, gazing thoughtfully over the dash at Jessop. "It'll be tough to prove."

"I don't think so. I bagged the rock, and it's still in my saddlebag. MacPherson's wounds will help, too, which is why I wrapped his head so carefully before we buried him. Your science techs shouldn't have too much trouble confirming my theory."

Nakai said nothing for a long time, but his eyes flicked back and forth, studying everyone. His deputies. Jessop. Slim. Dusty. The trail hands. The dudes huddled under the chuck tent.

Then he turned to me, flashed his teeth and said, "All right, girlfriend, let's go for it."

We climbed out of the Jeep and walked over to the deputies, where Nakai issued his instructions. Then, safety finally in numbers, we approached the chuck tent, where he made his announcement.

"Clinton Clayburn, Vern Pincus, Hester Schowalter, Bob Gately—you're all under arrest for the murder of Stephen MacPherson."

TEN

AFTER A MOMENT of shocked silence, Clinton Clayburn made a dash for his saddlebags, where I figured he had stashed Slim's Bulldog .44, but Dusty intercepted him and kicked the big man full-strength in the balls.

"Bastard tried to kill my girlfriend," Dusty muttered, inspecting his boots for fresh scuff marks as Clayburn lay moaning on the ground.

At that point, Nakai began to Miranda-ize the entire MacPherson Communications' board of directors while his deputies cuffed each in turn.

I looked toward Renée, expecting her usual emotional outburst. But for once the drama queen appeared stunned into silence.

Only Tiffany spoke. "You mean they *all* killed my stepfather? But *why?*"

As one of the deputies cinched the cuffs around Gately's wrists, Mr. Beautiful forced a chuckle. "Sheriff, I don't know what kind of wild story Lena told you, but if you ask me, that fall she took during the stampede rattled her brains."

"Oh, I don't think so, Mr. Gately," Nakai said. "If the autopsy on Stephen MacPherson's body proves Lena's claims, and I expect they will, he couldn't possibly have been killed by just one person."

I nodded. "All those wounds, that *overkill*, I'll admit it confused me at first. He'd been bludgeoned from different heights and angles, from the left and from the right. Try as I might, I just couldn't picture the murderer shifting that rock back and forth from hand to hand, first hitting Mac-Pherson from above, then crouching to hit him from below. The whole scenario was simply impossible for one person.

"The wounds weren't the only difficulty I had to grapple with. Given the number of people in camp, how could someone have stolen Slim's gun and cell phone without being seen? Again, it was impossible. The same impossible scenario was true for the gunshot that started the stampede. You were all riding together in a big clump at the back of the herd, and no one could have pulled that gun without the others seeing.

"Once I realized you all had to know who fired the shot, the next question was—why keep quiet about it? Ruling out the impossible, only the probable was left—you were all in it together."

Gately shook his handsome head and forced a smile. "You ought to be in Hollywood writing scripts for my wife."

I smiled back. "Sorry, Gately. *Murder on the Orient Express* has already been filmed, and I think it even won an Oscar or two. Anyway, it's been playing on the Mystery channel for some time now, which is where I saw it."

Only then did his composure began to slip. "I don't know what you're talking about."

I motioned toward his saddlebags, where he kept his paperback mystery novels. "While you were going through those mysteries looking for possible movie material, you came across that Agatha Christie book where a whole group of people conspired to kill one man. It gave you the idea, didn't it? And I'm betting that it didn't take too long to convince the others, either, considering the financial threat you were all facing. The brilliant part of the plot was that by roping everyone in on your plan, you made them all culpable in the eyes of the law. It insured everyone's silence.''

''Well, I'll be damned,'' Renée said, finally speaking up.

Hester, her face showing every one of her fifty-plus years, snapped, ''That's the most ridiculous thing I've ever heard. People like us don't commit murder! What do you take us for, a bunch of Hell's Angels?''

I tried to keep the pity I felt for her out of my voice. ''Apparently you're all willing to commit murder if your CEO is running your company into the ground. Not only that, but he was getting ready to call in everyone's personal loans to help finance even more buyouts, wasn't he? MacPherson was building a house of cards the Federal Communications Commission was certain to eventually knock down, and none of you wanted to go down with it. Gately wasn't thrilled about the idea of being financially dependent on his wife, Clayburn had all those ex-wives he was supporting, Pincus was overextended after helping his new wife finance those gyms, but you—''

''Gately's right,'' Hester snapped, interrupting me. ''You're crazy.''

I shook my head. ''Poor Hester. With you, it wasn't just a matter of hating to see MacPherson Communications destroyed. It was also personal. You loved the man, but he'd humiliated you with other women too many times. First with the socialite, then the centerfold, then the actress. After all those years of waiting for him, you were growing old alone. Now that someone new had popped up on the horizon, you finally admitted that you were never going to get your turn at being Mrs. MacPherson. You, alone of all the others, killed MacPherson because you loved him.''

Hester said nothing, but tears began to form in her eyes. I hoped she would be able to cry in court. Juries tend to be sympathetic toward weeping women.

Then I turned to Vern Pincus. "You murdered Mac-Pherson out of mixed motives, too, didn't you, Vern?"

Pincus's right shoulder twitched, revealing his attempt to pat the pocket where he kept the picture of his bouncing baby bride. The handcuffs prevented that.

"Gately's right," he muttered. "You belong in Hollywood."

I smiled. "Too much smog."

"Vern, don't say anything!" Gately warned him.

But Pincus didn't take Mr. Beautiful's advice. "Maybe I would be a bit strapped financially if Stephen called in my loan, but he and I were close friends. He wouldn't let me go under."

"MacPherson didn't have friends, just business associates. If he wanted your money, he would take it. Just like he was getting ready to take your wife."

That last was just an educated guess on my part, but the expression on Pincus's face revealed I'd scored a bull's-eye. "He... She... Stacey loves me! She's having my baby!"

I shook my head. "Correction, Mr. Pincus. I'm betting that DNA tests might show that she's having MacPherson's baby, not yours. Hester said he had a weakness for blondes, and you all worked out at the same gym together, right? Somehow I can't see MacPherson suddenly exhibiting a self-restraint he'd never been known for just because you had married his favorite aerobics instructor. And once Stacey got pregnant, well, that intensified things, didn't it? For some reason MacPherson had no children by any of his wives, and maybe he decided he wasn't getting any younger. Maybe he saw this pregnancy as his last chance to create a family."

Pincus's lower lip trembled. "Every marriage has trouble once in a while, but Stacey and I were working it out. All right, maybe she was a little dazzled by Stephen, and maybe they did...have a *thing*. But Stacey would never leave me."

Gately groaned. "Oh, Vern, you idiot. Don't say another word until you talk to your attorney."

Pincus finally fell silent, but too late. Nakai smiled across the chuck tent at me, and I figured he was having the same vision as I was: an entire squadron of high-priced attorneys winging toward Arizona in sleek Learjets.

I watched as two deputies helped Clinton Clayburn to his feet. Too bad I hadn't been the one to kick him. Given Clayburn's bulk, he had probably been elected to strike the first blow against MacPherson, and perhaps that first blow had been enough. But perhaps not. The autopsy would reveal at what point during the beatings the magnate had died. I was certain that Clayburn had been the one who'd stolen Slim's gun and cell phone, and fired the shot starting the stampede. Of the entire murderous group, he was the most vicious.

But Gately was the only one of them who knew enough about horses and saddles to cut Lady's girth.

I shivered. Which was more evil? Clayburn's hotheaded malice or Gately's cool planning?

Then, as I watched the deputies herd the entire MacPherson Communications' board of directors to the SUVs, a voice floated toward us, carried by the pine-scented wind.

"Hey, you bastards forget about me?"

Poor Jessop was still tied to the latrine wagon.

ELEVEN

THREE DAYS LATER I eased back in the saddle and breathed in the crisp mountain air as the herd, eager to enter the lush green pasture on the outskirts of Flagstaff, quickened its pace down the dirt road.

With the arrest of the MacPherson Communications' board of directors, our supply of trail hands had been seriously depleted, but word of our plight had reached the Mormon Lake ranchers. In the true spirit of the West, they had loaned us a few of their own cowhands, trail-hardened men who actually knew what they were doing.

No city slickers were present to help us celebrate the end of our journey. As soon as the four murderers had been loaded into the SUVs, Renée and Tiffany had driven back to civilization with Sheriff Nakai. According to Slim, who'd cadged a cell phone from one of the deputies, the grieving widow had flirted with Nakai all the way to Flagstaff. Unlike Dusty, though, the happily married Nakai was redhead-proof. Rebuffed, Renée had chartered a jet to take her to Southern California, where she was probably already hawking her story to the Hollywood studios.

Only one question remained.

Had Renée really killed Tiffany's father? I suspected she had, although I could do little to prove it. But life had a way of settling scores. If Renée was smart, she would watch her step around her daughter.

Just as if I ever found my birth mother, she should watch her step around me.

I forced my thoughts away from vengeance and murder, focusing instead on the surrounding symphony of mountain bluebirds, the whisper of the wind through tall Ponderosa pines. When all was said and done, these were the things that mattered.

"Well, we made it, didn't we?" Slim said as we approached the gate of Borrowed Time Ranch. "For a while there, I was beginning to think none of us would ever get here alive."

"Oh, it was never in doubt." I'm such a liar.

I heard hoofbeats behind me and turned to see Jessop coming up on the outside. After throwing me a look of pure loathing, he spurred his horse past us to open the gate to the ranch.

"He'll never forgive me," I said to Slim.

Slim laughed. "Oh, I think he'll mellow when he sees the size of the bonus I'm giving him. But why couldn't you just tell the poor man that you needed a scapegoat to convince the real killers they were off the hook? Knowing that everyone's safety was at stake, I'm sure he would have cooperated."

I shook my head. "Yes, he would have cooperated, but I doubted Jessop had the acting skills to pull it off. Knowing that one of the killers still had the gun, I was afraid to take the chance."

We reined our horses aside and let the cattle and horsemen file past us. "I guess you're right," Slim said. "Jessop's too much of a stand-up guy to put on a convincing act."

Dusty, though, had performed his part in my script with Oscar-winning style. Then again, he'd never been a stand-up guy, had he?

Except when it came to life and death.

I squinted my eyes against the sun as I watched the red cattle spread out over the green pasture. The sky was so blue it hurt my eyes. We had made the trip to Flagstaff losing only one bad man, one good horse and three cattle. A hundred years earlier, such a low death rate would have earned Slim's wranglers national acclaim.

Like everything else, our losses were all a matter of perspective. As was family. Or the lack of family.

And sometimes our friends—the loved ones we have chosen, not inherited—become our family.

"You look tired, hon," Dusty said as he reined the no-longer-lame Thunderball over to us. "Tell you what. Slim's trailering all the horses back to Scottsdale, so why don't we spend the night up here? I'll rent us a room with a Jacuzzi at the Little America Resort, and I'll even give you a hot oil massage. Tomorrow I'll rent a car and chauffeur you back to Scottsdale. If you're still tired, well, you can curl up and sleep in the back seat."

With that offer, I forgave him everything he'd ever done to me.

Even for convincing me that I needed a vacation.

EPILOGUE

Six months later

From *Variety*

Beverly Hills: Filming began today on *Death at Sundown*, an action-driven romantic suspense film starring Oscar-winner Renée Rodgers and her rumored real-life squeeze, Chip Cartwright. The biopic tells the true story of an actress who solves a murder case during a modern-day cattle drive and finds love in the arms of the handsome trail boss.

"When my beloved husband was murdered, I knew the only way I could forget my grief was to dive head-first back into work," said Ms. Rodgers during a recent interview, wiping away tears. "What better honor could I do Stephen MacPherson than to let the world know all about those horrible people who killed him, and how I risked my life to bring them to justice."

When asked about the child-abuse charges an Arizona woman has leveled against her, Ms. Rodgers waved them aside.

"Child Protective Services paid no attention to that crazy woman," she said. "Their investigation was mere window dressing, and those so-called home visits the social workers continue to carry out, well, state flunkies have to earn their money somehow, don't they? But let's not talk about those ridiculous charges. Let's talk about my picture.''

Ms. Rodgers continued to chat genially until she was called to the set, at which point her daughter, Tiffany Rodgers, took over the conversation. Tiffany plays a supporting role in *Death at Sundown*.

''I was drawn to the plot because it's about a real-life murder,'' Tiffany said. ''This is the second time someone I loved was killed. And just like my mother, I want to see the truth come out.''

The young beauty smiled her unsettling smile. ''I intend to follow in my beloved mother's footsteps. Oh, yes. I will follow her very, very closely.''

THE FIRST PROOF

by Terence Faherty

ONE

I WAS LATE getting to Penn Station. I left my Chevy in a park-and-ride lot near Matawan and took a bus into New York City, thinking it would let me relax and gather my wits for the ordeal ahead. It didn't. The bus became one small piece of a midmorning clog in the Lincoln Tunnel. My coping technique was to tell myself over and over that I was about to let down an old friend, about to screw up the first favor she'd ever asked of me.

I wasn't counting the times we'd had sex. I considered those long-ago occasions to be favors Marilyn Tucci had done for me. Which put me considerably in her debt. Now, in May 1988, she was calling in her marker. She'd asked me to be at the station in time to catch a certain train to Boston. And I was going to miss it.

When the bus finally broke through and deposited me at the Port Authority Terminal, I ran the maze that led down to street level. Then I stood in the cab line long enough to catch my breath and to satisfy myself that the hands of my watch were moving faster than I was. I headed south on foot, setting a pace that drew admiring glances from the native office workers in their business suits and Reeboks.

I reached the basement train station precisely at ten-fifteen, the scheduled departure time for the Patriot. I was hoping for the usual Amtrak delay, and I got one, though the big black information sign, whose entries flipped into place like the correct answers on a game show, was an-

nouncing an on-time departure. When I hurried down the
specified escalator to the specified platform, the train was
still there. Next to it stood Marilyn, alone amid the bustle
and noise.

She was wearing a black dress, as befitted a very recent
widow, though half the young women I'd passed on my
dash to the station had been similarly attired. She was bare-
headed, her thick, wiry hair pinned up tightly but unlikely
to remain that way. A few strands had already broken ranks.
In the draft of the platform, they were waving to me like
old friends at a reunion. Otherwise, she was perfectly mo-
tionless, her dark eyes, hidden by darker glasses, apparently
fixed on the dull aluminum siding of the train.

I was braced for a few choice words on the subject of
my late arrival, but when she finally noticed me, Marilyn
said only, "Owen, you're here. Good. Tony's on the train
already."

"Tony" was Anthony Corelli, Marilyn's late husband.
He was riding to Boston in the Patriot's baggage car—or
whatever the railroad now called the car in which bulky
items like coffins traveled. I felt a renewed surge of guilt
over not having gotten there in time to stand by Marilyn
while she saw the body safely on board.

She let me work a little of that off by carrying her bag
onto the train and stowing it and mine in an overhead rack.
The car she'd selected was half empty and new and very
nice, far nicer than the New Jersey Transit trains I was used
to, nicer even than the Amtrak trains I'd ridden to college
twenty years earlier. The interior's color scheme was white
and blue and gray, and the spacious seats had fold-down
tray tables like an airliner's. Several in our car were already
in use as laptop stands. I'd neglected to bring a computer
or even to buy a *Daily News,* so I made small talk.

"You holding up?" I asked the woman next to me.

"I'm fine, Owen," she said, using my first name for the

second time in as many minutes. She usually addressed me by my last name, Keane, and her failure to do so now made me concerned enough to press my question.

"Really?"

"Really." She removed her dark glasses to display her long-lashed eyes. They were perfectly dry and had been for a while, judging by their clear whites. Those eyes resided beneath heavy, Brooke Shields eyebrows that shone in the car's artificial light. Beneath the eyes and the broad, flat cheekbones, the face narrowed. Her lips were very thin. Lipstick would have helped, but Marilyn seldom wore any. The contrasting brows and lips gave the face an interesting internal contradiction, suggesting a struggle between the sensual and the business-like. At least it did to me, a guy who'd experienced both sides of her character at very close range.

By the time I looked away from that face, we were under way, sliding by the suddenly deserted platform. The train moved through an unlit portion of the station, then briefly into sunlight, then into the tunnel that would carry it beneath the East River.

I was careful not to mention our proximity to that river, but Marilyn thought of it anyway. She looked toward the car's brushed aluminum ceiling, picturing, I was sure, the muddy river bottom that was now somewhere above us. It was an apt moment for her to shed a tear or two. None came.

I was reminded of a nickname I'd come up with for Marilyn back in the earliest days of our relationship: "the unmoved mover."

I'd lifted it from one of the proofs of God that St. Thomas Aquinas had lifted from Aristotle, the first proof, in fact, the "proof from motion." Pared to the bone, the proof goes like this: everything moving is moving because it was prodded by something else, also moving. This chain of collisions can't be infinitely long; there must have been a point at which it was started by something unmoved but capable of moving everything else. This "unmoved mover" is God.

I've always felt drawn to that proof, doubter though I am. Any detective would feel comfortable with it, even an amateur detective like myself. I've often thought of it while rereading Raymond Chandler, while following Philip Marlowe as he sorts out all the collisions, random and intentional, that lead backward from some crime to its first cause.

I'd assigned the name "unmoved mover" to Marilyn, not because I'd had her confused with God, but because I'd been struck by her ability to move those around her—me especially—while remaining unmoved herself. Untouched, in fact. Uninvolved emotionally.

She was outwardly unmoved now, though the dark water where her husband had lately resided swirled above our heads.

TWO

THE PATRIOT stayed in the Empire State long enough to breeze through New Rochelle. Then it turned east, for Stamford, Connecticut, and the coast. We'd been traveling for more than an hour when we reached the next good-size town, Bridgeport. In that time, Marilyn had said exactly two words to me, "no" and "thanks." Those had been in reply to a question from me about coffee. I went off alone in search of a cup.

I drank it alone, too, in the glorified snack bar that constituted the train's dining facilities. Visible from the window near my plastic table were occasional glimpses of water, the little inlets and rivers the tracks crossed. More frequent were views of Route 1, the road the tracks shadowed, though it may be fairer to say that the old highway shadowed the older rail line.

Over my coffee and a bagel that might have predated both Route 1 and Amtrak, I reviewed the situation to date. I'd been informed of the death of Tony Corelli by a co-worker of Marilyn's named Jodie Kwan. I'd met Jodie and Tony on the very same evening, at a noisy party in the little Eastside apartment Marilyn and her husband were then sharing. Marilyn's stated reason for inviting me had been to set me up with Jodie, a very nice young woman with whom I had nothing in common except last initials. I now suspected that Marilyn had actually wanted to show off her husband, to show me the type of man I should grow up to be.

I'd found Tony Corelli to be a pleasant, dark-featured accountant who was very generous with his Scotch. When Marilyn had introduced us, she'd mentioned Tony's passions, sailing and racquetball and the Knicks, as though they were unusual accomplishments. But I'd known that, for Marilyn, their value lay in the fact that they weren't unusual at all, that they and the man they represented were ordinary. Almost commonplace.

Marilyn and I had first gotten together when I'd been successfully passing myself off as another ordinary guy. I'd been working as a researcher then. So had she, so we'd hummed along nicely at first. But when she'd realized that my personal researches involved things that went bump in the dark night of the soul, things that couldn't be cataloged or indexed or filed, she'd first dumped me and then tried to palm me off on friends like Jodie Kwan.

Jodie knew about my history with Marilyn. The night she called to tell me that Tony had been found in the East River, she moved quickly to her concerns about his wife.

"Nobody's heard from Marilyn since she called to say she needed time off," Jodie told me. "I'm worried about her, Owen. She's all alone in Brooklyn. She moved back there when she and Tony separated. Did you know that?" I hadn't. "She's not answering her phone if she's home. Somebody should go check on her."

Jodie's call had come in on a Monday evening. On Tuesday morning, I was knocking on the door of the apartment whose address Jodie had given me. The missing Marilyn answered the door herself, dressed in a slate-gray topcoat and carrying a shoulder bag.

"Keane," she said. "What the hell are you doing here?"

A lesser man might have wilted under that greeting. I said, "I heard about Tony."

She nodded. "I'm on my way to the medical examiner's office. I don't have time to visit."

"I'll go with you," I said without any real hope that the offer would be taken up.

Marilyn surprised me by saying, "Okay."

She insisted on driving us in her little Japanese station wagon. Then she insisted on leaving me in an outer office while she talked to the assistant medical examiner assigned to Tony's case. Getting me that close to a mystery without letting me all the way in was like taking a drunk bar hopping and making him sit outside on the curb. Marilyn knew that, but I still wasn't sure the slight was intentional. I already had the impression that she was sleepwalking through the whole business.

The solution to the news blackout came in the form of an assistant medical examiner named Graham. He'd seen me enter with the widow and chatted me up when I was left behind.

"Friend of the family?" he asked, guessing, I supposed, that a relative would have been treated better. "Terrible way to die, drowning. It makes me gag just to think about that first breath of water. Hard on him and hard on his wife."

Graham was a tall, spare man who towered above me from his perch on the arm of my sofa. It hurt my neck to look him in the eye, so I watched his hands, which were large, their dark skin smooth and unmarked.

"Still," he said, "it could have been worse. The body got snagged on a bit of old pier. A police patrol boat spotted it. Probably hadn't been in the water more than a couple of hours. If it hadn't snagged like that, it would have sunk. Then God knows where it would have ended up. I mean, first thing, it would have gone down to the bottom. And it would have been months before it came up again, the water as cold as it is out there. That would have been even harder on his wife."

He paused to let me agree with that and then asked, "Ever hear of a suicide by drowning?"

I'd once heard of one that had happened in the distant past. And I'd briefly thought that I'd witnessed another. I could still taste the lake water I'd swallowed during my unsuccessful attempt to save that "victim." But I said what I knew Graham wanted to hear. "No."

"Didn't think so. They're pretty rare. Almost all drownings are accidents. But it's awfully hard these days to accidentally fall into the East River."

"How hard is it to get thrown in?" I asked.

"Thinking of homicide by drowning?" His big hands pushed the idea to one side. "A lot rarer even than suicide. And there was nothing to suggest homicide."

Which implied that there was something to suggest suicide. "He left a note?"

"Nope. But there's the way his father died."

Graham paused again, this time to let me fill in the blank. When I didn't, he said, "His father drowned, too. What are the odds of that happening accidentally to both father and son? A million to one? Two million? But a son recreating the way his dad died, that's not uncommon. Hell, most of us do it, by working too much or drinking too much or watching television too much. Your friend just had a tougher example to follow."

THREE

WHEN MARILYN and the assistant medical examiner had finished with each other, she drove me to Tony's apartment, their old apartment, on East 56th Street. She told me she wanted to collect a suit for Tony to be buried in, though, after the damage done by the river and the doctors, I couldn't imagine anyone viewing the body.

During the short drive, I waited patiently for Marilyn to fill me in on what she'd learned. Instead, she quizzed me.

"You haven't asked me why I was living in Brooklyn, Keane. Why is that?"

"Marriages break up every day," I said before I'd really thought about it. After I had, I added, "It isn't the most pressing question."

That being, Why had Tony killed himself? I was trying to lead Marilyn back to it, but she wasn't a woman to be led.

"You probably saw that it wouldn't work out that first night. At the party. You saw the fake right away."

I was used to people underestimating my powers of observation or greatly overestimating them. I seldom corrected either mistake, since both could work to my advantage. But this time I tried. "What fake?"

We were at the apartment by then and Marilyn was back to not speaking. She let us in using a key from her own noisy ring. That suggested that she hadn't considered the break with Tony to be permanent.

Marilyn had brought up the party where I'd met her husband, but I would have been thinking of it anyway, the only other time I'd been inside the apartment. That night the place had been very full of life. Now it was very lacking in life, and that wasn't just me being fanciful. There wasn't a pet or a plant or the smell of an old meal or the drip of a faucet. The front room wasn't even messy. On my happiest day, I'd never kept an apartment that neat.

Marilyn paused near a desk on which mail had been stacked. "The box must be ready to explode," she said. She took a tiny key from a desk drawer and held it out to me. "Empty it for me, will you?"

I walked back down to the old building's lobby and opened the mailbox whose number matched the apartment's. It was full, with junk mail and bills, some of it addressed to Mr. and Mrs. Anthony Corelli despite the separation and Marilyn's refusal to give up her own name. One bill, the one that had popped out at me first, was addressed to Anthony Banfield Corelli. I stood considering that mouthful until I noted the postmark, which suggested that the bill had arrived that morning. Then I noticed that it was a phone bill and realized that I held a record of some of Tony's last calls.

After a little less than a second's hesitation, I opened the envelope. Only the long-distance calls were listed individually, and there were only three of those. All three had been made on the same evening, one week before Tony's swim in the river. The first and third calls had been placed to Pequod Point, Maine, but to different numbers. The first had run Tony more than four dollars, the second only thirty cents. The call in between those Maine calls, another one for four dollars, had gone to Scarsdale, New York.

I pocketed the bill so Marilyn wouldn't know that I'd been snooping. I knew from personal experience that the phone company would be happy to send another every few weeks until they got their money.

Back in the apartment, I heard Marilyn in the bedroom but didn't join her there. I didn't want the pressure of selecting a relative stranger's last pair of socks. I placed the new mail next to the stack on the desk. Then I flipped through the old mail, looking for a personal letter but not finding one.

Next to the mail was a framed photograph of Tony and Marilyn. They were seated on a beach somewhere, a beach with grassy dunes. They were wearing sweaters and their pant legs were rolled up and they were laughing. The picture was a little cockeyed, which led me to imagine Tony placing the camera on a rock or a piling, setting the automatic timer, and running back into the frame. And Marilyn laughing at his performance as I'd never once seen her laugh.

I looked from the photo to the wastepaper basket beside the desk and spotted a single cream-colored envelope with a hand-printed address. I retrieved it. It had been sent by someone named Towe who lived in Pequod Point, Maine, the same town mentioned twice on the phone bill. The envelope was empty. I searched the desk and then the room for a matching letter without success.

When I heard Marilyn approaching, I quickly pocketed the envelope. She entered carrying a souvenir of her own, which she held up to me.

"Know what this is?" she asked.

"A pill bottle?" I asked back, wary of an ambush. While I'd never seen Marilyn laughing on a beach, I had seen her angry. She was angry now, but not at me.

"It's Tony's prescription. His antidepressants. They're why I left him."

"I don't understand."

"I found out he was taking these, that he'd been taking them for years. And that he'd been seeing a head doctor for years."

"Why?" I asked.

"He wouldn't tell me. Wouldn't even talk to me about it. We had a big fight, and I left. But the fight was only an excuse. I left because of these." She shook the pill bottle, but it was too full to make much noise.

I remembered what she'd said in the car about me spotting a fake the night I'd met Tony. I said, "Because he wasn't normal? Wasn't ordinary?"

"Wasn't what he pretended to be," Marilyn said in summation. "I asked him to drop the pills and the doctor, but he wouldn't. Now he's dead."

I nearly walked into the trap, nearly said, "But he didn't stop taking the pills or seeing the doctor, so what happened didn't happen because you'd asked him to."

What stopped me was the muted sound of Marilyn shaking the pill bottle again.

"That's right," she said, seeing from my eyes that I'd gotten it. "This bottle's full. He got the prescription refilled a week before he died. There should be seven pills missing. He did what I asked him to do. He stopped taking them. And now…"

She didn't feel the need to finish the sentence, and I couldn't think of a comeback, so we just stood there for a time. Then she returned to the bedroom with me trailing her. We collected the clothes she'd laid out and left the apartment. Marilyn was locking the front door before either of us spoke again.

"Owen," she said, using my first name for the first time in years, "I need a favor. A big one. Tony's mother wants him to be buried in his hometown. I'm taking him up there Thursday, if I can get everything arranged. I'd like you to come with me."

Then, to cover her embarrassment, she turned travel agent. "I don't expect it will be much of a trip. May isn't really the time to visit Maine. And Tony came from a real jerkwater town. Pequod Point.''

I involuntarily touched the pocket where the phone bill and the cream-colored envelope were hidden. ''I'd be happy to come,'' I said.

FOUR

THE PATRIOT made it to the outskirts of Providence, Rhode Island, about one-thirty, only a few minutes late, according to the schedule I'd gotten from a friendly conductor. During Marilyn's protracted bouts of staring out the window, I'd consulted that schedule, a tall, narrow card minutely printed, often. And I'd wondered each time how long it would be before I was talking to it.

A train never goes in by a city's front door. I was reminded of that as we slid past Providence neighborhoods that were missing out on the decade's economic boom. Presently the run-down houses were replaced by old brick buildings with faded signage painted on their walls. The signs, advertising now dead products and businesses, had been aimed at the now dead passengers of now dead trains. Seeing those cave paintings, it was easy to believe for a moment that the rails were carrying us between two worlds, from the present to the past or from the land of the living to the place where Tony Corelli awaited us. Then the train entered the part of the old capital kept evergreen by the business of state government, and the illusion passed.

After Providence, the coastline went its way and we went ours, which was north into the underbelly of Massachusetts. The closer we got to Boston, the less Marilyn's silence bothered me, as I became more and more preoccupied with memories of my college days. Every little town we passed was a place I remembered or imagined I did. By the time we'd reached suburban Boston, I was remembering individual streets and bars and even passersby. Remembering them as familiar types, at least, as the 1988 versions of streets I'd once walked and people I'd once known.

The Patriot's last stop was South Station, a gray stone pile that had born the soot of ages when I'd last passed through it. It was in a section of the city, the area along Fort Point Channel, that was being revived for the benefit of tourists. As a part of that process, the station had been sandblasted sometime recently, and now looked like a new mausoleum instead of an old, neglected one.

Unfortunately, our next train, the Downeaster, left from North Station, which was clear on the other side of the older, historic tip of downtown Boston. We had three hours to make the connection, enough time to walk it, if it hadn't been for Tony. The Amtrak people assumed responsibility for transferring the coffin, along with all the other northbound parcels, but Marilyn was reluctant to trust them. She insisted on hanging around until her husband had been loaded into a railroad van. She would have joined him inside if regulations had permitted it. Luckily, they didn't.

A sympathetic Amtrak lifer directed us to a cab stand on Summer Street. But the van was long gone before we'd driven around to the station's loading docks. That gave me a chance to remind Marilyn that we hadn't had lunch. The cabdriver suggested Jimmy's Harborside and Anthony's Pier Four, both nearby.

"You pick," I said to Marilyn. I was curious to see whether she'd be drawn to Anthony's because of the name or turned off by it.

She said, "North Station," with so much of her old authority that the cabbie never even looked back to me.

North Station, like Penn Station in New York, shared its site with a sports facility. In North Station's case, it was the old Boston Garden. As a result, there were plenty of places to eat in the immediate neighborhood, most of them taverns. Once she'd determined that Tony had arrived safely, Marilyn consented to a brief stop at a lunch counter on Canal Street.

There I told her a story from my college days—a mystery, of course—while she hunted through the minestrone in her soup bowl without finding a piece of vegetable or macaroni that met her standards. The story concerned my long pursuit of a man the Boston press had called the Oldsmobile Bandit, because of the car he'd driven while preying on female hitchhikers. I hadn't a hope that it would distract Marilyn, but I prattled on anyway. I was afraid she was having second thoughts about asking me along. Canal Street seemed to be the perfect place for second thoughts.

When I ran out of story, I decided to try something more interactive. "Tell me about Tony's mother."

"I can't," Marilyn said. "I've never met her."

"She wasn't at your wedding?"

"No. None of Tony's family was. Well, one guy. A cousin of his dad's, who was about a hundred years old."

"You never went to Maine for Thanksgiving or Christmas?"

"No," Marilyn said. "Not for Easter or the Fourth of July, either. Tony never wanted to. I'm not close to my own family, so I didn't think much about it."

She delivered the last line to an autographed picture of Larry Bird that hung on the wall to my left, which made me skeptical.

Marilyn read my thoughts, looking me in the eye to say, "It's not that hard to believe. In all the hours I've listened to you talk, you haven't mentioned your family twice."

"You and I were never married," I said.

That might seem like a bold stroke, coming from a man who, only moments before, had been afraid of being sent home, but I'd gotten a lot more secure about my place at

Marilyn's side. Her willingness to discuss Tony's family, when she'd sat on every other conversation starter I'd tried, told me that the subject was weighing on her mind. And now that I knew she wasn't expecting to see a single familiar face in Maine, I couldn't imagine Marilyn casting me off.

"Okay," she conceded, "I did wonder about Tony's mother. When I first found those pills he was taking and heard about the doctor he was seeing, I thought of her right away. I mean, I thought he had some of those mother issues you guys like to wallow in. I never had the chance to confront her about it."

"Just as well," I said, thinking that the task before us was already awkward enough.

She looked back to Larry Bird and said, "Just as well."

FIVE

THE DOWNEASTER reached Portland a little after nine. Most of the trip north from Boston had been made in darkness, but that hadn't stopped Marilyn from staring out the window. I'd long since decided that, whatever she'd been looking at all day, it hadn't been the scenery. Back in Boston, I'd been careful to pick up a private-eye paperback and a pocketful of candy bars, so I'd given her her space.

In Portland, she snapped back to life a little. "Somebody's meeting us," she said as we stood in the vestibule of our car, waiting for the train to come to a full stop.

She sounded anxious about it, but she needn't have been. At the bottom of the car's steps stood a little man in a dark suit holding a sign that read "Corelli."

"Mrs. Corelli?" he asked Marilyn as we climbed down.

"Ms. Tucci," she replied. "I'm Tony's wife. This is my cousin, Owen." Marilyn had had eleven hours to prepare me for that surprise, and it had somehow slipped her mind. She was gesturing toward the back of the train. "Tony's—"

"All taken care of, ma'am," the little man said. "Mrs. Corelli—Tony's mom—made all the arrangements. My name's Wren. I'm the funeral director in Pequod Point."

Wren was the first funeral director I'd ever met who wore a beard. His was a natty, gray Vandyke that was a perfect match for his dried-apple face.

"Mrs. Corelli said I was to offer you a ride. If you don't mind riding in a hearse."

"We don't," Marilyn said.

She made it sound like a lifelong dream of hers. I was moved to take her hand, but she got away from me, hurrying down the platform at the brisk pace set by Wren.

His hearse was a burgundy Cadillac, maybe five or six years old and wide enough to hold the three of us comfortably on its single bench seat. The coffin was already secure in the back when we got there, though how Wren had arranged that I had no idea. He wasn't a man to waste time. Within ten minutes of the Downeaster's arrival, we were speeding through Portland on Interstate I-295. The low-rise downtown, which I watched go by through the passenger window, seemed very quiet for half-past nine.

I mentioned that, idly, and our guide said, "Come back in a month. It'll be lively enough then. And it'll stay that way until Labor Day. The whole coast of Maine's like that. We say up here that tourists were God's way of reconciling us to the winters."

He didn't speak again until we'd crossed a bridge that honored someone or something named Tukey. Wren's preliminary throat-clearing coincided so precisely with our arrival on the opposite shore that I decided he'd planned it that way, that he'd put off his announcement until then.

"I'm afraid I've got some bad news for you, Mrs., er, Ms. Tucci. Your mother-in-law, Ava, has been taken ill. I mean to say, she had a stroke, a bad one, early this morning."

"How bad?" I asked when Marilyn, who was sitting between Wren and me, made no comment.

"She's not able to speak or walk, but she can move her hands. Her right hand anyway. My information's a little out-of-date. I had to get things ready for Tony and then drive down here. She might be better by now or she might be worse."

We drove into a rain shower. Wren got the wipers going

and then said, "Of course, they can do a lot for stroke victims nowadays. Retrain them to walk and talk. For that kind of therapy, she should really be down in Portland. Maybe even Boston. But they'll have the devil's own time getting her to leave Corelli Memorial."

More silence from Marilyn. I said, "Corelli Memorial?"

"Our little hospital in Pequod Point. Best medical facility between Portland and Bangor. Mrs. Corelli had it built and equipped herself. You don't grudge a person having half the money they've printed when she spends it like Ava's spent hers."

I looked to Marilyn for some sign that she'd known of her mother-in-law's wealth. I couldn't even tell if she was listening. Her inattention made me decide to risk a slightly different line of inquiry.

"Corelli Memorial is named after who? Tony's father?"

"Right," Wren said. "The full name is the Victor Banfield Corelli Memorial Hospital, but we're too tight with our words up here to say all that."

I was confused. "Banfield was Tony's middle name. I thought it might be his mother's maiden name."

"Nope," Wren said. "She was Ava Custis, a local girl. She met Vic Corelli because his family came up here summers. His, Vic's, mother was a Banfield. That's where all the money came from, the Banfields. So it's only right that their name got on the hospital."

Which brought us to the question I'd been edging toward. "How did Tony's father die?"

"Boating accident. Way back in 1953. He was racing a Spinner Twelve—that's a kind of sailboat they build around here. A freak gust of wind blew her over on her beam ends. Vic's foot got tangled up in a line and he couldn't swim free. By the time the other boats got there, he'd drowned."

This time it was Wren who stole a glance at Marilyn,

perhaps to see if his indiscreet mention of drowning had bothered her. Then he hurried on.

"It was hard on Pequod Point. Vic was a favorite with everybody. Harder still on Ava. She was eight months pregnant with Tony. Already packed to head south to have the baby."

"In Portland?"

"No, Boston. She needed the best of care after everything that had happened."

We stayed on the interstate for another twenty minutes. Then we traded down to a modest two-lane. It was Route 1, the road that had been dogging our tracks all day. About the same time, the rain stopped. Wren relaxed a little behind the wheel and took up our conversation as though there hadn't been a break.

"Ava built that hospital mainly so the local women wouldn't have to go through what she went through—traveling miles and miles to have her baby. Lots of babies have been born there since. Now poor Ava's there herself."

After a stroke. I said, "Having to bury her son must have been too much for her."

"That and her other troubles."

"What other troubles?"

"Nothing you'd be interested in," the funeral director said, revealing himself to be one poor judge of character.

SIX

WHEN WE DREW CLOSE enough to Pequod Point to leave Route 1 behind, my two companions got around to discussing the funeral arrangements, which Marilyn already seemed familiar with, at least in broad outline. No church service was planned. A brief visitation at Wren's funeral home, from ten until ten forty-five, would be followed by some remarks from a local minister. Those would be followed by a very short procession to the cemetery and an even shorter graveside service.

"I asked Ava to consider a longer visitation," Wren said. "Tony had a lot of friends in this area. She has many more. I didn't think forty-five minutes would be enough time for all of them to pay their respects. But Ava thought that something, er, quiet was best, given the circumstances."

Given that Tony had taken his own life, he meant. Once upon a time, suicides were denied any kind of service as well as burial in consecrated earth. Now they got docked half a viewing. Marilyn didn't express approval or disapproval of the plan. Her flat profile, illuminated just then by a passing property's security light, gave me no clue to her thoughts.

Wren was wrapping up. "Now that Ava herself is ill, the timing may not be a problem. Those who want to see her will be going to the hospital to do it. That reminds me. Feel free to drop by there anytime to visit Ava. Don't worry about visitors hours. There aren't any, not for her. I think she'd especially like to see you before the service."

That last instruction was delivered in the gravel drive of the inn where we'd be staying, the Damascus Inn. From what I could see of it in the darkness, the inn was a white frame building with a deep front porch that ran its entire width. The porch was lit by a hanging lantern that seemed too big for the job.

We stood at the steps of that porch, next to our bags, until the Cadillac's taillights were completely out of sight. Only then would Marilyn allow me to lead her inside.

There the innkeeper, Mrs. Handshoe, fussed over us, first producing sandwiches from the officially closed kitchen and then escorting us to our rooms.

"Mrs. Corelli wanted you to have the best. You'll be in the Long Cove Room," she told Marilyn. "And your cousin will be in Christmas Cove." She misclassified me with no prompting whatsoever, which told me that my elevation to cousin hadn't been a last-minute inspiration on Marilyn's part.

I didn't call her on it that evening; we were both too beat. I retired to the Christmas Cove Room, whose combination of nautical and holiday motifs, though striking, failed to keep me awake. But the next morning, when Marilyn joined me in the inn's breakfast room, I greeted her with, "How did you sleep, coz?"

She wasn't amused. It wasn't the day to amuse her, of course. Or, I suspected, the year. She'd traded her black dress for a black pantsuit—Pequod Point had awakened to temperatures in the forties—and her auburn hair had escaped all restraint, perhaps in reaction to the sea air, and become the mane I remembered from our dating days.

"It was the easiest way to explain you," she said as she sat down. "Or would you rather be known as 'the guy who used to sleep with the widow'?"

Shortly after that, Marilyn sent me in search of Mrs. Handshoe, to ask the location of the nearest rental car agency. I was already pals with our landlady, a very slim blonde somewhere on the dark side of fifty. She'd found me hunting for coffee earlier and told me all about her Damascus Inn. The name was a reference to a ship that had wrecked near the point just before the Civil War. The inn had been built from the wreck's timbers, and there were other odds and ends of it about, like the front porch lantern.

"So," she'd concluded, "you were on the road to Damascus all day yesterday and didn't know it. Like Paul in the Bible. Any bright lights knock you from your horse?"

"Not lately," I'd said.

When I tracked her down now and asked her about rental cars, Mrs. Handshoe put pink-tipped fingers to her mouth. "I forgot. Winston, Ava's hired man, brought a car over for you yesterday. It's Ava's own car. She won't be needing it today, poor soul. She may never need it again."

The innkeeper collected the car keys from the desk that blocked most of the inn's center hallway. "Winston was so upset. He showed me the note Ava wrote him about the car, the handwriting all weak and scratchy. It about made me cry. But that's so like her. In a hospital bed and still looking out for others."

And doing more than right by them. Mrs. Corelli's loaner was a late-model Mercedes, whose silver paint was only slightly dimmed by the morning mist. In it, I drove Marilyn to Corelli Memorial Hospital, which was back up the peninsula, halfway to Route 1.

The hospital was small—very small in relation to its full name and to its manicured grounds. There was more than enough room on the broad expanse of double-cut grass for some comparable memorial to be thrown up for Tony. His father's namesake was a single-story brick structure with a jutting center section and matching, setback wings. Mrs. Corelli was in the east wing, in a private room almost as big as the dining room at the Damascus Inn.

The scale of the room suited the flower arrangements that surrounded the single bed. But not the bed's occupant, a tiny woman, frail and, I thought, frightened.

Mrs. Corelli already had a visitor, a slightly stooped man who was dressed as we were, for the funeral. He turned out to be Winston, the hired hand. He all but bowed to Marilyn as he made his way out.

I was reminded again of my secret nickname for Marilyn—the unmoved mover—when her actual meeting with her mother-in-law took place. Mrs. Corelli tried to speak. By that I mean, she moved her lips, which were drawn down on one side, her left side. Her left eyelid drooped in the same direction. Her right eye was fine and watched her daughter-in-law's face intently.

Marilyn said, "I'm sorry."

Mrs. Corelli scribbled something on a pad that lay by her right side. She handed the note to Marilyn. Over her shoulder, I read "I'm sorry."

The sufferer reached up with her good hand and touched Marilyn's sleeve. At the same time, tears rolled down her wasted face.

I looked for a miracle then: tears from the unmoved mover. None came.

SEVEN

THAT WAS IT for our interview with Mrs. Corelli. One of the squad of nurses bustling in and out explained that the old woman's doctor wanted her to be mildly sedated during the hours of the funeral, fearing some aftershock of her stroke.

"You wouldn't believe the number of friends who've been here already this morning," the nurse confided as she shooed us out. "Mrs. C's run through two pads of paper already."

We'd been granted only a single sheet, the one I'd read over my "cousin's" shoulder. I might just as well have hung back politely. Marilyn had handed me the note as soon as she'd finished with it. When I tried to return it in the hospital hallway, she said, "Throw it away."

In our wanderings around Pequod Point, we were guided by another piece of paper, a photocopy of a hand-drawn map of the area. The map was one of the perks of staying at the Damascus Inn. I'd consulted my atlas on the night before we'd set out for New England, and I knew that Maine had a ragged coast. So ragged that it looked as though Maine had been torn from a much larger state without benefit of a perforation or even a crease. Random tatters—little peninsulas and points—hung down from the coast along its entire length, dozens of them, large and small. On the atlas map, the rents that were inlets and bays appeared to be held in check only by the red thread of a meandering seam: Route 1.

Pequod Point had been a very minor tatter on that atlas page. On Mrs. Handshoe's map, it was huge and shaped a little like the bottom half of New Jersey, with a broad upper expanse giving way suddenly to a narrow, slightly cockeyed tip. The hospital was near the center of the upper bulge. The inn was near the place where the peninsula narrowed. The dot identifying the village that took its name from the point was below the inn, about halfway to the southernmost landmark, a lighthouse.

Driving the actual ground reminded me of my most recent visit to Cape Cod. I'd been struck then by how normal—how unshorelike—the countryside was. In New Jersey, the approach to the shore is marked by a warning track dozens of miles wide, a territory of sand and scrub pines. On Cape Cod there'd been much less notice of the ocean's proximity, and here in Maine there was none at all. The water just popped into view at will, with normal trees and normal grass running right up to the water's edge.

In architecture, the Pequod Point area was also like Massachusetts, with one interesting exception. Again and again I saw old houses that had barns or stables attached. Sometimes the barn would be connected with a structure like a sided breezeway. Sometimes it directly abutted—often dwarfing—the house. It said a lot about the local winters that people had been willing to live that close to their livestock.

The actual village of Pequod Point was on the eastern side of the peninsula, on hilly land overlooking a small harbor. Wren's funeral home was well up on one of the hills, in an old house, one without a barn attached. This particular house was a white brick Victorian with a mansard roof topped by a widow's walk. A ship captain's house, perhaps.

The rooftop lookout surely commanded a view of the water that we could only glimpse through the intervening trees.

We arrived at Wren's early, which was lucky, as it turned out. Someone was waiting for us there besides the owner and Tony Corelli. As soon as I parked the Mercedes in the home's sloping lot, he started for us, a man in his thirties but with the air of a kid.

A very big kid. He was well over six feet tall and heavy, maybe fifty pounds heavier than he'd been when they'd measured him for the blue suit he wore. His red, bumpy complexion detracted from otherwise regular features, as did his thick glasses. His sandy hair was as wild as Marilyn's, but because his hair was thinning, there was something desperate about the party it was throwing itself.

"Are you Tony's wife?" he asked Marilyn before she was even out of the car. "My name is Bob Towe. Tony may have told you about me. We were friends. We grew up together. I think I may have killed him."

I would have been interested in Towe even without that remarkable statement, having remembered his name from the return address of the envelope I'd found in Tony's wastepaper basket. Now, of course, Marilyn was interested, too. She led us inside and asked Wren where she and Towe could talk in private.

The little funeral director gave Towe a very unfriendly look. Then he showed us to an overfurnished room set aside as a break area for grieving families. Marilyn tried to shut the door while I was still outside, but I wasn't having any of that.

"Not if you expect me to be here when you come out," I said.

She shrugged and let me in. They sat in facing, matching armchairs, Towe all but overflowing his. I stood a little way off, feeling like a referee at a chess match.

Marilyn moved first. "What did you mean when you said you might have killed Tony?"

"By writing him about Dr. Sims coming back," Towe said. He was close to crying like Mrs. Corelli had cried. "I knew Tony would want to know. Wait a minute, I'm lying. I needed help. I needed someone I could talk to, someone who would give a damn. I never dreamed it would upset Tony that badly. He was the one who always kept it together for the rest of us."

Towe's near babbling was getting to Marilyn, who seemed ready to snap at him. She looked to me, her expression saying, "As long as you're here, make yourself useful."

I sat on one end of a sofa that crowded Towe's chair. "Start at the beginning," I said. "Who is Dr. Sims?"

"Dr. Merrill Sims," Towe replied, without asking me who the hell I might be. "He was the doctor here in Pequod Point when I was a kid. When Tony and I were kids. He was the one who sexually abused us, Tony and me and the others."

He looked from me to Marilyn, asking her permission, I thought, to air this in front of me. I realized then that he expected Marilyn to know all about the abuse. And then I saw from her collected expression that she did know.

"It's all right," she said to Towe. "Go on."

He turned back to me expectantly. I asked, "When did this happen?"

"In 1960. I was seven. So was Tony. Two of the others were only six. One was five. We were all patients of Dr. Sims. Everybody for miles around was. But he was only fondling boys our age. When one of the six-year-olds, Russ Beamer, told his parents about it, all hell broke loose. Wait, that's another lie. Hell should have broken loose. Our parents joined hands and held it back. They hushed up everything. They forced Dr. Sims to leave town, but they didn't prosecute him. And they didn't get any help for us. They thought we'd just forget it, I guess. We didn't. After a few years, the families of the other boys moved away. It was just me and Tony for a long time. Then he moved to New York City. Maybe he did forget for a while.''

Not if the antidepressants he was taking were any indication.

Towe had been okay while discussing what had been done to him. But as we returned to the subject of what he had done to Tony, he started getting worked up all over again.

"I bet Tony was getting along fine until I wrote to tell him that Dr. Sims had come back. I sent that letter about ten days before he drowned. When we heard about that, I knew I was the one who'd pushed him in the river.''

He said the last bit to Marilyn. She sat there not speaking. She might have been doing the same math I was doing. Tony must have gotten Towe's letter about the time he stopped taking his pills, if Marilyn's guess about the pills was right. Which suggested that he'd stopped taking them because of the letter. But why? Why had the news of Sims's return affected him so much?

"Why did this Sims come back?" I asked.

"He said he wanted to spend his last days here. He lived here a long time, and he said he had the right to die here. He said his old sins were all paid for.''

"How?" Marilyn asked.

"With prison," Towe said. He'd only displayed a trace of shame when he'd told us about the abuse. Now it weighed his head down.

"When Sims left Pequod Point, he went out to California and set up practice there. After a while, he started abusing children out there. And he got caught again. Only those California parents did something about it. They had him arrested and prosecuted and locked away.

"When Sims got out of prison, he came back here. Got himself a cottage with an ocean view. Everybody here knows the truth about him. All the old-timers, anyway. But nobody's doing anything about it. Just like the last time."

"Did you think Tony might do something?" I asked.

Towe shrugged. "I thought he'd be somebody I could talk to. Talking to Tony always helped. Now I'll never get to talk to him again."

It was the cue for a really good cry. Towe was poised for one, but Wren cut him off.

The little man did it by sticking his pointy beard into the room and saying, "People are coming in now, Ms. Tucci."

EIGHT

TOWE PULLED HIMSELF together and hurried out. Marilyn would have followed him, not hurrying, but I blocked her way.

"You knew about the sexual abuse," I said.

She took a step forward, backing me up, then changed her mind. "The assistant medical examiner told me," she said. "He'd spoken to the psychiatrist Tony'd been seeing, and she'd told him there'd been abuse. None of the details, though. The examiner expected to get those from me. But I didn't have any details. I had to get them from a guy who still wears his high school graduation suit. The examiner couldn't believe I didn't know, Tony's own wife. That was a nice interview."

I was thinking of a more recent one, thinking of how coldly Marilyn had behaved toward Mrs. Corelli. "You thought Tony's mother was involved," I said.

Marilyn didn't admit to the mistake. She pushed passed me and out of the room.

By the time I joined her in the viewing room, Wren's largest, it was already half full. It was completely full only minutes later, and I started to think that Wren's first guess—that the mourners couldn't be accommodated in the time allotted—had been right.

But after Marilyn had taken the widow's place of honor at the head of the receiving line, it was clear that timing wouldn't be a problem. The combination of Marilyn being an outsider, Mrs. Corelli being missing, and the coffin being screwed shut, kept things moving. There were none of the hugs and little conversations and tearful scenes that make the usual viewing line such an ordeal.

I made that observation from one side of the room, where I'd tucked myself between an old grandfather clock and a wire rack that held some of the smaller flower arrangements. I watched Marilyn shake every hand and nod to acknowledge every hackneyed condolence. And I decided that she was putting herself through a penance by playing her part so thoroughly, that this whole trip was a penance she'd allotted herself.

I was about to shoulder my way through the crowd to stand by her side when I spotted Bob Towe. He was on the opposite side of the room, hidden in a little nook as I was, his formed by a fireplace on one side and an easel on the other. The easel held a portrait of Tony Corelli, probably taken when he'd graduated from college. Both of them, Towe and Tony, seemed to be scanning the crowd.

I did my shouldering in Towe's direction. He didn't notice me until I was stepping onto the hearth next to him.

"Looking for Dr. Sims?" I asked.

"I wouldn't put it past him to come," Towe replied. "I wouldn't put anything past him. But I was looking for someone else, the other guys, you know. The other members of the Sims club. I thought they might have heard about Tony somehow and come."

It was a forlorn hope, and Towe made it sound like one. The way Towe had told it, Tony and the others had been all the support group he'd had. And now they were either dead or scattered.

"I feel like a cigarette," the big kid said.

I felt like one myself, though I didn't smoke. I followed Towe out, the passage made easy for me by the wide swath he cut through the crowd.

Once we were out on the old mansion's flagstone porch, he produced a pack of Vantages and shook one free for me.

"No, thanks," I said. "I've quit."

"I wish I could," Towe said. "My dad's always on me about it, always pushing the latest nicotine gum or whatever at me. He's a druggist, so he gets free samples. He doesn't understand that there's more to smoking than chemicals. He doesn't understand…."

His voice trailed off, making that last fragment an epitaph for his relationship with his father.

We stood for a time looking out at the village and the sky above it. The morning's mist had blown away, giving us a better view of an overcast sky that was low and threatening.

"Storm's coming," Towe said, echoing my view of the general situation.

I didn't contribute any observations on the weather. I was thinking of the men Towe had been scanning the crowd for, his fellow victims. Towe's mention of them had reminded me of a question I wanted to ask.

"The boy who spoke up—Russ Beamer?—he was a year younger than you and Tony, right?"

"Right," Towe said.

"How was it that he was the one who blew the whistle? Why wasn't it you or Tony?"

"We were too scared. Sims threatened us to keep us quiet, and Tony and I were old enough to take his threats seriously. Russell wasn't."

I was used to Towe's habit of giving himself the lie, so I wasn't surprised when he did it now.

"That isn't true," he said. "Russ Beamer was just braver than we were. Sims scared us, but he didn't scare Russ. Tony always felt bad about that, about not speaking out. He thought he might have saved the three younger kids if he had."

"How about the California kids? How do you think Tony felt about them when he read your letter?"

I was looking for the real trigger, the thing that had knocked Tony off his medication. Sims's return still didn't seem like enough. So I'd hit on the guilt Tony might have felt for the victims of another time, on another coast.

Towe was quick to point out the flaw in my reasoning. "There's no way Tony could have felt responsible for that. It wasn't Tony's fault that Sims got away. Our parents did that. Pequod Point did that. Whoever's responsible for what happened in California, it wasn't Tony."

He was right. I'd have to look elsewhere for my trigger. And, as it happened, I carried a jumping-off point for the search folded up in my wallet. I produced the phone bill I'd taken from Tony's mailbox and pointed to the two Pequod Point numbers.

"Recognize those?" I asked.

"That first one's mine," Towe said, referring to the number that had received the longer call. "The other one looks familiar, but I can't place it. What is that, a phone bill?"

"Tony Corelli's last phone bill," I said. "He called you the night he got your letter. You talked for a long time. You told him something over the phone you haven't told me. What was it?"

Towe had seemed genuinely puzzled at first. Now he seemed more than genuinely mad. Suddenly he didn't look anything like an oversize kid.

"I don't know what you're talking about," he said. "And neither do you."

Then he turned and marched back into the house.

NINE

BACK INSIDE, Wren and some volunteers were converting the viewing room into a chapel by adding new rows of folding chairs to the half dozen we'd started with. A small lectern had been set up next to the casket. Facing it and fronting the first row of chairs was a sofa, on which Marilyn sat alone.

Though busy, Wren had time to give Bob Towe another unfriendly look as the big man reentered the room. He then directed Towe with a jerk of his head to an open seat in one of the first rows. Towe squeezed in there between an older man and woman. His parents, I guessed.

I was surprised to get the same treatment from the funeral director, the dirty look followed by the jerk of the head. My jerk directed me to join Marilyn on the sofa. I'd been debating that very point and coming down on the side of taking a quiet chair in the back. I'd been sure there'd be other family jockeying for a place on that sofa, other Corellis or a Custis or two from Tony's mother's side. But none had shown up, and Wren's position seemed to be that none would. So I made my way up the center aisle that ended at the sofa's back and sat. On a good day, Marilyn could have given Wren lessons in the nonverbal expression of aggravation, but this wasn't a good day. She merely glanced my way and nodded.

Shortly after that, a man took his place behind the lectern. He was young by my late-thirties standards and nervous. He stood with his feet well apart, as though he intended to deliver a punch instead of a eulogy.

He led off with Psalm 23, the one that begins with "The Lord is my shepherd, I shall not want" and ends on another hopeful note: "I will dwell in the house of the Lord forever."

I got stuck on a line in the middle of the psalm, the one I always got stuck on: "Though I walk in the valley of the shadow of death, I will fear no evil."

By the time I came out of it, the speaker had moved on to a précis of the major events in Tony Corelli's life. He was too junior to know the facts firsthand, so he must have done his homework, a lot of it. I learned that Tony had been a track star and a summer-stock actor and that he'd raced the same kind of sailboat his father had, the famous Spinner Twelve.

That point interested me, but not as much as the idea that Tony had once been an actor. By then I was seeing Tony's whole life in New York as an act, a part he'd written for himself: the perfectly ordinary guy. It had to have been a relief to him to have lived somewhere where no one but a tight-lipped psychiatrist knew about his past, where there were no Bob Towes stopping by to compare symptoms. And he'd been good in the part. He'd fooled everyone, including the woman sitting next to me.

The preacher had left me behind again. He was now on the subject of forgiveness, telling us why he was sure Tony would be forgiven for whatever sins he'd committed. One of the planks in his platform was that Tony had earned forgiveness for his sins by being forgiving of the sins of others. The speaker quoted the "Our Father" next. "Forgive us our trespasses as we forgive those who trespass against us."

I sensed an uneasy shifting in the crowd behind me and realized that we were moving from the subject of Tony Corelli and his sins to something else. When the shifting didn't settle down, it told me what the new subject was. The sins of Dr. Merrill Sims. Though the nervous preacher hadn't mentioned him by name, the doctor had to be the one he meant, the one whose redemption was tied somehow to Tony's own.

"As we hope for Tony Corelli's sins to be forgiven," he was saying, "as we pray for our own to be forgiven, so we must be willing to forgive those of others."

I stole a glance at Towe to see how the pitch was going over. It wasn't. Towe had his fat jaw set and elevated. Even stonier was the expression I saw on Marilyn's face as I turned back to the speaker. She'd see herself damned and the rest of us with her before she'd buy a word he was selling.

It might have been the look in her eye that convinced the preacher to give it up. He returned to the formal part of the service with the words, "Let us pray."

Shortly afterward, we made our way out into what had become a windy, cool day, more a March day than a May one. Marilyn and I were herded into a burgundy limo that matched the burgundy hearse. We had even more unused space on its back seat than we'd had on the viewing-room sofa. Our long train ride, an eleven-hour class in sitting next to Marilyn without speaking, held me in good stead now. Actually, I probably would have managed it without the class. She was that lost in her thoughts.

We drove south toward the lighthouse, but only a very short way. The cemetery was just outside the village, on a little rise from which the ocean was visible. The water looked dark and angry, so it matched the mood of the gathering perfectly.

The gutsy young preacher conducted a short graveside service, but I didn't follow any of it. I was distracted at the start by the sight of an older man standing some way off from the rest of us. He was short, but he might not always have been. He had the look of someone who'd lost vertebrae with age. Also hair color. The hair I could see beneath his camel hat, which matched his winter overcoat, was white. Nearly as colorless was his jowly face. Every time the wind gusted, he reached out a gloved hand to the tree next to him to steady himself.

I decided that he must be Dr. Sims, come to stand on the sidelines of the funeral as a taunt or a plea. I was waiting for someone else to notice him, for word to spread through the crowd, and then, what? The suspense had me too nervous to listen to the words being said or even to breathe.

Then Bob Towe looked over at the old man, blinked, and returned his gaze to the grave. So the man wasn't Sims. I tried to focus on the service, but it was too late. The preacher had finished, and the mourners were beginning their slow shuffle past the casket. Each one who passed placed a carnation on its curved lid. I saw Wren moving through the crowd with a basket of the flowers. When he got to us, he pulled out a carnation for me and then produced a rose for Marilyn. I placed my flower on the impressive pile, wondering if I'd have even a relative stranger to perform the ritual for me. Marilyn hesitated over the casket, and I turned away to give her some privacy.

And there was the old man, standing a little closer but still on the fringe of things. I walked over to him, cinching my trench coat tighter against what had become a strong, steady wind.

I introduced myself, giving my name and my phony connection to the widow.

"A cousin," the old man repeated. "That's what I am, a cousin. Of Tony's father. It can be a strange role, cousin. You're family, but you're not really family, if you know what I mean."

"I do," I said. I wasn't the least bit concerned that his

odd remark might mean that he'd seen through my disguise. I wasn't sure he was even seeing me through his tears.

"You may remember me," he said very formally to Marilyn, who had stepped up beside me. "I was at your wedding. I'm Arthur Banfield."

"I remember," Marilyn said. "Thank you for coming all this way. You live in Rochester, don't you?"

"Oh, no," Banfield said. "Scarsdale."

TEN

IT DIDN'T ESCAPE ME that Arthur Banfield's place of residence, Scarsdale, was one of the towns listed on the phone bill I'd stolen. But Banfield himself did escape me. It happened because the officious Wren came up at that moment to remind us of the postfuneral reception Mrs. Corelli had laid on at a Pequod Point restaurant.

"She would have had everyone to her house," Wren said, "only…"

"We understand," Banfield said. "I'm sure under the circumstances this is best."

Leading me to believe that he would attend the reception, where I could get him away from Marilyn and quiz him.

Banfield declined a ride in the burgundy limo, but that didn't worry me. It only meant he had his own car. After the limo driver had deposited Marilyn and me at the Pequod House, a nice old place with authentically low ceilings and creaky floors, I scanned the sparse crowd for Banfield without spotting him.

Marilyn misinterpreted my search. "The bar's over there," she said, pointing to a cubbyhole off the reception room. She didn't place an order, which told me that she was letting me off my leash. "Have a drink," she was saying. "Have several. Go nuts. Go away."

It would have been a token act of rebellion to have passed on the drink, but I wasn't feeling that rebellious. I stood in line, collected a Scotch on the rocks and then resumed my search for Banfield.

Instead of the old relation, I found the young preacher who had laid such an egg at the service. He was standing alone in a corner of the main room, getting the cold shoulder from the locals.

The preacher's name was Theard, which I learned when I walked over and introduced myself. He was just out of the seminary and up from Boston, so we would have had two topics of conversation if I'd been willing to admit to a stranger that I'd once been in the seminary myself. I settled for telling him that I'd been an undergraduate in Boston, and we chatted about the Hub City for a time.

Theard was an intense-looking guy with a lot of forehead, close-set, almost browless eyes and a very thin nose that curved downward to a tip still red from the wind. He had a nice smile, but I saw it only briefly, when I mentioned some Boston association that registered for him. When I steered the conversation to the recent funeral, the smile went away and hid.

"I'm glad I said what I did," Theard told me, lowering his voice but resuming the combative stance he'd used behind the lectern. "This town has Sims on the brain. On the soul, I should say. Pequod Point will never get over Sims until it acknowledges that he's got a right to be here. It will never forgive itself until it forgives him.

"I saw you speaking with Bob Towe over at Wren's," Theard added. "He's a symbol for the whole town, as far as I'm concerned. Stuck in time because he's unwilling to forget and forgive and move on. Mrs. Corelli knows what Pequod Point has to do. She's the only one who spoke up for Sims when he came back."

And she ended up with a stroke. Had it been the result of the strain of resisting the entire town's impulse to toss

Sims out? Or had the stroke come from the internal pressure of trying to forgive the man who had damaged her son?

I thought about that after Theard had excused himself and left the restaurant, not quite shaking the dust of the place from his sandals as he went, but looking as though he wanted to. I was still thinking about it when Marilyn found me shortly afterward.

"I'm leaving," she said. Then she added something I'd never dreamed I'd hear a woman say. "I need the keys to our Mercedes."

I scanned the remaining mourners one last time for Banfield, my gaze lingering regretfully on the finger-food buffet I'd yet to sample. Then I said, "I'll drive you wherever you need to go."

Marilyn treated me to another of her winning shrugs, and we went out.

Wren's funeral home was in the same block as the restaurant, so we didn't need to hitch a ride to our borrowed car. And we barely needed the car for the short drive Marilyn had in mind. She started us back up the peninsula toward the inn. But just outside the village, she had me turn west on a road called Clifftop. It climbed steadily, winding through patches of forest. My guide had me slow down every time we came to a driveway. Most of the drives had signposts, and most of those bore whimsical names such as "Whispering Pines" and "Rocky Retreat." When we reached a sign for "Clifftop Cottage," she had me turn in.

I stopped at the foot of the drive. "Is this a good idea?" I asked.

"No," Marilyn said. "It's a bad idea. But it's something I have to do."

"How did you even know where to come?"

"I asked around at the reception until somebody told me. Now let's go. You can sit in the car if you're frightened."

That advice would have had me sitting in cars most of the time, I reflected as I shifted the Mercedes back into gear.

Clifftop Cottage turned out to be a very accurate description of the structure we found at the top of the drive. It was a small, clapboard saltbox, white with a rust-colored roof and bright red shutters. It might have been a cheerful spot if the sky hadn't been a roiling gray and we'd been there on any other errand. The property was certainly at the top of a cliff. The backyard simply ended in midair a dozen yards beyond the cottage. I could clearly hear the ocean at work not far away, even before I'd shut down the sedan's engine.

Marilyn was out of the car immediately and marching up the cottage's front walk, a pebbled pathway through pine needles and spreading juniper. I managed to catch up just as she assaulted the front door's knocker.

The man who answered the summons was as old as Arthur Banfield, but not as comfortable with his years. His remaining hair was dyed surf-bum blond, perhaps to match his eyeglass frames, and it was combed to cover as much of his scalp as possible. His nose was small but well-veined. The loose skin of his cheeks held both age spots and a rosy glow, recently applied.

His manners fell far short of Banfield's. "Who the hell are you?" was how he greeted us.

"Dr. Sims?" Marilyn asked.

"Not doctor," the old man said testily. "Not anymore."

"I'm Tony Corelli's wife."

Sims collected himself in the pause that followed. "Ah," he said. "You'd better come in."

ELEVEN

SIMS SHOWED US into a stuffy little sitting room that had as much to do with him as the Christmas Cove Room at the Damascus Inn had to do with me. This room's theme was the cottage itself. There was an oil painting of it and photos from several periods—from several decades probably—including a long shot that had to have been taken from a boat. It showed the cottage as a bright bump on the top of its cliff. At the base of the cliff, a fringe of rock formed a natural breakwater.

"How is your dear mother-in-law?" Sims asked after Marilyn had finally decided to sit. He asked it a little anxiously, which Marilyn probably didn't understand. I thought I did. Mrs. Corelli was one of the few locals who'd made an effort to forgive Sims. If he lost her, he'd be down to the Reverend Mr. Theard and change.

"She's holding her own," I said when Marilyn didn't answer.

"You've just come from her?"

"No," I said. "From the funeral."

Sims nodded. Seated, he seemed a little less of a wreck. His jawline was still scalloped by a series of sagging jowls, and the folds of his neck were barely held together by his tightly buttoned shirt collar. But his thin lips had ceased working soundlessly between sentences. The small, blue eyes behind his gold-rimmed glasses had also settled, no longer darting around nervously but holding steady on Marilyn.

"Your mother-in-law is trying her best to forgive me," Sims informed her. "She's a good Christian woman."

"I'm not," Marilyn said.

Sims got nervous all over again, reaching up to smooth his yellow combover. "Mrs. Corelli knows I deserve a little peace. She knows that I've paid for my crimes. My sins."

"How have you paid for what you did to Tony?" Marilyn asked. She asked it with so much urgency I knew it was the single question she'd come to ask. "You never went to jail for that."

"No," Sims said. "But while I was in prison out west, I suffered things I couldn't begin to describe to you. Punishments no judge had laid out for me. Sentences handed down by my fellow prisoners, again and again and again. That was how I paid for my crimes against Tony and the others."

Sims' reedy voice had risen an octave during that speech. I could see a sheen of sweat beneath the golden hair.

Marilyn just sat there, her hands balled into fists in her lap. The angry ocean filled the awkward silence. That had been my job all day, and I took it back now.

"Why would Tony Corelli kill himself because you'd come back?" I asked.

The former doctor blinked at me. If he was finally wondering who I was, he didn't ask.

"He wouldn't," he said instead. "The idea is ridiculous. There must have been something else."

He looked at Marilyn as though at a more likely cause. She was out of her chair in an instant, still holding her balled hands in front of her. Sims rocked backward, but I grabbed Marilyn's arm before she could take a step.

"I insist you leave now," Sims sputtered. "I'm not a well man."

I looked to Marilyn and saw that I'd been wrong earlier when I'd decided that her question on forgiveness was the only thing she'd come to ask. I could tell by the way her face was twisted that she was desperate to ask or say or do something else.

"I'll call the police," Sims said, regaining composure with every word.

I led Marilyn to the front door, my hand on her arm the whole way. When we were halfway down the pebbled walk, Sims called out to her.

"You've no children, I hear," he said. "Are you pregnant by any chance? No? That's too bad for you." And then, almost singing it, "Too, too bad."

On the last word, he slammed the door on us.

BACK AT THE Damascus Inn, they were battening down the hatches for the approaching storm. That is, they were taking in the lawn furniture and winding up the badminton net.

I sat on the deep front porch and watched the proceedings, the paperback novel from our train trip in my lap. The book was only a prop. I was actually out there guarding Marilyn, who was in her room behind a locked door, guarding her against the approach of any other cheerful locals like Bob Towe. At the same time, I was protecting Pequod Point from Marilyn. On the drive back from Sims's, she'd looked angry enough to tear the whole peninsula off the map.

I'd suggested a return visit to Corelli Memorial Hospital during that drive and gotten turned down flat. So I'd had to get my update on Mrs. Corelli's condition from Mrs. Handshoe, the innkeeper. The widow had made it safely through the hours of the funeral and was now resting comfortably. Mrs. Handshoe had answered another question for me. Arthur Banfield was not a guest at the Damascus Inn. I'd started to think of him as the one who got away.

The rest of my thinking was devoted to Marilyn. What

else had she wanted to say to Sims? I fell into thinking of the thing she had asked him—how had he earned his forgiveness?—and of the emotion she'd put into the question. Had she been hoping for some loophole she might also squeeze through, some way she might atone?

The penance she'd assigned herself, the funeral, hadn't seemed to do the trick. Earlier in the day, I'd actually hoped she might relax a little once Tony was in the ground. I'd pictured the two of us having a quiet dinner together, a dinner that would mark a new step in her grieving process.

But that dinner for two never happened. At Mrs. Handshoe's suggestion, I booked the early seating, just in case the storm knocked out the power. The long-in-coming rain was just starting to fall when I tapped on Marilyn's door at six. I tapped and went on tapping. Just when I'd begun to think she'd fallen asleep or slipped out, Marilyn opened her door.

"I'm not hungry, Owen," she said. "Try me for breakfast."

So I ate my lobster pot pie alone, feeling very conspicuous in the little dining room where every table but mine seemed to be occupied by a courting couple. Things got even more romantic when the power failed as promised and we were reduced to candlelight. I almost asked the well-preserved Mrs. Handshoe to join me. Luckily, she was too busy to do more than flit by my table.

After dinner I sat in the inn's common room for a time, watching sheets of rain lit by the very regular flashes of lightning. On my way to my room, I knocked again on Marilyn's door. I could barely hear the knocking myself against the noise of the rain and the wind, so I wasn't surprised when she didn't answer. I retreated to Christmas Cove, read for a while, and then turned in. My last act was to hide the keys to the Mercedes.

I slept fitfully, because of the storm and the day that had

preceded it, only really sinking in deep when it was very nearly dawn. As a result, I overslept. It was ten when I awoke to the sound of some serious knocking on my door. It was my traveling companion, I thought, ready to travel.

I was wrong. My caller was Mrs. Handshoe, looking every day of her age.

"The police are here," she whispered. "They want to talk with you. That terrible Dr. Sims is dead."

TWELVE

I DRESSED QUICKLY, hoping for a private word with Marilyn before we faced the police. But when I went out into the hallway, Mrs. Handshoe was still there. She might have been waiting to finish the speech I'd interrupted when I'd shut the door on her, because she started right in again, still speaking in a whisper.

"They found his body on the rocks below his cottage. Some fishermen coming down in their boat from Wascesset did. The doctor would have floated off in the storm, only the rocks held on to him."

I thought of Tony Corelli, snagged by a bit of rotting pier. What were the odds of that happening to both men? I suddenly understood why the police would be interested in Marilyn and me.

I started to knock on her door, but Mrs. Handshoe stopped me. "Your cousin is downstairs already," she said. "Sergeant Edgecomb asked for her first. I'll take you to them."

The sergeant, a second uniformed officer, and Marilyn were tucked away in a little glassed-in porch on the opposite end of the inn from the dining room, as far from her other guests as Mrs. Handshoe could put them. The trio sat in white wicker chairs at a little wicker table, the two policemen jammed in on one side and Marilyn, her back to the house, on the other.

The porch was even glassed on the house side, so the sergeant saw us approaching while we were still a room away. He gestured for us to stay where we were. The inn-keeper could have safely left me at that point, but she stayed to chat.

"The storm blew itself out around five. There's another one due in this evening. Until then, it's going to be fine."

It certainly was at the moment. Sunlight was flooding the little porch, but I hadn't noticed it until then. My attention had been fixed on the woman who sat with her back to me. That back was ramrod straight.

Mrs. Handshoe patted my arm and hurried off. Almost at once, the sergeant looked up and met my eye. After a moment, he waved me in.

"Mr. Keane, is it? Come in, come in. We're about finished. Ms. Tucci was just going to show Herman where he could find some coffee. Care for a cup?"

"Yes," I said.

Marilyn stood and turned my way. Her face was composed but very pale. As much as I wanted that cup of coffee, I would have traded it for a smile or a nod or a wink from her, some little sign that we were in this together. She looked right through me.

The younger and thinner of the two policemen got up and followed her out, leaving me facing an avuncular guy with a lot of gray in his reddish crew cut. He had a meaty face with lines around the eyes and mouth that were so sharp-edged they looked like slices cut in bread dough.

"Have a seat," he said. "My name's Edgecomb. You're Ms. Tucci's cousin, I understand."

I'd been wondering how I'd address that point ever since Mrs. Handshoe had called Marilyn my cousin in the hallway upstairs. I gave it a half second's more thought now and said, "No. I'm just a friend."

My experience with policemen had taught me that it was better to lie to them as little as possible. But what convinced me to avoid this particular lie was the memory of Marilyn's stiff back as she'd sat in the chair I now occupied. I was guessing that she'd exploded the cousin story herself—done it defiantly—and that I'd be in trouble if I stuck with it.

The sergeant's smile told me that I'd guessed correctly. "Ms. Tucci said you'd been more than friends once and she didn't care to explain that to Mrs. Corelli, among others. I can understand that.

"You've heard about Sims's body being found, I expect."

He was assuming that Mrs. Handshoe had passed along the gossip. That was my first thought. My second was that he'd instructed her to tell me. I didn't have a chance to build on that. Edgecomb was hurrying on as though he were wasting my valuable time.

"It's pretty clear that the doctor fell from the top of the cliff. Whether he died from the fall or drowned is something we won't know for a while. Unfortunately, the guys who spotted the body took it on themselves to recover it, so we never got to see it in place. Still, if they hadn't pulled Sims off the rocks, he might have floated away by now—the tide was coming in when they found him. Then who knows where he'd be."

I paraphrased the recent lecture I'd heard on the subject back in New York. "The body would have sunk," I said. "It would have stayed down for a long time, as cold as the water is up here."

Edgecomb nodded. "That's what someone might expect, someone who doesn't know the ocean. Thing about the ocean that's different from a lake or a river is it throws things out sometimes. Washes them up on shore, I mean, or onto some rock.

"You visited Dr. Sims yesterday afternoon, is that right?"

I started to describe the visit, but the sergeant wasn't interested. He held a stub of a pencil in one hand, and he was moving it up and down rapidly, like a conductor trying to get allegro out of a particularly slow bassoonist.

"We really don't need much detail now," he said. "Not before you've had your breakfast and all. I just have one quick question about that visit. Did Ms. Tucci give Dr. Sims anything?"

"Give him anything?"

"Yes, you know, did she take anything that she was carrying with her and hand it to him?"

"No," I said.

"Fine," Edgecomb said, writing my answer down in his notebook. "That's fine." He looked over my shoulder and decided he had time for a new subject.

By then I was smelling trap with every breath. The way Mrs. Handshoe had brought Marilyn and me down in order, the information she'd passed me, the coffee errand Marilyn and her escort had been sent on. I saw it all as chamber music Edgecomb had orchestrated. And now he was waving his little baton at me again.

"We understand you two have the use of Mrs. Corelli's car. Who has the keys?"

"I do."

"Have they ever been out of your possession?"

"No." I'd checked the keys before I'd scrambled into my clothes. They'd still been under the ceramic Santa Claus where I'd hidden them.

"About last night now. Did you drive anywhere after dinner?"

"No," I said.

"Take a walk, did you?"

"No, the storm—"

"That's right," Edgecomb cut in. "Quite a nasty night. When did you see Ms. Tucci last?"

"Before dinner," I said. "She told me she'd see me at breakfast."

"Fine," Edgecomb said, scribbling away. Then he looked over my shoulder again, this time seeing what he'd been watching for.

"Herman, finally. I was getting ready to send the blood-hounds after you."

The lanky officer stepped onto the porch carrying two cups of coffee. Marilyn followed him carrying a single cup. My cup. Just as Edgecomb had arranged for her to do.

"Ah, Ms. Tucci," he said. "As long as you're here, why don't you join us. I was just going to tell Mr. Keane about something we found on Dr. Sims's body.

"Those fishermen disturbing things was a problem from one point of view, but it did sort of jump start our inquiry, their delivering the body to our fishing pier and all. Otherwise, it might have been some time before we discovered this, if we ever did."

He dug in the pocket of his windbreaker and produced a plastic bag. In it was a small brown pill bottle. He held it out for Marilyn to see, getting it so close to my nose that I could read the label. It was Tony Corelli's prescription for antidepressants, the pills I'd last seen in the dead man's living room, in his wife's hand.

"Mind telling me how Sims came to have these?" Edgecomb asked.

THIRTEEN

"MR. KEANE, why don't you give Ms. Tucci your seat."

I stood, but Marilyn didn't move to claim my chair. I placed myself beside her, almost in the doorway to the porch. The junior cop had gone around to Edgecomb's side of the table, but he stayed on his feet, too.

In addition to not sitting, Marilyn was not answering. Specifically, she hadn't said a word about the pill bottle. After a little more of that, the sergeant continued.

"You told us just now that you'd met Dr. Sims only once, when Mr. Keane drove you over to Sims's cottage after the funeral. We think you went back to see the doctor last night. Here's why. Mr. Keane didn't see you or talk to you after you passed on dinner around six. A woman matching your description was seen walking on Clifftop Road, near Sims's drive, around nine. The cottage isn't all that far from here. A person could easily walk there in an hour, even in a thunderstorm. Mrs. Handshoe found water and mud tracked in the center hall when she got up this morning. As far as she knew, none of her guests went out last night. I suspect that we'd find wet clothes in your room if we went up there and looked.

"Then there's this." He shook the bag that held the pill bottle. "I'm guessing we'll find your fingerprints on this, if the ocean left us any. It's a recent prescription, filled at a New York pharmacy. Mr. Keane told us you didn't pass anything to Sims when you visited him yesterday afternoon.

So you had to have gone back there last night. Why don't you have a seat and tell us about it.''

Marilyn sat, the better to look Edgecomb in the eye. "I went back to Sims's cottage last night," she said, speaking slowly and clearly. "I walked there in the rain. Owen didn't know anything about it."

"Why didn't you tell us that before?"

"I didn't want to have my name connected with Sims's suicide."

Edgecomb sat back in his chair. "Is that what you think this is, suicide?"

"Of course," Marilyn said. "I went back there to tell Sims what he'd done to Tony. How he'd ruined Tony's life. How his sins were still alive and well, no matter how forgiven he thought he was. I did tell him. I shook that pill bottle under his nose. I'd gone there to do that yesterday afternoon, but I got too worked up to speak. I couldn't go back to New York without making Sims understand that he'd killed Tony. I did make him understand. That has to be why he killed himself."

"Let me get this straight. A young man kills himself by jumping into a river, and then an old man who abused the young man years ago kills himself by jumping in the ocean. That's a mighty big coincidence."

"Not coincidence," I said. "Cause and effect." I was thinking of St. Thomas Aquinas at that inappropriate moment, and of his first proof of God. We were dealing with a long chain of collisions and ricochets, leading backward to what? I thought, illogically of Tony's father, Victor, the first drowning victim in what appeared to be a chain of them. Wondering about that dropped me a step behind Edgecomb.

"In a book or a movie," he was saying, "having Sims kill himself like Tony Corelli killed himself might seem satisfying. Might balance things or close the circle. In real life, it seems plain unlikely, like the same lottery number coming up two days in a row.''

"If it wasn't suicide," I said, "why did Sims have those pills on him?"

"The person who helped him off the cliff might have insisted he take them."

I was ready for that one. "Signing her name to the crime?''

"She could have thought the body would sink or float away. Or she could have been too mad to think. Or how's this? Sims might have pocketed those pills on the sly, as a clue, a message to us."

Marilyn was finally getting it. "Are you saying I pushed Sims off that cliff?"

"He was a feeble old man. Anyone could have done it, even a woman.''

I felt more than saw Marilyn bristle over that remark. I jumped in quickly.

"A lot of people in this town hated Sims for what he did. One of the abuse victims still lives here.''

"Bob Towe? He was down in Portland last night on business. Who else you got? Want me to check to see if Tony's mom is faking her stroke?"

"Of course you don't. Because it all comes down to this. A lot of people were unhappy when Sims came back, but I know of only one person who was at Sims's cottage last night. That's you, Ms. Tucci.''

"You know about someone else who was in the vicinity," I said. "The person who saw Marilyn on Clifftop Road. Who tipped you to that?''

Edgecomb looked uncomfortable for the first time, his very solid face taking on a little of the red hue of his hair. "We don't have a name. The information came in anonymously.''

That admission changed the whole feeling of the little

room. The temperature dropped a degree or two, and the
sunshine seemed less like the bright lights of a third degree.
Edgecomb was on a fishing expedition, pure and simple.
That was why we were chatting at the inn and not at the
police station. If Marilyn broke down and confessed, fine.
If she didn't, he was only out an hour of his time.

Still, he didn't give up. "If you went to Sims's just to
talk to him, why did you sneak back in here at the Damascus
after everyone had gone to bed?"

"I didn't *sneak*," Marilyn said, bristling visibly this time,
as though sneaking were a worse crime than murder.

If I'd had any doubts about her innocence, this show of
temper would have ground them out. If this woman had
wanted Sims dead, she wouldn't have slunk back in the dark
to do it. She'd have throttled him at high noon, in the center
of town.

"I got lost coming back," she said, almost spitting the
words. "It was pouring rain and I took a wrong turn. I was
an hour getting straightened out."

The sergeant seemed as knocked off balance by Marilyn's
sudden anger as I was reassured. I took advantage of that
to ask him a question.

"What did you find at Sims's cottage? Any tracks leading
to the cliff?"

"No," Edgecomb said, his eyes still on Marilyn. "The
land behind that cottage is nine-tenths rock. And it poured
rain last night, as Ms. Tucci said."

"How about inside? Any signs of a struggle?"

My moment of opportunity had passed. Edgecomb
snapped his notebook shut and climbed out of his seat.

"If I think you need to know any of that, Mr. Keane, I'll
tell you. Were you two planning on leaving today?"

"Yes," Marilyn said.

"I'd appreciate it if you would stay around for a day or
so, to help us with our inquiry."

I expected Marilyn to tell him to come to Brooklyn if he wanted to talk with her again. Actually, I was afraid she'd say it. I wasn't ready to leave Pequod Point.

She surprised me by going along with Edgecomb's plan and mine. "We'll be here as long as you need us," she said.

FOURTEEN

MARILYN AND I LINGERED on the sunporch after Edgecomb and his stooge had left it. She'd come down to the interview in a simple, straight dress and sandals, the flat shoes making her seem smaller, which in turn made her seem more vulnerable. Or maybe that quality had more to do with the dark smudges under her eyes and the sallow cast of her skin.

She waited until the police were just out of earshot to say, "There's no reason for you to stay, Owen. I'm sure the cops aren't interested in you. Catch up with that sergeant guy and tell him you're leaving."

"No, thanks," I said.

The offer worried me a little. Worried me a little more, that is. Ever since the funeral and Marilyn's reaction to it, I'd been uneasy. If my theory that this trip was some kind of penance was right and if our adventures to date hadn't satisfied her, I was expecting Marilyn to come up with a new way to punish herself. She hadn't jumped at the chance to take the blame for Sims's death, but the idea might be growing on her. Sending away her only friend, a friend who had some experience of the police and their habits, could be a sign that it was growing on her.

Marilyn demonstrated that she hadn't simply forgotten my personal history—my long addiction to mysteries—by standing there, waiting for my inevitable questions.

So as not to disappoint her, I asked, "Did you see any cars on Sims's road last night?"

"No."

"How did you get into his place?"

"What do you mean by that? You think I broke a window?"

"We left there yesterday because he threatened to call the police. He was afraid of you. So why did he let you back in after dark?"

She thought about it. "I knocked and he opened the door like he'd been standing right on the other side, waiting. I pushed him back into the room and started to say my piece."

"He didn't ask who it was before he opened the door?"

"No. Why is that important?"

"He's a guy the whole town hates, and he opens his door after dark like he hasn't an enemy in the world."

"So?" Marilyn asked, her patience going fast.

"So maybe he was expecting someone. Someone who might actually have shown up after you'd left."

My audience shook her head. "He just didn't give a damn. He opened his door the same way to us yesterday afternoon."

Her objection was actually a clue, but I didn't spot that just then. I moved on to another point.

"When did you last see that pill bottle?"

"I've been trying to remember. I did shake it under Sims's nose. I wasn't kidding about that. I scared him, Owen. I think he expected me to stuff those pills down his throat. It made me sick all of a sudden to be taking things out on that excuse for a human being. It came to me that it was too late to punish him. It had to have happened back in 1960. Why didn't they do something then?"

"I don't know," I said. "What about the pills?"

"There was a little table next to Sims's chair. I didn't notice it when we were there earlier. It had a battery-powered lantern on it. That was the only light in the room."

"The power was out," I said.

Marilyn nodded. "I put the pills down next to the lantern. Something to remind him that the slate wasn't really clean. That it never would be. Then I left and got lost and came back here. That's it."

Meaning both that she'd run out of story and that our private interview was over. She told me she'd be in her room and left me.

The coffee Marilyn had brought me was now cold. I went in search of a new cup and found Mrs. Handshoe instead. She almost cringed when she saw me coming. Over the part she'd played in Edgecomb's trap, I thought. It was actually over something new.

"The sergeant told me you'd be staying over a day or more," she began.

A day to twenty years, I thought.

"The thing is, the reservation Ava made was only for three nights. And she wasn't even sure you'd be here for all three. But she never said four. Those rooms are booked for tomorrow night. The whole inn is, in fact."

"So you want us out of here by tomorrow."

"I could call around and find you rooms. I have a list of all the inns and bed-and-breakfasts around here. I do that sort of thing all the time."

"Could you do me a favor while you're calling around?" I asked.

"Of course," she said, but warily.

"A man came to the funeral yesterday from out of town. Arthur Banfield. I'd like to find out where he's staying, if he's even still around. He's a relative of Mrs. Corelli's," I added, stretching the point somewhat.

Mrs. Handshoe brightened at the sound of the magic name and told me she'd find Banfield without fail.

That left me with time on my hands. I drove into Pequod Point, where I found a storefront diner that was still serving breakfast. Over my pancakes, I decided that a talk with Bob Towe was in order. I was certain that Towe was holding something back, something he'd told Tony Corelli during the telephone call he wouldn't acknowledge.

The diner had a pay phone near the exit, and I stopped there on my way out and called Towe's number to see if he was home and receiving visitors. His line was busy on my first attempt. Also the second and third. So much for giving him fair warning. I dug out the cream-colored envelope on which Towe had printed his address and asked my late waitress for directions.

I ended up walking to the Towe residence, a dark-stained ranch, since it was only a block or two up the hill from the Pequod Point business district. Many of the yards I passed on that walk had people puttering in them on this Saturday morning, and the ranch's yard was no exception. A man was working his way down the front walk with an electric edger. I recognized him as the man Bob Towe had sat next to at the viewing, the man I'd guessed to be his father.

At first I thought the father had stopped by to help his son with some yard work. Then a likelier explanation occurred to me. Bob Towe still lived with his parents. That fit with my impression of Towe, a man the Reverend Mr. Theard had described as "stuck in time."

The elder Towe was a much sparer specimen, with gray hair, his son's irregular complexion, and glasses whose lenses were amber-colored on their upper halves and clear below. His edger was noisy—very noisy whenever the blade touched the walk's concrete—and he didn't notice me until I was almost up to him. Then he switched the thing off and removed one of his earplugs.

"Yes?" he said. And then, before I could start in, "Didn't I see you at the funeral yesterday? You're some relative of Tony's wife, aren't you? I'm sorry I didn't speak to you there. We were pretty upset. We're all so broken up about Tony. He was a wonderful boy, so kind to everyone. My name's Walter, by the way. Walter Towe. Are you looking for my son?''

"No," I said. That had been my original plan, but the idea that Walter Towe and his son lived under the same roof had redirected my thinking, suggesting a way to reconcile the record of Tony's long call with Bob Towe's insistence that he hadn't gotten a call.

"I'd like to talk with you, Mr. Towe. Tony called your number a week before he died. Did you or Mrs. Towe speak to him?"

"I did," Towe said promptly. "Gosh, we talked for some time. But Tony never even hinted that he might take his life. I would have called his mother right away if he had."

"Why did Tony call?"

"He was looking for Bobby. Tony had gotten a letter from him about Dr. Sims coming back. Bobby was out, so Tony and I got to talking."

While he'd answered, he'd unplugged the edger from the orange extension cord that ran to the house. Now he crouched and fiddled with a guard that covered most of the blade. The guard swung open, revealing a compartment stuffed with mud and grass, which Towe began to dig out.

"Really too wet to be doing this," he said, looking up at me through the amber part of his glasses. "But I couldn't stay inside. My wife's been on the phone all morning, spreading the word about Dr. Sims. I guess you've heard what happened."

Had I ever. "How did you hear?"

"Word of mouth," Towe said. "But it's been on the radio, too, I guess. On the Portland stations even."

"I understand that your son was in Portland last night."

Towe looked back to his work. "I sent him down there to keep him busy. Like I said, the funeral had us all upset.

Bobby especially. God knows how this new business will affect him."

"It might help him," I said.

"It might," Towe said without much hope. He snapped the guard back into place and stood. "Was there anything else?"

Only the one thing I'd come to ask. "What did you and Tony talk about that night? Was it just Sims coming back?"

"No. It was mostly Sims going in the first place. Tony wanted to know why we'd let him get away in 1960. The same question Bobby's asked me a thousand times. I gave Tony the only answer I have—we just didn't know any better. I mean, we tried to do what we thought was best. We thought it would only scar the boys worse to put them through testifying at a trial. That would have punished them almost as much as it punished Sims."

"Were all the parents in favor of hushing things up?"

"Those who weren't came around in the end," Towe said. "Ava Corelli thought it was the right thing to do, and that carried a lot of weight.

"You have to understand, not talking about sexual things was the rule back then. It would have gone against the way we'd all been brought up to have made a public circus of it. So we tried to bury it, bury it deep. The boys were young. We thought they'd forget it if we gave them a chance. Bobby never has. I guess Tony didn't, either."

FIFTEEN

So much for the first of my mystery phone calls. But I still had two others, the one I was now convinced had gone to Arthur Banfield and the last one listed, the very short call to the unidentified number in Pequod Point.

I hadn't tried the most obvious method of identifying that second local number, but I tried it now. Back at the diner where I'd left the Mercedes, I put some coins into the pay phone and tapped in the number. There followed four rings, a click, and a woman's voice. "Hi! You've reached Ava Corelli. Please leave your name and number after the beep, and I'll get back to you."

So that last call had been to Tony's mother. He might have gotten her machine, as I had. That would explain the length of his call. Whatever message he'd left had probably long since been erased, perhaps even from the memory of the stroke victim who'd received it. That left me with Arthur Banfield.

I called the Damascus Inn and Mrs. Handshoe came on, sounding like her old chirpy self. She didn't drop an octave when she heard it was me, which gave me hope.

"I found you rooms," she said. "They're north of here, up on U.S. One. A very nice motel. The rooms are even available tonight, so you could move up there right away if you want."

Sparing her any return visits from the police. I wondered

whether Marilyn's arrest on the premises would make some future history of the inn.

"How about Arthur Banfield?"

"Oh, yes. I found him, too. He's staying out on Marsty Island. At the Marsty Inn. I can give you their number."

"How do I get there?"

"You have to take a boat. Ask at the fishing pier in Pequod Point."

I did and learned that the tourist boat serving the nearby islands, the *Erin Marie,* had just left on a run and wouldn't be back for hours. A helpful fisherman suggested an alternative, what he called a "work boat," the *A. Renee.*

I found the boat, which was white with blue trim and broad and blunt-bowed but not particularly long, tied up near the pier's fuel pumps. The fueling process must have been over, because the two men working there were loading boxes into the boat's open bow. Both men wore yellow rain jackets. One of them, the one who responded to my hello, also wore yellow rain pants and a knit cap. This though the weather was quite mild.

"We're going to one of the outer islands, but we'll pass Marsty," he told me. "You're welcome to come along, but we don't have a heated cabin like the day trippers' boat."

I'd left my all-purpose trench coat back at the inn. That left me with the dark suit I'd worn to the funeral, transformed into weekend wear by the absence of a tie.

"I'll be fine," I said, and we worked out a price.

They stowed me in the open bow with the rest of the cargo. The stern was also open, though there was a protrusion from the center of the deck that was a little shorter and wider than Tony Corelli's casket. This housing covered the engine, or something else that emitted a great deal of noise and an occasional puff of smoke. Amidships was a tiny wheelhouse. The man in the knit hat, whose name was Arnie, took his place there while Juan, his one-man crew, untied us.

As we eased out past a row of tied-up fishing boats and cabin cruisers, I wondered where on the long pier they'd landed Dr. Sims. Juan, a dark-featured kid, happened to be coiling a rope near my feet just then, so I asked him. He pointed to a spot just ahead of us and blessed himself. The stretch of pier he'd indicated was now occupied by strolling tourists. As far as they were concerned, Sims was already forgotten. For the locals, he might never be.

The water that had looked so dark and angry on the afternoon of the funeral was now a beautiful deep blue and almost as calm as a lake. We passed small sailboats—dangerous Spinner Twelves, maybe—and speedboats, several of whose occupants waved to me. I waved back, happy for the moment to forget Sims and Tony Corelli and to pretend I was just another pleasure boater. And it was a pleasure. Arnie's comments about heated cabins seemed silly on this sunny afternoon. So did my unspoken fears about my sea legs. I even ventured from my seat, moving to the railing to get a better view of a group of fat, brown seals that were sunning themselves on a rock carpeted in seaweed. I could see an even bigger rock at the mouth of the inlet, one large enough to support pine trees and a cottage or two. If it was Marsty Island, we'd be there in ten minutes.

It wasn't Marsty. Nor were the next two islands we passed. Each one seemed to function as an indicator that we were one step nearer the open Atlantic. The swells became bigger and steeper as we cleared each pile of rock, and the wind colder. It never got quite as cold as the spray coming over the bows though.

The mate brought me a sheet of heavy plastic as we passed the third island. "Found a tarp," he said.

One used to wipe up oil spills from the look of it, but I

wrapped it around me gladly. "How much longer?" I asked. We'd been at it for over an hour by then.

"Not long," Juan said. "Twenty minutes."

That made the island dead ahead Marsty, which was a relief, as I'd begun to think it might be Iceland. It was the biggest of the islands I'd seen, both in breadth and height, its southern end almost a rounded peak. That knob had been a hazy blue when I'd first spotted it, but by the time Juan made me the gift of the tarp, other colors were coming through. I could make out a belt of green with gray rock above and below it. In the green were specks of white and red that eventually became houses.

The *A. Renee* headed straight for those houses, though I couldn't make out anything like a harbor below them. When we got closer, I saw that what I'd taken for the rocky shore of Marsty was really an out island, complete with its own trees and a blinking light atop a tripod. Behind it was a protected stretch of water in which several boats bobbed at buoys.

We tied up at a stone jetty. Arnie then addressed a subject to which I'd given insufficient thought.

"We'll be back in an hour, maybe an hour and a half. The *Erin Marie* should be here sooner, if you'd like a warmer ride back. My advice would be to catch her. The weather's supposed to kick up a little later on. If you decide to leave before we get back, have Spence up at the inn give us a call on the radio so we don't have to stop."

SIXTEEN

SPENCE AT THE MARSTY INN—its owner and manager and, at the moment I found him, a busboy in its restaurant—told me how to locate Banfield. The old man was staying in one of the inn's cottages, on a sandy hill above the main building.

I climbed a winding path and found Sternpost Cottage but no Banfield. I had a look inside the gray-shingled shack, since the place wasn't locked. The whole thing was two rooms plus bath, the main room arranged around a wood-burning stove that was almost hot to the touch. While I was checking the bedroom, I spotted Banfield through its single window. He was out back in an Adirondack chair that sat in a spot where the trees were thin enough to permit a view of the ocean.

When I came up behind his chair, I said his name and got no response. His head was leaning a little to one side. If this had been one of the mystery stories I loved so much, Banfield would have been dead in that chair, shot through the heart by someone who'd anticipated my trip to the island. As it was a different kind of story entirely, Banfield was only asleep, drool and not blood staining the plaid blanket he was wrapped in.

Instead of waking him, I got caught up in the view. The ocean that had lately felt like a roller-coaster ride looked smooth enough from the hill. At least it did until the *A. Renee* came into view, rounding the breakwater islet that protected the anchorage. The way the little work boat was bobbing up and down set up a sympathetic vibration in my stomach.

When I looked back to Banfield, his eyes were open and he was wiping at the corner of his mouth with a handkerchief.

"Good afternoon," he said in his formal way. "You were with Tony's wife at the funeral. We heard some disturbing news this morning from the mainland. About Merrill Sims. Is it true?"

"Yes," I said. For some reason, I hadn't expected Banfield to know about Sims's death. But I should have. Mrs. Handshoe had probably passed on the news to every inn and bed-and-breakfast she'd called.

"I'm afraid I've forgotten your name," the old man said.

"It's Keane."

"Of course. Someone at the funeral told me you were Ms. Tucci's cousin."

I'd told him that myself, but I didn't point it out.

Then he remembered without my help and smiled a rueful smile. "We chatted, didn't we?" To prove his memory wasn't completely shot, he added, "About how odd the job of cousin is."

I nodded. "You said a cousin is family but not really family." It was the place to admit I wasn't even a cousin, but Banfield cut me off.

"Exactly. You're connected but not an insider. More of a spectator than a participant. A spectator with reserved seating."

"Like you are with the Corellis?" I asked.

"Yes," Banfield said and sighed. "Can I offer you some tea?"

He led me back to the cottage at such a sedate pace I had time to tell him a lie. "Marilyn missed seeing you at the reception after the funeral."

"Yes, I'm sorry about that. But when you stay on an island, you have to accommodate the boatman's schedule. The way it was blowing up yesterday, I was afraid if I waited I might not get back."

Leaving me to wonder if he really had gotten back. I had time to wonder because we'd reached the cottage by then and my host was fussing around the wood-burning stove, adding a small chunk of wood to an impressive bed of embers. Then he filled a tin teakettle and placed it on the stovetop.

"No electricity to any of the cottages," he explained after he'd settled heavily onto a ladder-backed chair.

"How did you find this place?" I asked.

"It found me. Banfields have been coming up here in the summer since before I was born."

He launched into a series of reminiscences about Marsty Island that carried us through the tea-making, many of them involving the famous painters he used to spy on as a child. I listened with only one ear until he mentioned the name Corelli.

"Tony's grandmother was a Banfield, of course," he said as though I knew all about it. "My father's sister. She married a man named Corelli who owned some kind of restaurant or club in New York City. The Banfields were quite scandalized. It started a tradition in that particular branch of the family of marrying outside the social register. Tony's father, Victor, married Ava, a Maine girl he met up here while he was on summer holiday with the Banfield clan."

"And Tony married Marilyn," I said, thinking that it was yet another chain of actions and reactions.

"Yes. Exactly the same pattern. They all married for love instead of money or position."

"From what I hear, the Banfields already have plenty of money."

"Yes, we do," the old man said, making it sound like a bad break.

I said, "The other Corelli pattern seems to be dying young."

Banfield nodded. "Victor Corelli, my good chum, died racing sailboats. I was on this island when I heard about it. They hadn't run the phone cable out here in those days. A fisherman brought us the news."

I was getting to like Banfield. For one thing, he laced his tea with rum. And I didn't often meet a person who used the word "chum," an echo of half-forgotten Hardy Boys' books. Banfield seemed like an echo of the past in general, or at least like a man who heard those echoes all around him.

"And now poor Tony," he said, drinking deeply of his spiked tea.

"Did you know what Dr. Sims had done to him?"

"Yes. But I only heard about it years afterward. Tony told me about it himself."

"So you two were close."

"We were. I manage a trust that provided for Tony and his mother, so I had regular contact with them."

I'd never get a better lead-in than that. "In fact," I said, "he called you the week before he died."

Banfield stopped in midsip. "How do you know that?"

I showed him the phone bill. "I'd like to know why Tony killed himself." So as to sidestep the subject of Sims's plunge from the cliff, I added, "I think it would help Marilyn to know."

"I'm not sure about that," the old man said. "The truth doesn't always set you free. I think she'll have a bad time of it no matter what."

"Do you know why Tony did it?"

Banfield sat there while generations of his ancestors whispered warnings in his ear. Finally he said, "No."

"What did you and Tony talk about during that last call?"

He had to think about that one, too. When he spoke, he did it very carefully. "He had questions about some family business."

"What business?"

"About the trust I mentioned earlier, the one I manage. The Banfield family trust. I've been trustee since 1950, when I was just out of law school. It was unusual in those days to have a family member as a trustee. It was usually a bank. But it's always been a provision of the Banfield trust that a Banfield be in charge."

I decided that he was stalling. "What did Tony ask you?"

"He wanted me to explain some provisions of the trust. Specifically, whether his wife, your cousin, would be provided for in the event of his death. I told him that, as things stood at that moment, she wouldn't be."

"Because they were separated?"

"No, because they had no children. It's a peculiarity of the way the trust is set up that the surviving spouse of a Banfield, like your cousin, is only provided for if there is one or more living child."

"One or more Banfield," I said.

"One or more blood relative, regardless of surname."

"Is that all you two talked about?"

"Isn't that enough?" Banfield asked his teacup. And then, when I hadn't made sense of that, "He was all but telling me what he intended to do, that he intended to take his own life. And I didn't see. I didn't act. I should have done something, called someone. Gone to see him myself. Instead, I did nothing."

There seemed to be more than enough guilt to go around in connection with Tony Corelli's death. Everyone but Sims seemed to have taken some on.

I stood. "Thanks for the tea," I said.

SEVENTEEN

IT MIGHT HAVE BEEN the good night's sleep I hadn't had or the hearty breakfast I'd had late or the strange sensation I was experiencing that I was still on the rocking deck of the *A. Renee*. For whatever reason, what Banfield had told me didn't really register until I was sitting in the Marsty Inn, eating seafood chowder that Spence had scraped off the bottom of some pot and served in a slightly stale bread bowl. Until then, all I'd taken away from my talk with the old man was disappointment. His call from Tony might have been a hint that the younger man was thinking about suicide, but it wasn't an explanation.

I ran through it all again, sitting there in the inn's dining room while Spence, a whirlwind of a man who seemed youthful despite salt-and-pepper hair, bustled about setting tables for the dinner crowd. And when I got to the part about Marilyn being cut off from the trust money because she and Tony had no kids, I had the absurd feeling that someone had already told me that. It was absurd because I hadn't even heard of the Banfield trust until I'd come to Marsty Island. Wren, the funeral home owner, had gossiped about Mrs. Corelli's money, but he hadn't mentioned any trust. Neither had Marilyn, who'd been communicating through the whole trip as though she were being charged by the word.

And then the answer came to me. I remembered Merrill Sims's parting words as he'd stood shaking with anger in the doorway of his cottage. He'd asked Marilyn if she and Tony had any children and feigned sorrow over the answer he already knew. At the time, it had seemed to me that he was just getting back at her for scaring him by saying the nastiest thing a man with a taste for children could think to say.

Now I saw that he was taunting Marilyn over the Banfield trust. He knew she wouldn't see a penny of the money because she was childless. He'd even asked her whether she was pregnant. So he'd known the provision of the trust that the careful Arthur Banfield had mentioned, the one about a woman being covered if she was pregnant at the time her trust connection died.

Recalling that provision reminded me of something else I'd been told: Mrs. Corelli had been pregnant with Tony at the time of her husband's death. So she'd qualified for the Banfield inheritance, but only just. I didn't have to search my memory for the name of the person who'd told me that. I could remember the very words Wren had spoken as he'd driven us north that first night. I could even see the lights of passing traffic on his face as he'd told us the story of Mrs. Corelli's trip to Boston to have her baby.

Those remembered lights seemed to grow in intensity until they blinded me. I'd have been knocked from my horse, if I'd happened to be sitting on one.

I knew I had to talk with Wren right away. The *Erin Marie* was due at any minute, but I couldn't wait. I found Spence and borrowed the phone I knew he had, the one Mrs. Handshoe had used to reach him.

Wren answered the funeral parlor's phone himself.

"This is Owen Keane," I said.

"Oh, yes? Are you free to go then? I can't drive you to Portland myself. Mrs. Corelli's hired man, Winston, is going to do it. If you're free—I mean, ready."

So Wren knew about Sergeant Edgecomb's request that we not leave town. That confirmed my opinion of him as a premier source of information.

"We're not ready to go yet," I said. "I wanted to ask you about the time Tony Corelli was born. You said that Tony's mother went down to Boston for the birth, that she needed the best of care after everything that had happened. Were you referring to her husband's drowning? Was that the only reason she needed extra care?"

That was a crucial moment. Wren could have hidden behind good manners or New England reticence and declined to answer. Or he could have taken advantage of modern technology and simply hung up. But he didn't. The little insight into his character he'd given us during the drive up from Portland turned out to be absolutely accurate. He liked to talk, and Mrs. Corelli was a favorite subject.

"The only reason she needed special care?" he repeated. "It was enough, but it wasn't the only reason. There were the miscarriages, too. You know about them."

He knew I didn't, but I was happy to offer him the cover. "Tony mentioned them. How many did she have?"

"Just the two. They were both heartbreakers. She was nearly to term both times, and she was so anxious to have a baby."

For good reason, I thought. I knew the answer to the next question, thanks to Bob Towe, but I asked it anyway. "Who was her doctor back then?"

"Everybody around here had the same doctor," Wren said, paraphrasing Towe. "Merrill Sims."

"Did he go down to Boston with her?"

"Yep. Stayed through the delivery. Ava trusted Sims. Everybody did, in those days."

I thanked him, got back to a dial tone and punched in a long-distance number. I didn't clear this call with Spence, but I didn't think he would mind, as I was careful to reverse the charges.

The number belonged to a friend of mine named Harry Ohlman, a former New York lawyer who was now a full-time painter of blurry landscapes. I was hoping his seven-year-old daughter would answer the phone, both because I was sure she would accept the charges and because I wanted to hear her voice. Instead, I heard Harry's.

"Where the hell are you, Owen?" he asked after he'd agreed to take the call.

"Marsty Island, Maine," I said, certain he'd never heard of the place.

"Really? Andrew Wyeth used to paint up there," he said, naming one of the artists Banfield had mentioned. "So what do you need, Owen? I know you didn't call to say hello."

"How good are your connections in Boston?" It was another question to which I already knew the answer. Harry's Boston connections were in the Kennedy class. The only reason his father had set up practice in New York was the density of Ohlmans in Massachusetts.

"They're fine," Harry said. "All two hundred of them. Why?"

"How hard would it be to trace the records of a miscarriage in a Boston hospital and a subsequent adoption?"

That was the answer I'd come up with, the single answer to all the questions regarding Merrill Sims. He had accompanied Ava Corelli to Boston for the delivery of her child, her last chance to establish a connection to the Banfield trust. And the pair had come back with a baby. Only it hadn't really been Ava's. She'd lost her baby and, with Sims's help, she'd obtained a substitute, Tony.

That had set her up for a life of ease and philanthropy, but it had also put her in Sims's power. She'd surely paid him off with money—perhaps even with the promise of a fine new hospital—but when he was later accused of molesting the local children, she'd had to do more. She'd had to use her influence to see that he escaped unpunished. That answered the question that still haunted Bob Towe. Sims had gotten off because he knew Ava Corelli's secret.

It also explained why Sims had come back to Pequod Point. He knew he could count on his old coconspirator to protect him and to support him as long as he lived.

I described my suspicions to Harry in general terms. As usual, he wanted specifics.

"When did this miscarriage and adoption happen?"

"In 1953. I'm not sure of the month. I can find out."

"Sure you can. What was the name of the hospital?"

"I don't know."

"Okay," Harry said. "I'll get back to you this time next year. But only if the Boston relative I sucker into helping with this is very lucky. Look, Owen, you're talking about something that happened thirty-five years ago. Even if the records exist, they're going to be buried."

"What do you mean 'even if the records exist'? They have to exist."

"No, they don't. Back then they didn't always file a death certificate for a fetus, even a nearly full-term fetus. It was up to the attending physician. What do you think this Sims would have done?"

As little as possible. "How about the adoption?"

"Maybe, but my guess is they did that under the table, too. There was no shortage of girls having babies they didn't want in Boston in 1953. Sims probably just faked a birth certificate, and that was that. If someone had thought to investigate the birth back then, there might have been a chance of turning up something. But now…"

I would have pressed the question, but I'd spotted a dark green boat rounding the harbor's barrier island. Compared to the one I'd come out on, it was an ocean liner. The *Erin Marie*, surely, heated cabin and all.

I thanked Harry and told him to give my love to Amanda. "Bring her back a lobster hat," he said. "If they let you leave, that is."

EIGHTEEN

I PAID SPENCE for the call to Pequod Point and asked him to radio my regrets to the *A. Renee*. Then I hurried down to the stone jetty. The *Erin Marie* was tying up. Four day visitors to Marsty were waiting to embark, and I joined the line. They'd all made the trip out in her that morning, or so I guessed from the warm greeting they received from the large, bearded man who handed them aboard. I got the look he reserved for stowaways, until I explained my situation. After that, he wouldn't even take my money.

"You paid Arnie for a round trip," he said, "so I'll squeeze my fare out of him. There's laws against piracy, after all."

He was being so friendly, I decided to verify Arthur Banfield's alibi with him. He confirmed that he'd run the old man out to Marsty Island immediately after the funeral. As far as he knew, Banfield hadn't visited the mainland since.

I found my way to the passenger cabin, which was equipped with rows of plastic seats identical to ones I'd seen in Laundromats all over New Jersey, right down to the bolts that held them to the floor. Or rather, the deck. I was reminded of that distinction by the movement of this particular floor. As Arnie had predicted, the weather had gone steadily downhill. The day now resembled the afternoon of the funeral, with strong winds and a threatening sky.

I told myself that the motion would be easier once we were moving. At the moment, we were still tied up, awaiting two missing day-trippers. I took a seat with the other passengers to wait and immediately began second-guessing myself about the most recent step I'd taken. I should have insisted that Harry make a call or two. Instead, I'd let him off with some pointless excuses. He was right, of course. The investigation should have been conducted in 1953, but who had been around to do it?

The answer that came to me froze me for a few seconds. When I snapped out of it, I heard the bearded man calling to the missing passengers to hurry and then to Spence, that jack of all trades, to cast off a line.

I scrambled out of my seat, almost knocking down two women in matching denim suits as I rushed out of the cabin. The stern was already swinging away from the jetty. I shouted, "Changed my mind," to the bearded giant and jumped toward Spence, whose hand was raised in an aborted wave. For a second, I swayed with my toes on the jetty and the rest of me over the water. Then Spence grabbed my arm and hauled me in.

"Call Arnie and tell him to pick me up," I shouted to him as I ran for the inn.

"Haven't told him not to stop yet!" he shouted back. "And by the way, you're welcome!"

I hurried up to the main building and then to the sandy path beyond it that led to the man whose name had come to me on the *Erin Marie*: Arthur Banfield. He was the one who had investigated Tony Corelli's birth in 1953. He'd been careful to tell me that he'd assumed the management of the trust in 1950. So it would have been his job to investigate Ava's claim, if he'd had the least suspicion. And anyone who knew the circumstances of the birth—and who also knew the details of the trust—would have been suspicious.

I'd thought that Banfield had been stalling when he'd given me all the background on the trust, but he hadn't been.

He'd been trying to tell me the truth, in his own ancestor-ridden way.

I hadn't fallen into the harbor, but all the same I was wet by the time I reached Sternpost Cottage. Perspiration was trying to work its way out of my suit while a light rain tried to force its way in. I knocked once on the cottage door and then went in without waiting for a reply. Banfield was seated exactly where I'd left him. If he was surprised that it had taken me so long to work it out, he was too polite to say so. I spoke first in any case.

"Why didn't you just tell me what Ava did in '53?"

"She was the widow of a man I greatly admired," Banfield said, speaking a little too carefully now. The half pint of rum he'd used to flavor our tea stood on a table near his elbow, next to a teacup that now contained no tea to speak of.

"She's also the person who defrauded the Banfield trust," I said. "You've known that for thirty-five years. Why did you let her get away with it?"

"As you observed earlier, the Banfields have plenty of money. I wanted my cousin's widow to be provided for. I thought it was my duty to see that she was."

"But you did investigate her claim."

"Yes. I was curious. I hired a Boston detective agency. They traced Tony's real mother. An Italian, like his father and grandfather. So I had my answer, but I'd already made up my mind not to do anything about it. Later, when I was given the opportunity to get to know Tony, I was glad that I'd done nothing. He was a boy to be proud of, a credit to any family. Especially the Banfields. I guess you could say I was an accessory to fraud."

To more than that, I thought. "The night that Tony called you, he asked about the provisions of the trust that applied to widows, but it wasn't over Marilyn."

"No," Banfield said. "I thought at first that it was. But

he never mentioned his wife. I saw soon enough that his questions had to do with his mother. With himself. He'd begun to suspect the truth. Dr. Sims's return, which he'd heard about from some childhood friend, had gotten him thinking over the old questions. Why hadn't Sims been prosecuted? Why had Ava used her influence on his behalf? And new questions. What had made Sims come back to Pequod Point, of all the little towns on earth?''

We both knew the answers to those questions, so I moved us on. ''Why didn't you speak up when Sims molested the boys in 1960?''

''I told you the truth about that. I didn't learn of the abuse until years later. Tony told me himself.''

''When he called you the week before he died?''

''No, years earlier. When he was in college. I knew immediately what had happened, how Sims had used his hold on Ava. But it was too late then for me to do anything about it.''

''You could have told Tony the truth.''

''Yes, but I didn't see any good coming from that. Not then.''

''But when Tony called you for the last time, you did tell him.''

''Yes.'' The old man's chin was resting on his sunken chest. ''I thought it might be a chance for a new start for him. He could even meet his birth mother, if she were still alive. I thought it might be a relief to him to know that he wasn't related to Ava. Wasn't really a Banfield. Instead…''

That unfinished sentence hung in the stuffy air of the cottage for some time. Then we heard the sound of a boat's horn some way off.

''Your ride,'' Banfield said. ''You'll have to hurry if you don't want to spend the night.

"Take this," he added, holding out the half pint of rum to me. "You'll need it on a night like this."

"You'll need it more," I said.

"I've a lifetime supply," Banfield said. "The family has seen to that."

NINETEEN

HALF AN HOUR LATER, on the bounding deck of the *A. Renee*, I was glad I'd taken Banfield's rum. And it wasn't because of the weather, though it was ugly. The rain came and went in regular showers, but they were hard to distinguish from the constant spray kicked up by the wind and our passage through the waves. I was on the aft deck this time, for a little additional protection, but wrapped again in my borrowed tarpaulin. Me and my bottle.

What had me drinking from that bottle as regularly as the rains came were thoughts of Tony Corelli. I knew now why he'd stepped into that river. Thanks to Banfield, he'd learned the secret history of his birth. In fairness to the old trustee, Tony had probably suspected the truth. His mother's behavior toward Sims, in 1960 and since the doctor's return, had to have pushed his thinking that way. Banfield had only confirmed it. The old man had offered the truth to Tony as a gift, as a way he might distance himself from the Banfields and the Corellis. Most especially from Ava Corelli and her sins. Instead, the revelation had bound Tony to those sins. The truth doesn't always set you free, as a sadder but wiser Banfield had observed.

If I was guessing right, Tony had seen himself as responsible in some small way for Sims's escape in 1960. The doctor had gotten off because of the Banfield money, because of Ava's addiction to it, an addiction Tony's whole life had made possible. So he could have felt responsible for Bob Towe's stunted life, which might have turned out differently if Sims had been exposed and punished.

Far worse was what had happened to those nameless children in California. Towe had dismissed my idea that Tony might have felt guilty over what they'd suffered, preferring to blame the Pequod Point parents. Tony might have seen it differently. He knew that those children had been victimized because of the Banfield trust money, the money that had supported him and his mother in such comfort. All through my time in Maine, I'd been looking for the smoking gun, for the single reason Tony had killed himself. Now I thought I'd found it.

I'd also been looking for the first mover, the person who had set the whole long chain of events in motion. For a long time, it had looked as though the spark for that fuse had been Sims. Now I saw that it had really been Ava Corelli. She was the true unmoved mover, the one whose heart hadn't been touched by the suffering of any of Sims's victims, not even Tony's.

Unfortunately, she was also almost literally an unmoving mover, a stroke victim confined to a hospital bed. If she'd pushed Sims off that cliff, either to protect her secret or to belatedly avenge her "son," she had to have used another pair of hands. Working that out now, as the little boat reared and plunged, reminded me that there were things left to do.

I crawled forward to the tiny pilothouse and banged on its door until Juan, who was crammed inside with Arnie, noticed me.

"You okay?" he asked when he'd opened the door a crack. "You ready to switch?"

Back at the island, he'd offered to sit out on the deck, but I'd turned him down. I accepted his generosity now.

The pilothouse, though small, was surprisingly well equipped. It had a navigation system called a loran, for example, and a stereo that was currently blasting out the

Doobie Brothers. I was interested in another piece of hardware.

I pointed to the radio and asked, "Can you get the police on that?"

Arnie answered without taking his eyes off the blunt bow. "What police?"

"Pequod Point. Sergeant Edgecomb. Tell him I know who killed Dr. Sims."

I didn't think I'd have to explain that statement, and I was right. Arnie skipped right to questions of judgment. "You been drinking?"

"Sorry. Where are my manners?" I handed him the bottle.

He actually took a pull. Then he got on the radio and called Pequod Point.

SERGEANT EDGECOMB and Herman were waiting for us when we got in. They'd parked their cruiser at the parking-lot end of the pier, and we saw its flashing lights from a long way out, the last of a series of lights that guided us home.

On land the gale we'd sailed through seemed like nothing more than a stiff breeze. Just enough to whip the tails of Edgecomb's plastic raincoat around his legs as he watched me walk the pier.

"What happened to you?" he asked at the end of that walk.

I ran a hand through my wet hair. "Pirates."

"Is this on the level about you knowing who killed Sims?"

"On the level."

I told the two policemen my story in their squad car, me in the guest suite in back.

"I suppose you can prove all that about Mrs. Corelli and Tony," Edgecomb said when I'd finished. There was anger in his voice, much more anger than I'd heard him express over the death of Sims.

"No," I said. "But Arthur Banfield can." I was betting the old man still had the private detective's report from 1953. Probably still in the original envelope.

"That stroke of hers isn't a phony." The sergeant dropped his voice. "I checked."

"So she had an accomplice." Both Edgecomb and Herman shifted in their seats to look at me. "Her hired man, Winston."

I saw the light of admiration fade from Herman's eyes.

Edgecomb said, "Winston was with Mrs. Corelli last night. We checked that, too. He's been sleeping at the hospital, outside her room. The night nurse had him in sight the whole time."

I didn't have an understudy for Winston in mind. Edgecomb did.

"Your friend Ms. Tucci is still a good fit. She and Mrs. Corelli could be in this together. For all Ms. Tucci knew, they were avenging Tony. Mrs. Corelli was just using her."

He said the last part to soften it, but it was still too hard for me. "I was with Marilyn in Mrs. Corelli's hospital room. They didn't plot anything."

"They could have had it all worked out before Mrs. Corelli had her stroke. Before Ms. Tucci came up here."

I thought back to the near trance Marilyn had been in on the train. It was exactly how someone contemplating the murder of a stranger would act.

Meanwhile, Edgecomb was still selling. "And there's that pill bottle. If Sims put it in his pants' pocket to point to his killer, it could only be Ms. Tucci."

I'd forgotten that damn pill bottle, Marilyn's link to the crime. For a spiked heartbeat or two, I interpreted that clue as Edgecomb had. I saw Marilyn as guilty. I saw my long day's work as having tightened the noose around her neck.

Then I settled down. I started with the pill bottle and asked myself to whom among Ava's possible accomplices it might point.

"Walter Towe," I said, pressing both hands against the screen that separated me from the policemen. "He's a druggist, isn't he?" One who pushed smoking cures at his son.

"A pharmacist, right," Edgecomb said.

"For how long?"

"Forever."

"Since Sims was a doctor?"

"Sure. Why?"

"That's how Sims would have remembered him, as a druggist. On his way to be murdered, Sims grabbed the pill bottle so we'd find it and think of Walter Towe."

"What does Towe have to do with the Banfield trust?"

"Not one thing." I borrowed a piece of the case he'd just made against Marilyn. "Towe thought he was avenging Tony. And his son. Mrs. Corelli was using him."

Edgecomb picked up on the echo and grimaced. "I guess it wouldn't hurt to check," he said.

TWENTY

WE MADE the short drive to the Towe residence. Mrs. Towe, a very overweight woman with cheeks as ruddy as a doll's, answered the door. I wondered whether her husband brought her diet pill samples. Then that unkind thought was knocked from my head by the fear in her eyes.

"Sergeant, thank God. I was just going to call you. Walter went off somewhere hours ago. I was on the phone and looked up and he was gone. Didn't take the car. Didn't even take his raincoat. Bobby's out looking for him now. Can you help—"

A new fear cut her off. "You haven't found him somewhere, have you? He isn't hurt or—"

"No," Edgecomb said, sounding very grim. "We haven't found him. But we'll help you search."

I asked, "What were you talking about on the phone when your husband left?"

Mrs. Towe looked guilty. Over unkind thoughts of her own, as it turned out.

"The last time I saw Walter, I was talking to someone about that cousin of yours," she told me. "Tony's widow. About how the police were after her over Dr. Sims."

Edgecomb butted back in then to ask for a list of places Bob Towe had already searched for his father. It included the family drugstore, but not the place I was listening for. Not the place the sergeant had in mind, either.

"We've got to get up to the hospital," he said as soon

as we were back in the cruiser. "I'll bet you Towe's gone up there for a strategy session or a showdown with Mrs. Corelli."

"Not the hospital," I said. "Sims's cottage. Towe left his house tonight because he heard that Marilyn was being blamed for what he did. He's going to use that cliff again. He may have gone over already."

Edgecomb didn't waste time arguing. He drove us the two blocks to the Pequod Point police station so we could check there for Towe and pick up the town's spare police car. Then he headed for Corelli Memorial alone while Herman and I drove to Clifftop Road.

My driver followed his sergeant's instructions and used neither flashing lights nor siren. But away from Edgecomb, he did permit himself to speak.

"Why would he pick the same way to kill himself?"

The question startled me, and not just because it was the first time I'd heard Herman's voice. I'd been thinking just then of Tony Corelli's method of killing himself and wondering why he'd chosen drowning. All along, I'd thought it was because he'd wanted to recreate his father's death. But I now knew—just as Tony had known at the end—that the man who'd drowned in that overturned sailboat hadn't been his father. So why had Tony chosen the river?

I realized fairly quickly that Herman wasn't asking about Tony. His question referred to Walter Towe. Why would he choose to die as Sims had?

"No judge would do that to him," Herman said.

I thought of Marilyn. "Some of us are hanging judges where our own crimes are concerned."

We were on the cottage's drive by then. The little saltbox at the top of it was dark. It was now raining steadily. Herman had pressed an official police rain jacket on me back at the station, but I left it in the car when we climbed out.

The jacket was bright orange, and I thought it might be important just then not to glow in the dark.

Herman led the way around the cottage, moving quickly until we reached the back. Then he froze. Not far away—closer even than I remembered it—was the cliff. And on its edge was a man, just visible against the dark gray of the sky.

Without consulting me, Herman called, "Mr. Towe?"

Towe turned slowly. "Herman? Stay back."

I started forward before I could be given the same order. "I'm here, too," I said. "Owen Keane. We talked this afternoon."

Edgecomb had described the backyard as being mostly rock, and it was. It looked like a single outcropping, almost as smooth as a huge flagstone, its dips and cracks leveled by the pooling rain. I stepped up onto it and kept moving, slowly.

"I need to talk with you again, Walter. I've found out something about Tony Corelli that you should know."

"About Tony?" Towe asked.

I'd been careful not to mention his presence on the edge of the cliff, and he seemed willing to go along with the act. We were just two near strangers, meeting on a street corner.

"Tony wasn't really a Corelli. He wasn't really Ava's child. He was a foundling she picked up in Boston after she lost her own baby. She needed to have a child or her husband's family would cut her off."

"The Banfields?" Towe asked. Of course he'd know the connection, being an old-timer.

"Right, the Banfields. Ava wouldn't have seen a nickel of their money if she'd come back from Boston without a child. So she came back with Tony. Dr. Sims helped her set that up. That's what he had on her. That's why she talked the rest of you into letting him go in 1960."

"It didn't take much talking," Towe said. He looked

away from me and down at the crashing surf below him. Below us now, as I'd reached the edge myself. My spot on the ledge was a nonthreatening six feet away from Towe's.

"That's why Sims came back here," I said. "To blackmail Ava. And that's why she asked you to kill him. It wasn't because of Tony or Bob or any of the other boys. It was to protect her secret. She used you, Walter. She'd love to hear that you'd killed yourself. Then she'd be safe forever. Don't do her the favor."

Towe was still looking down at the water. I looked, too, and that was a mistake. The rocks below were much closer than I'd pictured them when I'd been told of Sims's plunge. The waves crashing against those rocks burst upward in electric blue explosions that seemed to reach almost to my shoes. I relived the dizzy moment on the Marsty Island jetty when I'd had more water than stone beneath me. Only this time I was swaying forward instead of back.

Then someone grabbed my shoulder. Herman, I thought, but it was Towe, standing as close to me as he must have stood to Sims.

"Come away from there," he said.

TWENTY-ONE

WE RENDEZVOUSED with Edgecomb at the police station. Other rain-soaked police showed up, by and by. First the chief of police, Edgecomb's boss and fishing buddy. Then a man and woman from the county sheriff's office. Finally, a matched pair of state troopers. For each layer of authority, Walter Towe patiently repeated his story, telling how Ava Corelli had enlisted him to avenge their sons. She'd assured Towe that he'd have no trouble getting into Sims's cottage, as the doctor was expecting someone with money from her—charity money, she'd told Towe, though he guessed now it had really been a blackmail payment. The money explained why Sims had been so happy to open his door, first to Marilyn and me, then to Marilyn alone, and then to Towe. Towe had seen Marilyn coming down Sims's drive during the storm and had reported it anonymously to Edgecomb, an act he seemed to feel worse about than the murder.

For proof of his story, he produced a note Ava had written in her hospital room after she'd had her stroke and Towe was having second thoughts. Though wet, the note was still legible: "Drown him for Tony."

I was able to produce the note Ava had written to Marilyn, so the collected police could compare the handwriting. I'd neglected to throw it away as Marilyn had instructed me. My note was also damp, having been in my pocket all day. Under the circumstances, its short message—"I'm sorry"—read like a confession.

It was all the confession the police would ever get from Ava Corelli. She died during the night of natural causes without ever hearing of Walter Towe's arrest. Died thinking she was safe at last, perhaps, or dreaming of the good works she'd do to make up for Sims's murder.

MARILYN AND I didn't stay for Ava's funeral. We were driven down to Portland by Herman on the morning after Towe's confession, early enough to catch the Downeaster's departure for New York. Though somewhat stunned by the rush of events, Mrs. Handshoe had personally supervised our checkout from the Damascus Inn. She'd even urged us to come back for lupine season, whatever that was.

Marilyn had been stunned herself. At least that was how I'd interpreted the calm silence with which she'd greeted the news of her deliverance. She was still quiet on the drive down to Portland, but I attributed that to Herman's presence.

I used the quiet time to think about Tony Corelli's last phone call. The last one listed on my souvenir phone bill, anyway, the very short call to his mother. Had he gotten her machine, as I'd earlier assumed? Or had she answered and then hung up on him when he'd started to tell her that he knew everything? I was leaning toward the hang-up, the curt dismissal, the acknowledgment that he'd served his purpose. Until I remembered the tears that had washed Ava's wasted face in the hospital. Then I gave her the benefit of the doubt and decided it was one more answer I'd never have.

I moved from there to a more important unanswered question, the one I'd puzzled over on the drive to Clifftop Cottage: why had Tony chosen drowning? Why had he emulated the death of a man to whom he had no real connection? Was it one last act of loyalty to Ava? Had he decided to help protect her secret by choosing a death that would seem right and satisfying to every old gossip in Pequod Point, to everyone who remembered his father? Or had he been reaching out to that father—hopelessly, the way he'd reached out to him all his life? Had he been trying to establish a connection where none existed, to fool the world for his own sake, and not Ava's, to fool himself perhaps? The drive ended before I'd chewed it through.

I might have started gnawing again as soon as we were on the train if Marilyn hadn't suddenly rejoined the living. Before we'd even started moving, before the throbbing in my fingers from Herman's parting handshake had completely died away, she turned in her seat to face me.

"Thank you, Keane," she said, and her use of her old pet name for me lightened my heart. So did the sight of tears in her eyes, the tears I'd been watching for for days.

She buried her face in the front of my suit and cried it damp all over again.

STAR
SEARCH

by Nancy Baker Jacobs

ONE

IT WAS A RAINY spring Saturday in Los Angeles when I got the phone call that promised to make me an instant millionaire. The voice at the other end of the line was a smoker's, scratchy, deep and male. I didn't recognize it.

"Yes, this is Quinn Collins," I replied in answer to my caller's query. I was a bit annoyed that my morning routine had been interrupted. When I'd rushed to answer the phone, I was hoping my caller would be that good-looking assistant director I'd met at last night's film screening, the tall, blue-eyed guy who'd asked for my home phone number. But no—this sounded more like a telemarketer about to launch into a sales pitch for some product I didn't want or need, something I'd never buy through a phone solicitation in any case. I got ready to hang up on him.

"Quinn Collins of the *Hollywood Star*?"

So it wasn't a telemarketer. This guy was calling me at home about my work. I bristled. The studios' P.R. flacks knew enough not to phone me here if they wanted to see whatever publicity they were pitching appear in the pages of the *Star*. The *Star* is the weekly trade paper where I'm a reporter and co-owner. I have an ironclad rule—contact me at the office or by E-mail, period.

"That's me, in the flesh," I snapped. That description was truer than my caller would ever know—I'd just stepped out of the shower and barely managed to wrap a towel around myself before sprinting into the bedroom and grabbing the phone off the nightstand.

"My name is Dwight Schultz," the gravel-voiced man said. He obviously wasn't a bit deterred by my testy tone. "I'm a lawyer here in Monterey, and I'm serving as trustee of the late Hugo Paxton's estate. I'm calling to let you know you're a major beneficiary of Mr. Paxton's trust."

I took a beat, now feeling completely disoriented. "*Whose* trust?"

"Hugo Paxton's."

"Sorry, you've got the wrong person. I don't know any Hugo Paxton." Still wet from my shower, I started to shiver in the cool bedroom.

"You *are* Quinn Collins?"

"I already told you so, but—"

"Well, obviously Mr. Paxton knew you, ma'am. He died last Thursday, and he very specifically left his Pebble Beach house and its contents to you. I've got the trust document right here in front of me."

My caller might as well have been speaking Swahili for all the sense I was making of his words. Maybe, I thought for a moment, this Paxton guy had been one of my old boyfriends and I'd forgotten him. But that didn't make much sense. I'd have to remember somebody serious enough about me to leave me his house, wouldn't I? Surely my memory wasn't that far gone. No, I was certain I'd never known Hugo Paxton, in the biblical sense or any other.

"Is this some kind of joke?" I asked. That seemed the only logical explanation. I glanced down and realized I was dripping all over the bedroom carpet.

"Absolutely not. The trust is quite explicit—I drew it up for Mr. Paxton myself. There's a bequest to his only living relative, and a trust fund set up for a close friend. Then he leaves his house and all of its contents to you." He read me the pertinent section, which referred to me as "Quinn Collins, born Quinn Foster, daughter of the late Sheldon Foster and Megan Collins, and currently a reporter for the *Hollywood Star* entertainment industry publication.''

''That's definitely me,'' I admitted. Maybe this really *wasn't* a joke. My parents died in an auto accident back in 1960, when I was only two, and I was raised by my mother's brother, Uncle Teddy. He'd legally changed my last name to his to lessen any confusion when I started school. All these years later, I really doubted that very many people still remembered my birth name was Foster. ''Was Hugo Paxton a friend of my parents?'' I asked.

''Sorry, I don't know about that, ma'am. Mr. Paxton hired me to draw up his trust a few years ago, but we had only a business relationship—we weren't social friends.'' Dwight Schultz explained that Paxton had been in his early eighties when he died of cancer and added, ''I don't normally work Saturdays, but I came in to the office today to try to track you down. Thought you might want to know about Mr. Paxton's memorial service tomorrow afternoon. But if you say you didn't know him, I suppose—''

''Give me the details,'' I said. ''Where is it and what time?'' We briefly discussed what he predicted would be a small gathering in a room at Pacific Grove's Asilomar Conference Center. I told him I'd be there, and he agreed to meet me with the house keys and directions to the place I'd supposedly inherited.

Before hanging up, I asked Schultz to fax me those pages of Hugo Paxton's trust document that mentioned my name. Not that I tend to be skeptical or anything, but Monterey is well over three hundred miles and nearly a day's drive away from L.A. I didn't want to find out when I got there that this was a sick joke after all. It still seemed possible that Dwight Schultz was a phony name chosen by a rival journalist at the *Hollywood Reporter* or *Variety,* someone who wanted to send me on an out-of-town chase while some big story broke here in L.A. Or maybe my caller was somebody in the industry who didn't like a particular article I'd written about him and was trying to get revenge by playing a dirty trick on me. There were more than a few people who might fit that description.

Before I'd managed to towel myself dry and step into a pair of jeans, the fax machine in my tiny home office spit out the portions of the trust document Schultz had just read to me. The display panel told me the call was originating in the 831 area code—Monterey's—and the cover sheet identified the sender as Dwight Schultz, Attorney-at-Law, with a Monterey address. It appeared to be typed on paper with a professionally printed letterhead. My hands began to tremble as I grabbed the pages out of the fax machine's tray. I knew Pebble Beach real estate was not cheap. Even if this house of Hugo Paxton's was a fixer-upper, a termite-infested dump, I figured the building's lot alone had to be worth somewhere in the high six figures, possibly even more.

It had been a few years now since I'd owned any real estate. I'd sold my Santa Monica house as soon as the market began to recover from the downturn after the 1994 earthquake, and I'd invested the proceeds in the *Hollywood Star*. I became my bosses' business partner—in a publication that was still struggling financially. But at least I'd saved the weekly for a while, not to mention my job.

Now I was living in the small guesthouse behind Uncle Teddy's place here in Pacific Palisades, an arrangement that worked well for both of us. I had to admit that, without Teddy's generosity, I'd probably be unemployed and bankrupt by now...or working at Starbucks. But maybe, just maybe, I began to calculate, with today's unexpected piece of financial good fortune, I'd actually be able to start a serious retirement fund or pay cash for a small condo or—

I caught myself up short. What was I doing here, mentally

adding up dollars and cents, greedily fantasizing about my meager bank account's suddenly becoming flush with dollars, while conveniently ignoring the fact that a man had died to make this possible? A man who'd thought about me long enough to will me his house, at that. I felt a hot rush of shame. Whoever the late Hugo Paxton was, I lectured myself, the least I owed him was my gratitude and a little respect.

AFTER I'D DRESSED and taken a dry towel to the soaked spot on the bedroom carpet, I went back into the main room of the guesthouse, which serves as my living room, dining room and home office combined, and booted up my laptop. I did a quick Internet search for Hugo Paxton, but came up blank.

Then I checked the on-line version of his local newspaper, the *Monterey County Herald*, and got lucky. A brief obituary notice had run in today's edition.

Pebble Beach
Hugo Paxton
Hugo Paxton, 83, a retired writer, died Thursday at Monterey County Hospice after a long illness. He was born January 12, 1920, in New York City and lived in Pebble Beach for forty-two years.

Mr. Paxton worked as a motion-picture scriptwriter in Hollywood until being blacklisted in the 1950s for his brief membership in the Communist Party a decade earlier. Unable to gain employment in Hollywood, he tried his hand at a different medium and wrote two novels, which were never published. In 1961, Mr. Paxton moved to Pebble Beach, where he retired.

He was active in several local nature groups and enjoyed playing golf and walking on area beaches.

Mr. Paxton is survived by a nephew, Charles Paxton of Los Angeles.

A memorial gathering will be held at Asilomar Conference Center in Pacific Grove at 3:00 p.m. Sunday.

The family suggests that donations in Mr. Paxton's memory be made to the American Cancer Society.

As I read the brief résumé of Paxton's life, I recognized at least one connection. My parents had been screenwriters whose names had ended up on Hollywood's blacklist during the McCarthy Era, too. Hugo Paxton could have been their friend—undoubtedly a very close one, if he chose to leave his house to their only child more than forty years after their deaths.

I examined the photo that accompanied the obit, which had to be close to forty years old. It showed a rather plain-looking man in youngish middle age. He had a thin face, a bushy mustache and a full head of curly dark hair cut in a style that had been popular in the sixties. Paxton was not smiling and I thought his eyes held a sad, or maybe just faraway, look. I felt certain I'd never seen him before.

Perhaps, I thought, Uncle Teddy might remember something about the man. I printed out the obit, slipped into my yellow rain slicker and headed out the door and around the swimming pool toward the main house.

TWO

As I OPENED the kitchen door, the smell of something wonderful in the oven hit me and I remembered I hadn't eaten breakfast. Uncle Teddy stood in front of his restaurant-size stove in his ever-pristine white chef's apron, his hands thrust into yellow oven mitts. He was removing two pans of blueberry muffins from the oven rack.

"Morning, sunshine," he said as I hung my dripping slicker on a peg by the door. "Have a muffin while they're hot." I crossed the room to give the dear old man a quick peck on the cheek.

"You don't have to ask me twice," I replied, picking up the teakettle. I filled it at the sink, set it on a burner and turned on the flame before taking a tea bag from a cupboard and plopping it into a mug. "You want tea, or did you make coffee?"

"Already have my morning caffeine fix there on the table," he told me as he transferred the steaming muffins into a cloth-napkin-lined basket. "Syl's coming over in half an hour, so I made extra. Says she wants to tutor me on the guest list for the party we're going to tonight." He gave me a sly wink and a grin.

I grinned back at him. Sylvia St. Clair, our next-door neighbor and Teddy's best friend, is about his age, in her mid to late seventies. A onetime starlet, she'd been married five times and now is happily widowed, financially secure and determined never to marry again. She swears my gay

uncle Teddy, whose life partner died a few years back, is
her favorite escort of all time. He's sophisticated, intelligent,
caring, courteous and every bit as much a Hollywood character as she is. Plus she doesn't have to listen to him snore
in her ear at night or have another facelift in an effort to
keep him attentive.

"What party is this?" I asked him.

"Some of Syl's old cronies from SAG. Cocktails and
dinner in Bel Air, followed by a screening of some new
Italian picture she's been raving about."

My guess was that Sylvia's friends from the Screen Actors Guild were all about her age and Teddy's, long retired
by now, but still avidly interested in the business in which
they'd spent their lives. At least one of them had handled
his money well if he could afford to retire in Bel Air in a
house big enough to include a screening room.

Teddy and I sat at the kitchen table and devoured a few
of his tasty muffins. Cooking has been his hobby since he
retired as an art director. He was always a good cook, but
now he enjoys experimenting with new recipes and he sub-
scribes to *Gourmet* and several other magazines aimed at
foodies. His enthusiasm for his hobby—he's constantly urging me, "Here, try just a taste of this, Quinnie, tell me what
you think"—makes it harder than ever for me to control
my already somewhat *zoftig* figure. By Hollywood standards, I'm not only over the hill as a forty-something female, I'm far too large. I'm five feet ten inches tall and I
weigh 150 pounds, which is well within the normal range
on any insurance company's weight chart. But certainly not
on Hollywood's. So, with my hometown's critical judgment
of my physique in mind, I suppressed a strong urge to have
a third muffin.

"You'll never believe the phone call I got this morning,"
I told Teddy, licking the last muffin crumbs off my finger-
tips. I described my conversation with the Monterey lawyer

in detail, then handed him the obituary notice I'd down-loaded from the Internet.

"Hugo Paxton…Hugo Paxton…" Teddy repeated as he examined the photo and obit with a puzzled look on his face. "That name's familiar somehow, and this blacklist connection is interesting. I want to say he was a friend of your father's, but I'm just not positive."

"Well, he must have known somebody connected to me pretty darned well if he willed me his house."

Teddy bit his lower lip as he reached for another muffin. Unlike me, he seems able to eat whatever he wants and never gain an ounce. I'm green with envy. "What I wonder is where the man got all his money," he said. "*Pebble Beach?* The blacklist survivors I knew were ruined finan-cially. Most of them never really recovered their careers, except maybe for Howard Fast and Dalton Trumbo, plus an actor here or there, like Zero Mostel."

I'd written an obituary notice for Howard Fast in the *Star* just a few weeks earlier, so I'd brushed up on the late writer's history. "I know," I said, "Fast's book was the one that broke the blacklist."

"*Spartacus.* But it wasn't the book that did it, really. There was never a true blacklist for writers in the book business, just in Hollywood, so Fast was still able to publish his books in spite of Senator McCarthy and his cronies. In this town, it's Otto Preminger and Kirk Douglas who get credit for breaking the blacklist. I remember when they did it like it was yesterday. They announced that they were go-ing to give Dalton Trumbo on-screen credit for scripting the movie adaptation of *Spartacus*, and they got away with it. Remember, Trumbo was one of the Hollywood Ten, so this was a very big deal." Teddy frowned as he slathered butter on his muffin. "Unfortunately, by then it was 1960, and most of the blacklisted writers and actors had been out of work so long that nobody remembered them. A decade is a lifetime in Hollywood, pumpkin, and without any recent credits, forget it.''

''That's what happened to my mom and dad.''

''Afraid so.'' Teddy dabbed the corner of his mouth with his napkin. ''Those were terrible, terrible days in this town.''

The Hollywood blacklist had been a result of Senator Joseph McCarthy's crusade, plus the House Un-American Activities Committee's hearings in the late forties and early fifties. McCarthy and HUAC contended that Communists had infiltrated the movie business and were placing subversive messages and anti-American ideas in Hollywood films in an effort to influence the audience. In the end, there was little proof that this ever actually happened, but a number of politicians quickly spotted an opportunity to further their own careers by ''fighting communism'' in as public a way as possible. If that meant ruining a number of people working in this crazy business I love, so be it. The careers of a group of filmland liberals meant nothing to the likes of Senator Joseph McCarthy and Congressman Richard Nixon and their cohorts. They played their big opportunity like a bunch of ham actors.

The truth was, many Hollywood folks had dabbled in communism in the thirties and forties, often for idealistic reasons. Some of them were union organizers. Others wanted to help the poor. A few even said they'd joined because the prettiest women in Hollywood were all members. There was a wide variety of personal motivations.

I remember reading an interview that one of them, Maurice Rapf, gave to a reporter a few years before his recent death. In his heyday, Rapf had scripted Walt Disney's *Song of the South* and the Spencer Tracy movie, *They Gave Him a Gun*. ''The thing that impressed me most and probably made me a Communist was that anti-Semitism was illegal in the Soviet Union,'' Rapf said years later, ''and that the

Soviets were very anti-Fascist, which the United States was not.'' Maurice Rapf was the son of Harry Rapf, a prominent producer who'd worked with Irving Thalberg and Louis B. Mayer in the twenties, at the time MGM was launched. But after he was blacklisted, Maurice Rapf's career abruptly ended. He never worked in Hollywood again.

HUAC hauled dozens of prominent actors and, especially, writers before its inquisitors, and insisted not only that they testify to their own Communist leanings, but that they also ''name names'' of others in show business who shared their leftist ideas. Ten who refused to cooperate with the committee were sent to prison for contempt of Congress, quickly becoming known as the Hollywood Ten.

From what I'd been told as a child, my parents, like so many others in the industry, struggled in low-paid jobs after being blacklisted. They moved to a cheap apartment in Venice Beach and pretty much lived hand-to-mouth, hoping things would change and they'd get their old lives back. Before the blacklist, my dad had been a screenwriter, while my mother mainly wrote publicity for the studios.

Teddy'd told me that my dad continued to write at night—perhaps, like Hugo Paxton, he tried his hand at penning novels—but as far as I know, he was never able to sell anything else he'd written. This, despite his having been nominated for an Academy Award for one of his scripts a decade earlier. My mother, on the other hand, probably had her hands full with a job selling cosmetics and, later, caring for me. As far as I knew, she gave up her own writing.

Then, one night in 1960, my parents were driving on a dark road in Malibu, my dad behind the wheel of their ancient car, when it plunged off the road into the sea.

I had to admit, all these years later, that I'd spent my life actively avoiding learning the details of their deaths. In my heart of hearts, I guess I was afraid to find out they'd had a suicide pact or, perhaps, that their violent end was a murder-suicide. What would that knowledge have said about the strength of their feelings for me, their baby daughter?

I honestly hadn't wanted to know, not if the truth would cut my heart to ribbons. But now, with this strange inheritance from a man I'd never even heard of—a blacklisted writer like my parents—old questions began to resurface in my mind.

"I've got it!" Uncle Teddy suddenly exclaimed, jolting me out of my gloomy reverie. "I thought I knew this fellow." He slid the computer printout he'd been studying across the table toward me.

"Well, don't keep me in suspense," I demanded.

"I was right, Hugo Paxton did know your dad—I think they might have worked together on a project or two while they both were blacklisted. Never got anywhere as far as I know. But that's not what I remember most about him." He planted a finger on Paxton's picture. "A long time ago, before I met Artie, I used to go to a gay bookstore in West Hollywood. This man used to hang out there, too. I'm sure of it. Looked a bit younger then, but this is definitely him."

Artie—Arthur Bates—had been the love of Teddy's life. They were a devoted, faithful couple for many, many years, more devoted to each other than most married people I've known. The majority of the years I was growing up here in Uncle Teddy's house, Artie lived in the guesthouse that's now my home. As far as the public knew, Artie was simply our tenant, but he was really a second uncle to me, as well as Teddy's life partner.

"So Hugo Paxton was gay," I said.

"Not openly, of course, not in those days—we all had to stay deep in the closet if we wanted work. I'm afraid this poor fellow had more than a Communist past he was hiding." Teddy grimaced. "Yes, my dear, Hugo Paxton was definitely gay."

That might explain the trust fund Paxton had set up for what the lawyer had called his "close friend," I realized.

Now, if I only knew what any of this had to do with why he'd chosen me as his main heir. Was it because he'd once co-authored something with my father? Or had Uncle Teddy known Paxton a whole lot better than he was letting on?

Or maybe there was still another explanation, a reason I couldn't yet begin to guess.

THREE

I WAS OUT OF BED by six o'clock on Sunday morning, still sleepy but ready and eager to begin my long drive north. I brewed a cup of strong tea in my tiny kitchen, wolfed down a couple of Uncle Teddy's leftover muffins, grabbed my laptop and the bag I'd packed the night before, and climbed behind the wheel of my trusty old Mercedes.

Because it was still early, there was relatively little traffic as I drove north on Highway 1 through Malibu, and I made good time. I told myself to try to relax and enjoy the beautiful day. The rain had stopped during the night and the color of the sea had changed from a troubled gray to rich turquoise. Southern California is always most beautiful after rain has washed the smog from the air. Now, the hills on my right were vibrantly green—this had been an unusually wet spring in California—and they were filled with wildflowers.

I expected to feel my spirits lift as I started off on a new adventure, whatever it turned out to be. My hyperactive nature has always craved excitement, change, that quick rush of adrenaline. Virtually anything new and different is preferable to boredom—that's been my motto since I was a kid.

So why wasn't I having fun yet?

I felt certain that was Harry's fault. Harry Radner, formerly my boss and now my business partner at the *Star*, and I had had a spat on the phone yesterday—nothing particularly unusual for us, but it was still darkening my mood.

I'd called him to tell him I wouldn't be in the office on Monday, and perhaps not on Tuesday, either, depending on how things went in Monterey and Pebble Beach. But, instead of celebrating my good fortune, Harry'd gone into one of his typical panics about our weekly deadline. Even my promise to spend Saturday afternoon writing and faxing my stories to the office before I left town hadn't pacified him.

"We can't afford to coast through with a bunch of rewritten press releases, Quinn, you know that," he lectured me. "With the economy in the crapper the way it is, we're drowning here."

As if I didn't already know that. "Look, Harry," I replied, "we've got until Thursday noon to put next week's edition to bed. I've already got three new film reviews in the can and there are a couple of features I can finish this afternoon with no more than another couple of phone calls." Then I had a brainstorm. "Plus," I proposed, "how about I start on a retrospective article abouf the Hollywood blacklist? Truth is, people like Hugo Paxton are old and dying. Pretty soon there won't be anybody from the McCarthy Era left to interview for that kind of piece." I began to feel a surge of excitement about my idea as I described it to Harry. "Yes! This is perfect. I can combine whatever I find out up north about my benefactor with—"

"Are you nuts?" Harry's already rather high-pitched voice rose another octave. The little man is nothing if not volatile.

"Exactly what's nuts about my idea?" I countered. "The blacklist is an important part of our industry's history and I think—"

"For God's sake, woman, don't you read the newspapers?" As the volume of Harry's voice rose, I was forced to hold the receiver away from my ear to avoid risking future deafness. "Don't you ever watch Fox News or CNN?"

The answer to my partner's first question was yes, and to

his second, not if I could help it. But I knew the queries he was shouting in my ear were merely rhetorical. "And your point is?" I demanded.

"This is *not* the time to rake up all that old stuff. Pay just a little bit of attention to what's been going on around you. Susan Sarandon and Tim Robbins just got uninvited to the Baseball Hall of Fame because they're liberals—not Communists, mind you, just plain old Hollywood peace-loving liberals. That producer from CBS's miniseries about the young Hitler was fired for telling a *TV Guide* reporter that the U.S. today looks a lot like Germany in the thirties. Clear Channel banned the Dixie Chicks' music from being played on its humongous chain of radio stations because one Chick made one negative comment about the president. For God's sake, doesn't all this tell you something, Quinn?"

"Sure as hell does!" Now Harry's sarcastic remarks were getting my own ire up, and I was tempted to start yelling back at him. But I forced myself to calm down before adding, "What all that tells me, Harry, is that the blacklist could happen again—maybe it's *already* happening—unless somebody speaks up."

"Well, it damn well better not be the *Hollywood Star*. We can't afford to lose one more advertising dollar. You know that. If the networks and the studios start pulling their ads from our pages, we'll be bankrupt before the ink is dry on your idiotic article."

I took a deep breath and shrugged off Harry's perpetual concern about offending our advertisers. He loved to use that excuse to avoid printing virtually anything I thought was good, investigative editorial content. But I was a full partner in this publication, too, and that had to be worth something. "I'll make you a deal," I told him. "You at least wait until you read my blacklist story before you piss on it, and I'll fax you those movie reviews and my two features this afternoon. I'll also keep you posted about when I'll be back from Pebble Beach.''

Then I hung up the phone before Harry could give me any more grief.

I STOPPED FOR GAS in Santa Barbara, then pulled back onto the highway and resumed my trek northward. By the time I reached Pismo Beach, I'd managed to push Harry's tirade to the back of my mind and my mood had brightened. I stopped at a small restaurant near the shore and sat on the patio while I ate an early lunch of local clams and fries. So much for today's cholesterol count. A glass of wine would have tasted good, too, but I summoned up a touch of self-control and settled for iced tea. I still had at least a couple of hours of driving ahead of me. Besides, it wouldn't be right to show up at a memorial service smelling of alcohol.

At San Luis Obispo, I ignored the signs for Highway 1 through Big Sur. The last time I'd been there, I'd been searching for a young actress hired for a location film shoot. Taking the scenic Big Sur route was tempting on such a gorgeous day, but it was also tediously slow. On a Sunday, I knew I'd likely be stuck behind somebody in a camper who was terrified of driving the two-lane road's cliffs and curves, and I couldn't be late for my date with the lawyer. So instead of retracing my earlier journey, I stuck to Highway 101.

The weather was markedly warmer on the inland route and I watched the temperature gauge on the Mercedes climb as it labored up the steep hill toward Paso Robles. Luckily, the old car seemed a lot happier after Paso Robles, where the terrain became more level.

I was driving through farm country now, still making good time as I pressed down on the accelerator while keeping an eye out for the highway patrol. It was just after one-thirty when I left Highway 101 and headed westward on

Highway 68 toward the sea and the cooler air of the Monterey Peninsula.

It wouldn't be long now, I thought, as I drove toward the resort area that came to international prominence some years ago, when actor Clint Eastwood was elected mayor of Carmel. But Eastwood wasn't the Peninsula's only famous resident. Doris Day had retired here, as had Merv Griffin and Joan Fontaine. Kim Novak once bought a home on a spectacular outcropping in Carmel Highlands, too, but she'd moved farther north a few years later.

Eastwood was now a partner in the Pebble Beach Company, which owned hotels and golf courses in the pricey, gated community where the annual AT&T Pebble Beach National Pro-Am golf tournament is televised from courses perched along the dramatic Pacific coastline. Over the years, the contest's amateur roster has included lots of golfers from show biz, including the late Jack Lemmon, Kevin Costner, Bill Murray, Glen Campbell, Andy Garcia and dozens more. I'm not a golfer myself—the game seems much too slow to me—but I can still remember when this tournament was called the Bing Crosby Pro-Am, in honor of the late singer who'd begun it.

Hugo Paxton's obituary notice mentioned he'd been a golfer, and he'd been lucky enough to live his later life in what had to be any avid golfer's version of heaven.

As I followed the road signs and eventually pulled my car into the parking lot at Pacific Grove's Asilomar Conference Center, where the memorial service was scheduled, I couldn't help wondering about something.

Had it bothered Hugo Paxton that show business—the very same industry that had banned him and his life's work because of his political beliefs—played such a major role in making his beloved Pebble Beach world famous?

Or maybe that was precisely why he'd moved here.

FOUR

Dwight Schultz was waiting for me outside the room where the memorial gathering was to be held, just as he'd promised. As soon as I spotted the portly lawyer standing there, puffing on a cigar and sneaking quick peeks at his wristwatch, I felt a huge rush of relief. Part of me still had expected today's chase north to be a practical joke, but now I could accept that it was real. I actually was going to be the owner of a house in Pebble Beach.

After we'd introduced ourselves and shared a quick handshake, Schultz asked me for some identification. He glanced at my driver's license, then held his cigar clamped between his teeth while he used both hands to open his monogrammed leather briefcase and pull out a large manila envelope. "The house keys are in here," he mumbled through the cigar's pungent smoke.

I pretended the stench didn't bother me—it didn't seem like good form to appear ungrateful.

"There's also a map I marked to show you where the place is," he added, "plus a gate pass. Just put it on your dashboard and it'll get you past the guards at any of the Pebble Beach gates."

The lawyer had me sign a paper testifying that I'd taken possession of the house keys, and told me I'd receive a copy of the deed in the mail after the change of ownership was recorded with the county.

As soon as I'd signed my name, Schultz extended his

hand a second time and I shook it. "Enjoy the house," he said, turning on his heel.

"Y-you aren't staying for the service?" I asked, a bit stunned.

He waved a pudgy hand in my direction. "Sorry, no can do," he replied over his shoulder. "Sunday—family obligations." He hurried toward the parking lot while I stood there with my manila envelope, smelling the lingering cigar smoke and feeling sorry for Hugo Paxton. Even if he and his attorney hadn't been social friends, somehow it seemed inappropriate for Schultz to duck his late client's memorial service.

I sincerely hoped the former Hollywood writer had had at least a few friends who cared enough about him to pay their final respects.

I NEEDN'T HAVE worried. I counted more than twenty people, mostly men, in attendance—not a bad turnout, really, for a fellow who'd lived to be well into his eighties. The memorial program was simple and completely nonreligious, and I was relieved to see neither an embalmed body nor an urn of ashes on display. Three elderly men took turns addressing the small crowd, simply sharing their memories of the man they'd known as a fellow nature lover, a golfing buddy or a neighbor. When they'd finished their short spiels, a fourth old man, leaning on a cane as he served as emcee, invited everyone to share in the refreshments set up at the back of the room.

"Our dear Hugo would have wanted all of us, the friends and family he appreciated so much during his lifetime, to share a toast to his memory," the man told the gathering. He took a quick breath, and I thought I spotted tears in his heavy-lidded eyes. He forced a smile onto his wrinkled face. "We've got enough of Hugo's favorite Carmel Valley Merlot for everybody, so let's all lift a glass to him before we part.''

I picked up my manila envelope and headed for the back of the room.

"Miss Collins!"

I turned and saw the white-haired emcee limping in my direction.

"Yes?"

"Miss Collins, I'm so glad you came. I'm Sidney, Sidney Hathaway, Hugo's life partner," he said. We exchanged a few pleasantries. "I just wanted you to know I made sure the house was cleaned for you," he told me, "fresh linens on the beds, just the way Hugo would have wanted. I took the liberty of clearing out his clothes, too, sending them to Goodwill." He shook his head. "That house holds so many happy memories for me. I hope it will for you, too." His lower lip quivered and once again he appeared on the verge of tears.

"How kind of you, Mr. Hathaway." I felt guilty. Somehow this didn't seem like the time to tell him I planned to sell the place. "But I'm confused," I told him, "if—if you and Mr. Paxton lived together in that house—it doesn't seem right, I mean, I would have thought he'd leave his house to you."

Hathaway patted his knee with one gnarled hand while leaning on his cane with the other. "Can't handle stairs anymore, my dear. You needn't worry about me. I moved into a local seniors housing complex when Hugo had to go into Hospice. Everything's on one floor at my new place. I can have someone cook my meals if I want, and I've got enough money to last the rest of my life. My dear Hugo didn't forget about me."

"That house should have been mine. You know that, Sidney."

I flinched as I heard the angry tone of a younger man who'd clearly been eavesdropping on our conversation.

"Hello, Charlie," Hathaway said.

I'd noticed the man earlier, sitting in the front row. Now he was holding a nearly empty wineglass. His complexion was noticeably ruddy—I wasn't sure whether that was a result of chugging his wine or his obvious displeasure.

Sidney Hathaway tried to make the best of the situation. "Miss Collins," he said, "this is Charlie Paxton, Hugo's nephew."

So this was my benefactor's only living relative. I felt my face flush with discomfort as I extended my hand in greeting. Charlie ignored it, and I let it drop to my side.

"I oughta see a lawyer about this," he snarled. "I might just do that."

I noticed that Charlie's words were a touch slurred and guessed he'd fortified himself before arriving at the memorial.

"Charlie, watch your tongue," Hathaway warned.

"What're *you* gonna do about it, you impotent old fag?" Hathaway flinched as Charlie shot both of us a venomous parting look and headed back to the refreshment table.

"Whew," I said. "What's *his* problem?"

"Don't worry about Charlie," Hathaway told me. "He's a part-time actor, likes to be dramatic. His drinking is just the first of his vices. He also likes to play the horses and the slots. Poor Hugo lent him money at least a dozen times over the years. Substantial sums, too, but that boy never paid him back a penny. Not one red cent. The trust forgives what Charlie owed Hugo, which is a great deal more than he deserves, if you ask me."

"Still, I'm really curious about why Mr. Paxton chose me to leave his house to. Maybe you can—"

"Of course, of course you're curious," Hathaway said, glancing around, "but I'm afraid this isn't the time or place." He reached into his jacket pocket and pulled out a small slip of paper. "Here's my new address, my dear. Come see me tomorrow morning, shall we say ten o'clock? We can talk privately then."

I read the address. "You live in Carmel Valley?"

"It's just off Carmel Valley Road. There's a sign that marks the turnoff. You won't have any trouble finding it." He grasped my elbow and steered me toward the food. "Now do help yourself to the refreshments. You must be hungry after your long drive. Meet some of Hugo's friends and neighbors." He went to greet some of the other attendees while I headed toward the food.

I grabbed a glass of wine and a couple of shrimp while I made small talk with two of Hugo's friends from a nature study group and surveyed the small crowd. There was only one face there that I recognized.

William Brooks stood at the other end of the refreshment table chatting with a much younger man who greatly resembled him. Brooks, now in his midseventies, was a hugely successful author I'd seen several times at industry events. He'd written at least a dozen, maybe as many as two dozen, bestselling novels over the years, at least five of which had been adapted for film. His potboilers were in no way great literature, but an international public seemed to crave them, and his writing had made him a multimillionaire. I seemed to recall that Brooks's last three or four books had been co-authored with his son, apparently an attempt to pass on the family business, now that he was getting along in years. Come to think of it, I was pretty sure the elder Brooks had written for the movies, too, during his early career. In fact, if I wasn't mistaken, he'd had a couple of the scripts he'd written nominated for both Academy and Writers Guild awards in the fifties, but then followed them with a couple of bombs in the early sixties. His far greater success had been with his books, not his films.

The two men caught me looking at them, so I smiled and waved. They headed in my direction.

"Lynn, right?" William said.

"Quinn. Quinn Collins of the *Hollywood Star*, Mr. Brooks. We met at the wrap party for the movie version of one of your novels—*Death and Roses*, I think."

"Of course, Quinn—unusual name. I was sure I remembered you from somewhere. Ms. Collins, this is my son, Jared."

Jared, who appeared to be about my age, gave me a bored nod.

"How on earth did you know Hugo Paxton?" William asked me, the crease between his eyebrows deepening. "Certainly you can't be here researching a story."

I gave the two men a brief account of my unexpected inheritance.

"How bizarre," Jared said, finally showing interest in something I said. Maybe money rated his attention, while meeting a middle-aged woman did not. "Any idea why Hugo chose you?"

"Not a clue, really, except I presume he was a friend of my parents during his Hollywood days. They were all black-listed during the McCarthy Era and lost their writing careers as a result." I scrunched up my cocktail napkin and tossed it into a nearby wastebasket. "How about you two? How did you know Hugo?"

"Hugo and I went way back," William said. "Met him when I was just starting out and still working in movies, back in the fifties…before you were born. We kept in touch off and on over the years."

"Then maybe you knew my parents—Sheldon Foster and Megan Collins?"

William took a beat, perhaps trying to remember who he'd known fifty years earlier. "Nope," he said finally, shaking his balding head, "can't say I did." He grasped the sleeve of his son's suit jacket. "Come on, Jared, it's been a long day. Your old man is ready to go back to the hotel." He nodded at me. "Nice seeing you again, Ms. Collins."

As I watched them make a beeline for the exit, I noticed that Charlie Paxton was staring at me again. Somehow I didn't think he was simply appreciating my girlish good looks.

Perhaps, I thought, it was time for me to get out of here, too. I was anxious to go check out my new house.

FIVE

I CLIMBED BACK into the Mercedes and sat in the driver's seat for a while, studying the map Hugo's attorney had given me. I quickly realized that Pebble Beach was bigger than its neighbors of Pacific Grove and Carmel-by-the-Sea combined, with a tangle of short roads winding around its rocky coastline and its well-known selection of exclusive golf courses. Luckily, the address I wanted wasn't too far from the Pacific Grove entrance into Pebble Beach, and I figured I'd be able to find it.

The bored-looking guard on duty at the gate barely glanced at the entry pass on my dashboard as he waved me on through. Apparently his security function was limited to collecting the $8.25 entry fee from the numerous tourists who wanted to cruise Pebble Beach's famous Seventeen Mile Drive.

I drove past the Inn at Spanish Bay, then veered to the right and continued on the scenic route between the rocky seashore and the Spanish Bay golf course. Stuck behind two slow-moving cars with out-of-state license plates, I had no trouble following the map as I drove.

When I spotted the sign for Point Joe, one of the many view turnouts along the coast, I saw that the turn I wanted would be the next left. I quickly veered onto Ocean Road and stepped on the gas as I started through the middle of the golf course.

Suddenly I saw movement in my peripheral vision and

slammed on the brakes. I managed to screech to a stop barely in time to avoid hitting two young male deer that sprinted across the road in front of me. They halted as soon as they reached the opposite fairway, bent their heads and began casually munching on the grass. Obviously the pair, with their fuzzy, newly sprouted antlers, didn't share my fright over our near collision.

The golfers nearby seemed to pay the deer no mind. Apparently they were used to sharing their links with the local wildlife.

After my shock had subsided and I stepped on the gas again, I had to smile at the stark contrast between this bucolic place and the frenetic Los Angeles I knew so well.

When I reached the far side of the golf course, I took a left onto Cormorant Road and began checking house numbers. I found Hugo's address on the inland side of the street, across from a row of gargantuan homes that, except for their close proximity to each other, wouldn't be out of place in the ritziest sections of Beverly Hills. These larger houses backed up to the golf course, over which they enjoyed a clear view of the Pacific Ocean, not to mention what appeared to be at least one free-ranging herd of deer. Most of these minimansions looked quite new, and they nearly filled the lots they were built on. I suspected they'd replaced smaller, older homes like Hugo's.

I pulled the Mercedes into the driveway of the house I still couldn't believe was mine. It was a two-story, Spanish-style affair, dwarfed by its neighbors across the street but still not terribly small—perhaps two thousand square feet. It definitely was not the termite-infested disaster I'd half expected, and it was at least three times the size of my little guesthouse back home. This place was quite attractive, with clean, white stucco walls and a red-tiled roof. It also featured a good-size, meticulously landscaped yard filled with ornamental grasses, pink-flowering ice plant and some bushy shrubs with yellow daisylike flowers I think are called marguerites.

I realized I'd have to ask Sidney to put me in contact with the gardener before I put this place up for sale. If I tried maintaining this foliage myself, these lovely plants would probably expire within the week. Besides, even if my thumb weren't black rather than green, I needed to get back to work at the *Hollywood Star* before Harry suffered a complete meltdown.

The inside of my new house was just as carefully kept as the outside, although I could see it hadn't been updated in many years. The draperies were heavy and old, as was the furniture, and the kitchen was 1970s-vintage. The refrigerator was relatively new, however, a side-by-side model complete with icemaker, and there also was a small modern microwave oven perched on the blue ceramic-tiled countertop.

The living and dining rooms were located at the front of the house, while at the back were the kitchen and a downstairs bedroom that Hugo apparently had used for his office—it held an aged oak desk with a vintage computer and two file cabinets, as well as a burgundy leather recliner chair and a floor lamp.

In a small wing of the house beyond the office, I found a bathroom and a comfy-looking den with a gas-log fireplace and large-screen TV. The den had tall French doors that opened onto a stone patio ringed by large potted plants I couldn't identify.

The upstairs was much smaller than the main floor, encompassing only a roomy master suite with another fireplace and a set of French doors opening onto an ocean-view balcony. I was touched to see that the king-size bed already had been turned down for me, and that there was a vase filled with fresh purple irises on the nightstand. Even in his grief, Sidney Hathaway had thought to provide everything I might need here—I'd even found an assortment of TV dinners in the freezer and a bottle of white wine in the refrigerator, so I wouldn't have to go out for dinner. The basic kindness of Hugo's friend reminded me of Uncle Teddy, and for a brief moment I felt homesick.

My bout of nostalgia didn't last long. What I felt most right now was completely exhausted. It had been a difficult, tiring day. Both my long drive over half the length of the state and the memorial service had taken a big physical and emotional toll on me. So I was grateful I wouldn't have to find a restaurant for dinner and a motel room for the night.

I went back outside and moved my car into the detached garage. Then I microwaved one of the frozen meals for my dinner and put a healthy dent in that bottle of wine before heading upstairs to bed. The fog was rolling in fast now, so I lit the gas log in the fireplace just long enough to take the chill off the bedroom. If I were inclined to make cozy seaside retreats on a regular basis, I told myself, I could hardly expect to do much better than Hugo's comfortable house.

THE BEDSIDE CLOCK said 2:16 a.m. when the sounds from downstairs awoke me. I lay still in the big bed, convinced at first that the faint noise was part of my dream.

But no, there it was again. Not loud, just a series of shuffling sounds and light thumps. Had I remembered to close the French doors off the den after I'd ventured outside following dinner? I'd spent ten or fifteen minutes on the patio, enjoying the sun setting below the fast-approaching marine layer and finishing my glass of Chardonnay. Now, hours later, I couldn't be a hundred percent certain I'd locked up again.

If there were herds of deer freely roaming this neighborhood, I realized, there probably were raccoons and rats and who knew what other native creatures. As I swung my legs over the side of the bed, I forced myself to stop imagining all the frightening critters that might have made their way inside this house.

I turned on the bedside lamp, slipped into my robe and crept down the stairs, my heart thumping in my chest. If I encountered a marauding raccoon, I wondered, what could I do about it? Try to scare it away? Snare it somehow and carry it back outside? I honestly didn't know. All I was certain about was that I couldn't let Hugo's home be damaged or destroyed because of my carelessness.

When I reached the bottom of the stairs, I realized the sounds were coming from the back of the house, from Hugo's office or perhaps the den. That part of the house was dark, which I saw as evidence that my intruder was not a human being.

"Shoo!" I yelled at the top of my lungs, hoping to scare the animal back outside without being forced to confront it at close range. "Get out of here! Shoo!"

The faint sounds ceased for a moment. I must have startled the creature that had made its way indoors. I trailed my fingers along the wall at the base of the stairs, searching for a light switch to illuminate the hallway without success. Where was it? Luckily there was just enough moonlight coming through the small window in the front door to outline the old-fashioned umbrella stand I'd noticed earlier. I grabbed one of the umbrellas, the only weapon I had, and carefully made my way down the hall.

"Go on, get!" I shouted again. "Get out of here!"

When I reached the open doorway of Hugo's office, I shifted the umbrella to my other hand, reached around the doorframe and felt along the wall for the light switch I was sure I'd seen there earlier. Ah, there it was.

As I flipped on the light, I blinked in the sudden glare, temporarily blinded. Before my eyes could focus, something hard slammed against the base of my skull and I stumbled.

I screamed as I lost my footing.

The useless umbrella fell from my hand as I careened forward and hit the floor hard—facedown.

SIX

TERRIFIED, I lay prone on the floor as my assailant stepped over me and fled from the room. All I managed to see was one large white Nike running shoe and the bottom of a leg clad in black sweatpants. Then he was gone.

I pushed myself to my knees, my head throbbing. Somewhere in the distance, a door slammed. Had he left the house? I fingered the back of my skull gingerly and was relieved to find no evidence of bleeding, although a lump was rapidly forming where I'd been hit. I was pretty sure I hadn't lost consciousness, and apparently I wouldn't need to be stitched back together. I told myself I'd been lucky. Yet somehow, at the moment, I wasn't feeling all that fortunate.

Still groggy, I crawled across the floor to the desk, climbed slowly into the chair and reached for the telephone. I picked up the receiver, prepared to dial 9-1-1 and summon the police.

There was no dial tone.

I felt a fresh rush of panic. Had the intruder cut the phone line? I tried to remember what I'd done with my cell phone and realized I'd left it my car's glove box. Calling the police would require venturing outside into the detached garage to retrieve the cell. Either that, or I'd have to wake one of the neighbors and ask for help. At this late hour, neither choice seemed all that attractive.

Think! I ordered myself. I tried to ignore the pounding at the back of my head and figure out what to do next.

First, I decided, I needed to determine whether the man who'd hit me really had left the house. Sure, I'd heard a door slam, but did that mean he'd actually gone, or was he still lurking in another room?

I took a deep breath, retrieved the umbrella—even a makeshift weapon had to be better than none, right?—and peeked around the doorframe into the hall. There was nobody there. I breathed a sigh of relief.

The pain in my skull slowly began to subside as I searched the entire house, room by room, and determined that I was alone. I found the front door closed but unlocked, so I shot the dead bolt. There was no other obvious point of entry—no smashed window or broken lock—so I had to suspect that the intruder had simply used a key to get in.

My second survey of the premises told me that this probably had not been a routine burglary. The TV was still here, as were the paintings on the walls. Even my laptop and my purse, which I'd left on the kitchen counter, hadn't been touched. My cash and credit cards were still intact, and I said a small prayer of thanks that my computer was safe. The only real disturbance I could find was in Hugo's office, where there were abundant signs of a speedy search—a file drawer left open, papers from the desk drawers strewed about, a few manila folders lying on the floor.

I began to form a theory—Charlie Paxton had come here, perhaps in search of a new will. He probably had a key to his uncle's house. I figured he simply refused to believe Hugo had cut him off, that the old man had actually left his house to a complete stranger, namely me. Charlie'd said as much at the memorial service, hadn't he?

Obviously, it had to be Charlie.

Unless, of course, there'd been something valuable in that office that I didn't know about, perhaps a pile of cash stashed in one of the desk drawers, or some stock certificates, or even bearer bonds. I'm not really sure what bearer bonds are, but I've seen villains kill for them in at least a dozen crime movies I've reviewed for the *Hollywood Star*. Bearer bonds must be valuable.

On reconsideration, my first theory seemed far more solid. The intruder—Charlie—had fled as soon as I showed up, and I didn't really think he was carrying a cache of loot when he stepped over me. I honestly wasn't worried that Charlie actually had found a second will. If there'd been one, certainly Hugo's attorney would have known about it.

My bigger problem was whether Charlie would be back to try again. I thought some more about making that trek out to the garage, retrieving my cell phone and calling the police. Did Pebble Beach even have a police force, or would I have to wait for somebody from the county to show up? Certainly the security guards collecting tourist dollars at the gates didn't constitute a genuine police force.

The idea of venturing out in the dark to get my phone, then waiting for the police to come, followed by who knew how much questioning, didn't hold much appeal.

So, instead, I wedged a dining room chair under the knob of each of the doors leading outside, swallowed a couple of aspirin and climbed back into bed.

I SLEPT FITFULLY, but at least I managed to get a little rest. Until about six o'clock, anyway, when daylight began to intrude into the bedroom. I got out of bed and took another quick tour of the house for reassurance that nobody had gotten past my makeshift security system.

Everything was just as I'd left it during the night, so I took a shower and got dressed for my ten o'clock meeting with Sidney.

I ran the brush through my hair with extra care—the lump on the back of my skull was still extremely tender to the touch. Still, I now felt certain I would live. Harry always complains that my head is as hard as a studio boss's heart. For once, I was forced to agree with him.

After I'd had a cup of tea and a piece of toast for breakfast, I went back into Hugo's office and took another look around. The labels on the file folders strewed across the floor indicated they'd held either income tax records or copies of personal correspondence, but they were all empty now. I stacked them on top of the desk, puzzled about why Charlie would steal the papers from these particular files. Of course, it was equally possible he'd found the folders already empty and simply tossed them aside in his hasty search. It seemed logical that Sidney would discard this sort of personal information soon after his partner's death. I made a mental note to ask him.

My inspection of Hugo's desk revealed nothing that drew my attention in any way. Certainly there was no sign of a new will here.

I turned my attention to the closet at the back of the office. It was bare, except for a collection of dusty manuscript boxes piled three deep on the high shelf along the back wall. Had poor Hugo continued to produce unpublished novels all these years?

As a fellow writer, I couldn't help identifying a bit with my benefactor. Long ago, before I landed my reporting job at the *Hollywood Star*, I'd tried my hand at freelance magazine writing. Sure, I'd managed to sell a few of my articles here and there, but mainly I'd collected enough publishers' rejection slips to wallpaper my bathroom. Still, all I'd ever written that failed to find a publisher was some articles—just a couple of thousand words apiece. I doubted I'd have had enough persistence, enough belief in my own talent, to write…how many books were here? I quickly counted eighteen boxes.

Eighteen! Yet, according to Hugo's obituary notice, not

one book he ever wrote was published. Was his writing really so dreadful that he'd never managed to sell even one of his books?

I pulled two boxes off the shelf and read the titles he'd carefully printed on their covers—*The Velvet Noose* and *The Scarlet Orchid.* Both titles sounded vaguely familiar, but I couldn't recall why. Probably variations on the titles of two bestselling books, I figured.

I opened the boxes and recognized the contents as typical draft manuscripts—typewritten with the author's revisions penciled in between the double-spaced lines. I read a few pages of each book. The writing really wasn't all *that* bad. It was potboiler stuff, certainly not the work of a literary genius, but both stories seemed promising and the writing had a certain commercial flair. It seemed odd that no book publisher had ever been willing to take a chance on Hugo Paxton's work.

I took two more manuscripts off the shelf and read the first chapters of each, which reinforced my initial conclusion. Now I was more curious than ever about Hugo's efforts to publish his work. I would definitely have to show Sidney these manuscripts and ask him about them.

Sidney! I glanced at my watch and realized it was getting very late. I had only twenty minutes to get to his house for our scheduled meeting. I took the four manuscript boxes I'd opened and stopped in the kitchen just long enough to collect my purse and computer.

My arms heavily loaded, I headed out the door.

SIDNEY WAS RIGHT. The entrance to his seniors' community was clearly marked, and I had no trouble finding it as I cruised east on Carmel Valley Road. I turned into the complex and followed the winding street past a series of small bungalows.

As I rounded a curve and spotted the house number he'd

given me, my heart skipped a beat. The road was blocked by emergency vehicles—a fire engine, a paramedics' van and two sheriff's cars. Had someone broken into Sidney's place, too?

I parked, got out of the car and rushed toward the uniformed officer standing outside the unit bearing Sidney's number.

"What's going on?" I demanded. "Is Mr. Hathaway okay?"

"You a relative or friend, ma'am?"

I briefly explained about my ten o'clock appointment.

"Better have a word with Detective Grabowski over there. Guy in the gray suit."

I approached Detective Grabowski, a tall, thin, fortyish man with a pockmarked face, and repeated my query. After I'd explained my tenuous connection to Hugo's partner, he shook his head.

"Sorry to have to tell you this, ma'am, but it seems Mr. Hathaway took an overdose of his sleeping medication last night."

I swallowed hard and stared at the paramedics' van. It didn't look primed to rush anybody to the hospital anytime soon. "Is he going to be all right?" I asked, fearing I already knew the answer.

"Sorry," he said again. "Mr. Hathaway died last night."

SEVEN

GRABOWSKI TOLD ME that Sidney's cleaning woman had found his body when she arrived for work this morning and immediately called the police. Sidney was slumped over his kitchen table, still fully clothed. He wasn't breathing. Near his body, the detective said, were both an open bottle of Scotch and an empty container for a prescription sleeping pill. He figured that Sidney'd had a few drinks before swallowing his nightly pills, not realizing how dangerous that combination could be.

Right, I thought. And that explains why the pill bottle was completely empty.

I suspected that Grabowski's true theory was that Sidney'd been overcome by grief over Hugo's recent demise and had committed suicide in the throes of depression. The cop seemed a decent enough guy, and I suspected he probably was doing his best to protect poor Sidney's reputation—at least until the county medical examiner issued a contrary opinion.

I, however, wasn't buying either theory, not after I'd been bashed over the head just a few hours earlier. I can swallow only so much coincidence before my gag reflex begins to kick in.

"Uh-uh, this was no accident," I told the detective, shaking my head. "It was no suicide, either. I'd bet you my last dollar Sidney Hathaway was murdered."

I spent the next twenty minutes telling Detective Grabowski all about my terrifying experience at the Pebble Beach house.

"Should've called us when it happened," he scolded me when I'd finished my tale. "Now the guy's long gone."

"So next time I'll remember," I snapped. My headache was rapidly returning, I was distressed about poor, sweet Sidney and I was in no mood to be lectured by a cop.

"Even if you're right about the nephew," the detective continued, ignoring my retort, "now I'm afraid we'll never get a conviction for either breaking and entering or assault—not unless you can identify him. Even if his fingerprints are all over his uncle's place, who's to say when he put them there?"

"I get your point, Detective, honest I do."

We went back and forth like this for another ten minutes, at the end of which I agreed to come into the station later and give a formal statement, even though there was no way I could possibly ID the man who'd attacked me. By then, I'm afraid I would have agreed to just about anything just to get away from there. I needed more aspirin. Bad.

In the meantime, Grabowski told me, I was free to go.

MY THOUGHTS SPUN as I drove back to Pebble Beach. I now was forced to conclude that whatever was going on had to be far more serious than a simple battle over who inherited Hugo's house. Even if the place was worth seven figures in the high-priced local real-estate market, what would be the point of killing Sidney? There was either a new will or there wasn't, right?

Unless Charlie had attempted to get Sidney to back his story about a second will, to get his uncle's lover to swear Hugo had left the house to Charlie, not to me. If Sidney had refused to cooperate with Charlie's scheme, could he have become angry enough to murder the old man?

I could see that my theory didn't add up much better than

Grabowski's. A murder like that would be a rage killing, something that happened in the heat of the moment. Yet clearly this had been a very cold-blooded homicide, something carefully staged to look like a suicide or accident. What would Charlie possibly have to gain from that?

I quickly discounted another possible motive, as well. From the way Sidney had talked to me about Hugo's nephew, there'd been no love lost between the two men. So certainly Sidney would never have left his own estate—whatever it might consist of—to Charlie. Murder for financial gain seemed unlikely.

No matter how I massaged the few facts I had, I couldn't envision a motive for Charlie to murder Sidney, at least not in this particular way.

BY THE TIME I drove through the Spanish Bay golf course on my way back to the Pebble Beach house—this time on full alert for any roving deer that might suddenly sprint across my path—my head was throbbing. I couldn't be sure whether my pain was physical or emotional or a combination of the two. All I knew was that I was beginning to regret ever having taken this trip north. I longed for my cozy little guesthouse back in Pacific Palisades, for the life I'd been living as recently as two days ago, for a chat with Uncle Teddy over one of his comforting meals, even for another of Harry's frequent putdowns of what I always thought were my brilliant story ideas for the *Star*.

Why hadn't I just stayed home?

Those were the melancholy thoughts romping through what was left of my rattled mind as I took the left turn onto Cormorant Road.

But as soon as I rounded the corner, I had to slam on the brakes.

This time, it wasn't a pair of young bucks that halted me.

This time, my route was completely blocked by half a dozen emergency vehicles.

My first thought was that I was hallucinating, that my groggy brain somehow was replaying the earlier scene from Sidney's cottage—police cars, fire engines, and all.

But then I got a whiff of the pungent smoke in the air. I parked at the curb and got out of my car more than a block away from my new house. I had no choice but to go the rest of the way on foot.

There were several more fire trucks here than at Sidney's, I saw as I approached. And this time their hoses were unrolled and rigid as they sprayed gallons of water on the orange and yellow flames that leaped skyward from the windows of a red-tile-roofed home a few hundred feet farther down the street.

For a moment, my exhausted mind refused to process what my eyes were seeing. Finally, it hit me.

The house rapidly burning to the ground was mine.

EIGHT

I JUST STOOD THERE for a few minutes, feeling helpless as I watched my new house being destroyed by fire, a fire I was instantly convinced was arson. This might have happened last night, I realized with a shudder. This place could have gone up in flames while I was upstairs asleep.

I could have been burned alive!

Even if the arsonist hadn't struck until this morning, I could have been killed. But for my appointment with Sidney, I might be dead right now.

Briefly, I felt so frightened I was nauseous. But soon a seed of anger began to sprout inside me. I promised myself that whoever was behind all this—last night's break-in and assault, kind Sidney's murder, and now the torching of the house—was going to pay big-time. I would see to that if it was the last thing I ever did.

I sloshed across the wet groundcover in front of the house, my shoes quickly becoming soaked, and approached the fire chief directing his men.

"Gas explosion," was his hurried answer to my query about what had happened here. That explained why a truck from Pacific Gas & Electric was parked across the street. The chief turned away from me, sprinted over to one of his trucks and began shouting orders.

I looked around and realized that several windows in the house next door had been cracked by the impact of the explosion, although so far the fire had not spread to any neighboring structures.

A gas explosion. There was no way this was my fault, I reassured myself. I'd been extra careful in turning off the gas log in the upstairs fireplace before I went to bed. If there'd been a gas leak, I'd have smelled it. I'd never even touched the den fireplace or its gas connection, plus I knew I'd extinguished the flame on the stove burner after boiling the water for my breakfast tea.

No, this was not due to any mistake I'd made. My mental survey of the house, however, confirmed one essential fact—it had several gas outlets, located on both floors and well dispersed throughout the place. All an arsonist really needed to do to destroy the house was open the gas jets, wait until the place filled with fumes and toss in a match. Or quite possibly there was a way to set off an explosion well after the arsonist had left the scene.

I was no expert on arson—I'd always specialized in reporting stories about show business, not crime. Of course, there are people who believe there's not much difference between show business and crime, but I've never been one of them.

Was Charlie the logical culprit here, too? I found myself focusing on Hugo's nephew for the dozenth time since last night. Was Charlie angry enough about not inheriting this house that he was willing to blow it up—and perhaps me with it—just to keep me from owning it? I shuddered to think about the kind of malignant rage that would result in murder and arson.

I shifted my gaze toward the small gathering of people watching the firefighters work. I saw only one slightly familiar face, a small, elderly woman with short, curly white hair and a kind face. I approached her.

"Hi, I'm Quinn Collins," I said. "You were at Hugo's memorial service, weren't you?"

The old woman nodded, neither turning away from the fire nor shaking my extended hand. I pulled it back.

"Right. I'm Mona Gleason," she said after a moment's hesitation. She seemed both frightened and fascinated by everything the firefighters were doing. "I live across the street." She pulled her hunter-green cardigan more tightly around her small body for warmth. "Sure glad Hugo isn't here to see this," she said. "He always loved this house so." She shook her head sadly and asked what I was doing there.

When I told her I'd inherited the house from Hugo, she finally tore her gaze away from the action and actually looked at me. "Really? Oh, you poor girl! Then this is your house now."

"It *was,* anyway." However briefly. "Do you know anything about what happened here, Mona? Did you see who started the fire?" I felt a surge of hope that I might have found an actual witness.

"What do you mean, who started it?" Her thin shoulders jerked. "I—I thought it was an accident. I heard a big boom—nearly shook my mother's priceless porcelain figurines right off their shelf. Almost like a bomb. I looked out the window and saw the flames, so I called 9-1-1 right away. At first, I thought it might be those terrorists striking the West Coast this time, but the fire chief says it was just an ordinary gas explosion."

"And you didn't see a car speeding away or a man running down the street right afterward?"

"No, no, of course not. I saw nothing of the kind. Are you *sure* this wasn't an accidental fire?" Her eyes widened and her face flushed. "This is Pebble Beach!"

I couldn't really see how that fact was relevant. Did Mona believe that, because she lived here, in great affluence and away from a large urban center, she was safe from burglary, arson, murder? Yet the idea that terrorists might attack this neighborhood had obviously occurred to her. Go figure.

"Somebody broke into this house last night and hit me over the head," I told her, fingering the sore lump on the back of my skull. "My guess is, it was the same guy who burned down the place." I decided not to add the fact of Sidney's murder. Not yet, anyway. I didn't want Mona Gleason having a stroke. Her shock and disbelief were clearly written across her wrinkled face.

"I—I don't know what…" Mona took a quick step backward. "I better get back home." She made her way across the street and into one of the largest of the neighborhood's houses as fast as someone her age could reasonably move.

If I had to guess, I'd bet she was calling her security company right now, ordering whatever additional reinforcements they could sell her to restore her wavering sense of invulnerability. I tried not to feel too guilty about having frightened a skittish old woman.

After all, I had my own problems.

I SPENT THE AFTERNOON being interviewed by the police about my suspicions regarding Sidney's death as well as the gas explosion and fire at the house. I really wasn't able to tell them much that seemed immediately useful, other than my hunch about Charlie Paxton and the clear resentment of me he'd expressed at the memorial service. I'm not at all sure I even managed to convince the cops that any real crimes had taken place.

It's always so much easier to write something off as an accident, a suicide, a natural death, than it is to investigate assault, murder and arson, isn't it? Besides, other than the lump on the back of my head—which I guess, from the cops' point of view, could have happened in a number of different, even self-inflicted, ways—I had no real proof to bolster my story that someone had broken into my house last night and attacked me. Now, with the place in ashes, it couldn't even be fingerprinted. Plus, my accusations about Sidney's death and the gas explosion seemed even more tenuous as I detailed them to my apparently doubtful listeners.

As I left police headquarters, still wearing my wet shoes and smoke-permeated clothes, I had the strong feeling I was being written off.

Maybe the cops' pointed questions, such as, "The house you inherited was still fully insured, wasn't it?" had something to do with my impression—actually, I didn't have the answer to that query, but I suggested that Hugo's attorney probably would.

I could be wrong, of course, but as I left the sheriff's office, I felt I'd just been tagged as yet another Hollywood nutcase, somebody merely acting a part, a woman craving publicity through any means available.

That seemed the best-case scenario.

The worst was that the cops really did believe murder and arson had taken place in the last twenty-four hours, and that I'd just somehow managed to make myself their prime suspect.

As I CLIMBED into the Mercedes, I glanced at my watch and recognized why my stomach was growling so loudly. It was four o'clock, and I'd had nothing to eat since that lone slice of toast at breakfast. I'd also lost my suitcase, my extra clothes and all my toiletries in the fire. I felt dirty.

I was drained, both emotionally and physically.

I gathered what little energy I could just long enough to make a quick stop at the Macy's store in the Del Monte shopping center, where I bought a pair of jeans, a shirt, and some underwear on sale, along with a new pair of sandals— thank goodness for credit cards. I changed into my new clothes in the store's women's room, putting my smelly old ones into the shopping bag. Then I stopped at the Whole Foods store across the parking lot. I bought some take-out food, a bottle of wine and a few essential toiletries, just enough to get me through another night on the Monterey Peninsula.

No way was I stupid enough to attempt the drive back to Los Angeles tonight, exhausted as I was. But first thing in the morning, I vowed, I was going home.

In the meantime, I checked into the nearest motel that appeared habitable. I parked in front of my assigned room, grabbed my purse and took my laptop out of the trunk. I told myself I should be grateful that those things, too, hadn't perished in the fire.

As I was shutting the trunk, I noticed the four manuscript boxes I'd carried out of Hugo's house earlier today.

How sad, I thought. All that now remained of my strange inheritance from Hugo Paxton was a charred piece of ground in Pebble Beach and four of the former blacklisted writer's numerous unpublished novels.

WHEN I AWOKE with a start, the bedside clock told me it was two in the morning. I'd been having a disturbing dream about writing a book. An image of myself at the computer, rewriting the same sentence over and over and over again began to fade as I rolled over in the motel room bed and tried to get back to sleep.

I listened for strange sounds as I lay there, but I heard nothing unusual. The night was silent except for the occasional hum of a car's engine as it passed by on Munras Avenue. What had awakened me so abruptly? Probably nothing more than someone in another of the motel's rooms flushing a toilet, I told myself.

Unless what had startled me awake had something to do with my dream. I tried to remember more about it, but the only detail that surfaced was a strong sense of frustration as I tried to write the perfect sentence, craft a publishable book.

A *book?* Why a book? I wondered. I'd never written a whole book, or even tried to, in my entire life. I'd always been happy reporting and writing article-length pieces. Perhaps I would write a book someday, after I retired from the *Hollywood Star.* Maybe then I'd write my memoirs or a novel about show business.

It must have been Hugo's stacks of unpublished manuscripts that triggered my dream, I figured.

I sat upright in bed, a prickly feeling coursing down my spine. Hugo's unpublished manuscripts. Was there something important about them I wasn't seeing? I pondered the reasons I'd carried them out of the house, why I'd intended to ask Sidney about them.

Two things came to mind. First was that there'd been so many boxes in that office closet. How many had I counted? Eighteen, that was it. Eighteen are a helluva lot of books to write without one's ever being published. And, to me, the quality of the writing in the portions I'd read hadn't seemed all that bad. Had Hugo never tried to sell any of his work after his first failures back in L.A.?

The second reason, I recalled, was Hugo's choice of titles. They'd somehow seemed familiar. At the time, I simply assumed they were generic thriller titles. I mean, how many mystery authors use variations of nursery rhymes to label their books? Or included words like terror, mystery, death in their titles? How many romance authors use words like love or passion or romance in their titles? Writers choose words like those to let readers know what kind of book they're getting.

Still…

I lay back down and pulled the covers up to my chin. But within just a few minutes, I realized I wasn't going to get back to sleep until I'd resolved whatever subconscious issue still nagged at me.

I got up, put on my new clothes and sandals—my night-gown and robe had burned in the fire, so I'd been sleeping in my underwear—and peeked through the motel room's window before opening the door. The well-lighted parking lot outside appeared deserted, so I decided it would be safe to venture as far as my car.

I opened the trunk of the Mercedes and took out the four manuscript boxes, then made another quick visual survey of the area. The parking lot was silent, and there were no lights on in any of the other rooms. I tried not to slam the trunk lid as I shut it, so as not to wake my neighbors, then fled back to the safety of my room.

Using my wireless Internet connection, I booted up my laptop and called up an on-line bookseller's Web site. In the space under Search, I typed in the title printed on the first of Hugo's manuscript boxes—*The Velvet Noose*—and clicked Go.

My foggy memory had been right. There had been a book with that title published, all right, way back in 1974. The hardcover was long out of print by now but, amazingly, the paperback version remained available in a fairly recent re-print edition. My jaw dropped as I read the author's name.

Maybe it was just a coincidence. I searched again, this time for *The Scarlet Orchid*, the title written on Hugo's second box. I saw that a hardcover book with that title had been published in 1985 and, again, there was a reprint pa-perback edition still available.

The Scarlet Orchid had been written by the very same author as *The Velvet Noose*. This was getting very weird.

I searched for the titles written on the last two manuscript boxes and found similar results. The hardcover versions of these novels had been published in 1988 and 1995 respectively, and their paperback reprint editions also were still for sale.

I shut down the laptop, realizing I would have to stop at a bookstore on my way back to L.A. Until I took a look at these actual books and compared them to the manuscripts in the boxes, I really couldn't be certain about anything.

In the meantime, I could do little more than wonder.

What had Hugo Paxton been doing with the original manuscripts of the novels written by world-famous author William Brooks?

NINE

"MAYBE BROOKS SIMPLY stored his manuscripts at Hugo's house," Uncle Teddy suggested as he peered at me over his coffee cup.

I'd driven straight through from the Monterey Peninsula, so I'd had time to stop at a bookstore and buy the paperbacks on my way home. As soon as I saw him, of course, I filled in Uncle Teddy about my disturbing experiences during my trip. As always, he was extremely solicitous about my welfare, repeatedly worrying aloud about the bump on my head and how I might have been burned to death in my bed. He also had more than a few things to say about how he should have been there to protect me. I'm really not sure what he thought he could have done, given that he's well over seventy and smaller than I am, but who am I to disillusion an old man with fantasies of his own heroism?

Visibly fretting, Uncle Teddy was obviously miffed that I refused to go to the hospital to have my head examined—allegedly for physical, not mental, damage. Now, as we sat side by side on his living-room sofa after dinner while he finished his coffee, he kept stroking my arm and patting my hand, as though to make sure I was still there, still breathing and, at least physically, burn-free. All this concern was starting to get on my nerves, which was why I'd brought up the subject of the manuscripts. Anything to distract my dear old uncle from the fact that, as he kept reminding me, "I could have *lost* you!"

"What reason would Brooks have to store anything at Hugo's house?" I countered. "Especially when he had to know Hugo was dying and Sidney was moving out? All Brooks had to do was go over there and get his manuscripts, then bring them back to L.A. or wherever he lives nowadays. Besides, I'm not sure why he'd even want to keep those manuscripts after all these years. They stink of mildew." I wrinkled my nose in distaste. "It's not like some library is going to want to display the pages when Brooks is dead, right? They're just pulp fiction."

"I guess you have a point, sweet pea," Teddy said, reaching for my hand again.

I pulled away, stood and began pacing the room. I'd had about all the patting I could take.

"So maybe," Teddy suggested, "Hugo worked as William Brooks's editor."

"Sure, Teddy, that's possible," I conceded, feeling a touch guilty as I strode across the room. My uncle means well and I don't know what I'd do without him, but occasionally I find his concern about me to be suffocating. Maybe that's why I never married—too much closeness tends to make me feel like taking the first flight out. "I suppose Brooks could have paid Hugo handsomely to get his manuscripts into shape. But I've got to tell you—those handwritten changes don't look like any editor's markings I ever saw. Most editors have very neat handwriting, which this isn't, plus they use blue pencils and special editing symbols to alert the author and typesetter to exactly what they want done. These manuscripts, on the other hand, are full of arrows and cross-outs and red ink and new paragraphs handwritten on the backs of pages. They look like an author's revisions, if you ask me." I plunked myself down in a chair just out of Teddy's reach. "I *am* a writer, you know."

Teddy shrugged. "Then I guess we're back to square one. What logical reason would there be for Hugo to have a closetful of William Brooks's manuscripts?" Teddy's brow furrowed as he set his cup on the coffee table, sank back against the sofa and stared down at his freckled hands. He seemed not to know what to do with them, now that I was firmly out of reach.

"My bet is because Hugo's the one who really *wrote* those books," I said. "Remember, he couldn't get work in Hollywood anymore because of the blacklist, and he never managed to get his own first two novels published, either. But, what if he had William Brooks's name and Academy Award to use as a credential? Any publisher would be far more willing to take a chance on a book with Brooks's name on it than Hugo's."

"You think William Brooks was Hugo Paxton's front?"

"I think there's a darned good chance, although for all we know, it might have started the other way around. It could have been Brooks who wanted the money and fame but maybe couldn't manage to pen a publishable novel. Screenwriting and book writing are very different skills, you know. Could be Brooks knew Hugo'd written a couple of passable novels, plus it certainly was common knowledge in this town that the man had tanked professionally. So maybe Brooks hired Hugo as his ghostwriter, figuring they'd split the profits from the novels if they sold well."

"Which would explain how Hugo could afford to go live in Pebble Beach, I guess, how he could 'retire' at such a young age despite the blacklist."

"Precisely."

Teddy scratched his head. "So it sounds like you think it was Brooks who burned down the house to destroy the evidence, Quinnie, in an attempt to keep his fans from finding out he'd had a ghostwriter for all those years.''

I pulled on my lower lip as I thought about it. ''I'm honestly not sure. Given the manuscripts, I guess Brooks is as good a suspect as Charlie. But the truth is, I don't see how either William Brooks or Charlie Paxton would benefit enough, whatever their individual motives, to risk going to prison for assault or burning down a house. And I especially don't get why they'd murder Sidney Hathaway.''

''In the case of Brooks, because Sidney had to know the truth about who wrote those books, that's why. No way could Hugo have kept that secret from his partner all those years. As for Charlie, I don't know. Maybe he thought it was Sidney's fault he was cut out of his inheritance?''

''It still seems an awful stretch.'' I got up and began to pace again.

''Maybe,'' Teddy said, ''but remember, sweetheart, you don't really know for sure that Sidney was murdered. Maybe the poor man really did commit suicide, like the cops seem to think.'' He had a faraway look in his eyes. ''He might have missed Hugo more than he could stand.''

I knew Teddy had to be thinking about Artie. ''Sure,'' I said, ''that's possible, but something doesn't make sense to me. Why would Sidney take his own life just before he was scheduled to see me? And why would he go to all the trouble of moving to a seniors' community first? Why wouldn't the man just swallow his pills as soon as Hugo was gone if he felt suicidal over losing him? Save himself a lot of trouble.''

Teddy rubbed his eyes, perhaps to keep me from seeing they were wet. ''I can't answer that,'' he said a moment later, after taking a deep breath. ''But just for the sake of argument, let's say Sidney wasn't murdered. Let's take that part of it off the table. The motive for the house break-in and fire could be envy and revenge—that would be Charlie's. Or for William Brooks, it could be to avoid the embarrassment of having the public know he didn't write the novels that bore his name. I mean, they *were* bestsellers. That kind of subterfuge surely would make the national news if it came out, maybe the international news. And with a journalist inheriting the house along with whatever papers Hugo had there, it seems pretty likely to be exposed sooner or later. Brooks might have burned down the place simply to keep you from finding what was in that closet."

"I guess," I said. I now felt sure the boxes I'd taken from the house held the original manuscripts of the Brooks novels. I'd already compared the first chapters of the paperbacks with the manuscripts from Hugo's closet. They were the same, even including the inserted, handwritten paragraphs. "But what I don't get, Teddy, is why exposure of this secret would be such a big deal after all these years? I mean, Robert Lindsey wrote every word of Ronald Reagan's supposed autobiography. That one involved the President of the United States, for heaven's sake, and nobody got killed to keep that secret from coming out. Truth is, every politician alive probably has a ghostwriter, and so does every movie star who publishes a so-called autobiography. Besides, the two latest Brooks books have Jared's name on them along with his dad's, and the Brooks Web site says the novel coming out this fall will be Jared's alone, that William's retiring. Hugo was sick for the last few years, so I really doubt he wrote the books with Jared's name on them. Maybe the son can actually write his own novels."

"Still, it would have to be embarrassing to have his fans learn that William Brooks has been using his name on a blacklisted writer's work all these years."

I waved away Teddy's insistence. "After all this time? Uh-uh, I don't buy it. It's just not enough," I said. "And even if it were, why wait until *now* to prevent that news from coming out? Why wait until I inherited the house and there was a substantial risk of public exposure? If William Brooks had a key to that place, why didn't he remove all the evidence of his fraud a whole lot earlier?''

Teddy stared up at me. "Maybe you just answered your own question, Quinn."

"What? How?"

"Maybe William—or William along with his son Jared—didn't think there was going to be a problem…until they found out about you. Think about it—how would they know you were going to inherit Hugo's house? They probably figured Sidney would continue to live there, or that it would go to Charlie and he'd sell it, gamble away the proceeds. Neither of those two would be a threat to the Brookses." He shook his head. "But a show-business reporter? That's another kettle of fish altogether."

I nodded, thinking over what Teddy was saying as I sank back against my chair. I was suddenly completely out of energy, even the nervous variety that had been keeping me going for the past few days. "You're probably right," I agreed. "I suppose the Brookses wouldn't have any way to know the details of Hugo's trust. Since the trust wasn't a regular will, there wouldn't be any probate, and the bequests wouldn't be open to public scrutiny even after Hugo's death. So until I showed up at that memorial service—"

"Exactly."

I realized I was right back at the beginning, back to the question I'd been asking myself over and over since Saturday morning.

Why had Hugo Paxton left his house and its contents to me?

TEN

"USUALLY A PRETTY WOMAN like you gets to know me a whole lot better before she decides not to like me," Jack said with a charmingly innocent-looking smile. He was tall and dark-haired, dressed in a gray jacket that looked like cashmere, a white shirt and a maroon-striped tie. He slowly twirled a tall martini glass in his well-manicured fingers. The image he presented was the height of sophistication for his day.

The camera cut to a close-up of pale blond Jennifer's lovely, expressive face, and the audience could see her initial resistance to her handsome suitor beginning to soften. "So," she asked him, flirting a bit, "are you suggesting I should get to know you a whole lot better?"

"Why not? We could try having dinner together—maybe someplace with soft music and candlelight—before you try to make such a momentous decision. What do you say?"

Jennifer laughed, obviously tempted.

The scene was a lavish party in a penthouse on the Upper East Side of New York City, complete with a tuxedoed man playing Gershwin tunes on a baby grand piano. The gathering was filled with snooty socialites, but the hero and heroine, of course, weren't at all snooty. I was only twenty minutes into the old film and already I—the woman who'd fought marriage all her adult life—was rooting for them to split from this pretentious cocktail party, have dinner together, fall madly in love and live happily ever after.

I was thoroughly enjoying these characters and their story, yet there was something about this movie that was bothering me. I couldn't quite put my finger on it. I picked up the remote, reversed the videotape and replayed this portion.

It was the dialogue, I realized, finally. Jack's come-on line for the blonde was a bit too familiar. I was certain I'd heard a very close variation on it in an earlier movie, one that, like this one, had been nominated for at least one major scriptwriting award. That film had been a suspense drama, in which the private-investigator hero would soon have to fight off a couple of crooked cops. If I remembered correctly, his line went something like, "Hey guys, usually people get to know me a whole lot better before they decide to hate me." Then he ducked a punch from one of the cops and managed to land the first blow himself.

I might not have the words exactly right, I knew, but I was positive I remembered the gist of the P.I.'s line. I should remember it—I'd certainly seen that particular film enough times. And I realized that bit of dialogue wasn't the only more-than-slightly familiar line in this film, either.

Suddenly I felt chilled to the bone.

I shut off the VCR and peered out the guesthouse window to see if I could spot any activity over at Uncle Teddy's house. It was early on Saturday afternoon and he always did his grocery shopping on Saturdays. It still seemed quiet over there.

After returning from the Monterey motel, I'd spent the rest of the week doing penance for my two-workday absence from the *Hollywood Star*. I'd managed to write three movie reviews, an interview piece with a hot new director, and financial stories about three different production companies, plus I spent Friday afternoon researching the in-depth feature I planned to do about the lives of those blacklisted industry workers who were still alive.

Now, thanks to a friend of Teddy and Sylvia's whose hobby was collecting old movies and transferring them to video, I was watching vintage films scripted by Hugo Paxton and William Brooks.

The one that bore Hugo's name was inane, an entirely forgettable vehicle about a mermaid and a sailor released in the late forties. The four by Brooks were a mixed bag. The first two, made in the fifties, were excellent—the love story with the familiar dialogue, and a touching story of a New England family faced with rearing a handicapped child. Both films had been nominated for major writing awards. The later two, produced in the early sixties, however, were pretty fluffy stuff, both featuring the kinds of stereotypical characterizations and overuse of plot coincidences common in Brooks's novels.

I suspected the two later scripts were ghostwritten by Hugo Paxton and that they probably represented at least one reason it had been necessary for William Brooks to start a new career writing popular novels. Two bombs in a row and you're through in Hollywood.

I heard a car door slam and hurried out to help Uncle Teddy unload his groceries.

I waited while he put the last of his purchases in the cupboard. Albertson's had a sale on garbanzo beans, and Teddy'd bought a dozen cans. He likes to stock up whenever there's a sale, convinced he's saving money and obviously not worried about living long enough to consume his entire cache. Often his cupboards look more like they belong to a survivalist than to a man in his seventies.

While he unpacked his grocery bags, I made us some tea.

"So what's on your mind, pumpkin?" he asked when he was finished with his task and settled into the chair across from mine at the kitchen table.

"Am I that obvious?"

"When was the last time you came galloping across the pool deck to help me carry my groceries in from the car?"

"Point taken." I shifted in my seat, feeling uncomfortable about the questions I planned to ask him after all these years. I hated the idea of upsetting this man who'd sacrificed so much for me. But there was no point in delaying any longer, I told myself. It was time. Heaven knows, if I'd had the stomach for what I feared I'd find out, I'd have explored this subject years ago.

I screwed up my courage. "I want to hear everything you know about how my parents died," I said.

The stunned look on Teddy's face didn't really surprise me. After all, it had taken me more than forty years to ask him for these details. Both of us had gone so far out of our way to avoid this subject that he must have figured it was closed forever.

"L-like what?" he asked.

"Let's start with where I was that night."

"Here, in this house, with me. You were right here, Quinnie. Your mother asked me to baby-sit, said she and your dad had an important dinner meeting to go to." Teddy looked down at his hands. "She never told me exactly where it was."

"Was that unusual?" I didn't really know very much about my life before I came to live with Teddy.

"Asking me to baby-sit wasn't—I was happy to help your folks out whenever I could. Money for baby-sitters was tight for them, and they couldn't afford to go out all that often. Besides, I adored having my baby niece around."

"So what was?"

"Was what?"

"Unusual."

"I guess not giving me instructions on how to reach them was strange. Your dad carried you in from the car and dropped you off along with your diaper bag. At the time, I guess I just figured they were running late, that they forgot. And it wasn't like I was some teenage nitwit who wouldn't know how to handle an emergency.'' Teddy squirmed in his chair. ''But later…''

''Later what?''

He looked away, avoiding giving me the answer I was certain I already knew.

''Later what, Teddy?''

''I—I don't know. It's nothing, really.''

''You figured they committed suicide, right?''

When he turned his gaze back toward me, I could see his eyes were wet. ''I could—could never be sure about that.''

''But you thought it likely, didn't you?''

The old man nodded slowly. ''I—I guess so.'' He chewed the end of his thumb. ''I'm so sorry, Quinnie. I hope it was an accident, I really do. I never wanted you to know about my suspicions. You shouldn't let them color your memories of your mom and dad. I know they were both crazy about you. I could see with my own eyes how much they loved you.''

I reached across the table and placed my hand over my uncle's. Now that the unmentionable had actually been mentioned, I didn't feel the devastation I'd feared—I actually felt a measure of relief. ''I think I've always known a suicide pact between my folks was a strong possibility, Uncle Teddy,'' I told him, ''ever since I found out how hard their lives had become, how much they lost when they were blacklisted. And if you want to know the truth, I have no memories of my parents at all…except for what you've told me about them, I guess. I was just a baby when they died.''

He wiped away a tear.

''It's okay, really it is,'' I told him. ''All I want is to know the truth about what happened. Tell me why you suspected they committed suicide.''

I waited while Teddy composed himself.

"Their not telling me where they were going was just one part of it," he said with a sigh. I gestured for him to continue. "See, I've done a lot of reading about suicide since it happened and I—I think maybe it's because they both, especially your dad, they seemed happy in the days before the—before it happened."

"Happy?"

He nodded. "Like something had been settled, like they'd made a decision. From what I've read, a lot of suicidally depressed people act that way—relieved, even happy—once they've made the decision, once they've finally decided to end it all."

So Teddy found it strange for my parents to be *happy*. Frankly, that revelation hit me harder than his suspicion that they'd had a suicide pact. Subconsciously, I'd always known about the possibility of suicide. But how terribly discouraged, how depressed they both must have been to never look or act happy. "They must have had some explanation about what had changed in their lives, if the change was actually that noticeable—"

"Well, sure, sweetheart, but what they said didn't make a whole lot of sense to me. It was pie-in-the-sky kind of stuff."

"Like what?"

"Your dad had this notion about how Dalton Trumbo's getting credit for scripting *Spartacus* was going to change everything for him and your mother. Sheldon seemed convinced that they suddenly would be employable in the industry again."

"And you didn't agree."

He shook his head. "It had been years, *years* since either of them had a writing credit. They'd been working at low-wage jobs all that time. You can't just show up almost a decade later and expect to be welcomed with open arms, not in this town. I tried to warn Sheldon about that, but—"

Teddy's hand jerked away from mine and he clapped it across his mouth, seemingly panicked that he'd said too much.

"But what?"

His eyes teared up again.

"But *what*, Teddy?"

He sighed deeply. "It's just that I know I never should have discouraged him, sweetheart. Not that your dad ever listened to me all that much—he seemed so certain this would be the break he'd been waiting for. Still, I can't help thinking I should have kept my big mouth shut, that I thoughtlessly robbed him of his last glimmer of hope, however false that hope might have been."

Teddy leaned forward, buried his face in his hands and began to weep. I walked around the table and put my arms around his thin shoulders, holding him as he sobbed with years of secret regret.

"It's okay," I told him, planting a gentle kiss on the top of his head. "It's okay, Teddy. Nobody kills himself over a few discouraging words, trust me. Whatever happened to my parents, it's definitely not your fault."

When Teddy regained his composure, he told me he'd long thought there were two possibilities about what happened that night. One was that my folks never had an important dinner meeting at all, that they'd simply left me in safe hands, driven out to Malibu and aimed their car off a cliff into the churning sea below. His other theory was that there was indeed a dinner meeting, and that it had been with someone they'd hoped would hire one or both of them for some kind of writing job. When they were rejected this last time, even after the blacklist supposedly had ended, they made the final decision to die together.

"What about a suicide note?" I asked. Wouldn't my mother and father have left a message behind for their only child? Something to explain their actions, to tell me they'd loved me despite their decision to desert me?

"They never found any note," Teddy said. "Of course, it might have been in the car with them. Th-the car windows were open, so the water might have washed it away."

"And there was nothing in the Venice apartment, either?" Perhaps they might have left a final message for me there, I thought.

"No, we never found anything. Of course, the apartment was burglarized the next day, as soon as the crash made the newspapers."

My heart skipped a beat. "Burglarized? That's certainly strange."

Teddy took a sip of his tea. It had to be lukewarm by now, but he didn't seem to notice. "Not all that strange, apparently," he said. "The police told me it happens all the time, right after somebody's death is written up in the paper. Apparently there are burglars who look for that sort of thing. Figure they'll break into the dead person's home and make off with whatever they can find. They know they're not going to find the place occupied, I guess, plus maybe they hope nobody knows what kind of loot was there in the first place. Makes it easier to fence whatever they steal, I suppose."

This was the first I'd ever heard about somebody breaking into my parents' apartment after they died. And now, I thought, all these years later, Hugo Paxton's house had been burglarized—on the very night of his memorial service.

Police theory or not, I really hate coincidences.

"From what you've told me about my folks' financial situation," I said, refilling our cups from the teapot, "there couldn't have been very much in their apartment to steal, could there?" I added a squeeze of lemon to my tea and sank back into my chair.

"That's what I told the police," Teddy said. "Only real

thing of value your folks owned by that time was that one small life insurance policy with you as their beneficiary. Otherwise, they'd already sold everything from their good times that was worth anything.''

I made a quick mental connection that somehow I'd missed before. ''If their deaths had been ruled suicides, that insurance policy probably wouldn't have paid off, would it?''

Teddy glanced away and didn't answer for a while. I waited him out. ''I don't know for sure, but I'll admit I was concerned about that.'' He looked at me again, his eyes begging me to understand. ''I just wanted what I thought would be best for you, Quinnie. The cops seemed anxious to write up the crash as an accident, and I wanted the insurance money to give you a nest egg for your future. Besides, I figured you didn't need to grow up with the—with that kind of stigma. Life is hard enough.''

Teddy had nothing to be ashamed of regarding that insurance money. He'd invested it for my benefit, and eventually it bought me my house in Santa Monica, the place I'd lived for most of my adult life. By the time I sold it and used my profits to keep the *Hollywood Star* from folding, Artie had died. So I moved back here, into Teddy's guesthouse. My uncle certainly had never profited financially from having me in his family. In fact, quite the opposite was true.

''Look, Teddy, don't beat yourself up about this,'' I insisted. ''If I had to lose my parents, you know I couldn't have asked for a better replacement than you and Artie. You—''

Teddy blanched visibly. Had my mention of his dead partner upset him?

''What's the matter?'' I asked. ''I didn't mean to remind you—''

''No, no, it's not you, Quinnie. It's—the fact is, Artie and

I—I was scared to death the police would call Social Services or whoever, that they'd send you to a foster home. I was afraid somebody official would find out you were being raised by two gay men and snatch you away from us. I suppose I should have…''

I reached across the table again, patted Teddy's hand and looked him straight in the eye. "Listen to me, Teddy. I want you to hear this. As far as I'm concerned, you should have done exactly what you did do. I honestly can't imagine what might have happened to me if I'd gotten caught up in the foster-care system. And, if you hadn't done whatever was necessary to keep me here, that's exactly what would have happened.''

Despite my words, which I hoped would reassure him, he looked old, tired, filled with self-doubt.

"Truth is, I just wanted the cops to go away, leave us alone, Quinnie. I wanted them to close the file and forget about us before somebody came and stole you. So I—I never pushed them on anything.''

At first, apparently nobody questioned Teddy's right to keep his sister's baby girl, at least not officially. Maybe after a time, and because he made sure we had the same surname, people assumed I was his child. I do know that Teddy never tried to adopt me, however—I doubt the courts would have allowed that, at least not in those days. Still, we did just fine as a family, thank you very much.

"Hey," I said, shooting him as close to a smile as I could still muster, "you were the best parent a girl could have, Teddy Collins. Now let's just close the subject, okay?''

"You sure? You have the right to know.''

"I'm absolutely sure.''

I don't think I ever saw my uncle look so relieved. He'd just been let off what was for him a very emotionally uncomfortable hook.

The subject of my parents' deaths and the possibility the

car crash that killed them was no accident might be closed between my uncle and me, but there was still more I needed to know about that night and the events leading up to it.

I didn't have to tell Teddy, but as soon as I could decently take my leave and head back to the guesthouse, I planned to make a very tardy phone call to the Malibu Police Department.

ELEVEN

"ORDER WHATEVER you want. This dinner's on me," I said.

"Damn straight," Detective Tracy Lewis told me as his eyes surveyed Moonshadows' menu. "You owe me for this one, Quinn. My nose is still full of dust." He glanced up at me with a hungry grin and rubbed his ample belly. "I'll have the T-bone with baked, all the trimmings, and the salad bar, thank you. Then maybe I'll have some dessert, too." He'd already started on the double Scotch sitting on the table in front of him.

It was Tuesday night, and we were sharing a window table at the Malibu seaside restaurant. The waves slammed against the broad pillars that held the building several feet above the churning tide. Our table vibrated ever so slightly each time a wave hit. Our meeting tonight was the result of a favor I'd begged from Tracy on Saturday, when I'd asked my pal from the Malibu sheriff's station to pull the file on my parents' fatal car crash.

"And this happened *when?*" he'd shrieked into the phone in response to my request.

I repeated the date.

"Nineteen sixty—hell, Quinn, you gotta be kidding. That's more than forty years ago!"

"I can do math, too, Tracy. Hey, I know it won't be easy to find, but Sheldon Foster and Megan Collins were my parents and, trust me, there's an urgent reason I need to know what's in that file. It has to be somewhere in your department's storage area, right?'' I heard an exasperated sigh on the other end of the line. "I really do need this favor, Tracy. Please?" I added, cringing as I heard the wheedling tone in my voice. I'm not the begging type.

In the end, though, I didn't even need to pull out my trump card—the fact that Tracy had shown up late the last time we'd worked together and his tardiness had nearly cost me my life. Maybe I should try this damsel-in-distress routine more often, I thought, then quickly realized it probably wouldn't work all that often—not when used by a woman well beyond the coquette stage of life.

For a cop, Detective Tracy Lewis was a decent enough guy in his early fifties. Plenty of industry folks live in Malibu, his territory, so frequently our paths have crossed on our jobs. He'd been a source on more than one of my *Hollywood Star* stories, and I'd given him a couple of laudatory tear sheets for his career scrapbook. Given his age, I figured Tracy'd put in a good twenty-five years in the department, managing to maintain a reputation for integrity. I felt certain he had not forgotten his earlier screwup, which was probably why he agreed to help me out here.

After we'd returned from the salad bar, Tracy put his briefcase on the chair next to his, opened it and pulled out an ancient, slim manila folder. "Can't let you keep this, Quinn—gotta get it back to the dead files room tomorrow morning—but you're free to take a look." He held it out.

My hand shook a bit as I reached for it. Suddenly I wasn't sure I really wanted to read all the gory details about my family's demise after all. If this file was about somebody else's father and mother, I wouldn't bat an eyelash, but this was about my own flesh and blood. Whole different deal. I took a big gulp of my Chardonnay, attempting to screw up my courage before opening it. "Have you read what's in here?" I asked Tracy, putting off the inevitable.

He nodded. "Not a whole lot there, I'm afraid."

"Any photos?" I was thinking autopsy shots, knowing I didn't want to see anything like that.

"Nope." Tracy stared at me for a moment, sensing my discomfort. "Want me to sum it up for you?"

I breathed a sigh of relief. "That would be great." I hoped Tracy's synopsis would make this small collection of papers a bit less intimidating, give me time to brace myself if it promised to be too disturbing.

He finished the last of his Scotch and signaled the waiter to bring him another. "You having another one of those?" he asked, pointing at my wineglass.

"Sure, I could use a refill." It was probably a good thing I don't like the taste of hard liquor. Otherwise I could end up drunk on a night like this.

"The case was written up as accidental death due to brake failure on your folks' car, a 1949 Buick," Tracy told me when the waiter had left. "Pretty steep piece of terrain they were traveling out there in that part of the district. Even today, there's not much chance to recover if you're heading downhill at any kind of speed and you suddenly lose your brakes. My guess is the road was in far worse shape back in the sixties."

"Brake failure," I said. "How does something like that happen?"

"Hey, it was an old car." Tracy stabbed at his salad. "Could be it wasn't maintained properly, that the brakes were shot and your folks didn't realize. Or could be there was a sudden failure of the brake line. You know, a rapid loss of brake fluid. No way could you stop a car on that incline if your brake fluid was gone. Cars weren't built as well back then, either. Didn't generally have those red lights on the dashboard to warn a driver about something like low brake fluid." Tracy plopped a forkful of salad into his mouth and began to chew.

I glanced outside for a moment and noticed a fishing boat

returning to harbor, the sun setting on the horizon behind it. The scene was a peaceful contrast to the violent event we were discussing. "So how would the police determine that's what happened?" I asked, turning my attention back to Tracy. "Did they have somebody examine the brakes on the car?"

"No indication of that. Probably just fished the vehicle out of the water and shipped it off to the junkyard. The book on your basic car accident would be closed pretty quickly, 'specially back then. You gotta realize, Quinn, this is guesswork on my part. All I got to go on is what's in that file—guys that worked the case are long gone by now."

"So give me your best guess, then. What indication would there be that the brakes failed?"

Tracy looked momentarily uncomfortable. "You sure you really want to talk about this stuff?"

I drew a deep breath. I'd looked forward to this meal, but now my appetite was gone. "Better you explain it to me, Tracy, than I wade through this file and then have to bother you all over again with my list of questions." Right. My motivation here was really to save Tracy's valuable time.

"Okay, your call, and you're buying the dinner. First off, there was no other banged-up car on the scene, so they'd rule out something like a collision where one of the vehicles ended up over the cliff." He broke off a piece of roll and began to butter it. "Second thing they'd look for would be skid marks on the road—evidence the driver tried to stop but lost control of the car and went over the side."

"And there weren't any skid marks, either?"

Tracy shook his head and pointed at the folder. "Not according to what's in that thing. Means either the driver had no brakes or he didn't actually try to stop, like maybe he had a heart attack or was drunk or fell asleep, whatever."

"And for some reason, the cops on the scene concluded

brake failure rather than a medical reason. Since there weren't any skid marks on the pavement.''

"Right.'' Tracy avoided my eyes, concentrating on buttering the other half of his roll. "Plus, nothing in the autopsy report to indicate there was any physical problem with the driver—your father, I mean. Remember, that piece of road is pretty short. You'd have to fall asleep no more than a few minutes after leaving Highway 1. Doesn't seem all that likely.'' Like Uncle Teddy, I could tell, Tracy was thinking suicide.

I, on the other hand, was not. Not yet, anyway. "Could the brake line have been cut?" I asked him.

He almost choked on his bread. *"Cut?"*

"As in severed, sliced, slashed.''

"Well, sure, I suppose, but that would make this murder.''

"Precisely.''

Tracy dropped his fork and stared at me like he thought I'd suddenly lost my mind. "But why—''

"I'm still working on the why, but I've got a theory. And,'' I warned him, "if I find what I think I'll find, I'm going to need a lot more of your help before this is over.''

I pushed my untouched salad aside and reached for the file. With luck, this wouldn't be the last fancy dinner I'd be buying Detective Tracy Lewis.

TWELVE

OTHER THAN FITTING IN a few phone calls, I found little time to complete the research on my theory before Friday morning—after the *Star* had been put to bed for the week. Wednesday afternoon and evening had been taken up by screenings of the latest techno-thriller, an animation flick, and a feature about a comic-book character currently being played by an accomplished actor who obviously was bottom-feeding in this turkey. At this time of year, I tend to think it's a shame I can't simply turn in generic reviews for the bulk of the summer movies I have to see. If I could, they'd definitely contain phrases like "may be hazardous for mature adult viewers" and "even worse than last year's crop of mindless hot weather pictures."

But no such luck. I'm required to write a full critique of each and every film I preview, no matter how brain-numbing it might be, and I also have to make each write-up sound different from all the others. Sometimes I believe this little exercise forces me to display significantly more creativity than many of these movies' screenwriters and directors.

By the end of Thursday, I'd managed to finish the three reviews, plus write a couple of features and rewrite a stack of press releases—after checking their facts personally, of course. By the time I'd made my weekly deadline, I was bushed.

Now, on Friday morning, I was pining to sleep late, or

maybe spend a couple of hours at Uncle Teddy's pool, swimming some laps and afterward relaxing on the pool deck with a good book. Often I take Friday mornings off to make up for having to cover the industry's social events on weekend nights.

But not this week. Instead, following a strong hunch, I headed back into the office.

"WHAT ARE YOU DOING HERE?" Lucy asked me as I came through the doorway of the *Star*'s offices. Lucy Flint is our sole secretary and our resident mother hen as well. A gray-haired woman "of a certain age," as she likes to describe her longevity, she's grateful for the job, and she works both cheaply and efficiently. I think her salary is probably the best investment Harry and I ever made for this newspaper. "You need your rest. You're supposed to be taking the morning off," she scolded me.

"I *am* taking it off," I replied. "In fact, I'm taking the whole day off. I just need to use the office computer's database to check something, and then I'll be gone. Pretend I'm not even here, okay?"

Lucy pointed at the closed door of Harry's office and lowered her voice to a whisper. "Then you better not let Harry hear you. He's in one of his moods again—ranting at the poor sales department about another production company cutting its ad budget, from what I could gather."

Our "sales department" consists of two part-time college students, plus Harry himself. I wondered what good he thought throwing a tantrum could possibly do.

"Thanks for the warning," I said, slinking into my office and shutting the door behind me as quietly as I could.

It took me only a few minutes to locate the information I needed by accessing the public records database. As I read the list of properties owned by my prime suspect over the years, the final pieces of the puzzle began to fall into place in my mind. Now all I needed was a way to prove what I felt certain was true.

I printed out the list, successfully avoided the still-raging Harry as I sneaked back out of the office and headed for Malibu.

IT MIGHT SEEM ODD that I'd never before visited the section of the shoreline where my parents died, but that's the fact. I'd avoided this place—always speeding past on the highway while averting my eyes from the water—because I didn't want to think about my painful suspicions.

Today, however, was a different story. I no longer believed my folks had a suicide pact, or that my dad had killed my mom along with himself. So the time had finally come for me to see the site where Sheldon Foster and Megan Collins had lost their lives. The place where the two of them had been murdered to keep their dangerous secret buried.

I pulled off Highway 1 and, no more than three minutes later, parked only a few feet from the spot where my parents' Buick had careened off the cliff. There was a rusty white metal barrier here now, but I knew from the police file that it hadn't been here back in 1960. Nor had the three lavish houses I'd just passed between Highway 1 and this spot. This section of the beach community had been far more rural forty years ago, with only the one huge home dominating the hilltop back then.

I got out of the Mercedes and forced myself to walk over to the edge of the precipice. My palms were sweaty and my stomach churned as I looked down at the turbulent sea. The drop-off was sheer here, at the spot where the steep, U-shaped road made a sharp turn before heading back uphill. Depending on the tides that night, I could see that the old Buick would have landed either on the huge rocks below or directly in the churning water.

I hoped my parents were either killed instantly by the

impact of the crash or knocked unconscious and quickly drowned. The other night at Moonshadows, I'd skimmed the autopsy reports in the file Tracy handed me as quickly as I could, so I wasn't sure whether the coroner had found water in their lungs. All I really wanted to know was that they died quickly, and that my father hadn't been driving drunk.

Anything more would feel like rubbing salt in my lifelong wounds.

I SPENT THE AFTERNOON at home. After making a call to Hugo Paxton's attorney in Monterey to confirm a few more financial details about the burned Pebble Beach house, I settled down in front of my home computer to write a lengthy feature story. If everything went as planned, I intended to print it in the next edition of *Hollywood Star*, no matter how apoplectic that action might make Harry. What I was writing not only would help restore my parents' stolen reputations, it was genuine news.

I rewrote my story half a dozen times, inserting a fact here, moving a paragraph there, until I'd covered the whole story. By the time I finished, I'd managed to combine the bits of information I'd gleaned from my talks with local survivors of the blacklist days, the facts surrounding the murder of my parents, some long-buried secrets, my recent experiences in Pebble Beach, including the killing of Sidney Hathaway, and the reason Hugo Paxton had left the bulk of his estate to me.

Now, I figured, it was up to me to use my research and writing to see that justice was done—justice that went far beyond mere public exposure in the *Star*.

I was aiming for the kind of justice that puts murderers and arsonists behind bars.

I printed my article, reread it and felt satisfied with what I'd written. I might still have a few facts slightly cockeyed, I knew, but there would be time to correct them before publication. Certainly the gist of what I'd written here was true—there simply was no other logical explanation for what I'd uncovered.

Even allowing for an error or two, I hoped the sheets of paper I now held in my hands would prove to be irresistible bait for my quarry.

It was time to put my plan into action. I took a deep breath, picked up the telephone and started making calls.

My first was to Detective Tracy Lewis. I'm not stupid—I knew I'd need professional backup. He gave me his usual argument, of course—I should give him my information, then back off and let the pros handle things. But when I pointed out that I was the only one even remotely capable of baiting the guilty into a confession, he relented. In the end, Tracy was quite willing to have solving three murders and an arson added to his already impressive career record. Besides, he still owed me for last time.

As soon as Tracy was on board, I worked up my courage, dialed Charlie Paxton's home number and nervously drummed my fingers on the desktop as I waited for Hugo's angry nephew to answer the phone.

THIRTEEN

I'D MADE THE APPOINTMENT at the Malibu house for three o'clock on Saturday afternoon, but I drove my rented van around the sharp curve in the road, by the spot where my parents died, a good fifteen minutes early. I wanted whatever small advantage that approaching my quarry a bit before the appointed time might give me.

I wasn't taking any chances with backup, not this time. Rather than simply counting on Tracy's being at the crucial place at the agreed-upon time, I met him on my way to Malibu, at Gladstone's beachside parking lot in Pacific Palisades. He left his car there and now he was hidden in the back of the van, sitting next to the special recording device he'd brought with him. This high-tech gadget was designed to pick up and record whatever was transmitted by the tiny microphone hidden in the normal-looking pen he'd given me. I had the pen in my purse alongside my reporter's notebook.

"Hey, watch it!" Tracy complained. "Slow the hell down or you're gonna kill us before we get there."

"Okay, okay, I'm sorry," I said, pressing on the brake pedal. I'd taken the sharp turn a little too quickly, even for my own comfort. I wasn't used to driving this big van, which I'd rented because, unlike my Mercedes, it offered a way to keep Tracy out of sight in the back. I'm usually a pretty good driver, but today I was a nervous wreck and it showed. After all, it wasn't every day I planned to look my parents' killer in the eye and accuse him of murder.

I applied the gas again as I drove up the other side of the steep hill, toward the only house that had been here on that fateful day in 1960.

I stopped the van at the wrought-iron gate blocking the entrance to what could only be called an estate. The grounds surrounding the big Spanish-style house occupied the entire hilltop, probably five acres of prime ocean-view real estate. I rolled down my window and reached out to press the intercom button on the stucco post next to the gate.

"Who is it?" I recognized the disembodied voice coming through the speaker.

"Quinn Collins."

"Okay, go ahead and pull in. You can park in the circular drive."

The gates opened electronically and I drove through, stopping the van in the circular drive as directed. I made sure its rear end was facing the house, in case Tracy had to exit quickly to save my hide. We'd agreed that he'd come to the rescue the minute he heard any sign of danger on the earphones connected to his recorder. Until then, we figured, the solid sides and back of the van should keep his presence from being detected by anybody watching from inside the big house.

"Okay, Charlie, show time," I said, grabbing my sheaf of papers and stuffing them into my purse.

Charlie Paxton gave me a leery stare from the van's passenger seat. "They expecting me, too?" he asked. He'd been virtually silent ever since we'd left Malibu Village, where Tracy and I had met him.

Charlie wasn't acting angry and belligerent this time. Instead, after hearing the details in the draft of my article, he seemed as nervous as I was. However, as I'd expected, my promise to give him fifty thousand dollars of my inheritance from his uncle—half when he showed up at Malibu Village on schedule and half after this bit actor with a gambling habit had played his co-starring role in my scheduled drama—had enticed him to come along. He might be frightened, but his fear clearly had been trumped by his greed.

"Not hardly," I told him, "but it's not going to be a problem. Just remember your lines, the way we discussed. Otherwise, keep your mouth shut and you'll be fine. If there's any trouble, Tracy's here to take care of it."

"I'm on it," Tracy said from the back seat. He sounded a bit too cocky for my taste.

As though touching a talisman, Charlie patted the back pocket of his chinos, the place where he carried his wallet containing my initial twenty-five-thousand-dollar check. I'd taken the money from the insurance settlement Dwight Schultz, Hugo's lawyer, negotiated for Hugo's burned house.

Charlie sighed loudly as we both got out of the van and he followed me to the front door. I knew how he felt.

William Brooks opened the door personally. Apparently his servants—assuming he had servants here at his beach house as well as at his main home in Beverly Hills—were not in residence. Did that mean he didn't want any witnesses to our meeting? I'd probably aroused his suspicions when I insisted on meeting him in Malibu. My anxiety level ratcheted up another notch.

He blinked in confusion when he spotted my companion. "Charlie, what the hell are *you* doing here?"

"Mr. Paxton is one of the major sources for the historical feature I'm writing for the *Hollywood Star*," I answered before Charlie had a chance to speak. "Just in case you think I've got any of my facts wrong, I thought I'd bring him along. He can corroborate a good part of what I've found out."

''That right, Charlie?'' I thought I saw a flash of fear on William's face, quickly followed by anger.

Charlie nodded. ''All I told Miss Collins here is what my uncle told me.''

''Humph. Well, old Hugo had a pretty vivid imagination, I'll say that much for him.''

''Why don't we come in and we can all talk about it,'' I said.

William held the door open and ushered us inside. ''Jared's waiting for us in the den,'' he said. He shut the door and led the way through the foyer, then past a large living area and into a cozier side room furnished with a leather sofa and matching chairs. Bookcases lined the walls and I noticed that an eye-level shelf of each one held a row William Brooks's novels, displayed face out.

Jared Brooks stood as we entered the room.

''Apparently Charlie is supposed to be some sort of news source,'' William informed his son, his voice thick with sarcasm.

Jared's eyebrows rose a fraction. ''That so.''

William indicated that Charlie and I should sit together on the sofa. He took a chair facing us, near Jared's. ''So, Quinn—may I call you Quinn?'' I nodded. ''Just what is the subject of this article you phoned me about?''

I took a copy of my draft from my purse and placed it on the coffee table in front of the sofa. ''I'll leave this here with you, so you can read it carefully,'' I said. I also took my reporter's notebook and the bugged pen out of my bag and set them next to the article. Tracy'd instructed me to make sure the pen was positioned so its hidden mike would transmit a clear signal.

''Basically,'' I said, screwing up my courage, ''it's an exposé. It begins with the story of how Hugo Paxton ghost-wrote the last two of your movies, William, or how you served as his front during the blacklist, if you prefer. It also reveals the fact that Hugo was the real author of your novels, at least up until the last few, when he got sick and you began sharing credit with Jared here.''

William blanched. ''That's downright libelous!'' he spurted. ''You print anything of the kind and I'll sue you blind.''

''Feel free. Charlie will back up everything I'm saying, won't you, Charlie?''

Charlie looked anything but certain. ''Uh, sure. That's what Uncle Hugo told me.''

It wasn't hard to see why Charlie hadn't made it big as an actor, at least not if he'd ever been required to do any improvisation. Luckily, the Brookses didn't seem to notice his discomfort.

''Look, just because Charlie claims Hugo said some asinine thing does *not* make it true,'' Jared said. He bolted out of his chair and grabbed my article off the coffee table, waving it in my face. His action bumped the pen and it rolled off the far side of the table and onto the carpet. I suppressed an urge to stand up and retrieve it. ''You can't get away with writing garbage like this,'' Jared continued, ''tarnishing my father's valuable reputation based on the word of a dead old man's notoriously unreliable nephew!''

''You're absolutely right,'' I said, ''about that much. But luckily, I have other evidence. A lot of other evidence.''

Jared plopped back down in his chair and began to skim what I'd written. I leaned forward, trying to see over the coffee table and spot where the pen had landed, but I couldn't see it. Oh well, I told myself, at least now it probably was closer to the Brookses. It should be able to pick up their part of the conversation that much better.

''Like what?'' Unlike his son, William had not become volatile. He'd turned cold.

''As I'm sure you well remember, gentlemen, Hugo willed his house and its contents to me. When I got the news, I had no idea why. I'd never even heard of the man.

But then I found all those original manuscripts in his closet, and I began to figure out what had been going on for more than forty years.''

William leaned forward, his old eyes darting nervously between his son, who was still reading my article, and me. ''What on earth are you talking about?''

''The original manuscripts of the books Hugo wrote, the ones that were published under your name, the ones that became bestsellers and made you rich and famous. Hugo kept them all.''

''That's just crazy,'' Jared protested, slamming down my article on the lamp table between the two chairs. ''Hugo did *not* write my father's books.''

''Actually, it's not crazy at all,'' I countered. ''There they were, right where Hugo left them for me to find—all eighteen manuscripts, neatly lined up on the his closet shelf. Each one typed and then marked up with his handwritten changes. Charlie confirms that the handwriting is his uncle's.'' I turned to Charlie and watched him slowly nod in agreement. ''And, we have quite a few other examples of Hugo's handwriting, as well, of course,'' I added. ''If it comes to that, we can have this all validated by an expert.

''Then I compared the manuscripts to your published books, William, and guess what? They're all the same, word for word. No doubt about it—Hugo Paxton was the real author of your books.'' Okay, so I was exaggerating a little here. But I felt sure the other fourteen manuscripts—had they not burned in the fire—would have been the same as the four I actually had.

Jared grew red in the face while William became paler. They exchanged a glance.

''Even if that were true, which I'm not admitting for a minute,'' William said, ''it's no crime to hire a personal editor or a ghostwriter. People do it all the time.''

''I know, I know—celebrities love to make people think

they write their own books, even though they hardly ever do. But that's not really my major point, William, which I'm sure you must realize by now.'' I shook my head. ''Hugo Paxton didn't leave me his house because he wanted posthumous credit for his work, although I'm sure that also must have entered his mind toward the end.

''He left me his house as his way of letting me know he hadn't been the first person to ghost your work for you. He wrote your two movies that bombed. But my father wrote the two earlier ones—the ones that got you your award nominations. You worked as my father's front because he'd been blacklisted and could no longer get hired under his own name.''

William didn't answer, he just stared at me, so I kept talking. ''Sheldon Foster's screenwriting made your reputation, William. I can prove it. I made a list of similar dialogue in the early movies that bore his name and the later ones he wrote for you.'' I reached back into my bag and retrieved a copy of my list, but this time neither of them seemed anxious to take my evidence. I set it on the coffee table. ''My guess is, my dad was probably a dreamer, an idealist—thanks to you, I'll never really know for sure. When the blacklist ended, he decided the time had come to reveal the deception he'd shared with you. To tell the whole world you'd fronted his work and reclaim the credit he thought he was due. He believed he could resume his own career and probably that my mother could get back her old P.R. job at the studio, too.

''But what he didn't count on was your reaction, isn't that right, William?'' I leaned forward and glared at this man who'd lived his entire adult life feeding off others' talent and becoming both vastly wealthy and world famous in the process. ''On that night when my father and mother came out here, to this very house, to tell you his plan to reclaim his writing credits and his career, he never fathomed that your reaction would be to cut the brake line on their car and send them to their deaths, did he?''

There still was no answer.

I sighed before continuing. ''So that's why Hugo Paxton willed me his house, William. He found out you killed my parents to shut them up. Hugo might have been your ghost-writer—goodness knows he had no other way to make a living. Not only was he a blacklisted writer, he was a gay man at a time when gays had to keep their lives hidden. You had two ways to blackmail him into silence. But he also was basically a decent man, and he wanted the facts to come out, even if it wasn't until after he was dead and gone. Hugo knew I'm Sheldon Foster's daughter and he knew I'm a journalist. He had to figure I'd be curious enough about this strange inheritance to start asking questions. That was his way of putting things in motion, of getting me to travel up to Pebble Beach and do enough poking around to find out the truth—about him, about you, and, most important, about what really happened to my folks.

''So that's what I did, and now that I know all this, I fully intend to tell the whole world. I included it all right there in my article.''

''That's nuts!'' Jared bolted out of his chair again, sweeping my article off the lamp table and onto the floor. As he rushed toward me, his shin rammed into the coffee table, nearly capsizing it. I heard faint a crunch and wondered whether he'd splintered the table or his leg. Right then, neither would have bothered me much. ''You damn bitch!'' he shouted at me.

''*Jared!*'' William's voice boomed. He sounded like a man half his age.

The son stopped in his tracks and rubbed his shin, a pained look on his face. I reached back into my bag, but yanked my hand out again quickly when I saw William open the drawer of the lamp table, pull out a handgun and aim it at Charlie and me.

I swallowed hard. "What are you going to do, William, shoot Charlie and me to keep us quiet?" I said, speaking loudly enough that I hoped Tracy would have no trouble hearing me.

"You stupid girl—you're exactly like your old man," William said, sneering at me. "Just can't leave well enough alone, can you?"

Charlie shrank back against the cushions of the sofa. His fear had a rancid smell.

"So you're willing to murder two more people to keep your secrets and your wealth, are you, William?" I faked a laugh. My bravado sounded hollow even to my own ears. "You didn't think I was stupid enough to give you the only copy of my article, did you?"

Jared turned and looked at his father. "Dad?"

"No one's going to believe anything she wrote, not after she commits suicide in the same spot where her parents died," William said. "The news stories—should there be any—will simply reveal that Quinn Collins, reporter for a failing industry rag, became depressed and delusional, so she decided to die in the same place her mother and father took their own lives. With luck, people will even believe she was so disturbed she burned down Hugo's house."

I stared into the barrel of the gun. I'm not all that familiar with firearms, except what I see in the movies, of course, but I thought I'd best assume the thing was loaded. "Don't you think the number of so-called suicides you're racking up here is getting pretty suspicious?" I asked, stalling for time and desperately wondering where Tracy was. He was supposed to be rushing to our rescue by now. "You already fed Sidney Hathaway that overdose. The police are plenty suspicious about that, you know, there being no suicide note and all."

"You can't prove I killed Sidney. The man had plenty of reasons to do himself in—he was old and sick, and his lover had just died. The cops up there have already chalked him up as a suicide, note or no note, and you know it."

"Don't forget, you've got assault and arson on your list, too. I'm assuming you pulled Jared into your clumsy cover-up, that he was the one who broke into the house that night, ransacked the office and knocked me down. That was probably right about the time you were feeding Sidney those pills, right, William? And which one of you torched Hugo's house? My guess is you got Jared to do that dirty job, too. At your age, William, you couldn't really figure on being able to run fast enough to avoid getting burned, could you?"

"Jared, go get that roll of plastic packing tape from the kitchen," William ordered, his gun hand still remarkably steady for a man in his midseventies.

"You throw me off a cliff bound and gagged, guys, it's hardly going to look like a suicide," I said. Accommodating me, ever willing to point out the flaws in the game plan.

William made a dismissive sound and glared at me. "The tape's not for you, you idiot."

Charlie flinched.

"Bind Charlie's hands behind him," William ordered as soon as Jared returned with the tape. The older man continued to hold the gun on both of us, so there didn't seem to be much we could do. It was starting to look like Charlie and I had the choice of being shot here and now or taking the chance that we could escape later.

Where the hell was Tracy? I was beginning to wonder if the Brookses had an accomplice after all, if somebody stationed outside had spotted Tracy and removed him from the equation.

"What," I said, "if Charlie goes off the cliff with his hands bound, that's not going to look suspicious?"

"Charlie we can take care of later. With his well-known

bad habits, all we have to do is shoot him and dump him in some seedy neighborhood. It'll look like his gambling debts finally caught up with him, like he crossed some trigger-happy loan shark once too often."

Charlie began to whine and beg for his life, promising to change his story, but Jared quickly shoved him against the back of the couch and pressed a length of tape across his mouth.

I began to think maybe Jared hadn't needed all that much direction from his father after all. He had a pretty wide mean streak himself.

"At least let Charlie go," I said, as I saw the bound man staring at me, his eyes widening in desperation. I'd gotten him into this and, as much as I believed he was a complete jerk, I never intended to get him killed. "Charlie won't rat on you."

Jared sneered at him. "Yeah, right. Charlie's always cool...right up until the next time he needs a buck. Then he'd sell his soul for a nickel. A promise from this loser wouldn't be good for a bloody week."

Jared continued to rail against Charlie. What was this, a battle between two crown princes? Both were approaching middle age and, as far as I could see, neither of them had amounted to much of anything on his own.

Finally, Charlie seemed to have had enough of this verbal abuse. He bolted up from the sofa and head-butted Jared in the stomach.

In the chaos that followed, I added my own two cents' worth by kicking Jared as hard as I could in his already bruised shin.

"Argh!" Reflexively, Jared took a step back. The coffee table caught him in the back of the knees. With a loud crash, it splintered as he fell backward onto it.

In my peripheral vision, I saw that William was momentarily distracted. He continued to wave the gun between

Charlie and me, but Jared was in the way now and William obviously didn't dare shoot. He stepped closer to Jared, as if to come to his son's aid.

In that split second, I skirted the fallen Jared and the shattered table, grasped my fists together and used them as a club to shove William's gun hand skyward. Reflexively, he squeezed the trigger and the gun fired, the bullet lodging in the ceiling. My nose caught the sharp odor of gunpowder.

The old man looked stunned by the ear-shattering sound, but he didn't drop the gun. I grabbed the hand that held it with both of my own and clung to it for dear life, using all my strength to keep him from aiming the next bullet at Charlie or me.

Jared rolled over and slowly pushed himself up off the floor. "You son of a bitch," he said. With one quick punch, he hit Charlie in the jaw. His hands still bound behind him, Charlie had no way to defend himself. He slumped to the floor.

Jared was heading for me when I heard a second shot split the air.

"Police! Hold it right there!" Tracy stood in the doorway, legs apart, his police revolver in his hand.

Jared grabbed my arm and Tracy fired a second time. This time, it was no warning shot. Jared yelped, grabbed his leg and fell to the floor.

"Drop the gun!" Tracy said. *"Now!"*

William's fingers relaxed and he let go of his gun. As soon as it fell to the carpet, I kicked it aside and backed away from him as he stooped to aid his son.

"Well, hallelujah," I said to Tracy. "You certainly took your sweet time getting here."

I decided it would be rubbing salt in the wound to add the fact that, if his bullet had hit just a foot to the left, he'd have shot me and not Jared.

I QUICKLY LEARNED it was the sound of the gunshot that
finally brought Tracy running to the rescue. It seems that
faint crunching sound I'd heard earlier, when Jared ran into
the coffee table, wasn't either shattering wood or his shin-
bone—it was the pen with the hidden microphone being
crushed beneath his shoe. Literally, with one misstep, our
sophisticated sound system had bitten the dust.

Now, three hours later, William had been booked into
custody while Jared and Charlie were being treated at the
nearest hospital. Jared, of course, was being held under sheriff's guard there.

Tracy and I were back at Moonshadows, relieving our
tensions with some mild—or in his case, not so mild—li-
bations on the seaside deck.

"Only trouble is," Tracy told me as he started on his
second Scotch, "I'm not sure how we're ever really going
to prove William murdered your folks."

"Why not?" I bristled. "I virtually got the guy to admit
it."

"*Think*, Quinn," he said, sounding irritated. "Exactly
when did you get that ancient piece of scum to fess up? Had
to be after Jared stepped on the pen mike, because I didn't
hear any of it out in the van. And if I didn't hear it, it's not
on the tape. And without the tape—"

"But it is on tape!" I said, finally remembering. "Sorry,
in all the confusion, I completely forgot about this." I pulled
my purse onto my lap and took out my minirecorder. Just
in case, I'd reached in and pressed the record button right
before Jared rushed me. My tape had run out hours ago,
shutting off the recorder, but the dialogue we needed would
be toward the beginning of the cassette.

"What the hell is that?" Tracy looked as though I'd just
revealed I'd been carrying a stash of illegal drugs in my
purse.

"What does it look like? It's a tape recorder, and it should have everything you need on this tape."

Tracy set his glass down, hard. "Let me get this straight—you went into William Brooks's house with this Radio Shack special in your bag. After I went to all the trouble of supplying you with a high-tech setup?" He did not look happy.

After the day I'd had, I was in no mood. "I'm a reporter, Tracy. I *always* carry my recorder when I go to an interview. Besides, it was your high-tech setup that almost got us all killed," I reminded him.

"Only because you let the pen get away from you."

"Maybe so, but I still managed to record what you need to convict these creeps, didn't I?" I ejected the cassette from the recorder and handed it to him. "Try thinking positive for once, why don't you? You just saved a couple of lives, mine included, plus you got yourself a few more brownie points with the brass at the sheriff's department and you're about to get some priceless publicity as well. As for me, I'm not only still breathing, I just got myself a very, very big story that also happens to be extremely personally satisfying. So we're doing pretty darned good, aren't we, Tracy?"

He grumbled something unintelligible, then added, "Okay, I guess, but don't forget, you owe me another big, expensive steak dinner." He slid the tape cassette into the handkerchief pocket of his sport jacket.

"No argument there." I grinned at him, feeling a slight buzz, probably the result of two glasses of wine mixed with a big dose of relief. "Okay, Detective Lewis, let's go chow down."

I stood and led the way into the dining room.

FOURTEEN

MY STORY appeared on the front page of the *Hollywood Star*'s next edition. Because of William Brooks's fame, the facts I'd uncovered were picked up by the Associated Press and CNN, then by a number of the foreign news media. Briefly, the Hollywood blacklist was once again a subject of general conversation. In addition, the *Star* was momentarily famous—because I was part of the story, almost all the newspapers and broadcast stations that carried it mentioned the *Hollywood Star* quite prominently.

This last made Harry ecstatically happy, for once. I honestly don't think my partner is capable of experiencing a calm emotion—with him everything's either heaven or it's hell. He immediately began trying to use our sudden recognition to generate increased advertising sales for the *Star*, predicting this would bring in enough extra revenue to keep us afloat for the rest of the year.

What I cared about far more than advertising bucks, of course, was the vindication I managed to get for Sheldon Foster and Megan Collins, the parents I'd barely known. The Writers Guild readily agreed to head the fight to have my dad's screenwriting credit substituted for William Brooks's on those two award-nominated films he ghostwrote back in the fifties. Right now, the odds look pretty good.

As I write this, both of the Brookses remain in jail while the district attorneys in Los Angeles and Monterey counties negotiate what charges to file against them. I figure Jared will probably be free someday—the most the state can probably pin on him is assault and arson. Conspiracy to commit murder would be a stretch, Tracy tells me, unless William rats out his son, and that isn't likely to happen.

In any case, William Brooks will be going away for good. The main thing that still bothers me is that "for good" won't be all that long, considering his age.

As for Hugo Paxton's estate, I paid Charlie the rest of his promised fifty grand, plus I agreed to foot his medical bills for wiring his broken jaw back together. That's only fair, I figure.

I plan to use some of the remaining insurance money to clear the Pebble Beach property before I put it up for sale.

The rest, along with the proceeds from the sale of the lot in Pebble Beach, will not end up in my retirement fund or buy me a condo here in L.A. after all. Considering everything I know now, it simply feels too much like blood money.

So, as soon as I get back from another trip to the Monterey Peninsula to hire a real-estate agent and settle the final details of Hugo's estate, I've decided to begin contacting a variety of show-business-related entities.

I plan to use my newfound wealth to endow some sort of memorial to all those industry workers whose careers were destroyed by the Hollywood blacklist. Perhaps it will be a new screening room at the Motion Picture and Television Home or at the Writers Guild's headquarters. Or maybe some sort of special classroom or library facility in the film school at either USC or UCLA. I'm not really sure yet.

What I *am* certain about is that the first names listed on the plaque that will hang just inside the door will be Sheldon Foster, Megan Collins and Hugo Paxton.

DEATH ON THE SOUTHWEST CHIEF

by Jonathan Harrington

ONE

New York City

WHEN THE UNDERTAKER closed the lid on Owen Michael McDonahue's casket, Danny O'Flaherty was certain that it was the last time he would ever see his uncle. He was wrong.

The sky over New York had been scrubbed clean by a morning rain as Danny and Fidelma Muldoon walked briskly under her bright red umbrella and ducked into Good Shepherd Catholic Church in Upper Manhattan.

The priest held his breviary against his chest and began to pray: "You have called your servant Owen from this life." He sprinkled holy water on the casket. "Save him from final damnation and count him among those you have chosen."

When the first funeral mass for Owen McDonahue ended, those gathered began to drift away toward waiting cars while Danny and Fidelma stayed beside Danny's aunt Bertie. Danny, on summer break from his teaching position at John F. Kennedy High School in the Bronx, had been savoring his first week out of school when he received the sad news about Uncle Owen.

After accepting the condolences of the mourners, Bertie said to Danny, "I need to speak to you about something."

"Excuse me," Danny said, taking his hand out of Fidelma's, who nodded with understanding. He moved closer to his aunt, took her hand in his own and patted it. "He was a wonderful man."

"Yes, he was," she agreed.

"I'll see you at the cemetery," Danny said.

"No, you won't. That's what we need to talk about. We're not burying Owen in Gates of Heaven."

"No? But I thought…"

An enormous woman in a black dress and a black hat bustled up to Bertie, enveloped her in a smothering embrace and broke down crying. "He was a lovely man…a saint, God rest his soul."

Danny stepped away toward the back of the church where Fidelma waited for him. He had loved his uncle—and had known him well. He had been many things in his life, but Uncle Owen was no saint.

"We're not going to the cemetery," Danny whispered to Fidelma.

"Why not?"

"Not sure. Change of plans, apparently. Let's wait outside."

When Bertie exited the church she strode directly toward Danny, put her arm on his and leaned heavily against him. "I've got a favor to ask you."

Danny's aunt, Bertha, was dressed in a conservative black suit, a most unusual outfit for her since she inclined more to orange lipstick and dangly earrings. She fished in her purse for one of her imported clove cigarettes. She was nearly seventy years old and retired from the office of the Chief Medical Examiner of New York.

Danny took a deep breath and looked around, feeling trapped. He certainly owed his aunt Bertha a favor since she had helped him countless times in the past, most recently in finding an autopsy report that had been useful in his investigation of the murder of Fintan Conway, grand marshal of the St. Patrick's Day Parade. But even on the day of his uncle's funeral, Danny was not inclined to get involved in one of his aunt's wild schemes.

But she did not wait for his response. "We found a note this morning among Owen's things."

"Oh, really?"

"He had one final request."

Danny braced himself. Of all his relatives, Bertie and her husband, Owen, were the most eccentric among Danny's large extended Irish-American family. What was Owen's final request? Danny wondered. To be cremated and his ashes spread over the infield at Yankee Stadium with a crop-duster? Or did he want one of those burials in space that the Russian space program offered?

"He wants to be buried in California." Bertie reached into her purse and took out a handwritten note. "We found this just this morning."

Danny took the paper and read the note in Uncle Owen's shaky hand:

My dearest Bert—
We never got to go on that trip out West that we so much dreamed about. Maybe you'd honor this final request of mine and bury my body in Los Angeles. That way, we can have our last trip together. I love you. Your Owen.

"Strange," Danny said, looking up from the note.

"Why strange?" his aunt asked defensively. "We always talked about taking a trip out West."

"Uncle Owen never stepped foot in Los Angeles," Danny said.

"That doesn't matter. All the more reason to be buried there. Will you help me?"

"Bert, now is not the time for a decision like this."

"Will you help me?"

"Of course, I'll help you," Danny said, feeling cowed. "But how?"

"First," Aunt Bertie began, "I've talked to Bill Cooney. The body will be shipped to California via Amtrak."

"You're not serious?"

"I most certainly am. You and I will take the same train out to Los Angeles."

"The train?" Danny asked, incredulous. "All the way to the West Coast?"

"Danny, don't argue with me at a time like this. Of course the train, you know I'm terrified of flying."

"But...when?"

"Immediately, of course. Bill and I discussed shipping the body, and he said he'd make the arrangements for it to go out today. All you need to do is get your own ticket for today's train."

"Today?" Danny shouted. "Bert, come on!"

"Please?" his aunt pleaded, which was not an easy thing for her to do.

"I don't know if I can just drop everything and go to L.A."

"You're not teaching this summer."

"But, Bert!"

"Thanks, Danny. See you at the station."

TWO

The Lake Shore Limited
New York to Buffalo

THAT AFTERNOON at 2:45 Danny kissed Fidelma goodbye at Penn Station, looked around desperately for his aunt, then finally boarded the Lake Shore Limited, bound for Chicago.

Danny had contacted Bill Cooney, who now owned the O'Flaherty funeral home, and Bill explained that he had arranged for the body to be put aboard the Lake Shore Limited from New York's Penn Station to Chicago, then on to Los Angeles on the Southwest Chief.

Danny stuck his head out the open door of the train, but still could not see Bertie. As usual, she was late. Damn it, where is she?

"All aboard," the conductor called.

"Where the hell…?" Danny muttered.

Another passenger raced down the stairs to the platform and climbed aboard with his baggage into Danny's car. The man's hair was greased back, and he had pointed sideburns reaching nearly to the corners of his mouth. He wore an ice-cream-white jumpsuit with the jacket open to his belly button, exposing a set of gold chains buried in his chest hair. The suit had gold-beaded piping, and sequins up the legs of the pants. He carried a guitar case and wore oversize sunglasses.

"It's Elvis," the woman seated in front of Danny shrieked.

"A tribute artist," the man said in a Brooklyn patois as he walked past them through the train. "But thank you, thank you very much."

Just as the doors began to close, Danny saw Aunt Bertie coming toward the train. You could hardly miss her. She wore a bright red sleeveless summer dress printed with white hibiscuses, a huge straw hat with a basket of plastic fruit atop it à la Carmen Miranda, a turquoise necklace and earrings that touched her shoulders. Hardly an outfit for a grieving widow, Danny thought.

Aunt Bertie pushed a wheelchair in which sat a man wrapped in a shawl. She was trailed by two porters carrying her luggage on hand trucks. "Over here!" Danny yelled down the platform to his aunt, who stood about three train cars up the tracks. He was used to his aunt picking up strangers along the way, so it did not surprise him that she was helping the disabled passenger find a seat.

"All aboard the Lake Shore Limited to Chicago. Station stops at Albany, Utica, Syracuse, Rochester, Buffalo, Cleveland, Toledo, South Bend, Chicago and intermediate points," the conductor called. "All aboard the Lake Shore Limited."

Bertie pushed faster, and with the help of the porters lifted the man and his wheelchair up into the train and threw her luggage aboard just as the doors shut behind her and the train moved out of Pennsylvania Station.

Danny met her at the front of the car and gathered her bags. "I thought for sure you were going to miss the train. Who's the guy in the wheelchair?"

"Let's just get settled in," Bertie said. "I need a drink."

Bertie was dealing oddly with the death of her husband, but then again, thought Danny, she dealt oddly with most things in life.

When he had finally settled Aunt Bertie's sleeping companion into the seat beside her, Danny took his own across the aisle from them, pushed back his wide reclining coach seat, heaved a sigh of relief and closed his eyes. My God, he thought, I've got almost four days of this ahead of me.

Aunt Bertie had covered the man's head with the shawl and reclined his seat for him.

"So, who's your friend?" Danny asked.

"Like I said, I need a drink. Be a sweetheart and get me a white wine from the café car."

Danny heaved himself out of his seat and made his way back to the café car. The gentle rocking of the train bumped him against the seats as he walked through the train. The Lake Shore Limited headed north, right through Danny's neighborhood uptown in the Inwood section of Manhattan. Danny lived on 207th Street above the O'Flaherty Funeral Parlor. Before his death in 1995, Danny's father had run the funeral home and the family lived above it. Danny lived alone in the two-bedroom apartment above the business, now owned by Bill Cooney, his father's former partner. His father had only one living sibling—Aunt Bertha, called Bertie or Bert by family.

Danny finally found the café car, just opening, and bought his aunt a miniature bottle of white wine and a plastic cup.

When Danny got back to their seats, the shawl had been removed from the head of the man next to Bertie, and he was staring fixedly in front of him. As Danny leaned over the seat to hand his aunt the wine, he nearly screamed with fright.

The man seated next to Aunt Bertie was Danny's dead uncle Owen.

"Wh-wh-wha…" Danny stammered, nearly passing out as he fell back into his own seat. "What are you doing?"

"Opening my wine," his aunt responded. "I would have preferred zinfandel. I thought you knew that."

"Are you out of your mind?" Danny responded.

"Not at all. I like zinfandel."

"Not that! What's he doing here?"

Aunt Bertie looked around, genuinely perplexed. "Who?"

"Uncle Owen!"

"We're taking him to California for burial, of course."

"I know that, but I thought he was—" Danny faltered for a moment "—you know, in the baggage compartment, or freight, or whatever you call it."

"My husband is not going to lie in a baggage compartment for three days," Bertie snapped. "We've been planning this cross-country trip for years, and I'm sure he did not intend to see America from the baggage compartment."

Danny dropped his head into his hands, then looked up. "You really are mad, aren't you? You're not just eccentric, Bert. Even my father told me once that you were stark raving mad!"

"I wish this wine was a little colder. This kind of white needs to be very chilled."

"How in God's name did you get him here?"

"With the wheelchair. I rented the wheelchair in the neighborhood," his aunt said. "We have a very good medical supply shop there."

"But how did you get him from the casket..." Danny couldn't even complete the sentence. He was too outraged to think about how she had shifted him from the casket to the wheelchair.

"I asked Bill Cooney if I could spend some time in the chapel after the funeral mass, alone with Owen, before he was shipped out West. It wasn't easy to get him out of the casket, but I managed. Of course we'll put him back in at the end of the trip. I just didn't feel good about him being alone like that."

"But surely the shippers must have noticed how light the coffin was."

"Don't worry, I took care of that. I filled the coffin with his beloved fruit crate label collection. He had so many of those old labels they weighed as much as he did."

Danny looked around the train nervously. There were half a dozen other people in the car: two soldiers, an elderly Asian couple, a businessman working at his laptop, and in front of them a woman of about Aunt Bertie's age. The businessman looked up from his laptop and seemed to be watching Danny and his aunt.

"Bert," Danny finally said, "I know how close you and Owen were."

"Do you really, Danny?" She looked pensively into her plastic cup. "Do you know what it's like to be married for fifty years?"

"I know you loved him a great deal. But this is outrageous. We've got to get this all straightened out."

A conductor made his way down the aisle. "Tickets. Tickets, please."

"Oh, my God!" Danny gasped. His heart pounded, keeping time with the wheels of the train. "What are we going to do now?"

Bertie looked up from her wine. "About what?"

"The conductor is coming, for God's sake. What are we going to do?"

Aunt Bert looked puzzled. "Don't you have your ticket?"

"Of course, I have my ticket," Danny shouted, then lowered his voice when the businessman with the laptop turned and gave him an inquisitive look. "But what about him?" Danny whispered, turning his head to Uncle Owen.

"Tickets, please!" The conductor was already upon them, and he loomed over the seat. "Tickets."

Danny's hand shook as he reached into the inside breast pocket of his blazer and took out his ticket. He glanced over at Uncle Owen whose head had begun to slide down the window.

The conductor took Danny's ticket, punched it with a hole puncher, then gave it back.

"What's on the menu in the dining car tonight?" Aunt Bertie asked pleasantly, handing the conductor her own ticket. "I'm famished."

How in the world, Danny wondered, could his aunt sit there thinking about dinner when the corpse of her husband was propped up—actually starting to slump down now—in the seat next to her and the conductor was there to collect tickets?

"Ticket, sir," the conductor said, addressing Uncle Owen.

Danny took a deep breath and stared out the window. Despite the morning's rain, it was a bright afternoon. The sun had broken through a mass of clouds moving in from the ocean and illuminated the brownish smog hanging over the city. Danny knew Bertie would get him into some kind of trouble on the train. Bertie and Uncle Owen had always been a little off their rockers. He remembered the time years ago when the O'Flaherty family had gone to a lodge in the Catskills with Aunt Bertie and Uncle Owen. The entire family went down to the lake while Aunt Bertie stayed to take sun on the front yard of the lodge. When they came back from the lake, Danny noticed a commotion in front of the lodge where a crowd had gathered and people were pointing. Finally, Danny could see his aunt Bertie stretched out face-up on a lounge chair taking sun without a stitch of clothes on. The owners of the lodge said theirs was a family business and the O'Flahertys checked out sheepishly and went back to the city. Uncle Owen and Aunt Bertie thought it was a big fuss over nothing and laughed all the way home.

But of all the embarrassing and dangerous situations Aunt

Bertie had subjected Danny to over the years, this one was so far over the top it even surprised Danny.

"Sir, sir," the conductor persisted, "ticket, please."

What laws were there against sneaking a body onto a train? Danny wondered. Could they go to prison for this? Transporting dead property over state lines.

"Sir, ticket, please!" The conductor, now irritated, had raised his voice as he leaned toward Uncle Owen.

Aunt Bertie patiently put down her wineglass and looked over the top of her half-lenses. By now, Owen's head had slid down the length of the window, and he looked as if he were going to topple from his seat.

"Please don't disturb my husband," she said. "He's dead...tired. It has been...well, let's just say it has been a very trying couple of days."

Aunt Bert reached over and flipped open Uncle Owen's sport jacket, dug into his inside pocket and came out with a ticket. "Here you are."

The conductor punched the ticket without further comment, handed it back to Aunt Bertie and stepped down the aisle. "Sorry to disturb you," he said. "Have a pleasant trip." Then he stopped and turned. "I recommend the salmon, ma'am. It's excellent."

When the conductor was out of earshot, Danny hissed at his aunt. "This is crazy, Bert. We can't go all the way to California playing this charade. Besides, we have to change trains in Chicago."

"What's a four letter word for a pre-Columbian indigenous people of Mexico and Central America?"

"What?"

Aunt Bertie had opened the *New York Times* and she nodded at the crossword puzzle. "You're the history teacher."

Danny taught history and social studies. "Maya," Danny said, annoyed. "Now would you put down that damn puzzle and listen to me."

"Watch your tongue, Danny."

Just like her, Danny thought. She sneaks a body onto a train but reprimands *me* for saying "damn."

"Let's at least move him into a sleeping car before we figure out what we're going to do."

"I'm afraid I tried to reserve a sleeper, but there are none available until Chicago."

"Oh, great!" Danny said, falling back against his seat.

Feeling tired, he nodded off, lulled by the gentle rocking of the speeding train.

Nine hours after departing Penn Station, the Lake Shore Limited pulled into Buffalo.

THREE

Buffalo to Toledo

WHEN DANNY WOKE, the Lake Shore Limited raced along Lake Erie just outside Cleveland. He looked at his watch. Three-thirty in the morning. The moon was bright and as the train sped along the lakeshore, Danny could see the shimmer of moonlight on rippling waters. Then the lake disappeared behind acres of car lots, a maze of railroad tracks, highways and corrugated steel warehouses. Danny drifted off again.

Two hours later he woke again as they pulled into Toledo. He looked over at Aunt Bertie. Jeez, I really slept, he thought, bringing his seat to its upright position. There was a decided kink in his back from sleeping in an uncomfortable position, and he couldn't turn his head to the left.

Uncle Owen leaned on Aunt Bertie's shoulder. Bert and Owen looked peacefully in love as they slept against each other. Suddenly, Danny was jolted out of his reverie when he remembered what a fix his eccentric aunt had put them in. He was relieved, at least, to see that almost everybody in the car was asleep. Bertie and Owen looked quite innocent—an elderly couple still in love after fifty years of marriage. Only the slightly stiff posture of Uncle Owen would have indicated that the husband of this loving couple was actually...well, stiff.

Danny consulted his watch again. Five-thirty. The train

paused to take on passengers and would depart Toledo in ten minutes. They were due to arrive at Chicago's Union Station at 9:10 a.m. Once they got on the train to L.A., thank God, they had a family sleeper reserved and could get Uncle Owen into a bed and away from the constant scrutiny of other passengers.

The train left Toledo and rocked gently left to right like a top wobbling to a stop. The clatter of the wheels on track was barely discernible above the white noise of air-conditioning. A sleeping passenger a few seats in front of Danny had left her Walkman playing, and Danny could barely hear hip-hop pounding its way out of the earphones on the seat.

He stood and walked the length of the car to stretch his legs. When he passed the seat where the businessman had been sitting, he noticed the man was gone but had left his laptop behind. A stupid thing to do, Danny thought. He must have gone to the bathroom. But still it seemed odd for a man dressed so conservatively and exuding an air of a securities trader or investment banker to leave a valuable laptop on the seat unattended.

Danny slipped open the door between cars and entered the next car, which held more people than his own. Most slept fitfully but some had their overhead lights on and were trying to read. A group of tipsy soldiers at the front of the car played a rather loud game of Twenty Questions.

Apparently they had picked up more Elvis Presleys along the way, since there were now four Elvis look-alikes in this car alone. His curiosity got the better of him. "Why all these Elvises?" Danny finally asked one of the men in dark glasses, coiffed hair and a white suit. The man pulled off his headphones, which blared, "You Ain't Nothing But a Hound Dog," and shouted, "What?"

"Why all the Elvises?"

"Bunch of phonies," the man said in a thick German

accent. "We're all on our way to the Elvis impersonator showcase and convention in Las Vegas. But I *am* Elvis. I *am* the King! I'm alive. I'm making my appearance in Las Vegas for the first time. It's really me. You don't believe me? Why doesn't anyone believe me?"

Danny moved away from the man, who continued ranting, and as he entered the next train car the man yelled after him, *"I am the King!"*

Danny approached the café car hoping to get a cup of coffee, but it was closed and would not open until later.

What was he going to do about Uncle Owen—and Aunt Bertie for that matter—? Danny wondered as he made his way back to his seat. If they could just get Uncle Owen into the sleeper car in Chicago, then they'd have two days to figure out what to do. Maybe he could convince Bertie to explain to the train authorities that there had been a mistake. Well, maybe mistake wasn't the right word—*"Excuse me, sir, but my aunt mistakenly put her dead husband in the seat next to her rather than in the baggage compartment and now you see—"* No, that was not going to work.

When Danny passed the businessman's seat again he saw that the laptop was gone. He remembered he had left his own Walkman on the seat next to him and hoped no one had come along and grabbed it.

As Danny reached his seat, he saw that Uncle Owen's head had fallen off Bertie's shoulder and was hanging at an awkward angle over her breast. Danny moved quickly to rearrange his uncle's head so that it was not so conspicuously out of joint. But the body was stiffer than he expected it to be, and when he moved Owen's head against the window his uncle's entire body moved with it so that his right arm stuck out at an unusual angle. Danny managed to get it into a halfway normal position then covered it with the shawl.

"Still awake?"

Danny whirled and faced the woman who had been seated in front of Bert and Owen.

"Yes," Danny said sheepishly. "I was just covering them…it's getting a little chilly."

"That's so sweet of you," she said as she brushed past, apparently headed for the bathroom.

Danny fell back into his own seat as the train raced toward Chicago.

FOUR

Toledo to Chicago

"GOOD MORNING!" Bertie said cheerfully as Danny opened first one eye then the other.

The crick in his neck had spread to his back. They had been on the train for nearly eighteen hours, and Danny could feel it. Thank God they were getting a sleeping car in Chicago. He'd never last three days sitting like this.

"Morning," Danny said wearily.

"Sleep well?" Aunt Bertie nursed a cup of coffee.

"Not particularly." Danny rubbed the back of his neck and glanced at his watch. 7:00 a.m. "Where are we?"

"South Bend, Indiana."

"Lovely," Danny grumbled. "Where did you get the coffee?"

The woman in the seat in front of them leaned across the aisle and said, "I'm going to the lounge car now. Can I get anything for you?"

"That's okay," Danny said hastily. This was the same woman he had talked to earlier. She seemed a little too interested in them, he thought. Was she just lonely, or nosy, or suspicious of them?

"Are you sure you don't want a coffee or a soda? It's really no trouble at all."

"I think I'll get one myself," Danny said. "I need to stretch my legs."

"How about you, sir?" she asked Bertie's husband.

Uncle Owen's face was turned away from the woman and he stared fixedly out the window, his head resting against the back of the seat, as if mesmerized by the scenery.

"It's really no trouble at all," she persisted.

But Uncle Owen stared out at Lake Michigan in silence.

"Thank you very much," Aunt Bertie said. "My husband's not thirsty, I'm quite sure."

"Just trying to be helpful," the woman said pleasantly. As she squeezed past Aunt Bertie, the woman whispered, "Your husband's not very talkative."

"Strong, silent type," Bertie answered, forcing a smile. "Actually, he's embalmed."

"Poor thing. I've been sober for fifteen years. He needs to get help."

"You don't understand."

"Believe me, I do. I've been there. Down as low as you can get. Hit bottom. I just got sick and tired of being sick and tired."

"But he's dead."

"No, no," the woman said, patting Aunt Bertie on the shoulder. "Don't give up on him. He just needs help." With that she disappeared toward the lounge.

"Would you quit telling people he's dead?" Danny said, looking around to see if anyone else had heard. "We could get thrown into jail for this."

"You worry too much. You're like you're father. The poor man gave himself an ulcer."

The train entered an industrial area outside Hammond, Indiana. The sun was up and already the sky was colored with a chemically phosphorescent bluish glow. The Indiana landscape outside the huge window of the train looked like the back of a radio. Danny stared at the power transfer stations, smoke stacks, transmission towers and scrubby brush along the banks of polluted creeks. It looked more like the outskirts of Newark, New Jersey, than the wide-open spaces he had been looking forward to.

"How long do we have to wait for the train in Chicago?" Danny asked.

Aunt Bertie pulled out her schedule, adjusted her half-lenses and said, "We arrive in Chicago at 9:10 a.m. The Southwest Chief leaves at 3:15."

"In the afternoon?" Danny nearly shouted. "Oh, no!"

"What's wrong? You know, since we have time to kill I was thinking of going to see the Powers, my mother's family in Des Plains."

"Don't be ridiculous. What are we going to do with Uncle Owen?"

"He'll come with me, of course. I'm sure they'd love to see him one last time. None of them could make it to the wake."

"Good God, Bert. Get a grip. You can't go driving around Chicago with a dead body in the car."

"You know I don't drive," Bertie said. "We'll take a cab."

"Not me."

"Suit yourself."

"And not you, either!"

"I'm not one of your students, Danny."

Danny fumed silently as the train sped toward Chicago. Already they had come into the suburbs to the southeast of the city.

At a little after nine in the morning, the Lake Shore Limited pulled into Chicago.

Chicago's Union Station, located on Canal Street between Adams and Jackson, was one of America's last great turn-of-the-century train depots. Built in 1909, its waiting room was illuminated by vaulted skylights and its stone columns brought one immediately back to an older more refined era.

Danny finally convinced his aunt to follow him to an

obscure part of the waiting room and sit there on one of the polished wooden benches with Uncle Owen. Danny paced nervously, bringing his aunt things to eat and drink while doing his best to keep Bertie from striking up conversations with people.

Danny thought that only a blind man would not recognize that Owen was dead. But Danny rearranged the scarf around him and bought a *Chicago Tribune* and put it in his uncle's lap. Danny also bought a can of soda, drank half of it and put the rest in the cup holder on the arm of the wheelchair. After that, he felt confident that people would mistake Uncle Owen for an elderly traveler who had fallen asleep in his wheelchair. When a police officer strolled by on his rounds inside the station, paused in front of them and asked pleasantly, "Everything okay?" Danny nearly jumped through the roof.

"My husband's tired," Aunt Bertie volunteered. "We're going to Los Angeles."

"Long trip," the cop said, then moved on.

Danny's heart throbbed, and he moved Uncle Owen and Aunt Bertie to another part of the station. By the time three o'clock rolled around, Danny couldn't wait to get Uncle Owen into a locked sleeping car and out of public view.

FIVE

The Southwest Chief
Chicago to Kansas City

"AMTRAK SOUTHWEST CHIEF now leaving from Track 2, serving Kansas City, Topeka, Dodge City, Albuquerque, Lamy, Flagstaff, Barstow, Los Angeles and intermediate stations," the conductor called. "All aboard!"

The Viewliner Bedroom in the Southwest Chief is designed to accommodate a wheelchair and three adult passengers. Danny and his aunt moved Uncle Owen into the lower berth. Bertie said she would sleep in the upper berth and Danny could stretch out on the small sofa. There was also a portable table where Danny set out some of his clothes. A private toilet and shower were next to the room, and there was a video monitor for watching movies.

When Danny and Bertie had gotten Owen into the bed Danny said, "I need a drink. I'm going to the café car."

Aunt Bertie looked at her husband lying peacefully in bed and suddenly she began to cry. "He was my life, Danny. The only man I ever loved."

Danny put his arm around his aunt and pulled her close. It was as though the reality of her husband's death had just now hit her. As if all this time she really did believe he was alive as he sat propped up in his wheelchair. "Come on, Bert, let's go get a drink."

As Danny walked behind his aunt toward the café car, he

noticed for the first time how old she had become. She shuffled along, slightly stooped, and when the train took a curve, she balanced herself feebly by gripping the back of a seat.

In the café car Danny bought his aunt a white zinfandel and himself a Rolling Rock. He ushered her to one of the plastic tables and opened their drinks. Six Elvis impersonators in the lounge argued loudly nearby. Two of them contended that the real Elvis had been abducted by space aliens in the early seventies and replaced with a clone. So the real Elvis was actually alive and being held captive on another planet, but was going to make his first appearance on Earth at the upcoming convention in Las Vegas.

The other four Elvises maintained that was all a bunch of ridiculous hogwash. Of course, Elvis had been abducted and cloned—everyone knew that—but the real Elvis was coming back when Christ returned, and Elvis was going to do the music for the Second Coming.

"I'm sorry, Danny," Bertie said after she'd taken a sip of her wine.

"Sorry? For what?"

"For putting you through this."

Danny felt a surge of sympathy for his aunt. "It's nothing, Bert. But now, maybe we can explain to the train personnel exactly what has happened and get Uncle Owen put back—" Danny hesitated for a moment "—where he belongs."

"You're right."

Danny was surprised by his aunt's reply. He had expected her to put up a fight.

"I think all the stress of the last couple days just sort of affected my mind," Bertie admitted. "You'll explain it to them, won't you?"

"Of course I will, Bert. Now let's just finish our drinks, and then we'll get this whole thing straightened out."

Danny and Bertie gazed out of the large picture window

of the café car to the landscape rolling past outside. They had left the suburban sprawl of Chicago and entered the immense, flat farm country of Illinois. Danny and his aunt sipped their drinks and stared at the undulating prairie…the birthplace of Abraham Lincoln.

To Danny, this marked the beginning of their great westward adventure. Once Uncle Owen was safely settled back where he should be, Danny could relax and maybe enjoy the rest of the trip. With a sleeping car booked through to Los Angeles, he could finally have a good night's rest. Now that Aunt Bertie was acting a bit more sensibly, Danny was already beginning to enjoy the trip.

"I'm glad I came along, Bert."

"You're a sweetheart for saying so, Danny."

"I mean it."

"Let's have another drink before we have to face the music," Bertie suggested.

Danny looked at his watch, then consulted his timetable. "We'll be arriving in Galesburg, Illinois, soon."

"Oh, come on. One for the road."

"These drinks aren't cheap, Bert."

"Good God, you *are* just like your father. That man pinched pennies so hard you could hear Lincoln squeal."

Danny sighed, got up and bought another beer and a wine for his aunt. When he sat down he could tell that everything was finally catching up with Bertie—the funeral, the trip—and the realization that her husband of fifty years was gone forever. "He was a wonderful man, Bert," Danny said.

But rather than consoling her, the remark seemed to trigger her grief. "I just couldn't bear not having him with me on this trip. I mean on the seat next to me. The thought of him down there with the luggage…"

"I know, Bert, I know. Let's just do what we have to do and try to enjoy the trip."

Danny vetoed the idea of a third drink when his aunt

brought it up—she did like her wine—and they made their way back to their sleeping compartment so they could check on Uncle Owen and decide exactly how to bring the situation to the attention of the conductor.

But when they pulled the covers off Uncle Owen's body, they were in for the shock of their lives.

Uncle Owen was gone.

Instead, the body of a middle-aged man who, by the looks of the bruises on his neck, had been strangled to death, lay there.

"Oh my God!" Aunt Bertie screamed.

"Keep your voice down," Danny said firmly.

A letter was pinned to the corpse's jacket.

"What's this?" Danny murmured as he unpinned it. The handwriting had been awkwardly disguised.

Hello, Folks—
Hope you are having a pleasant trip so far. When I noticed your traveling companion was not moving around much I wondered what you two were up to. (Forgive me for my natural curiosity…some people have called me nosy). When I figured out what you-all are doing, it gave me an idea. I won't get into all the whys and wherefores, but suffice it to say my business partner is, and always has been, a complete pain in the behind. I can assure you that he is really better off now—frankly it was a mercy killing…the poor guy was just insufferable. If it's any consolation to you, I had no intention of killing him when we left New York. Actually, I got the idea after I realized what you two were doing.

Anyway, here's the deal. If you'll do me the favor of accompanying my friend the rest of the way across country, I'll be glad to make sure your—is it Uncle

Owen?—is safely returned to you so that he may have the proper burial he so richly, I'm sure, deserves.

Now, the problem for you, as I see it, is three-fold. A) If you alert the authorities aboard the train, you'll be in the uncomfortable position of convincing them that you had no hand in murdering the dead man now resting in your sleeping compartment. B) If you are successful in convincing the authorities, you would need to further explain where the supposedly live person you did get on the train with is now. C) If you intend to come clean with the train officials—I think generally Mother was right when she said honesty is the best policy—in this case it would probably be extremely awkward explaining what you were doing on board with a corpse to begin with. D) Maybe you'll decide to go the Boy Scout route and tell the truth—in a way I would admire you if you did live up to your principles.

But the downside is that if you do decide to blow the whistle, you will never see your Uncle Owen again. That sounds cruel...but at least I didn't have to say you'll never see your Uncle Owen again...alive. I didn't know Uncle Owen—do you mind if I call him that?—but I somehow feel that he deserves better than to be buried in an anonymous shallow grave—or worse, to be pitched from a moving train.

So, there it is, folks, in a nutshell. Don't do anything rash. I always make it a practice to sleep on any major decision I have to make, then decide once and for all after breakfast the next morning when I am clearheaded and fresh. Anyway, it's your choice. However, I just want you to know I appreciate your help in this matter. If you had known the deceased, I am confident that you would agree with me that he deserved to die. If it makes you feel any better, the guy was a complete schmuck, really. Trust me on this one.

Anyway, we'll meet up in Los Angeles—stay posted, I'll let you know where. We'll do the old switcheroo there...I'll give you back Uncle Owen and you can give me back my ex-partner. Oh, yes, did I mention that I *do* need the body back so don't even think about shoving him from the train. If you do, of course, I'll not hesitate to give Uncle Owen the heave-ho. Then you'd be in the position of trying to explain where he went off to...I'm sorry I've made this so complicated for you, but you have to take some responsibility for this in trying to pull off such a bizarre caper yourselves.

In closing, I apologize for any inconvenience this turn of events may cause you. You seem like nice enough folks, albeit with rather bizarre funeral customs. Really, it's all my partner's fault. He was a pain in the ass to everybody and has proved to be an inconvenience even in death.

Stay calm, and hope you enjoy the rest of your trip— the scenery really is stunning, isn't it? Best wishes...

"WHAT IN GOD'S NAME?" Aunt Bertie gasped.

"Just stay calm," said Danny, who himself was shaking. "Let's just stay calm and use our heads."

He looked again at the body in the bed and recognized him as the businessman with the laptop who had been with them on the Lake Shore Limited from New York to Chicago. He was a big man, not fat by any means, but he filled his blue three-piece suit in such a way that it was obvious he had never missed a meal. His gray hair had receded to nearly the middle of his head, and he was clean-shaven except for his sideburns that grew below his ears and then were shaved back so that they curved around under his ears. It was a style that Elvis had made popular in the fifties, and was sometimes seen today on very young people. But on this man in his late fifties with his conservative suit, it gave him a look of perhaps being from another country.

Even though his face was purplish and engorged with blood, his nose and mouth seemed slightly small making him look somewhat rodentlike. Nevertheless, he would probably have been considered handsome by some women. Finally, his still-open eyes were startling. The eyeballs protruded horribly and were speckled with small bright chips of blood. The eyes were such a washed-out shade of blue that they looked almost transparent in the weak light of the compartment. To Danny, the face suggested a life of cunning.

Danny looked down again at the letter.

"What are we going to do?" Aunt Bertie interrupted his thoughts.

Danny didn't answer for a long time, then he said, "We've got to find the murderer."

"But I thought we were going to explain to the train authorities…"

"It's a little late for that," Danny answered angrily.

Aunt Bertie sat on the small couch wearily. "Oh, dear. I suppose so."

"I remember seeing this man on the train from New York."

"You do?"

"Yeah. Do you remember him?"

Bertie looked at the corpse on the bed. "Yes, now I do remember. He was working on a computer when I first got on the train."

"Did you see him with anyone else?"

"Yes, I did. When I went to the café car, he was sitting at a table with that nosy woman who had been sitting in front of us."

"Really?" Danny glanced back at the letter. Somehow,

it didn't sound as if it had been written by a woman. Besides, could the rather frail woman he saw sitting in front of them have strangled such a large man? The amount of physical strength it took to block off someone's throat long enough to kill him while the victim struggled to fight off his assailant was considerable. Looking at this man, Danny doubted that he himself would have the strength to do it. It seemed highly unlikely that the woman who had been sitting in front of him would have had the strength to do it, either.

"Did they seem like they knew each other?"

"No, I don't think so," Bertie said. "It seemed like they had just met."

Danny loosened the dead man's tie. It was knotted with a single knot. Danny always tied his own with a double Windsor, a skill his father had taught him. He unbuttoned the top two buttons on the man's shirt and opened up the collar so that he could see the strangulation marks on his neck better. A horizontal blue-black bruise completely encircled the neck. About three-quarters of an inch wide, it looked as if a tie or belt had been wrapped around the man's neck and pulled tight until the vessels supplying oxygen to the brain were shut off. Danny was sure that something had been used to strangle the man. If the murderer had used his bare hands, the imprint of his fingers where he had crushed the man's trachea would have been left on the neck.

Two beads of blood had formed just outside the man's nostrils and above the bruise mark on his neck, the skin had ruptured and bled slightly.

Next, Danny looked carefully at the man's hands. They looked like the hands of a lawyer or an accountant or someone who never used them for anything but signing documents or pushing buttons on a calculator. His nails were neatly manicured, and he wore no rings. However, one nail on his right hand was ripped, and under the forefinger and middle finger of the man's left hand Danny could see blood.

Most likely the man had scratched his assailant while trying to fight him off as he was being strangled.

Danny turned the man over and searched his back pockets for a wallet but found none. Then he searched the rest of his pockets, his coat, his shirt and shoes. The dead man had obviously been stripped of any identification.

"What are you looking for?" Bertie asked.

"Trying to find out who he is. If we know who he is, we should be able to easily find out who his partner is."

"I don't believe it was really his partner who killed him. Why would he say so in a note. I think he was just trying to throw us off."

"Maybe so."

Danny continued to examine the body carefully while Bertie got up and paced around what now seemed like a horribly claustrophobic compartment. Both Danny and Bertie nearly leaped out of their skins when a knock sounded at the door.

"What are we going to do?" Bertie whispered.

Danny held his finger to his lips.

The knock came again, more persistently.

Danny whispered. "Ask who it is."

"Who is it?"

"Sleeping car attendant. I have your dinners for you."

"Tell them we don't want any," Danny whispered.

"But it comes with the room," Bertie snapped back. "We've paid for it and besides, I ordered some nice salmon steaks."

Danny glanced over at the corpse on the bed. He rearranged the blankets around the dead man.

"Okay, let him in."

Bertie opened the door. The sleeping car attendant held a tray of food and smiled at them. "Hi. My name's Harry. I'll be taking care of you folks for the next couple days."

The sleeping car attendant wore black shoes and pants,

white shirt and dark blue tie knotted with a single loop, and a white coat. He set out the plates on the small table while keeping up a cheerful patter. Then he noticed the body for the first time. "Just two of you eating?" he asked.

"That's right," Danny jumped in a little too quickly. "He's asleep."

"Does he always sleep with his shoes on?"

Danny glanced over and realized that the covers had slipped down revealing the dead man's wing tip Oxfords.

Danny pointed his thumb at his mouth in a quick motion to indicate that the man was drunk.

The attendant smiled, then produced a bottle of wine from his coat pocket. "You ordered zinfandel, right?"

"More?" Danny asked, looking at Bertie with exasperation.

"It's been a trying week." She sighed.

"But, Bert!"

"Good gracious you *are* your father all over again. Nag, nag, nag."

The attendant reached into his pocket again, removed a corkscrew and deftly opened the bottle with his left hand, then set it on the table beside the food and waited while Bertie dug in her purse for a tip.

"Do you have any change, Danny?"

Danny lunged for his wallet, anxious to get rid of the guy, pulled out a ten-dollar bill and reluctantly gave it to him when he realized to his dismay that he had nothing smaller. Then he gently pushed the man out the door.

"Gee, thanks."

Danny closed the door, then snapped the lock behind him and heaved a sigh of relief. "Close one."

"What are we going to do?" Bertie asked, pouring herself a glass of wine.

"I'm going out into the train to find out who the hell has

Uncle Owen. That's what I'm going to do. While you sit here and get toasted."

"Eat your dinner first, Danny."

"Bert, I'm not hungry."

"Danny, sit!"

Danny sat with resignation beside the corpse on the bed, wolfed down his meal, tossed back a glass of wine and stood. "I'm going to take a look around out there."

"Danny, don't bolt your food. You'll get indigestion."

"Too late for that, Bert. I've had indigestion ever since you told me we were going on this cockamamy trip."

"Well, why didn't you say so?" Bertie reached for her purse and began riffling through it. "I've got these lovely little papaya extract pills that your uncle used to always take. Loved the curry, he did, but it just didn't love him." She passed a pill into his hand.

"Bert, I…" Danny began.

"Danny, take it!"

With a sigh Danny popped the pill into his mouth.

"Don't swallow. Chew it."

He did, then chased it with another cup of wine. He stood. "I want to take a look around out there."

"Good luck." Bertie went back to her salmon.

As Danny made his way through the first passenger car it began to dawn on him that he faced a daunting task. At least thirty passengers were in the car. Most sat reading or chatting quietly with the person next to them. Danny studied each person as he passed his or her seat, not sure what he was looking for.

"Did you lose something?" someone asked.

"What?"

"I'm just wondering why you're looking into every seat."

The man who spoke these words appeared to be in his

early thirties, and though he was seated, he looked as if he were wound up tight and about to explode.

"Dropped my pen," Danny said, moving quickly past him. He went through the next car and decided to just explore the layout of the train.

On this particular run, the Southwest Chief's two locomotives hauled eleven cars between Chicago and Los Angeles: five passenger cars, two freight cars, a crew car, a baggage car, a dining car and a café car. Danny estimated there were thirty or more passengers in each passenger car. That would mean that the murderer was one of 150 people. Given the wounds of the victim, Danny was certain the murderer was a man. The male-female ratio seemed generally even, so that brought the number of potential suspects to seventy-five. Eliminate the children, who made up roughly twenty-five percent of the passengers, and he was left with maybe fifty-five men with the potential to strangle another fully grown man to death.

But some of the passengers in coach would have sleeping accommodations. They did not spend the entire time in the sleeping compartment but passed part of the day in coach, or in the café car or the dining car.

Over the public address system Danny heard, "Next station stop, Fort Madison, Iowa."

He glanced out the window as the train passed over the Mississippi River on a steel bridge that must have been at least three thousand feet long. A full moon had just risen, and it cast a golden river of moonlight over the Big Muddy. This was the true dividing line between East and West, Danny thought. Since leaving Chicago, they had stopped at Naperville, Mendota, and Galesburg, Illinois. Now they were approaching Fort Madison, Iowa. Even though he was a New Yorker, Danny knew Iowa meant more than cornfields and prairie. He thought of their famed Writer's Workshop in Iowa City and remembered that Bix Beiderbecke, the cornet player, was born in Davenport and trained on the showboats that plied the Mississippi.

After Fort Madison, Iowa, the train entered the prairie. Danny felt he was truly in the west now. It was almost 7:00 p.m., and silos rose out of fields like gigantic rockets. The train sped westward, clipping the southeast corner of Iowa and racing across Missouri toward Kansas City.

A little after ten o'clock, the Southwest Chief pulled into Kansas City, Missouri, starting point for the old Santa Fe Trail. Danny imagined for a moment that he was riding with Wild Bill Hickock or Bat Masterson heading west. Instead, Danny had less than thirty-four hours to find Uncle Owen on a moving train and to discover who had killed the man who now lay dead in their sleeping car.

SIX

Kansas City to Topeka

THE TRAIN PULLED OUT of Kansas City at almost 10:30 p.m. Danny worked his way methodically back through the train starting up front at the locomotives. As Danny made his way through the cars, several people caught his eye. First, the young man who had been so defensive about Danny checking out the train cars. He was in his thirties, with an earring in his left ear, an almost militaristically severe haircut, and a half-inch scar under his right eye. Danny noticed that the young man had fresh scratches on the backs of both hands and forearms.

In the lounge car two men sat across the table from each other. Both had the stereotypical looks of East Coast mobsters. The tall guy wore a dark suit with a skinny necktie. He had a long, thin face with an angry red scar from the lobe of his right ear to the corner of his mouth. The short guy wore a pair of black Italian loafers, pleated gray Armani slacks and a navy-blue golf shirt open at the front, showing three gold chains around his neck. He had about a ton of gel slicking back his dark black hair and talked like he had a mouth full of marbles.

Danny bought a cup of hot water and a tea bag, and slipped as inconspicuously as he could manage into a seat near them. Danny had to smile. There was a time, before he visited Ireland for the first time as an adult, when he hated tea. Now he drank it more regularly than coffee.

"So," the short guy said, "I'm sitting in the 53rd Street Cigar Bar off 7th Avenue feeling grand, minding my own business, puffing a Purofino Blue Label Pyramid, and sipping from a snifter of Courvoisier when I see the headline of the *Daily News* on the seat next to me—Cigar Vendor Smoked In Hoboken. Holy moley, I'm thinking. I know that gal. Name's Debbie Burns. The cop quoted in the story says the murder had all the earmarks of a Mob hit. But let me tell you, Debbie Burns ain't no mobster, and the cops can't figure the motive for the crime. Well, let me tell you, I know why Debbie got smoked, and to tell the truth I'm feeling a little guilty about it."

"Come on," his buddy said. "You guilty?"

Danny pricked up his ears.

"Hey, I'm busted up about the poor kid."

"So what happened to her?"

"Just listen, it's a long story."

"Hey, I got nothing to do until I get to Tinseltown."

Danny turned and looked out the window so these two guys wouldn't notice he was listening.

"Just yesterday, swear to God, not twelve hours before they lug Debbie's body out of her apartment zipped into two separate body bags, a cigar stuffed down her throat and another one up her wazoo, I'm on my way to see a buddy of mine owes me money."

"Cigar in her—"

"Just shut up and listen to this. I come out of the OTB on 9th Avenue where I dropped a couple dead presidents in the fourth race at Aqueduct on a loser named Rich Reward. My buddy, you might know him—Eddie Ferman."

"Talk about losers…"

"Yeah, well, anyway, Eddie leases a suite of offices on 57th Street between Broadway and 8th Avenue where he's got some kind of pyramid scheme going. Don't ask me the details…it's all Greek. Just as I enter the lobby, I spot Debbie and suddenly I remember the cigars. She vaults over the counter of her kiosk and races toward me, pushing aside customers, so I haul butt to the elevator, get inside just as the door closes and hit the button for the fifteenth floor. Let me tell you, I'm sweating bullets.''

"You afraid of a woman?" The tall guy sneered.

"This ain't no ordinary woman. Anyway, the elevator door opens and Debbie steps inside and shoves me against the back wall. 'Hey, watch the shirt,' I tell her.''

"Who is this broad?"

"Runs the concession inside the lobby of the building selling cigars, humidors, pipes, cutters, punches, stuff like that. She has a hold on my brand-new navy-blue polo shirt my main squeeze give me the week before on my birthday.''

"Hey, happy birthday."

"Yeah. Right. She tells me, 'Screw your shirt.' I tell her, 'Watch the tongue, Debbie.' She don't think that's funny. No sense of humor at all on this babe. She snatches at my collar, shoves me back against the wall again and reaches back and pushes the Stop button. Debbie's over six feet tall in black motorcycle boots laced to the knee. She's got on black leather pants and her arms look like sides of beef. She's wearing a T-shirt with red lettering across her boobs—'Don't Ask Me 4 Shit.'''

"A real charmer."

"You bet. She always wears a silver chain looped to her belt. Holds a wallet the size of a sub sandwich crammed into her back pocket, and she sports a gold nose ring, has a shaved head, and speaks fluent Bronx. Debbie Burns ain't no freaking debutante, let me tell you.''

"I hear that."

"She bounces my head off the elevator wall, and her face goes through four different shades of purple like one of them mood rings they used to sell way back when. All she says is, 'I want my money,' then she gives my head another jolt for emphasis and adds, 'Today.''"

"You're making this up!"

"I kid you not. I tell you, I ain't never smacked no woman, but I'm seriously considering making an exception in this case. 'Let's just talk about this,' I say to her, trying to calm her down. She says, 'We are talking.' So I says, 'I mean in a little classier place. Lemme buy you a beer.' I would have offered her a coffee, but I figure she's already had one cup too many. Still, the offer puts her off guard, at least long enough for me to figure how I'm gonna spring for a beer when I dropped my last two presidents on Rich Reward, which is why I'm going to see my buddy in the first place.''

"Ferman?"

"Right. Anyway, she don't want no beer. All she wants is her money."

"What did you do, rip her off?"

"Are you kidding? You don't rip off a broad like that. But still, she had a right to be pissed. Like I say, she ain't no debutante, but she ain't no gangster, neither. She's actually a respectable small business person. She inherited the cigar shop in the lobby of the building and specializes in fine and expensive cigars. I've known Debbie ever since my buddy moved his operation into the building and I started picking up a J. Cortes here and a Crispin Patiño there in her little shop. When cigars caught on in the last couple years, Debbie starts raking in more green than she ever imagined the shop could produce.''

"Get to the point, Shorty. How did all this get her clocked?"

"Relax. I'm getting to it. You know me, I'm always on the lookout for opportunity and I spotted it, or so I thought. One day this Rican guy in my hood offers to sell me twelve boxes of Cuban cigars—Hoyo de Monterrey Double Coronas, to be exact—at a price that was, as it turned out, too good to be true. With my priors, I ain't exactly tearing up the financial world as far as the job market goes. You hear what I'm saying? I do a bit of this, a bit of that, but my income's been spotty since getting back from Rikers.''

"Hey, believe me, everyone appreciates your taking the rap on that one. Lots of people owe you for that.''

"Yeah, yeah. Anyway, I ain't pulling no more jobs—I'm clean—so I make do with minor stuff. What my girlfriend likes to call my 'little schemes.' But with this cigar deal, I'm thinking I could pick up some extra change, and maybe kiss my hustling days goodbye. Get into something respectable, like Amway, maybe.''

"You, respectable? Gimme a break.''

"I knew you'd laugh, but you know, when I was doing time I started thinking about years ago when Princess Diana cashed in her chips.''

"Princess Diana?'' the tall one repeated, laughing. "Shorty, you getting loopy on us?''

"Seriously, man. I start thinking…what the heck am I doing with my life, anyway? You know what I mean? That gal had class written all over her, but she had a heart for the little guy, too. Next thing you know, she buys the farm. Stuff like that makes you stop and think. Evaluate your life, like.''

"Oh, yeah? Look, Shorty, I don't get it. You got some dyke who wants to beat your butt and now you've got Princess Diana into the story. What in the world does any of this have to do with murder?''

"Don't rush me. Anyway, just to set the record straight, ain't nothing illegal about holding Cuban cigars. Even though they threw down this embargo against Cuba back when Fidel shook things up in bananaland, there ain't a single thing in the law says you can't *possess* Cuban cigars in the United States. I ain't no dummy. What the law says is that it's illegal to *purchase* a Cuban cigar and *bring* it to the U.S. You follow me?'

"I think I'm starting to get the picture."

"So anyway, you think I ask this Rican guy where he gets his cigars, or how he gets 'em to the States? Forget about it. None of my business. Instead, I call around to some cigar experts in Manhattan. Find out he's offering to sell me the cigars at one-quarter their value."

"Nice."

"I fell for it. I could kick myself, but we all make mistakes in life. Bummed the dough from my old lady, copped the cigars and turned around and sold them to Debbie Burns for $250.00 per box. Tripled my investment—actually my girlfriend's investment—overnight. No-brainer, I thought. Course, Debbie couldn't legally sell them through her concession, but she still has lots of cigar-smoking friends. To be exact, a family in Canarsie named Capasso, with connections to the Genovese Family and a huge appetite for fine cigars. The mother goes through something like three boxes of Purofinos a week."

"I know the Capassos. Now I'm starting to get it."

"Ok, listen to this. Hoyo de Monterrey Double Coronas come in boxes of twenty, and the street value of the cigars is something like fifteen bucks per cigar. Debbie sold the whole lot of them to Papa Capasso."

"Okay."

"Anyway, I'm shoved up against the wall of the elevator and Debbie Burns pulls my face toward hers and says 'You knew those cigars was fake when you dumped them on me.'"

"Wait a minute," the tall one says, looking around nervously. "You're responsible for a bunch of phony cigars being dumped on the Capasso Family?"

"How many times I got to tell you? I never even heard

of counterfeit cigars when I bought 'em. Well, let me tell you, I learned everything I needed to know about them too late. Since the boom in the cigar industry, pricey Cuban cigars like Hoyo de Monterrey Double Coronas are copied in places like Tampa, Florida, right down to the packaging and labels and sold as the real thing. A cigar expert can tell the genuine article from the phony with a couple puffs. The real cigar has a cocoa and coffee-bean flavor, backed up by a smooth, woody and leathery aroma.''

"You should work for *Cigar Aficionado*," the tall guy said. "That is if you live long enough.''

"It ain't my fault! Debbie made the mistake of not actually smoking one until she sold the shipment to someone higher up the cigar chain. Big mistake. Apparently the Capasso Family wasn't too happy about the sale. In the meantime I paid my sweetie back the cash I owed her, threw a couple bills to a shylock in Jersey City who was breathing down my neck and spread the rest around at Aqueduct. Then one day a couple weeks ago Debbie brings the problem to my attention.''

"In the elevator, right?''

"Exactly. She's all up in my face saying she wants her dough. I'm looking straight into Debbie's mouth and notice some decay. 'You should see a dentist,' I tell her. She says, 'I might do some dental work on you right now.' And her face is getting all twisty with rage. Then she says, 'I don't know why I ever listened to you. If I don't give these spaghetti heads back their money, I'm dead meat.''''

"Spaghetti heads? What? She prejudiced?''

"You know, at the time, I got the impression that the money meant less to her than her wounded pride. She got greedy, bought the cigars without trying one first, and she got burned. Come on—we both did. For that she couldn't forgive herself. So, naturally, she takes it out on me.''

"My girlfriend's shrink calls that transferring guilt,'' said the tall one. "Maybe this Debbie might have benefited from therapy."

"Yeah, well, anyway, I tell her I'm really sorry about the whole misunderstanding. And I mean it. It has to be one of the most dumbest schemes I ever pulled off, and even my relationship with my old lady changed over the deal. She keeps talking to me about getting my life together. Fact, that seemed to be the theme of my birthday celebration when I got the new polo shirt. She never said it straight out, but what I was hearing was either I get something right for a change or I get lost. Well, I kept thinking when I made a score on this cigar deal she'd be singing a different tune. Meanwhile, this Debbie has a one track mind that she states over and over again in four words—'I want my freaking money!'"

"That's five words."

"Whatever. So I tell her, listen, Eddie Ferman upstairs owes me money. I'm going to collect right now. You wait, and I'll have a substantial down payment on the money I owe you. In ten minutes."

"She go for it?"

"What I'm really thinking is I need to get out of New York like yesterday. Every time I turn around there's loan sharks busting my balls, and I'm sick of the cold and sick of the city. I need a couple weeks in Las Vegas."

"So, *that's* what you're doing on this train?"

"Didn't want to risk the airport. Thought I'd go out to Vegas and unwind over the slots. Anyway, Debbie lets go the collar of my shirt but still stands with her face too close to mine, breathing hard. Her breath smells like French fries."

"Liberty fries, Shorty."

"Yeah, right. Anyway, she says, 'You think I'm that stu-pid? I'll wait in the lobby. You don't come down here in five minutes with my money—all of it—you're dead meat. You got that?'

"Upstairs, my buddy slips me a couple hundred and gives me the bum's rush out of the office. Mr. Big Shot. No time for his old friends anymore.

"I pocket the money, and as casually as possible I ask the secretary does she know where the freight elevator is? She's a good-looking West Indian woman with colored beads in her dreadlocks and long fingernails painted apricot—or is it peach? She's punching buttons on the switchboard and I can't believe how she can do it with three-inch nails hanging off the ends of her fingers. But she looks at me the same way all these snooty bitches with desk jobs do and says, 'what do you want the freight elevator for?'

"'Well, I'll be honest with you,' I say. 'There's this woman downstairs in the lobby I'd like to avoid.'

"Secretary looks at me like she's gonna start laughing.

"'You know how it is,' I say. 'She's after my body.' I can barely stifle a laugh myself on that one. It's true. Debbie Burns *is* after my body. She wants to make mincemeat out of it.''

"I'll bet.''

Danny inclined his head toward the two wise guys, straining to hear every word.

Just then, a large middle-aged man in a dark blue suit entered the car, looked around, then backed out and slammed the door after him.

"Anyway, Miss Jamaica seems interested all of a sudden. So I lay it on thick. Yeah. She won't leave me alone. Always calling me, chasing me around the city. Fatal attraction stuff. She hates it when I come up here. I wink. Thinks I'm seeing someone here in the building. Now, I got the secretary giggling. I can't tell whether she's buying this bullshit, but she seems to enjoy the story. 'Down the hall to the right,' she says.''

"You always could tell a good story, Shorty."

"It's the Irish in me. Anyway, I go down the elevator, exit the building through the loading dock and pick up a cab on Broadway just as Debbie races out the lobby of the Fisk Building toward me, screaming. That's the last time I ever seen Debbie Burns. Until yesterday, when I reach over, pick up the *Daily News* and open up to page two where they got a high school yearbook picture of Debbie looking sweet and innocent and kind of beautiful, even. Broad's dead as a doornail."

The tall guy gives a long, low whistle. "Capasso?"

"Of course. But it ain't over."

"Oh, no."

"I'm sitting there looking at the picture when I hear someone ask 'your name Sawed-Off McEvilly?' I spin in my seat, knocking over the snifter of Courvoisier. This greaseball in a four-hundred-dollar suit."

"Shorty, can you lose the ethnic slurs? You know I'm Sicilian."

"Yeah, right. Okay, this *wonderful* Italian-American individual smoking a cigar the size of a Polish sausage is staring at me staring at the *Daily News*. 'Who wants to know?' I ask. He says, 'Shame about Burns getting clocked, huh?'

"I shrug, but my heart's hammering. What's it to me? I don't know the stiff.

"Greaseball...oops, I mean Joe Italiano, smiles and flips his head toward the door. The cigar bar is all windows along 53rd Street, and there's a black stretch Lincoln double parked outside. 'I think you do know about her. What say we take a little ride over to Hoboken.' I tell him, 'No, thanks. I got a free transfer coming on my Metro card.'

"'Come on, Sawed-Off,' this guy says. He flicked me a smile, then shut it down quick as a switchblade. 'I promise it won't hurt a bit.'

"'The name's Shorty,' I told him."

Suddenly the short guy whirled and glared at Danny. "I hope you're enjoying this story, buddy."

Danny looked up, alarmed. "Excuse me, I—"

"How 'bout grabbing your tea bag and taking a hike!"

Danny stood, knocking over his cup of tea. "I was just leaving."

"We know you were. Have a nice trip."

Danny's heart thumped as the train raced toward Topeka across the vast Kansas prairie. These two criminals were bad news. The short one was on the run from the Mob for getting some poor store owner killed in Manhattan. The tall one was a rough character, too. It was pretty obvious that if anyone on this train had strangled someone to death with his belt it was one of these guys.

Ten more Elvis impersonators had gotten on board at Kansas City. None of them seemed to get along, and they argued incessantly about arcane Elvis trivia. By Danny's calculation that brought the number of Elvis look-alikes on the Southwest Chief to at least one hundred.

Danny went to the Railfone—the onboard telephone—at the head of the car, inserted his credit card and dialed New York information. "I'd like the number of the 34th Police Precinct, Detective George Washington, please."

"Hold for your listing."

When Danny got the number, he punched it in with some difficulty as he rocked back and forth with the moving train. Detective Washington was now the senior supervisor of detectives at the 34th Precinct in Washington Heights. He was a tall, well-built black man approaching sixty who always wore a crisp blue suit, white shirt and blue necktie. Danny knew him from his involvement in the investigation of the murder of the grand marshal of the Saint Patrick's Day Parade as well as the theft of Saint Valentine's Diamond. It was almost one in the morning—four in the morning in New

York—and Danny hoped Washington was working the night shift.

"Washington, here."

"Hello, this is Danny O'Flaherty."

"Danny Boy," Washington said, surprised. "How are you?"

"I could be better."

"I see." There was a pause on the line. "You never call unless you're in trouble."

"Well, that's what the police are for," said Danny.

"What's up, O'Flaherty?"

"Right now I'm on a train crossing Kansas."

"You mean as in 'Toto, I don't think we're in Kansas, anymore'?"

"That's right."

"O'Flaherty, I'm afraid that's about five hundred thousand blocks beyond my jurisdiction."

"I need some information."

"Call me when you get back to Washington Heights."

"It can't wait. Please."

Detective Washington sighed deeply and Danny could hear a chair scrape the floor, then squeak loudly as Washington lowered his considerable weight onto it. "What you got?"

"Two hoods on this train, one of whom may have been involved in the murder of a woman named Debra Burns."

"Oh, yeah. The boys at the Midtown precinct are working that one," Washington said, sounding interested for the first time. "Who are they?"

"One guy's named Shorty McEvilly."

"You mean Sawed-Off?" Washington asked.

"Yeah."

"Man, that's some tour you're on. What are you doing, anyway?"

"Actually, I'm with my aunt delivering the body of her dead husband to Los Angeles."

"Why does this not surprise me, O'Flaherty?"

"It's not exactly the way it sounds." Danny laughed. "It's worse."

"Spare me the details."

"What I need to know," Danny said, "is who was this Debbie Burns?"

"Small-time cigar dealer."

"Legitimate?"

"Squeaky clean, O'Flaherty."

"One of these guys sold her a box of phony Cuban cigars," Danny explained to the detective. "She turned around and sold them to someone in the Capasso Family. When they found out they were counterfeit, they whacked her."

"Ouch."

"Yeah, big ouch. Then they went looking for Shorty McEvilly. Apparently he got away and hopped on the train to Las Vegas."

"That's good information, O'Flaherty. I'll share it with the boys in Midtown. Now, what can I do for you?"

"I think this Shorty might have strangled someone to death on this train."

"You think?"

"I can't go into the details right now. I just need to know if Shorty works with a partner."

"Let me see what I can pull up about him."

Danny could hear Detective Washington pecking away on a keyboard. After a long wait, Washington said, "This guy usually works alone. He's also a gambler. Did time in the seventies for burglary. Then he did another stretch of one year in Rikers for contempt of court. He was supposed to give evidence in a murder trial against a capo in the Mob but when he took the stand he refused to answer questions."

Danny scribbled the information on the back of an envelope. "You ever hear of a guy named Eddie Ferman?"

"Can't say that I have," Washington answered.

Danny glanced at his watch. "Listen, I have to run. Can I call you again?"

"Just let the authorities handle this, O'Flaherty."

"I'm afraid it's not that simple."

The train pulled into the station at Topeka.

"It never is with you, is it, O'Flaherty?"

SEVEN

Topeka to Trinidad, Colorado

DANNY SCANNED the passengers' faces as he made his way through the train back to the sleeping car. But he could hardly keep his eyes open from lack of sleep.

He knocked on the door of their compartment and Bertie let him in. "Oh, thank God you're here," she said. She started to pace the tiny compartment, wringing her hands. The dead man reclined peacefully on the lower bunk.

"What's wrong?" Danny asked.

She thrust a sheet of paper into his hands.

"What's this?"

Danny took the folded paper, unfolded it and read:

Hello again—
Well, we're not off to a very good start, are we? I'm just afraid that if you don't listen to me, I'll have to put poor Uncle Owen off at an unscheduled stop. First, let's stop the Sherlock Holmes/Doctor Watson routine. I'm watching you, and I don't appreciate the way you are going around the train asking questions and eaves-dropping on people's conversations.

Danny looked up from the letter. Eavesdropping? It must have been one of those two wise guys in the lounge who wrote this. But if it was, they certainly didn't write the way they talked. And if it wasn't, who else was in the lounge car when he was eavesdropping on the two hoods?

As he recalled, there had been only one more person in the car—an elderly gentleman with tousled gray hair and a crooked bow tie who had been sipping from a can of soda and nibbling on a packet of crackers. He seemed to barely have the strength to lift the can of soda to his lips. He certainly didn't have the strength to strangle anyone. Many people had entered the car while Danny eavesdropped on the hoods. They would buy something at the counter, then return to their seats. Any one of them might have noticed Danny listening in on the conversation.

But then Danny remembered the rather large middle-aged man who had entered the car, looked around quickly, then exited, slamming the door after him. Danny tried to recall details of the man's appearance, but all he could conjure was that the man seemed powerfully built beneath his plain, dark blue suit. Then Danny remembered something else. He had caught a glimpse of a wire snaking from beneath the collar of the man's shirt and disappearing into his right ear. Danny had been so intent on the hoods' conversation that he had dismissed the detail at the time. Perhaps the man wore a hearing aid.

He looked at the letter again.

So let's keep the monkey business to a minimum, shall we? We want Uncle Owen to rest in peace. But at the rate you're going, I think he might end up at the bottom of the Grand Canyon. Let's be a little more cooperative. Okay? Otherwise, I hope you're having a relaxing trip.

Danny looked at Aunt Bertie and handed her back the note. "I think the guy's crazy."

"Of course, he's crazy," she said shrilly. "Do you think a sane person would strangle his partner to death?"

"Do you think a sane person would take her dead husband aboard Amtrak?" Danny snapped back.

Aunt Bertie's face fell and Danny put his hand on her shoulder. "I'm sorry, Bert. The stress is just getting to me. Where did you find the letter?"

"It was sitting on the body when I got back from taking a stretch."

"You mean, someone's been in here?"

"Obviously. Now, what have you found out so far?"

"There are two guys up front who were talking about a woman who got murdered by the Mafia back in New York."

"Oh, really?"

"Yeah, they're like small-time crooks. The one guy was selling counterfeit cigars and the Mob got a hold of a couple boxes of them and murdered the woman who sold them the cigars. Now they're looking for this guy because he's the one who sold the woman the cigars."

"Counterfeit cigars. Imagine that!"

Just then the train rumbled into Dodge City, perhaps the most notorious town in the West. It was known as the "wickedest little city in America" back in the 1800s. Out the window of the compartment, Danny could see the train unloading passengers and a crush of new travelers dragging their luggage on board. A knock sounded at the door.

"Cover him up," Danny whispered, thrusting his chin in the direction of the corpse on the bed. "Who the hell could that be?"

After Bertie had covered the body she sat at the head of the bed as if to guard it while Danny opened the door a crack and peeped out.

A hand thrust an ID through the crack in the door. "Open up, FBI."

Danny glanced down at the ID—William James, Federal Bureau of Investigation, Kansas City—then opened the door.

It was the powerfully built man in the dark blue suit. He removed his dark glasses and looked around the sleeping car. He let his eyes rest on the bed. "Who's that?"

"My husband," Bertie said too quickly.

"What's the matter with him?"

"He's had too much to drink."

The man considered that a moment and then said, "My name's James. William James. I saw you listening in on those two hoods in the lounge. You know 'em?"

Danny shook his head.

"Then why are you so interested in their conversation?"

"My nephew has always had a curious nature," Aunt Bertie began. "I remember the time when he was three—"

"Spare me the family sagas. You know who those guys are?"

"I heard a few things," Danny said.

"One of them goes by the moniker Shorty. Used to be known as Sawed-Off McEvilly. Ran with Featherstone's bunch in Hell's Kitchen. Ever heard of the Westies?"

"Of course," said Danny and his aunt in unison. "We're Irish."

The Westies was an Irish mob that ran Hell's Kitchen in New York.

"Wanna know how Sawed-Off got his name?" the FBI agent asked.

"It's pretty obvious," Danny said. "He's only about four foot nine."

"Wrong! One time he and another goofball whacked some guy in Brooklyn and tried to cram him into a trunk to get rid of the body. But the trunk was too small. So McEvilly took a meat saw and sawed off the guy's legs so he'd fit into the trunk."

"Good Lord," Aunt Bertie gasped.

"Yeah—Sawed-Off McEvilly. Funny, huh?"

"Hilarious," Danny said.

"Well, we're doing an undercover operation on this train and you just about blew it for us, O'Flaherty."

"How do you know my name?"

The FBI agent twisted his neck as if he were trying to get a kink out of it, shoved his chin forward and put his shades back on. "Don't worry about how I know your name. I just want you to stay away from those guys before the fireworks start. You got it?"

"What have they done?"

"Let's just say enough to put them away for a couple lifetimes."

"Do you think they've killed someone on this train?" Danny asked.

The FBI agent looked at Danny for an uncomfortably long time. "Why? You know someone who got killed on this train?"

"Of course we don't," Aunt Bertie said. She moved her hand and pulled a corner of the blanket back over the body where it had begun to slip off.

"All right, then. Don't worry about it." Agent James turned on his heel and started out the door. "Oh, and one more thing. I think your husband needs help."

"My husband?" Bertie asked, confused.

The agent nodded at the corpse. "Anybody who gets so tanked he passes out like him needs help. He's hardly breathing."

Bertie started to object, but Danny interrupted. "We're putting him in a rehab program in L.A."

"Good idea," the FBI agent said. "Poor guy looks like he's dead."

EIGHT

Trinidad to Santa Fe

DANNY COULD BARELY keep his eyes open as he let the FBI agent out. Bertie had already crawled onto the top bunk and was snoring. Danny stumbled over to the tiny couch, dropped onto it and was soon dead to the world.

He awoke the next morning as the train pulled into Lamy, station stop for Santa Fe. Aunt Bertie was not in the sleeping compartment, and Danny got up to find a cup of coffee. Another group of Elvises got on at Santa Fe, then the train raced the short distance toward Albuquerque. None of the Elvis impersonators seemed to get along. The bloated and beer-bellied older ones who impersonated the Elvises of the seventies seemed to resent the trim, coiffed younger ones who looked and dressed as Elvis did in the late fifties and early sixties.

After Danny had gotten a cup of coffee from the café car, he decided to change tack. He was getting nowhere trying to find which of the passengers was the killer. He needed to figure out who the dead man was. If he could find the laptop, certainly it would have letters or memos on the hard drive that would give him some clue as to the dead man's identity and even the murderer's.

He walked back to where the victim had been sitting when they left Chicago. Danny had seen him only one time on the Southwest Chief, but he remembered the seat. It was the first seat on the left in the third car back from the locomotive.

When Danny found the seat again, he was relieved to see that no one was sitting in it or even across from it, so he sat in the seat himself. He pulled aside the curtain to let in more light and turned on the overhead light, as well. He looked through the magazine pocket attached to the back seat in front of him and found nothing more than Amtrak's *All Aboard* magazine. Then he looked around under the seat and on the floor, but there was nothing.

Then he dug into the crack between the seat back and the seat itself and came up with a scrap of paper. It was a receipt from the U.S. Post Office. He glanced quickly at the date and saw that it was dated the thirtieth, the day they'd left New York. The time on the receipt was 12:35 p.m. It could have been dropped by the dead businessman, since the visit to the post office was a good two hours before the train left Penn Station.

The receipt read, "United States Post Office/Welcome to Ansonia Station... Cashier: KMQ4Q6. Cashier's Name: Chao." And it gave the phone number of the post office.

Then it listed the transaction as Media Mail: "$1.84/Destination 90005/Weight 1 lb 9.60 oz/Postage type: PVI/Total Cost $1.84/Base Rate: $1.84. Etc."

The man had given two dollars to the cashier and received sixteen cents in change.

Danny pocketed the receipt and walked back to the Railfone, inserted his credit card and dialed Fidelma Muldoon's number in New York. The train was just beyond Santa Fe. Danny glanced at his watch. It was two o'clock in the afternoon, five o'clock in New York.

"Hello?" Fidelma answered.

"Hi, Fidelma, it's me."

"Danny! Where are you?"

Danny looked out at the Sangre de Cristo Mountains. "Right now we're on the way to Albuquerque. Just leaving Santa Fe."

"How wonderful. Wasn't there a song like that... 'Do You Know the Way to Santa Fe?'"

"No," Danny said. Just as Fidelma had to teach him a lot about Ireland when he was over there, Danny was always correcting her misconceptions about America. "It's 'Do You Know the Way to San Jose.'"

"Are you sure? Anyway, are you enjoying the trip?"

"Not exactly. But, listen, I'll explain all that later. In the meantime, can you do me a favor?"

"What's wrong, Danny?"

"It will take longer than I have right now to explain. I just want you to find out a few things for me if you can. One of the passengers has been murdered."

"Oh, my God, what happened? Are you all right? Is your aunt okay?"

"Please, Fidelma, it's a long story. The dead guy dropped a receipt in his seat for a package he mailed from Ansonia Station on June thirtieth at 12:35 in the afternoon. The cashier's name was Chao. And the package was going to 90005."

"I have a zip code book right here in the office. Hold on. Ah, blast it all. Can you fix this desk drawer for me when you get back? It sticks all the time."

"Yes, yes, I'll fix the drawer."

Danny heard a loud crash. "Got it," Fidelma said. "Now, what was the number?"

"Nine, three zeros and a five."

"Let's see. This might take some time." Fidelma was silent for at least a minute, then said, "Here it is. That's Los Angeles."

"Aha," Danny said. "Good. Thanks. Now, if you can find out somehow who mailed this package or to whom it was mailed, it would help a lot. Anything you can find out will be wonderful. I'll call you a little later."

"All right," Fidelma said, sounding worried. "Be careful."

"Thanks, Fidelma, I will."

NINE

Santa Fe to Albuquerque

DANNY CALLED Fidelma back at home later in the day as the train sped toward Albuquerque. When she picked up the phone, he said, "Did you find out anything?"

"I certainly did. First, as I said, the zip code—90005—is Los Angeles. I spoke to the woman at the post office, Evelyn Chao, a lovely Chinese-American woman. Anyhow, I told her my boss had a client in L.A. who was expecting a package and he never got it and asked me to see what I could find out. I told her the time and date it was mailed and that it weighed about a pound and a half.

"She said that normally she wouldn't be able to remember a specific package, but she did remember that one because the package was being mailed to a Mr. Crumpacker at the Mid-Wilshire Plaza Hotel in Los Angeles. She remarked to the man who was mailing it that Crumpacker was a funny name.

"The man seemed upset when she said that, and he had snapped at her. 'What's so funny about it?' She was surprised that he reacted so strongly until she noticed the return address was the same name, so she realized she had hurt the man's feelings. Obviously he was mailing something to himself so that it would be waiting for him in Los Angeles. She said she was sorry, she hadn't meant any harm. But the man snatched his receipt and walked away."

"Wow!" said Danny. "You *are* good."

Fidelma laughed. "Sure, a little Irish charm goes a long way in New York."

"Did you get his first name?"

"No, sorry. I don't think she remembered the first name or maybe it wasn't even on the package. Now, can you tell me what this is all about?"

"I don't know yet," said Danny. "But I *do* know that Mr. Crumpacker won't be picking up his package at the Mid-Wilshire Plaza Hotel."

"Why not?"

"Because someone strangled him to death on the train somewhere between Chicago and Galesburg, Illinois."

"Oh, my Lord!"

"Listen, Fidelma, I've got to see what I can find out about this guy. We'll talk later."

"Okay, let me know if you need anything else."

"Thanks, love," Danny said, then, "Oh, can you conference us to L.A. information?"

"Sure."

When Danny had gotten the phone number of the Mid-Wilshire Plaza, he hung up and called the hotel and asked for the reservations desk.

"How can I help you?" came the professionally cheerful voice on the other end.

"I just want to confirm my reservation for tomorrow night," Danny said. "The name is Crumpacker."

Danny could hear the clerk typing on a keyboard. Then she said, "Here it is—Archibald Crumpacker."

Danny scribbled the first name on a scrap of paper.

"You're booked for one night, single room."

"What a relief," Danny said. "I wasn't sure if my secretary had made the reservation for me."

"You're all set, sir," she said.

"Thank you," Danny said. "You've been very, very helpful."

"My pleasure."

"Oh, one more thing. I've forgotten my organizer and left my secretary's number behind. Did she leave the number with the hotel?"

There was a long pause, and then the woman said, "You don't know your own office number?"

Danny laughed nervously. "Well, you know it's funny but I never call myself."

"Surely you carry a business card."

"Forgot that, too. I'm getting a little forgetful with age."

"We're not supposed to give out this information." There was another uncomfortable pause.

"I understand," Danny soothed. "It's just that, well, today's my secretary's birthday and I wanted to call and tell her to close the office early and go home."

The clerk seemed to soften a bit so Danny drove the nail home. "I've wired a surprise bouquet to her house, and I want to be sure she's there to get it."

The woman at the hotel gave him the number quickly as if afraid someone might overhear her, then she hung up without waiting for a thank-you.

Danny dialed the number of Archibald Crumpacker and a woman with a perky voice and a faintly English accent answered the phone: "Crumpacker, Inc."

"Yes," Danny began, not sure where he was going with this, "this is the Mid-Wilshire Plaza Hotel in Los Angeles."

"How's the weather out there?" the secretary asked enthusiastically. "I've always wanted to go to L.A. It's raining like mad here in New York. But I can just imagine out there the sun must be—"

"Weather's beautiful, warm, lots of sunshine."

"You're lucky to live in such—"

"Listen, we're trying to update our records," Danny cut in. "Mr. Crumpacker has not yet arrived and—"

"He won't get there until tomorrow morning at about 9:00 a.m. your time," said the secretary.

"Oh, yes. Yes. Now, let's see we have your phone number. Can you tell us your address and the nature of Mr. Crumpacker's business?"

"We're at 400 Park Avenue South, Suite 10. Archibald Crumpacker is the heir to the Crumpacker pickle fortune."

"The what?"

"You've never heard of Archibald Crumpacker? And you're from L.A.? His pickles are incredibly popular out there. He's even been called the pickle purveyor to the stars. His grandfather was *the* Archibald Crumpacker."

Danny did seem to vaguely remember seeing Crumpacker pickles in the supermarket.

The secretary went on glibly, "I can't believe there's anyone on the planet who never heard of Crumpacker pickles. His grandfather practically invented the process of using a lactic acid bath in the brining tanks. That allows the natural sugars in the cucumbers to help them ferment." She sighed like a woman in love. "That man was a genius."

"Do you know why—" Danny began, but was cut off.

"And let me tell you something," she said, warming to what was obviously her favorite subject, "you'd never know Archie Crumpacker was the most important pickle purveyor on the planet. He's so down to earth. He's really a wonderful man. He's never let his pickles go to his head."

"Let me ask you something, just out of curiosity." Danny's head was spinning with all this information. "If he's so wealthy, why doesn't he fly out to L.A.? Why take the train?"

"You don't know?" she gasped. "I thought everyone knew that Archie had an episode of that...what do you call it? Deep vein thrombosis on a flight to London several years ago. Now that alone would not have prevented him from flying, but after his operation his doctor advised him to take the train from then on. He takes the train to Los Angeles every other month in order to check on a new pickling facility being built out there.''

"What operation?'' Danny asked.

"You mean you didn't read about that in the paper?'' The secretary laughed. "Where in the world have you been?''

Danny was getting a little bit annoyed. "Listen, I don't keep up on the latest developments in the pickle industry.''

"But it was in all the papers, not just the specialized pickle press. It was a page six item in both the *Post* and the *Daily News*. Archie wears a pacemaker that is the first of its kind in the world. In fact, the only one of its kind. Some of the most important doctors in the world operated on him at Columbia-Presbyterian Medical Center. There's a biotech firm here in New York with a patent on this pacemaker. Right now it's so expensive that Archie is the only one so far who has ever gotten one. Although we heard recently that the crown prince of some Middle Eastern country is supposed to receive one soon. Oops...'' the secretary said, "I've got another call. Was there anything else I can help you with?''

Danny puzzled over the information and stared out the window of the train at the beautiful Sangre de Cristo Mountains.

"Sir? Is there anything else I can help you with?''

"Oh.'' Danny snapped back to the telephone conversation. "No, I don't think so. Thank you.''

When the secretary hung up, Danny walked back through the train cars to his sleeping compartment, wondering why in the world anyone would want to murder a pickle baron.

TEN

Albuquerque to Gallup

AN HOUR-AND-TWENTY-MINUTE layover in Albuquerque allowed for the train to be serviced, refueled and washed. Most of the passengers got off to shop for crafts and souvenirs being sold at the station by Tiwi Indians from the nearby towns.

Danny and Aunt Bertie got down from the train, and Bertie made directly for the souvenir stands featuring silver and turquoise jewelry, colorful blankets and pottery.

Train personnel scurried about on the platform helping passengers disembark and taking luggage off the train. Danny saw the attendant from their sleeping car helping another employee push a hand truck overflowing with baggage into the station.

"Listen, Bert," Danny said to his aunt, "I need to make a few phone calls while you shop for trinkets."

"Suit yourself."

Danny found a phone booth and called New York.

When Detective Washington came on the line he did not sound happy to hear from Danny. "Now what?"

"Do you know anyone on the Los Angeles police force?"

"Are you kidding? With the cutbacks in the city it seems like half the guys I went to the academy with have moved out to Tinseltown and joined the L.A.P.D. Why?"

"Because I'm expecting some fireworks when this train

gets to L.A., and I'd like to have some help from the police when we arrive."

"Listen, O'Flaherty," Detective Washington said, obviously annoyed, "we have bigger fish to fry out here than to get involved in one of your wild schemes."

"But there's a murderer on this train and someone needs to meet the train in L.A. to arrest him."

"So then tell the conductor!" Washington sounded overworked and irritable. "Let the train authorities handle whatever is going on out there. I've got my hands full here. There's been a rash of break-ins at Columbia-Presbyterian, and some nut is going around threatening the doctors."

"Can you please," Danny pleaded, "just get in touch with someone in L.A. and have some police meet the Southwest Chief when it arrives. Please? I know I've led you down a few dead ends, but I was ultimately right. Right?"

Washington let go a huge sigh. "This better be good, O'Flaherty. If this is another wild-goose chase, I'm going to have you brought up on charges, like interfering with a police investigation."

"I promise this is—"

"What time does it arrive?

"We're running slightly late but we should be at Union Station in Los Angeles tomorrow morning at about nine."

"Where is it?"

"Downtown, 800 North Alameda Street."

"I'll tell you what, O'Flaherty. I'll have a couple detective buddies of mine out there send someone over. But if this is all a waste of their time, then I'm going to instruct them to put you in cuffs as soon as you get off the train. You got that?"

"Got it."

Danny spent the rest of the time in Albuquerque trying to drag Aunt Bertie away from the souvenir sellers. She had already bought a full set of Albuquerque souvenir shot glasses and was bargaining with another Indian for a six-foot-tall, wooden, hand-carved statue.

"What in God's name do you need a life-size wooden Indian for?" Danny asked, exasperated and pushing her away from that stand only to be stopped at another.

When he had finally yanked her away from another Tiwi Indian trying to sell her a purple poncho, they grabbed some burritos and tacos from a lunch wagon and raced back onto the train.

ELEVEN

Gallup to Flagstaff

"ALL ABOARD Southwest Chief to Los Angeles," the conductor roared. "Station stops at Gallup, Winslow, Flagstaff, Williams Junction, Kingman, Needles, Barstow, Victorville, San Bernadino, Riverside, Fullerton and Los Angeles. All aboard!"

They carried their tacos to the café car where Bertie got a white wine and Danny a Rolling Rock. As they pulled away from the station, Bertie pointed to a hand truck loaded with baggage sitting beside the station house. "Look!"

"What?" Danny looked carefully and then he realized what Aunt Bertie was pointing to. At the bottom of the stack of luggage he could see the end of a casket jutting from under the mountain of baggage.

Danny put his arm around his aunt. "Aunt Bertie, there are lots of people who have to ship their loved ones this way. We're not alone."

Bertie fought back tears as she put down her burrito and dabbed at her eyes with a tissue. "But that looked exactly like Owen's coffin."

"Now, Bert, don't be silly. They all look alike."

"No they don't! You're the son of an undertaker, and I know you know better than that. When Bill Cooney showed me around the showroom it was as confusing as picking out a new car. All these makes and models. And that one out there looks just like..."

"Drink your wine, Bert."

"But what if they accidently put off his casket back there, and it's full of his beautiful collection of rare fruit crate labels?"

Good God, Danny thought. She's worried about his freaking fruit crate labels. Fruit *cake* labels is more like it. "Bert, we have a lot more to worry about than that. His casket is safely stored in the baggage compartment. What we have to do is find Uncle Owen!"

Aunt Bertie threw down her burrito and wept openly.

"And we only have about fourteen hours to do it!"

As Bertie went into hysterical fits of weeping, people in the café car looked up from their snacks and drinks and stared at them.

"Come on," Danny said, gathering up the spicy food. "Let's get you back to the sleeping car. You're making a scene."

Back in the sleeping car, Bertie sat on the corner of the bed, beside the dead man, and Danny paced the small interior of the compartment. "We have to think," he said. "I've found out a few things so far. This guy's name is Archibald Crumpacker."

"The pickle mogul?" Bertie asked, astonished.

"You mean, you've heard of him?"

"Of course, I have. Anybody who hasn't been living in a cave for the last hundred years has heard of Archibald Crumpacker. Owen used to buy a quart of Crumpackers every week at Fine Fair."

"I see," Danny said absently. "Now, why is a pickle kingpin taking a train instead of flying across country? Because he has a weak heart. He wears a pacemaker and he has suffered DVT in the past."

"What's DVT?"

Still smarting from the cave remark, Danny retorted, "I thought you worked for the Medical Examiner's Office? Deep vein thrombosis. It happens sometimes on long-distance flights. Blood clots develop in the deep veins of the legs. Every once in a while someone dies of it, usually because the clot travels from the legs to the lungs, which causes the lungs to collapse and then leads to heart failure.''

"Oh, yeah. I knew that.''

Danny let it go. "Now, his partner strangled him to death somewhere between Chicago and Galesburg, Illinois.''

"He *said* it was his partner. Maybe it wasn't a partner but someone who was going to inherit his money,'' Aunt Bertie suggested.

"Right. I thought of that. But if so, why did he take Uncle Owen's body and replace it with Archie Crumpacker's?''

Aunt Bertie tucked the bedclothes tenderly around the body. "Now that I know who he is, I'm starting to feel sorry for him.''

"Why would he take Owen's body and leave Crumpacker's here?''

"It's so weird,'' Bertie said.

Danny looked at his aunt for a long time. Weird? He thought. If you hadn't tried to sneak your dead husband's body on this train we wouldn't be in this predicament in the first place. That's what I call weird. But he let it go. "Why did he exchange the bodies? I've been racking my brain trying to figure it out. Either way if he's caught he's got a dead body on his hands.''

"Sure,'' Bertie said. "But he didn't kill Owen. That's easy enough for him to prove. Could we prove that we didn't kill Archibald Crumpacker?''

"Point.''

"But still,'' Bertie went on, "why does he want this body back?''

There was a knock at the door and Danny's heart jolted. "Christ, I wish the service wasn't so damned attentive. Yes?''

It was the sleeping car attendant. "Snacks, sir.''

"We don't want any,'' Danny said.

"Yes, we do," Aunt Bertie countered. "I'm hungry."

"Good gracious, Bert, you just wolfed down two burritos."

"I always like a snack before I turn in," she said, unlocking the door and letting the sleeping car attendant inside.

"Good evening."

The attendant looked quickly around the compartment, his eyes alighting on the bottom bunk. "Is he *still* sleeping?"

Danny moved swiftly to cover his feet and stood protectively in front of the corpse. "Of course not," he said. "He was up and about most of the day."

"*Was* he?" the attendant said cryptically as he laid out a plate of cheese, crackers and slices of pickles.

"Then he wasn't feeling well," Aunt Bertie added quickly. "So he went back to bed."

"I see," said the attendant, distracted by his work.

Danny, trying to change the subject, picked up a slice of pickle and brought it to his mouth, asking, "What kind of pickles do you serve on this train?"

The attendant stood up and looked at him intently for a moment. "We serve only Crumpackers, sir. Nothing but the best."

"Oh." Danny regretted bringing up the subject. He was beginning to feel deeply inadequate about the fact that everyone on the planet but him knew about Crumpacker pickles.

"Anything else, sir?"

"No, I think…"

"How about a half carafe of white zinfandel?" Aunt Bertie suggested.

"No, everything is fine," Danny put in abruptly, glaring at Bertie. "Everything is fine. We'll be turning in soon."

By the time the train arrived in Flagstaff, Arizona, it was nine-thirty at night.

TWELVE

Flagstaff to Needles

"Good God, Bert, would you lay off the wine! I think this guy suspects something."

"Oh, he does not."

"Didn't you see the way he looked at the body, and the way he was asking questions? And even that sarcastic tone when I said he was up and about all day, he asked, *Was he?* Like he didn't believe me."

"You're imagining things."

"He's on to us, I know it. And he's probably telling the train authorities right now."

"Oh, you're just being paranoid."

"We've got to get this body out of here."

"Out of here? But where? Danny, just calm down."

"Calm down, my foot. I'm getting him out of here before that guy comes back with the conductor."

"How will you explain where he went?"

"I'll tell him he got off in Flagstaff. At least that will buy us some time."

"But what in the world are we going to do with him?"

Danny paced back and forth in the tiny compartment trying to think. Then, all of a sudden he stopped in his tracks and started for the door. "I'll be right back."

"Where are you going?"

"Just sit tight, and don't let anyone in this compartment

under any circumstances. Remember that song, 'McNamara's Band'?''

"Well, of course, I do," said Bertie, beginning to sing the old song off-pitch.

"Right, right, right." Danny stopped her. "I'll knock out that rhythm on the door when I get back. Don't open up the door unless you hear that."

"Okay. I hope you know what you're doing."

"Believe me, I hope so, too."

Aunt Bertie was dozing on the tiny couch in the sleeping car for perhaps an hour when she heard the knock. She woke abruptly, then heard it again, the first fifteen notes of "McNamara's Band."

When she opened the door, Danny pushed quickly into the compartment carrying an armload of clothes. "Did anyone else try to get in?"

"No, I don't think so. What are those?"

"Don't ask," Danny said abruptly, stripping the covers off the corpse and beginning to remove Crumpacker's shirt and tie. "Help me strip him."

"Where did you get those clothes? What in God's name are you doing?"

"Just help me. I had to buy these from another passenger. It's a long story. Hurry, take his pants off."

Bertie gasped. "Of course, I can't do that. Owen's been dead less than a week. What kind of woman do you think I am?"

"Take his pants off," Danny shouted, then lowed his voice. "Please, we're running out of time."

Danny and Aunt Bertie quickly stripped Archie Crumpacker of his clothes and awkwardly put on the white pantsuit, white open collar shirt, white jacket with gold sequins running up the lapels. They pulled him to a sitting position on the bed and put his shoes back on him.

"Not bad," Danny murmured.

Most of the other passengers were sleeping when Danny and Aunt Bertie moved Archibald Crumpacker to a coach seat and propped him up with his head against the window as if he were sleeping.

Danny placed a pair of sunglasses on Crumpacker's face and a gold medallion around his neck. Then he stood back to admire his work.

Danny nodded appreciatively. Despite the black wing tips, Archibald Crumpacker looked remarkably like Elvis Presley.

THIRTEEN

Needles to San Bernadino

THE TRAIN ARRIVED in the dusty desert town of Needles, California, at 1:30 a.m. This was the station stop for Las Vegas, and Danny watched as hundreds of Elvis look-alikes clambered off the train in the dark with their baggage, guitars, white pantsuits, coiffed hair, beads, beer bellies, gold jewelry and their individual, peculiar obsessions. They were met by other Elvis impersonators, so that the entire station looked, in the dry heat of night, like either a bad dream or a mass hallucination.

A shuttle bus would whisk those registered for the conference to the Lady Luck Casino in Vegas to witness either the second coming of Elvis or the shattering of their delusions. No matter which one, Danny was glad he would not be a part of it.

Not that the nightmare he and Aunt Bertie were caught up in was any better. Now, he had to act quickly, because in the morning, someone would notice that there was still one Elvis impersonator who had not gotten off in Needles.

Bertie snored loudly from the top bunk of the sleeper while Danny spent the entire time between Needles and San Bernadino searching the train for some sign of either Uncle Owen or of the murderer of Archie Crumpacker. Finally, he could not keep himself awake any longer and went back to the sleeping compartment to catch a few minutes' sleep. He was awakened by a knock on the door.

Danny raised his head groggily and saw that it was just getting light outside. When he opened the door, the sleeping car attendant had a tray of breakfast for them. Now Danny was relaxed, glad that he had gotten rid of the body, but the sleeping car attendant's reaction threw him for a loop.

"Where is he?" the car attendant asked in an agitated voice as he set down the tray.

"Where's who?"

"The...the...your friend. What did you do with him?"

"He got off in Needles."

"He got off?" The car attendant looked around, dumbfounded. "He got off?"

"Yeah."

The attendant pointed an angry finger at Danny. "What are you two up to?"

Danny looked into the dismayed eyes of the attendant, then at the knot on his tie. A double-knotted tie has a symmetrical triangle shape. A single-knotted tie is slightly asymmetrical, like half of a triangle. The sleeping car attendant had tied his necktie with a single knot.

As the train pulled into San Bernadino, suddenly, it all fell into place.

FOURTEEN

San Bernadino to Los Angeles

THE ATTENDANT SLAMMED the door of the sleeping compartment behind him and raced up through the train. Danny went to the nearest Railfone, called Fidelma—it was about four in the morning in New York—and woke her up.

"Yes?" Fidelma answered in a groggy voice.

"Fidelma, there's an emergency."

"Who is this?"

"It's Danny!"

"What time is it?"

"Please, Fidelma. You've got to get in touch with Detective Washington."

"Who is this?"

"It's me! It's Danny. I'm running out of time. Get in touch with Detective Washington at his home. I don't care what it takes. Just call him, or go to his house if you have to. Tell him to get in touch with someone at the Albuquerque police department and get them out to the Amtrak station. There's a dead man in a casket back in Albuquerque, and he still may be at the station."

"What do you mean? I'm sure they put dead men in caskets out in Albuquerque just like we do here."

"Fidelma!"

"Now if there was a live man in a casket, I could see the problem…"

"Have Washington see if he can get the police out there to find the casket in Albuquerque. Then have the L.A.P.D. meet the train in Los Angeles. I'll explain everything to the police in L.A."

"Danny, be careful. I'll get in touch with Detective Washington right away. I actually have his cell phone number from last time. We're growing quite chummy."

"Good. Just keep ringing until he wakes up. Whatever it takes. This is serious."

"But who's in the casket in Albuquerque?"

"Uncle Owen," Danny said, and he hung up.

FIFTEEN

Los Angeles

THE TRAIN pulled into the Art Deco and Spanish-styled Union Station in Los Angeles. Danny heaved a sigh of relief when he saw a troop of uniformed L.A. police officers waiting on the platform.

Barely waiting for the train to stop, he hopped off and ran toward them. "Someone on board has been murdered," he shouted breathlessly.

"Be careful, Danny," Aunt Bertie yelled from the train door.

"Are you O'Flaherty?" one of the officers asked.

"Yeah."

A few of the cops started chuckling.

What did Washington tell them? Danny wondered.

"I think you better come with us, sir," one of the cops said.

"No, you've got to get on the train," Danny protested. "Somebody on board strangled a man named Archibald Crumpacker to death."

"Is that the pickle guy?" another of the cops asked. "I love Crumpackers!"

A plainclothes officer among them pointed at one of his men. "Montejo, you take this guy's statement while we search the train."

"But I have to go with you to point out the killer," Danny said. "We've got to hurry before he gets away."

The plainclothes officer pushed a finger between Danny's eyes and said, "You just stay put, Sherlock, while we straighten out this mess." Then he led two of his officers onto the train.

Just then, among the people crowding the platform, Danny saw one lone Elvis dressed in a white pantsuit, white open-collar shirt, and jacket with gold sequins being wheeled rapidly in a wheelchair down the platform and into the station.

"That's him!"

The cops looked toward the wheelchair and back at Danny. "Elvis?"

"No, he's dead."

"No shit, Sherlock. Been dead since '77."

"I mean that's Archibald Crumpacker dressed like Elvis and he's dead...Crumpacker, I mean. The man pushing the wheelchair murdered him."

The cops took off in the direction of the wheelchair just as it disappeared into the crowded station. Danny sprinted after them. He elbowed his way through hundreds of travelers loaded down with luggage. He spotted the wheelchair being pushed through the front doors. A van was double-parked in the crosswalk.

"They're out there," Danny yelled to the officers, who bolted through the revolving doors in pursuit, almost mangling someone's grandmother.

The van's side doors were open and the man pushing the chair raced toward them. One of the L.A. cops caught up with him, grabbed him by the shoulder and spun him and the wheelchair.

The man reached into his inside pocket and drew out what looked to Danny like a gun. Six L.A. cops drew their weapons, pointed them at the man and yelled in unison, "Drop it!"

The man let go, and the wallet he held dropped open to reveal a badge. "FBI!" he shouted.

As Danny approached, he saw that it was Agent William James.

When he was close enough he finally got a good look at the man slumped over in the wheelchair. It was not Archibald Crumpacker. It was the sleeping car attendant, his face a mottled purple, his eyes shot with blood. His tie was still twisted around his neck, knotted with a single loop. A gold medallion sparkled on his chest. He was unmistakably dead.

The cop named Montejo came up behind Danny, slapped handcuffs on his right wrist and pulled his left hand roughly behind his back. "You have the right to remain silent," he intoned as he put Danny's other hand in cuffs. "Anything you say—"

"Wait a minute," Danny pleaded, "I can explain everything. Archibald Crumpacker suffered deep vein thrombosis. That's why his doctor wouldn't let him fly. He always crossed the country by train. Makes this cross-country trip every other month. The sleeping car attendant knew that. Probably met him on an earlier trip. Crumpacker wears a pacemaker. First of its kind and the only one in the world currently being worn by a living human being."

"What's that got to do with anything?" Montejo asked, pushing Danny toward a waiting police cruiser.

"Crumpacker was the first and only patient in the world to receive the device," Danny said, his head twisted backward toward Officer Montejo. "The pacemaker is patented by a company in New York. The operation took place at Columbia-Presbyterian Medical Center. They've had a rash of break-ins this week at the hospital. You can check with Detective Washington in New York! Doctors were threatened. Somebody wants that pacemaker. I'm sure it was the sleeping car attendant who offed Crumpacker. That's why he needed the body back. For the pacemaker."

"Well, somebody killed your chief suspect," Montejo said. "We're locking you up until we get to the bottom of this."

As Montejo pushed Danny into the back seat of the cruiser none too gently, another cop ran up with a walkie-talkie to his ear. "The cops in Albuquerque found the casket with this guy's uncle in it."

Montejo leaned into Danny menacingly. "You kill your own uncle, too, you scuzbag?"

"No!" Danny squeaked. "Uncle Owen was a great guy. Used to take me to Coney Island!"

"I can explain."

The cops turned as Aunt Bertie approached, dressed in her sleeveless red summer dress printed with white hibiscuses, straw hat with a basket of plastic fruit atop it and turquoise earrings that touched her shoulders.

"Who's this, Carmen Miranda?" one of the cops asked, snickering.

"This is my aunt," Danny said angrily. "Bertha McDonahue."

"Hoo boy!"

"It's all my fault," Bertie began, sniffling and touching a tissue to her eyes. She blew her nose loudly and put her tissue away. "You see, my husband always dreamed of seeing California…" For the next ten minutes she narrated everything that had happened between New York and Los Angeles. "So," she concluded, "I'm really the one to blame. If I hadn't brought Owen aboard—"

"It's not your fault, Bert," Danny cut her off. "I knew when the killer wanted the body back that it must be about the pacemaker. Why else would he kill someone but need to keep the body?"

"This all sounds a little far-fetched to me," Montejo said, but he stepped back from Danny.

The cop with the radio squawking in his ear spoke up. "I think this guy's on to something. They just booked some-one in Albuquerque who was supposed to pick up a body. He fingered some kind of industrial spy who had given him a lot of money to pick up a body at the train station. The spy wanted the pacemaker out of this guy. Ain't that sick?"

Officer Montejo looked at Danny, then back at the cop with the radio.

"Anyway," the radio cop went on, "the guy delivered the casket that the sleeping car attendant took off the train. But when the spy opened the casket and saw the body, he went ballistic. Looks like this sleeping car attendant double-crossed him and gave him this guy's uncle's body instead of the one with the pacemaker in it."

Montejo pushed his hat back on his head and scratched his nose. "Why would he do that?"

Danny spoke up. "He was probably trying to sell Crum-packer's body twice. Once in Albuquerque and once in L.A."

"How can you sell the same body twice?" Montejo asked.

"You can't, of course," Danny explained. "That's why he gave the group in Albuquerque the body of Uncle Owen, pretending it was Archibald Crumpacker. He saved the real Crumpacker for a second payoff in L.A."

The FBI agent, William James, had been silent through-out this whole exchange. Finally he spoke up. "This guy O'Flaherty's close to it. The sleeping car attendant's name is Harry Tessler. He strangled Crumpacker. We've been watching these industrial spies for some time now. Two competing biotech firms, Century BioSolutions, Ltd. and an-other outfit called Millennium Biological Technologies, Inc., are both anxious to get this new type of pacemaker that

Crumpacker was wearing, probably so they can study its design and launch their own line of devices. Industrial spies from Millennium broke into Columbia-Presbyterian in New York this week attempting to find plans or any other information. Then, the surgeon who performed the operation on Crumpacker reported that he had been offered a lot of money from someone connected to Century to give information about the design. When he refused, they threatened him in order to make him reveal something about the device's workings. Instead, he reported these incidents to the police."

"So when did the FBI get involved?" Officer Montejo asked.

"The investigation has been going on for more than a year. But I've only been on the case a couple months. I've been trailing Crumpacker on every one of his cross-country trips because we thought someone might try something like this. I'm sorry we weren't able to prevent his death."

"Yeah, that's too bad. I love his pickles."

"We thought it might be Shorty McEvilly or his buddy, Screwball Salerno, who was going to try to knock off Crumpacker and cut the pacemaker out of him, that maybe Millennium or Century had taken an old-fashioned hit out on him. Shorty Mac's pretty handy with a meat saw."

"I think I'm going to barf," one of the cops said.

"Screwball Salerno?" Montejo asked.

"Yeah, that's the guy Shorty met up with on the train. We'd been tipped off. Now I'm beginning to think it might have been one of Shorty's enemies who gave us a false tip. Anyway, about halfway through the trip we got some interesting information about Harry Tessler. He's a compulsive gambler with major debts in Vegas. We think Tessler met Crumpacker on a previous trip. Maybe Crumpacker told him about the pacemaker, maybe Harry T. read it in *Time* magazine. Anyway, he puts two and two together, and figures there might be a way to make some money off this deal. I guess he was right.''

Danny shifted in the seat, trying to ease the strain on his arms. ''The way I see it, after Harry Tessler strangled Crumpacker with his own necktie, he found out what my aunt and I were doing, and he realized he now had a perfect place to hide Crumpacker's body...in Uncle Owen's empty casket. I realized he was the only one who would have access both to our compartment and to the baggage compartment. What I couldn't figure is why he needed the body back and why he would have switched bodies in the first place. I racked my brains trying to figure out why anyone would murder someone and then want the body back. That's when I found out about Archibald Crumpacker's pacemaker and it all started to make sense.''

''It did?'' asked one of the cops, leaning on the door.

''But you still couldn't figure out why he would switch the bodies, could you Danny?'' Aunt Bertie was looking at Danny with pride.

''You know,'' she said to the policemen and the FBI agent, ''my nephew teaches history, but he has also solved a couple of crimes before. Haven't you, Danny?''

Danny blushed slightly and went on. ''When I saw a casket unloaded in Albuquerque, I thought maybe it was Uncle Owen's.''

''No, you didn't,'' Aunt Bertie said. ''I was the one who told you it was Owen's.''

Danny sighed. ''Okay, but I did realize you were right.''

''Well, you didn't say that, did you?''

''I was getting around to it.''

''No, you weren't, you passed right over it.''

''Okay!'' Danny exclaimed. ''Aunt Bert realized they had taken my uncle's casket off in Albuquerque.'' He glanced pointedly at Bertie. She seemed content.

''Thank you,'' she said. ''You know I always taught you

to give credit where credit is due." She leaned confidingly toward Officer Montejo. "The male ego is a fragile thing, as I'm sure you know. I always had this same kind of problem with my late husband."

"Can we get back to the story?" Montejo grumbled.

Danny resumed. "Then I realized that maybe Harry Tessler was trying to pass off Uncle Owen as Archibald Crumpacker to someone in Albuquerque," Danny continued. "I figured he could sell Uncle Owen's body in Albuquerque to someone, then sell the *real* Crumpacker corpse in L.A. Or cut out the pacemaker himself. He'd double his profits that way."

"Two heads are better than one," one of the cops remarked. No one laughed.

"This is sick stuff," said the cop with the radio.

"Apparently O'Flaherty was right," Agent James said. "Tessler did try to pass off Uncle Owen as Archibald Crumpacker and he *was* saving the real Crumpacker for Millennium Biological Technologies, who wanted the device."

"I get it now," Montejo said. "So when Tessler got found out, somebody on board must have been notified and whoever that was murdered Mr. Tessler. Maybe it was this Shorty guy, or his buddy, Screwball."

"Nobody murdered the sleeping car attendant," Danny said.

All eyes turned to Danny. "Say what?"

"He wasn't murdered."

"What's he doing, then?" asked Montejo. "Faking?"

A couple of the cops guffawed.

Danny pointed his chin at Agent James. "See the way he ties his tie?"

"What?"

"Look at the knot in Agent James's tie."

"What's this all about?"

"He uses a double loop to knot his tie, just like I do. A

double Windsor. Just like my father taught me. If you'd take these cuffs off I could show you.''

"You ain't going nowhere, O'Flaherty," Officer Montejo said.

"Okay. I'll explain. When I tie my tie, first I cross the two halves of the tie, then the half in my right hand goes under, then down through the loop. Then it goes over, up and through. Then straight down through the two sides of the knot. It leaves a perfectly symmetrical triangle-shaped knot. Dad used to call it a double Windsor.''

"Fascinating," Montejo said, stifling a yawn.

"When I saw Crumpacker for the first time working on his laptop," Danny continued, "his tie was looped with a double Windsor. I always notice that on men, since the day my father taught me how to tie a tie.''

"You *are* just like your father!" Aunt Bertie beamed. "That man paid attention to every little detail. It's what made him such a good undertaker. I remember the time the Widow Daley died—"

"Aunt Bertie, please." Montejo silenced her.

"When Harry Tessler dumped the body in our compartment, Crumpacker's tie was tied with a single knot. You bring the half of the tie in your right hand over the other half and all the way around it one and a half times. Then draw it up behind it and down through the loop once. The tie will have a single knot more or less like half of a triangle.''

"That's the way I tie my tie," Montejo said.

"Me, too," said another cop.

"I knew whoever killed Crumpacker had strangled him with his own tie. Then when he retied it, he used a single knot, not a double, like Crumpacker wore.''

"Okay," Montejo said. "So what? There's two of us here that tie our ties like that. What makes you so sure it was Harry Tessler?''

"Because," Danny went on, "on a right-handed person, the top corner of this single knot is on the person's left-hand side."

Danny saw one of the cops making motions in the air as if he was tying his tie.

"On a left-handed person it's just the opposite. I start tying my tie with the long fat part of the tie hanging on the right side of my neck."

Agent James had whipped off his own tie and was following Danny's instructions.

"A left-handed person starts with the long, fat part on the left side of his neck. And he ties a single loop in the exact opposite direction as a right-handed person. When he knots the tie, the top part of the top corner of the half triangle is on the right."

The other cop was still going through tying motions in the air but finally gave up and shook his head, confused. Agent James, meanwhile, had awkwardly tied his tie with a single loop with his left hand according to Danny's instructions. When he finished, he said, astonished, "Gee, he's right."

All the cops looked at the FBI agent's tie. The top corner of the half triangle was on his right-hand side.

"That's clever, O'Flaherty," Montejo said, reaching behind Danny and taking off the cuffs.

"Thanks," Danny said. He stood and rubbed his wrists.

"Now I get it," said the cop who had been making tying motions in the air. "The sleeping car attendant was a lefty."

"That's right." Danny pointed at the knot on the attendant's tie. "This tie is tied exactly the way the attendant wore his. See, the upper corner of the triangle is on the right. He tied this himself. Nobody strangled him and retied his tie. He never took this tie off. My guess is he hanged himself with his own tie."

"Now that's a stretch!" Montejo said, evoking guffaws from his fellow officers.

"He's right again," Agent James said. "I found him in one of the bathrooms. I think he knew it was over for him. Decided to end it before he had to face the music in L.A. He was dressed like this when I found him. I think he was going to try to sneak off the train, but then decided to cash it in."

"You're telling me," Montejo said, "that you removed the victim from a crime scene?"

"I had my orders," Agent James said. "This is a federal case."

"This is Los Angeles, buddy. This is L.A.P.D. territory."

"But where is Archibald Crumpacker?" Aunt Bertie asked, interrupting the two men who looked as though they were ready to have a fistfight. "The poor man. And where's my husband?"

"Your husband is coming in on the next train," said the cop with the radio.

The plainclothes cop who had gotten aboard with his two officers walked up. "We found Crumpacker," he said. "He was stripped of all his clothes and buried under a whole pile of these in the baggage compartment."

The plainclothes officer held up one of Uncle Owen's precious rare fruit crate labels.

"Oh, my Lord." Aunt Bertie sighed.

EPILOGUE

"YOU HAVE CALLED your servant, Owen, from this life." The priest held his breviary against his chest and prayed.

Only Danny and Aunt Bertie stood next to the open grave in a distant suburb of L.A. for the second funeral of Uncle Owen. The sun shone brightly and birds chirped in the palm trees. Danny put his arm around his aunt.

"Save him from final damnation and count him among those you have chosen."

They blessed themselves, and Bertie bit back tears. The priest shook their hands, turned and walked toward a waiting car.

Danny and his aunt stood silently for another five minutes. Then Bertie said in a small voice, "Thank you, Danny, for everything."

Danny squeezed his aunt's shoulder. "Oh, Bert. That's what family is for."

Then they turned their backs on the Pacific and looked East, already anticipating the long trip home.

ED GORMAN
EVERYBODY'S SOMEBODY'S FOOL

A SAM McCAIN MYSTERY

When local bad boy David Egan is accused of murder, lawyer Sam McCain finds himself saddled with a new client…and another tale of small-town murder in Black River Falls, Iowa.

But McCain's client dies a fiery death in a car accident—an event that becomes murder when it's discovered the car's brake lines were cut. Working to clear Egan's name, McCain follows a trail of shattered dreams, cheating spouses, dark secrets to a body lying lifeless in a bath and to a tale of murder that embraces the vast human emotions that drive lovers to love…and killers to kill.

"…a fascinating time machine, recalling the arcana of a more innocent time.'
—*Publishers Weekly*

Available June 2004 at your favorite retail outlet.

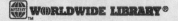